The Oxford Book of

HEBREW
SHORT
STORIES

The Oxford Book of

HEBREW SHORT STORIES

Edited by

Glenda Abramson

Oxford   New York

OXFORD UNIVERSITY PRESS

1996

Oxford University Press, Walton Street, Oxford OX2 6DP

Oxford New York
Athens Auckland Bangkok Bombay
Calcutta Cape Town Dar es Salaam Delhi
Florence Hong Kong Istanbul Karachi
Kuala Lumpur Madras Madrid Melbourne
Mexico City Nairobi Paris Singapore
Taipei Tokyo Toronto

and associated companies in
Berlin Ibadan

Oxford is a trade mark of Oxford University Press

Published in the United States
by Oxford University Press Inc., New York

First published 1996

Introduction, selection, and editorial material © Glenda Abramson 1996
Additional copyright information appears on pp. 411–12
The Publisher acknowledges the assistance of the Institute for the Translation of Hebrew
Literature in preparing this anthology

British Library Cataloguing in Publication Data
Data available

Library of Congress Cataloging-in-Publication Data
The Oxford book of Hebrew short stories / edited by Glenda Abramson.
    p.   cm.
Translations from Hebrew.
1. Short stories, Hebrew—Translations into English.
I. Abramson, Glenda.
PJ5059.E8096 1996   892.4′30108—dc20   95-51792
ISBN 0–19–214206–2

10 9 8 7 6 5 4 3 2 1

Typeset by Graphicraft Typesetters Ltd., Hong Kong
Printed in Great Britain
on acid-free paper by
Bookcraft (Bath) Ltd.,
Midsomer Norton, Avon

1997

Acknowledgements

Many hands have assisted in the compilation of this anthology. My thanks are due to the editors and translators at the Institute for the Translation of Hebrew Literature. Thanks to those who made useful comments regarding the inclusion of certain stories, not least of all the authors themselves. Dr David Patterson's advice and Dr George Mandel's careful and detailed reading of some of the material are much appreciated.

My editor, Judith Luna of Oxford University Press, has endured more than is required by an editor's brief. Her unfailing cheerfulness and encouragement throughout have been a sustaining force. To Judith, therefore, my most grateful thanks.

My husband, David, became a very good cook during the last stages of the preparation of this book. It was a matter of political correctness being allied to the need for survival. My thanks to him for a different kind of sustenance.

Contents

Introduction

I

Before the establishment of the State of Israel, few people associated the Hebrew language with fiction. Poetry rather than prose had always been regarded by Jewish scholars and teachers as the supreme form of creative expression. It was a fitting vehicle for the Sacred Tongue, mainly because of its long tradition from the time of the Hebrew Bible and its value as liturgy. Fiction in Hebrew had no such tradition or value; it was not produced at all until the early nineteenth century. Rather than being the end result of a continuous narrative development or, as in other cultures, the progression of the secular saga, romance, or epic, Hebrew fiction is a relatively new departure, its own story-line fragmented by certain historical events which altered the direction of Jewish culture.

The development of Hebrew fiction spans less than two centuries, during which time it underwent many changes: it was produced in various geographical locations and in a minority language within different host cultures until its establishment in its own territory. It is important, for this reason, to have some idea of its history, if only to explain the sharp thematic and linguistic changes that took place through the course of its peripatetic evolution. In some ways Hebrew fiction is comparable to American literature, which discarded its British cultural ancestry when its development began in its own territory. So too did Hebrew literature reject certain aspects of its diaspora heritage when it finally settled in its ancestral land.

It was not until the mid-nineteenth century, in Russia, that the first full-length work of imaginative fiction was written in Hebrew, a result of what could be called popular demand. During that time modern romances rendered into Hebrew began to appear in Russia, establishing in the Hebrew reading public a taste for fiction. The enormous success and repeated editions of of Eugene Suë's *Les Mystères de Paris* in Kalman Shulman's Hebrew rendition (1847), for example, proved that Hebrew readers were ready for pastime literature, fiction in place of serious writings. However, the task of *creating* modern fiction of aesthetic value in a language which had not been used as the vernacular for centuries was almost insurmountable. Writing fiction in Hebrew demanded the invention of a world of the imagination without the vocabulary to describe it, using a language which for almost two thousand years had been almost exclusively textual rather than spoken and colloquial. Hebrew was inadequate for authentic creative expression: its exalted nature and its biblical lineage were a bar to the exercise of the literary imagination. For this reason Hebrew versions of popular nineteenth-century fiction were adaptations, accounts, rather than accurate translations. Another problem was that fiction was disdained and often proscribed by the Jewish religious authorities. Nevertheless, the first novel in Hebrew was not long in following the Suë–Shulman best-seller: *The Love of Zion* by Abraham Mapu, a secular romantic tale about two young lovers, set in the time of the prophet Isaiah, was first published in 1853. At this time Dickens's *Bleak House* was being serialized, and Dostoevsky and Flaubert were a few years away from their own masterpieces. Mapu, the obscure Russian-Jewish romantic novelist, was a writer of a quite different order; but despite its high biblical style, which today seems ridiculous, his novel was acclaimed by its readers and reprinted more than sixteen times. *The Love of Zion* signalled the birth of modern Hebrew fiction in the form of the novel; the short story emerged a few years later.

II

Without doubt the greatest impetus to the development of Hebrew fiction was a Jewish cultural movement known as the *Haskalah*, the Hebrew Enlightenment of the eighteenth and nineteenth centuries. It was influenced by the intellectual fashion of the *Aufklärung* (German Enlightenment), from which it drew its ideas, adapting them to Jewish social and cultural needs. The *Haskalah* set out to educate the Jewish masses out of their servitude to so-called 'obscurantism', the over-reliance on religious control. It encouraged the liberation of the individual from certain historical, social and religious systems which were perceived as being contrary to reason, and it championed the claims of humanism and notions of tolerance. It signified the reappropriation of those rationalist traditions which Jewish culture had adopted in the Middle Ages, together with a strong interest in science. The movement, which had begun in Prussia, had its greatest development in Galicia and Russia.

Before the *Haskalah*, Jewish intellectual activity had been confined almost exclusively to the study of the canonic Jewish texts, the Bible, the Mishnah, Midrash, the prayer-book, and the great legal system of the Talmud and its associated writings. The intellectual élite of the Jewish communities were drawn from the students of the religious high school (*yeshivah*), all male, who were the authentic Jewish aristocracy. It seems strange that modern secular Hebrew literature should have arisen indirectly from these pious ranks, yet it is logical: these men were the most educated and learned, with a thorough knowledge of the Hebrew language. Two of the greatest Hebrew fiction-writers, Uri Nissan Gnessin and Yosef Hayyim Brenner, among many others, were graduates of the *yeshivah*.

Yeshivah education was perceived by many of the enlighteners as being one-sided and narrow. For example, books outside the sphere of Jewish religious studies were seldom permitted in the *yeshivot* of Russia and Poland. Many *yeshivah* students and teachers regarded such 'external' knowledge, including knowledge of a non-Jewish language, as something potentially threatening to Judaism. Some religious authorities even banned the study of Hebrew as an ordinary language that possessed rules of grammar and syntax, and proscribed its secular literature. They feared as anti-Judaic the use of Hebrew for modern, secular needs, and they suspected any incursion of modern ideas into the controlled space of religious education. However, new ideas were able to find their way into these preserves of religious scholarship. We see in M.Y. Berdyczewski's description of the agonizing dilemma of a young *yeshivah* boy ('Without Hope') the extent to which the grip of Jewish tradition clashed with the boy's need to experience an intellectual world and a life outside it. In a series of autobiographical stories, Mordechai Ze'ev Feierberg similarly described the disillusionment of his young protagonist with his religious confinement, and his attraction to the lure of the external world.

The majority of European Jewry resided in the areas demarcated for Jewish settlement in Russia, known as the Pale of Settlement. The accession of Alexander II to the Russian throne in 1855 led to substantial improvements in the political situation of the Russian Jews. For example, they were permitted wider rights of residence throughout the Russian empire, and were able to obtain a modern education for the first time. The challenge offered by the rapid changes in their lives and communities and their need—encouraged by the Enlightenment —to grapple with the ideas of the modern world encouraged Jewish intellectuals to establish literary journals and newspapers in Hebrew throughout the empire, which aided the spread of modern ideas. These also included works of romantic fiction in serial form with cliff-hanging instalments (masking the authors' educational, 'enlighten-ing' intentions), which proved extremely popular among Hebrew readers.

Eventually the continuing development of the literature, together with the efforts of the enlighteners, led to a movement away from lit-erary romanticism, which glorified the past, to realism, which excori-ated the present. The realist writers attacked the ornate, elevated biblical style of their predecessors and urged the creation of realistic portraits of life in their communities. A little over a decade after the publication of *The Love of Zion* a young writer, S.J. Abramowitz (1836–1917), published a realistic novel entitled *Fathers and Sons* (1868). Abramowitz was among the first to introduce the diction of the Talmud and the Midrash into Hebrew fiction, rendering the language a little more amenable to the description of Jewish life and character in Eastern Europe. Abramowitz, who later adopted the pseudonym 'Mendele the Bookseller' (Mendele Mokher Sefarim), is credited as having been the first to write a short story in Hebrew. He was undoubtedly the most accomplished and influential fiction-writer of the time in Yiddish and in Hebrew. It was he who refined the art of satire into a precisely honed tool of the *Haskalah* and who established realism in Hebrew literature. Mendele's writings have been characterized as a 'museum of ghetto misery'; at the same time, in accordance with the *Haskalah*'s reformist design, they are superb, detailed portraits of life in the Pale of Settlement. Like all good satires they blend humour and pathos, and in them Mendele displays an indulgent love of his people which is untainted by his often exasperated mockery of their world.

After Mendele the short story became an accepted literary form, attempted by every author writing fiction in Hebrew. Portraits of life in the East European Jewish *shtetl* (small Jewish town) have come to us in stories from many authors, including Dvora Baron, Yitzhak Dov Berkowitz, Gnessin, Feierberg, Brenner and Shmuel Yosef Agnon, some writing with nostalgia of the structured, cohesive lifestyle lost to them for ever, some conveying with accuracy the life in crowded, impov-erished, often squalid conditions, both the pleasures of traditional stability and the dismal, wretched details of everyday existence.

The greatest crises for East European Jewish life towards the end of the nineteenth century were the anti-Jewish pogroms which fol-lowed the assassination of Alexander II in 1881, and the gradual dis-integration of the unified traditional communities. Some of the most accomplished of the Hebrew writers moved to Western Europe after spending short periods in Palestine. They continued to write in Hebrew for a shifting and precarious constituency whose members were no longer learning the language: what they were expressing was, in fact, this very shift, the breakdown of the old Jewish world in Eastern Europe. In addition, these writers depicted their own deracination, the distress of the Jewish intellectuals who found themselves uprooted and adrift in Europe while their communities were disintegrating. They also described an altered relationship between the artist and his world, and embarked on a journey of thematic and stylistic experimentation. Not only was their subject-matter powerful and tragic, but they created out of Hebrew a richer linguistic and literary tool by experimenting with the language according to the European literary models which they were encountering, some for the first time.

One of this group, Micha Yosef Berdyczewski (1865–1921), expressed his disillusionment with the entire value system of traditional Judaism. He attempted to introduce into Hebrew literature entirely new ideas about Jewish cultural development. He contrasted the 'desire for a natural and healthy life' and the political aspirations essential to national existence with the Jews' exaggerated spirituality. While somewhat idiosyncratic in his literary style and inconsistent in his cultural philosophy, Berdyczewski was one of the most profoundly analytical of the Hebrew writers whose influence can be discerned in all subsequent Hebrew literature.

As a result of their disillusionment with the Haskalah's naïve belief that Jews, once educated, could integrate into Russian society, a belief shattered by the pogroms of 1881, a large segment of the Russian-Jewish community turned to Jewish nationalism with the hope of creating a national home in Palestine. In the 1880s the new 'Love of Zion' (Hibbat tziyyon) movement proposed the creation of a national and political centre in Palestine, where Hebrew would be revived as the national language. Many Hebrew authors supported the movement, which greatly influenced the new literature.

The Hebrew language became one of the cornerstones of this movement and of Zionism generally. Throughout the nineteenth century the Haskalah educators and writers had been committed to Hebrew, the language of the biblical prophets. The writers viewed it as one of the most fundamental and revolutionary elements of early Zionism. Yiddish (contemptuously termed 'the jargon' by its critics), the lingua franca of the East European Jewish masses, was not to be identified with the demand to remove Jewish culture from the political and cultural margins of non-Jewish societies to centrality in a politically self-determined Jewish state. Hebrew, not Yiddish, had historically been the language of political autonomy. Peretz Smolenskin (1842–85), the advocate of the first positive programme of nationalism, declared: 'We feel no shame in clinging to the ancient language that has accompanied us from country to country and in which our seers and poets have sung.' Eliezer Ben-Yehuda (1858–1922), also a nationalist, founded the movement for the revival of Hebrew as a *spoken* tongue. He concluded that Hebrew could not be sustained as a literary language alone, but that it would certainly survive as a language of day-to-day speech. Of the many phenomena accompanying Jewish national revival in the nineteenth century, the revival of Hebrew as a spoken tongue is one of the most remarkable. The language had endured, first on a biblical vocabulary of about 5,000 words, then grown to some 14,000 words after absorbing loans from Aramaic, Greek, Latin and Persian after the second century CE and from Arabic in the Middle Ages. It had survived as a written language and through its liturgy, but not as a vernacular, being spoken only on certain formal occasions. Nevertheless, it was capable of being transformed into a spoken colloquial language within a few decades at the turn of the twentieth century.

With the waves of emigration from Eastern Europe to Palestine after the events of 1881, Hebrew literary activity spread to the newly established *yishuv* (Jewish settlement), first under Ottoman rule (1905–1917) and then, after the First World War, under the British Mandate (1917–48). The *Hibbat tziyyon* movement further augmented the Jewish population in Palestine. There was a perceptible difference between the fiction of the *yishuv* and that written in Europe, not least because of the Middle Eastern landscape which many of the writers encountered for the first time. Early in the *yishuv* period the pioneer writers first saw the land which for generations had been portrayed as a cross between the biblical paradise described in the Song of Songs and something resembling a seventeenth-century Arcadian fantasy. It was, of course, neither: the writers realized with some shock that the country was in fact hot, primitive and often dangerous, barren and malaria-ridden. Brenner (1881–1921) was one of the few fiction-writers who portrayed it realistically, incorporating the experiences of the early settlers, the Jewish bureaucracy and the life of settlement during the First World War, caught between the British and the Turks. Brenner was an ex-*yeshivah* student who brilliantly manipulated Hebrew into the configurations demanded by literary modernism. His desolately introspective works, which lean heavily on autobiography, express his personal pessimism which even living in Palestine did not relieve. Having adopted naturalism as his genre, Brenner wrote caustically about his own people, as in his story 'Travel Notes', discovering little virtue in them and urging them, without much confidence, to effort and endeavour. Brenner believed that Palestine would either produce a 'new Jew', free from the burdens of the past, or fail altogether. His central characters were, in the words of the scholar Uzi Shavit, 'maladjusted young men who rebelled against the traditional ways of their parents' generation and were desperately and vainly looking for a new philosophy that would replace their shattered system of beliefs'. Brenner's prose is clear and lucid, conveying his brooding anger, his chronic anxiety and his almost fond cynicism when observing the behaviour of his fellow Jews. The development of the language as a vernacular is illustrated by the spareness and clarity of his style when compared to the floridity of the earlier, European Hebrew fiction.

A writer who reached Ottoman Palestine in 1908, a year before Brenner, was Galicia-born Samuel Joseph Agnon (1887–1970), whose work constitutes something of a junction between the East European *shtetl*, the Central European Jewish milieu and modern Israel. Agnon is the only Hebrew writer to have won the Nobel Prize for literature. His novels and short stories are situated in three locations: the Jewish districts of his native Galicia, which he eulogized, lamenting their destruction; Central Europe in the 1920s; then Palestine and Israel. Agnon's descriptions of East European Jewry are elegiac epitaphs on a lost cultural world. His nostalgic yearning for the *shtetl* of his youth and family culminates in the despairing conclusion in his novel, *A Guest for the Night* (1938), that there is no going back. His writing encapsulates the major tension between the Jewish historical past and the Israeli cultural present. Many of his stories depict surreal experience in which an unnamed hero wanders through an incomprehensible world, unable to proceed because of real or imagined obstacles. At the same time Agnon's writing is founded upon a strong traditional base, revealing his familiarity with the Jewish sources and blending together Jewish mysticism, folklore and Orthodoxy. He was a master of the allegory, the modernist short story, the sustained novel-length narrative and the folk-tale. His language is deceptive: apparently guileless and direct, it is in fact constructed of layers of complex allusion combined with terse description and a form of dialogue which lays bare the very essence of character. To my great regret Agnon is not represented in the present anthology because the Institute for the Translation of Hebrew Literature was unable to negotiate terms for the reproduction of his story 'The Garment'.

European-born writers of the post-war period arrived in Palestine during the 1920s and 1930s. The First World War and the Bolshevik Revolution had totally disrupted East European Jewish life, and Hebrew and Zionism had become outlawed in the Soviet Union. Nevertheless these writers, like those of the previous generation, counted themselves socialists, their literature, too, having adopted some of the assumptions of Soviet literature. For many, socialist Zionism had replaced traditional Jewish Orthodoxy. Tel Aviv became the new centre of Hebrew literary activity, replacing the great centres in Russia, Lithuania, and Poland. Hebrew had become the writers' spoken language and their writing reflected its vocabulary and rhythms of speech. Their works, moreover, reflected a variety of European modernist movements, and their poetry in particular was strongly influenced by Russian Symbolism and German Expressionism. Under Brenner's influence many of these writers attempted to describe life in the early Settlement and, just as their forebears had written in detail about existence in the East European diaspora, they concentrated on the minutiae of daily living on the *yishuv*. Some of this writing was still ingenuous and excessively romantic, but the best of it was experimental, both technically and thematically, and linguistically inventive. Many of the writers were innovators who enhanced not only the language but also the variety of genres and styles adopted by the evolving fiction. Hayyim Hazaz (1898–1973), with Agnon, dominated the fiction-writing of this period. In contrast to Agnon's multi-layered prose and surrealistic style, Hazaz was influenced by German Expressionism. Unusually for the literature of the time, he set a number of his stories within the Yemenite community in Palestine. His story 'Rahamim' illustrates in spare but precise detail the difference between a weary European intellectual and the innocent optimism of a simple Kurdish porter.

III

When Hebrew creative literature was ultimately able to develop in its own territory where the readership was enlarged, it rapidly became a viable literature, taking its place on the world stage as a mixture of Jewish traditional sources, European models and elements that had grown with the new culture of the new Middle Eastern nation-state. Israeli fiction rose on the political barricades following the War of Independence and the establishment of the State of Israel in 1948. It proclaimed its own uniqueness in an experimental language which moved between almost vulgar colloquialism and high-flown rhetoric. It was established by a group of writers, the first literary generation of the State, loosely and inaccurately called the *Palmah* writers (*Dor hapalmah*), after the *Palmah*, the élite corps of the Israel Defence Force. This popular sobriquet is largely a generalization, for this generation does not constitute a homogeneous artistic 'school'; its representatives fall into several categories, distinguished by their choice of theme or by the poetics that distinguishes one literary convention from another. Even so, there is a certain unanimity in their response to the establishment of Israel and the nature of its society after the War of Independence.

The poet Ayin Hillel (Hillel Omer, 1926–90) claimed that the Israeli writers of his generation—those born between 1915 and 1930—share what amounts to a common biography, and in the broadest possible sense this is true. Those who were not *sabras* (native-born Israelis) had immigrated to Palestine at an early age and begun to speak Hebrew. They joined youth movements, graduated from high school; many moved to *kibbutzim*, then joined the army. Many distinguished themselves in the War of Independence (although not necessarily in the *Palmah*) and all saw the proclamation of the State of Israel while still in their teens or twenties. They were the first generation for whom Hebrew was the mother tongue; many of them had no other language. They were also the first generation of writers to have grown up within the Israeli landscape, which they regarded without the romantic idealization of the enlighteners and the pioneers. Their attachment to the land and identification with the land were axiomatic. They were defined by other characteristics: they were predominantly male, Ashkenazi, socialist, kibbutz-orientated, collectivist, and secular. Other writers of the same chronological generation who were female, Sephardi, individualist instead of collectivist, urban rather than *kibbutznik*, were marginalized in favour of the stalwart representatives of the literary *Palmah*.

Late nineteenth-century Hebrew fiction had revealed a number of inner tensions: for example, its educational usefulness as opposed to purely aesthetic value and its promotion of the collective in the face of the need for individual expression. After the War of Independence, Israeli literature examined each of these propositions and concluded that the ideology of the collective was an anachronism once political self-determination had been achieved. It was the dismissal of this communal ideal that brought about one of the great social reversals of the time: the disintegration of the group. This conflict was internalized by the early literature of the State, which examined it through the male hero's identification with, or rejection of, his inherited ideology. Also, the writers of the 1950s and 1960s defined their new social identity as a civic and political identity which freed their literature from its ancient obligation of concern with the spiritual life of the Jewish people. With the loss of concern for a *Jewish* culture, the literature was able to establish an *Israeli* culture which reflected present circumstances rather than the Jewish exilic past, and which differed from modern Western literary culture only in language and locale. East European literature had provided the predominant model for Hebrew letters throughout the later nineteenth century. In the twentieth century, Western Europe, America and Britain offered to the young Israeli literature new possibilities of style and linguistic usage, and varieties of experimentation.

The writers' alienation from the diaspora led to the manifestation in Israeli literature of a negative view of the Jewish exilic past and an ambivalent attitude towards the victims of the Holocaust, who represented the old Jewish world. The writers were determined to create a literature that would reflect their own lived experience in Israel. It was to be a positive literature of endeavour and achievement, a literature that signified redemption and rebirth. The social and intellectual context of Israeli fiction and drama was clearly defined: it directly reflected the new State and its dominant ideology, Labour Zionism, its polyglot society, its political conflict and its rural and urban life. The landscape was at its heart; its people were native Israelis, often in confrontation with immigrants from Europe ('Strange Fire'), North Africa and the Middle East ('Dr Schmidt', 'Rahamim'), and its wars provided an omnipresent and sinister background ('The Last Commander', 'Together With Them', 'The Swimming Contest').

During the 1960s, especially after the Six-Day War, the so-called New Wave writers (including Amos Oz and A.B. Yehoshua) began for the first time to question the Zionist ideology that underlay the establishment of the State; and after 1967 they emerged with accusations against the State itself, writing fiction, later known as 'Israeli naturalism', that was devoted to the nation's major social and political problems. The political upheaval following the rise of Likud in 1977 brought into focus the Sephardi communities which until then had existed more or less on the cultural margins of the society. Their increased activity and prominence led to greater pluralism within the society, which suddenly was no longer exclusively Ashkenazi, socialist and secular. The literature swung away from its earlier collectivist identity into a greater individuality both of theme and of style. Women novelists achieved prominence. Mainstream writers devised narratives of every kind, including stories of marital disintegration, depression and aberrant relationships. Amos Oz, for one, explored the darkness deeply rooted in humanity's soul (for example, in 'Strange Fire') and Yehoshua Kenaz offered grotesque vistas of early adolescence. The 'new wave' writers were rebelling against their *Palmah* forebears, against their realism, their often glib nationalism and their nostalgic pastoralism. The new stories juxtaposed individual 'heroes' or spokesmen and their society. These 'heroes' displayed growing confusion about a number of issues, in particular about the values they had inherited from a tradition that no longer appeared relevant in their circumstances; the phrase 'Zionist dream and Israeli reality' loomed large in Israeli criticism. They were confused about their identity in relation to that of post-Holocaust diaspora Jewry, about their relationship with their Arab enemies and their treatment of them, and about their relationship with the national entity of which they were a part.

IV

Those Israeli writers who began writing shortly before and after the establishment of the State were, by and large, masters of realism, one of the most evocative of these being S. Yizhar, whose powers of description, particularly of the landscape, remain unequalled in modern Hebrew prose. Benjamin Tammuz, too, provided realistic and elegiac evocations of the *yishuv* before the 1948 war. Realism later gave way to experimentation with a variety of literary genres: Tammuz, for example, wrote impressionistic stories, some of which reflected his flirtation with the politico-cultural movement of Canaanism in the 1950s; Yitzhak Oren, who remains unfairly neglected today, weaves intricate surrealistic tapestries incorporating humour, pathos and the grotesque. Symbolism is popular with writers such as Yehuda Amichai and Amalia Kahana-Carmon. Amichai, noted as Israel's leading contemporary poet, also creates atmospheric fiction, expressionistic stories concerning love and war, while Kahana-Carmon has invented her own unique, hermetic style, presenting the viewpoint of women always confounded in their search for self-understanding. Yitzhak Ben-Ner discovered an almost journalistic style of prose description that is always strong and evocative. Aharon Appelfeld, whose central concern is Jewish fate in the twentieth century, introduced the subject of the Holocaust into Hebrew fiction, using the approach that he himself characterizes as 'indirect': he 'surrounds' the Holocaust, evoking the pre- and post-Holocaust world but leaving the event itself unmentioned. In his early fiction A.B. Yehoshua created bizarre characters whose most consistent trait is tiredness, a sense of being suspended between waking life and a dream (see 'The Last Commander'). Yehoshua has devised a series of non-linear narratives, experimenting with narrative viewpoint and chronological logic, and he is also a master of allegory and the cultural epic. Other writers extend a broader thematic base, including myth: Amos Oz, for example, introduces exotic mythological material and ideas into his evocations of Israeli life; he symbolizes the landscape so that it becomes a dynamic shaper of his political allegory. Oz is a powerful synthesizer of polar opposites, from which his unique picture of Israeli society is drawn: tradition and secularism, Israel and diaspora, intellectual and worker, group and individual, man and woman. Yaakov Shabtai's novels of memory, set in modern Tel Aviv and microscopically tracing his protagonists' inner worlds, are written in the stream-of-consciousness style, while his short stories are realistic vignettes of city experience, including the unhappy relationship between Jewish past and Israeli present ('The Visit'). David Grossman's writing moves through political confrontation, Holocaust experience and personal pain, the latter reflected in his story of sexual betrayal, 'Cherries in the Icebox'.

For many years Israeli fiction's continuing sense of commitment expressed itself in a preoccupation, almost an obsession, with the political reality of the country. For the first time since the War of Independence even the poetry, which had avoided any kind of confrontation, entered the arena of distinctive Israeli 'naturalism' and emerged as a voice of protest after the war in Lebanon in 1982. Intense attention to sociopolitical life dominated fiction and drama throughout the 1980s. However, in the 1990s there have been clear signs of change. Israeli writers have become increasingly aware of the ambivalence of Jewish existence within Israel and outside. Hebrew fiction appears to be returning to its origins. Gershon Shaked writes: 'Young people with the hunched back of exile are certainly less attractive than the tall, clear-eyed youths of whom their fathers dreamed . . . Nevertheless the portrait of the new Hebrew as the old Jew is perhaps more authentically complex than the portrait of the Israeli as a young goy.' The diaspora, derided by the early literature as the site of 'oppression, defamation, persecution, martyrdom', in the words of one of Hazaz' characters, is now being admitted into the Israeli consciousness and accommodated as an integral part of the Israeli personality. The literature's 'new Hebrew' is an amalgamation of the Israeli and the old-world Jew, hero and martyr, religiously observant and assimilated. Moreover, the fiction is being produced by writers other than the Ashkenazi men who generally constituted the mainstream group: the mid-1980s and 1990s saw an increasing number of Sephardi writers and women writers. Recently, even A.B. Yehoshua, always regarded as part of the Ashkenazi intellectual mainstream, has been exploring his Sephardi roots, presenting the Ashkenazi–Sephardi conflict in his novels *Molcho* and *Mr Mani*. Sephardi writers concentrate on their experience in the dominant Ashkenazi intellectual and social milieu.

The emergence of young women writers in the 1990s exemplifies this tendency away from the well-worn 'Israeli naturalism'—the political writing of the previous three decades. Yehudit Katzir, Savyon Liebbrecht, and Orly Castel-Bloom are three of the most prominent of the younger female writers, creating unusual and imaginative fiction. There has always been a small core of distinguished women novelists and poets in Israel, who in their own way have been trailblazers. The poet Leah Goldberg, the fiction-writers Amalia Kahana-Carmon, Yehudit Hendel, Ruth Almog, and Shulamith Hareven, to cite only a few examples, are to this day unequalled in originality. Orly Castel-Bloom is particularly noteworthy in bringing the influence of the French avant-garde to Israeli letters. These and their followers, today's postmodernist female writers, are not afraid to deal with female experience in a strongly and traditionally male-dominated literary society, taking the principal components of Israeli literature and recasting them, often with underlying hostility, from a woman's perspective. They withdraw from the so-called 'Zionist experience'; if they do contend with Jewish or Israeli experience, it is made abstract, almost as a protest against the customary engagement with social issues. If they use allusion, it is certainly not to biblical or traditional sources, but to films, television advertisements, and popular songs. The issue of Jewish identity is irrelevant to their world, although Jewish history does sometimes impinge upon their protagonists' consciousness. If their pessimism and inner darkness are no less acute than those of their literary forebears, their source is different—neither Jewish nor Israeli, but the effects of urban living in the late twentieth century, relationships inside and outside marriage, the response to personal experience, and the millennial fear of the destruction of the self.

By the time the State of Israel came into being there were fewer than one million Hebrew speakers and readers; today there are over three million in Israel alone. From the stilted, mannered, and self-conscious prose of Mapu, the incorporation of recognizable biblical quotations in Mendele's stories, the relentless realism of the fiction of the 1950s, Israeli fiction now uses a jazzy, unemotional, unallusive literary idiom whose starkness is perfectly suited to the contemporary bleakness of the experience it describes. Oz's lush, layered expression has given way to a linguistic translucence which none the less incorporates neologisms and calques, Americanisms and Arabisms, a language drenched not only in the multilingual colouring of its own society but also in Western culture imported through cinema and television. According to the scholar Dan Miron, this is an act of literary purification, to eradicate all the 'swollen symbolism' of earlier generations. Some traditionalists would disagree with his definition of 'purification', but the language has without doubt freed itself from the overblown rhetoric which characterized much of the earlier writing.

V

An anthology of this nature suggests the existence of an established short-story canon. Certain authors are unquestionably canonical, and appear repeatedly in anthologies both in Hebrew and in translation. The popularity of these writers is due to a combination of aesthetic and political qualities. Amos Oz and A.B. Yehoshua, for example, perfectly embody the stresses which typify their own milieu, particularly the tension between social commitment and individualism and between Israel and the diaspora. This suggests that a canon is constituted by the expression of cultural, social and political features current in the literature's society. This is not always the case, but it is true of Israel. Throughout the development of Hebrew literature many writers have been nominated as representative because they exemplify a political consensus or a dominant ideology, and many others have been omitted because they are perceived not to have done so. Writers such as Aharon Megged, Moshe Shamir, Natan Shaham and S. Yizhar perfectly represented the qualities both expected of and demonstrated by the first Israeli literary generation, primarily those concerned with their social and political outlook. Their exact contemporary, Yitzhak Oren, did not: at a time of committed, dialectical, social-realistic writing, he indulged in unlocalized, Kafka-like fantasies and therefore remains largely unknown in Israel. When social or political circumstances change, some neglected writers enjoy a 'revival' and are deemed suitable to the spirit of the age. This has not yet happened to Oren.

Neither a historiographical nor an ideological agenda has motivated the choice of the stories for inclusion in this anthology. Merit is the single criterion. Needless to say, the task of selecting thirty-two stories from hundreds of equal quality is not an easy one. They have been chosen primarily for their aesthetic quality, their narrative texture and colour, the combination of language, innovativeness, and, above all, impact. While some of the canonical or at least popular works are offered here, other stories appear for the first time in an anthology in English translation. Despite the non-programmatic choice of stories there is, however, an inevitable embodied history, not only of the literature but of the people who have written it. For example, the reader is unlikely to obtain a portrait of the *shtetl* and *shtetl* life from an Israeli writer, to whom one looks, rather, for insight into life in the young state. Also, the fiction reveals an interesting recurrence of certain motifs which constitute a thematic trait shared by many Hebrew authors in all the periods of the fiction's composition. One of these is the theme of childhood, which recurs almost obsessively in every generation of writers and which, in its Israeli evolution, may point to the relative youthfulness of the culture itself and its struggle for maturity and knowledge. It also reflects the primacy of the family in Jewish/Israeli fiction. It may, on the other hand, indicate an unacknowledged nostalgia for the national past, a time of innocence before the getting of (political?) wisdom, as illustrated, for example, in Tammuz' poignant story of the swimming contest and in Yizhar's 'Habbakuk'. Childhood is a time—or a state of being—in which the realization of the Zionist dream is still believed possible.

The most characteristic works of certain authors have had to be omitted because of their length: for example, the novella was a much favoured form of many of the *fin-de-siècle* writers. Gnessin, for one, is better known for his novellas than his stories, but novellas are disproportionately long for an anthology of this nature. An influential literary innovator, Gnessin could not be omitted altogether and he is therefore represented by a short story, a form he perfected in his maturer years. Some authors are untranslatable, for their writing is so linguistically specific that translation would not do it justice. Even some of those included, such as David Grossman and Amalia Kahana-Carmon, have presented immense problems for the translators.

Over little more than a century, from the stilted biblical Hebrew of Mapu's love story to the truncated rhythms of contemporary prose, the accomplishments of writers in Hebrew are astonishing. Above all, this anthology offers a taste of the rich imaginative diversity that constitutes Hebrew short fiction.

Mendele Mokher Sefarim (S.J. Abramowitz)

BURNED OUT

Mendele (1836–1917) was born and raised in Lithuania. He was orphaned at a young age, spent a few years in a yeshivah, and then began a life of wandering. Later he settled down, completed his education and began to write literary criticism in Hebrew. His first realistic novel, also in Hebrew, was published in 1862. Under the influence of the Haskalah Mendele began writing in Yiddish, and assumed the persona of 'Mendele', a peripatetic bookseller who sells his wares in three fictional towns, all the while acutely observing life in the Jewish communities, their customs, behaviour, and institutions. It was in Yiddish that he produced two of his most accomplished and ideologically radical works, 'The Mare' (1873) and The Travels of Benjamin the Third *(1896) which, in the style of Cervantes, parodied the lives of the Jewish communities. In 1888 he composed one of his masterpieces,* Fishke the Lame *(in Hebrew,* The Beggars' Book*). From 1905 Mendele was engaged in revising and translating his Yiddish works into Hebrew; he produced two quite distinct canons which stylistically and linguistically shaped the future course of modern Hebrew and Yiddish prose. 'Burned Out' is typical of Mendele's didactic style tempered with gentle humour. The language is a mixture of modern Hebrew and allusions to and often quotations from the biblical text which, in the context of the story, become strongly ironic.*

The story I am about to tell you, gentlemen, took place in the first year after the Great Fire of the Holy Community of Beggarsburgh.

That conflagration is inscribed in the chronicles of the community, and the Beggarsburghers date every event in their lives from it. They say, for example: 'So and so was born, or such a one was married and buried in this or that year of the Great Fire; the *yarmulka* decree, the decree on ordination and elementary education, the death of children because of the sins of the city, the stinking mildew, the scraping of the ritual bath and of the polluted river—all took place in this or that year of the Great Fire.' There are still old men and women in these precincts from the time of the Great Fire, and sometimes, when they sit by the stove in the House of Study at twilight, the young people thirstily drink in their words, and their eyes are flooded with tears.

I myself was not in town during the Great Fire. I was far afield, wending my way from place to place in my wagon laden with books. In those days there were no newspapers among the Jews as there are today, no writers, no glib stylists, no composers of articles, and the like. They didn't publicize the plight of abandoned wives, they didn't eulogize the dead, and they didn't write up fires in high tones. Husbands deserted their wives, the dead died and were buried in secrecy, and homes and bathhouses burned to the ground with no one to proclaim it to the world. Therefore Beggarsburgh burned down, and I knew nothing of it.

One day it chanced I was slowly proceeding alongside my horse, who was taking small steps at the side of the road, tearing off clumps of grass and munching complacently. It was *Lag B'omer* the one summer day when a Jew mustn't mourn, and all of lovely creation in its splendour, crowned with great glory, is permitted for his enjoyment. Behold, I was raising my feet, walking and regarding the gracious trees and ploughed fields, meadows, vegetable gardens, and grain. The mandrakes gave forth their fragrance, and winged creatures sang sweetly to me in exultation. I listened and imagined violins and timbrels, flutes and trumpets, the shepherd's pipe and the cymbal —musical instruments giving voice for grooms and brides today in all our settlements, wherever Jews live. There I was, sharing their joy and sending them greetings and blessings from afar, wishing that their matches be good ones, that they flourish and multiply, just like the grass of the field. While I was contemplating the Lord's bounty in the world of the living and enjoying it within my heart, bands of people appeared before me, walking along the road, staffs in their hands, bundles on their shoulders, having the appearance of absolute beggars. True, it is common enough to encounter beggars on the road, and it is a law for Israel for all eternity that beggars must constantly wander through the towns within their confines, but such a huge abundance of beggars, in such long processons—that was a great astonishment, even greater when I got a close look and saw they were Beggarsburghers, my fellow townsmen!

'Alas! Beggarsburgh is on the march!' I called out, frightened and confused at what I saw: that great horde of men and women, children and suckling babes, all of them with their clothes torn, barefoot, hungry and thirsty, their faces as sooty as the bottom of a pot. 'What is this, my brothers, and what is the cause of it?'

'Alas, our city has been destroyed,' they all answered at once. 'We are Beggarsburghers, but Beggarsburgh is no more!'

'Devastation hath come from the Lord, a decree of heaven!' The sound of weeping came from among the women.

'The Lord hath waxed sorely wrathful against Beggarsburgh!' the people lamented.

'In the multitude of our sins,' the city notables began recounting, 'For our sins the soot in a chimney caught on fire . . .'

'In Naftali the Redhead's chimney,' others interrupted them, 'it wasn't swept, and it wasn't trimmed, and the fire was borne on the wings of the wind, it spread to the thatched roofs and piles of straw, and to the low walls of the wooden houses, jammed close together, and they all burned at once. A great outcry rose in the city, turmoil and great confusion—and no one extinguished the blaze. Alas, what has happened to us? The Lord hath not had mercy on the dwellings of Beggarsburgh, from on high He sent fire and burned our city!'

'Brothers,' I waxed furious and began arguing vehemently against them, 'you began by talking about a fire in Naftali the Redhead's chimney and ended with fire from on high! What do flames from heaven have to do with it?'

'Fire from heaven descended upon us by means of the Redhead's chimney,' my brethren replied ingenuously. 'They are one and the same. Here's proof: how many years has his chimney stood unswept and untrimmed? Nevertheless, by the Grace of the blessed Lord, nothing ever happened . . . Certain simpletons explain the fire, saying it came because of the sin of building houses close together, cheek by jowl till there was no room left, and for the sin of thatched roofs and faulty stoves, and for the sin of the firemen, of whom there is neither hide nor hair in our township, but those fools have neither understood nor set it in the tablets of their hearts that Beggarsburgh passed many years as it was, and from the time it was first built it knew no evil . . . The truth is, as it is written, "If the Lord preserveth not a city, in vain shall the guardian labor." "If the Lord sendeth fire from on high, even many waters shall not extinguish it."'

No wisdom, no understanding, and no argument can stand before the written Word, hence I bent my head and kept my peace.

The Beggarsburghers were tired and weary, trudging and stumbling as they went, and my knees too failed me with the travails of the road, so we stopped to rest a bit by a grove of trees near a small pond. The Beggarsburghers hung their bundles and rags from the willows by the water, and they prostrated themselves upon the earth. The men moaned and groaned, provoking one another, and arguing about the situation. The women lamented, cursing their day and making their voices ring. Suckling babes groped for their mothers' breasts, seeking milk to restore their souls, and there was none—the breasts were withered. Young children asked for bread and wept. There was Leyzril, the perennial village idiot of Beggarsburgh, for he too was among the exiles of his congregation. His clothes were tattered and his hair unkempt, his hat was all awry, slipping down over his neck. He wandered about, going up to one person after another like a cow seeking her calf, with his mouth wide open, staring, occasionally making strange noises through his nostrils, not saying a word. I sat silently among the downtrodden Beggarsburghers, distraught and mournful about their great disaster, and the lovely world of the Holy One, blessed be He, was darkened for me. Alas, what good does that creation do for me now, with all its beauty? It gives its glory to the others, not to us Jews. The sun's warmth no longer restores my soul, for it is a blazing fire. The fresh air has become a pestilence for me, and the fragrant incense of the harvest and the mountain plants is acrid smoke in my nose. Flames blaze in my thoughts. I see a vision of fire, wind, and pillars of smoke. The birds' song becomes mourning, and their melody the sound of weeping!

'Where will you go, my brothers?' I opened my mouth after a long silence and spoke with great pity.

'Where can burned-out Jews go?' replied the members of the band with a nod of their head and a sigh. 'Where all our paupers go, to the settlements of our merciful Jewish brethren. We have certificates signed by the Chief Rabbi of our holy congregation, granting us the right and privilege of begging for alms from door to door. The community leaders worked diligently on behalf of the burned-out people and divided the cities of Israel among them by lot. Many groups wandered off in the other direction, and we've taken this one. Now we must make a further division among ourselves, as to who will go where, but there is dissension in our ranks. Some of us wish to go to one place, but all the rest do too. So we're clinging to each other in one big bunch, arguing, irritated, and angry on our way. Everyone vexes his companion and annoys him. Perhaps, Reb Mendele, you might act as judge and decide for us!'

'Scatter, beggars!' I told the Beggarsburghers gently. 'Split up for your own benefit and pleasure. Why are you bunched together, crowded, fighting, squabbling and annoying each other? You're only harming yourselves. Everyone is interfering with everybody else, and too many poor souls are picking at the same crust of bread. You'll manage yet to stir up an outcry. People will complain that you're descending like locusts, and you'll be a burden on the community. Spare yourselves and split up, Jews!'

When I saw my words were going unheeded, I ceased addressing them. I shook my head and said to myself: 'Not even fire will separate you, Jews!'

'They're fobbing off the Idletown District on us, and they're skimming off the cream, Foolsville and its surroundings. We too have a share and a holding in Foolsville!' they cried out.

'We won't forfeit our right. We too have Jewish souls, and our lineage is as good as yours!' the others shouted.

'Drop dead!'

'A curse on your ancestors!'

'Sweet Jews,' I said to the Beggarsburghers who were shouting loudest, 'Are you too among the burned out? You were never householders.'

'What difference does it make whether we were householders or tenants? Now we're all destitute,' they responded sensibly. 'We owned no homes, but we had dwellings. We used to live in Yankev-Shimshon's basement, a man and his children in his own corner, and when his house burned down, we were deprived of our dwelling. Now where shall we go?'

'I used to live in the House of Study,' shouted Azriel the idler, 'and since it was burned down, I have nowhere to sleep, and I am like everyone who was burned out.'

If fleas could talk, they would lodge the same complaint, I thought to myself, for they too live in people's houses and beds.

'The fire murdered me and throttled me at the same time,' complained Dovid-Yehuda the storekeeper. 'In normal times, when the Beggarsburghers lived in their houses, I would rent a store, and customers would come my way. With the destruction of Beggarsburgh, my luck turned bad, and my livelihood was lost.'

'I'm a miserable, poor man, as you can plainly see,' explained Nochum the teacher, speaking tastefully and intelligently. 'When there were householders, I used to teach their sons in my schoolroom, and I barely scraped by. Now that there are no householders, where will pupils come from? Without pupils, there can be no schoolroom, without a school and Torah, there's no flour.'

'Just what I say: if there are no houses, there are no *mezuzas*.' Yoysef-Shimshon the scribe spoke downheartedly. 'When Beggarsburgh stood,

I used to write parchment scrolls for *mezuzas*, and now, since there are no houses, who needs scrolls?'

'And we,' put in several Beggarsburghers, known among us as clerics: beadles and cantors, public functionaries, their helpers and their relatives and the relatives of their relatives, various sorts of office-holders, marriage-brokers, grave-diggers, students of Mishnah and professional reciters of psalms in honour of the dead, orators and the like from the burial society. 'Now we are like shepherds with no flock, like moss with no wall, like fish with no fry oil. Woe is us, and alas for our children and babes, there is neither food nor clothing, no householders and no governors. We are for the Lord, and now our eyes are turned to our relatives and redeemers, our acquaintances and generous donors. Let them take care of our children, let them support us until the Almighty takes pity on Beggarsburgh and rebuilds our city so we can return to our livelihood.'

'There is no sorrow like ours,' lamented Shloyme the windbag, pouring his heart out to me. 'My sorrow is that of a daughter! Look ye and see my shame, my devastated daughter Hinda-Rochel over there. She was engaged to a man, and the wedding was set, according to the prenuptial agreement, for this *Lag B'omer*. Everything was in order between the parents-in-law. What did the Holy One blessed be He do? The Holy One blessed be He made a great fire in the city, and quite a few people suffered damage, including me. One mustn't question the Holy One blessed be He and ask why He did that, and He certainly knows what He's doing. Since I suffered damage, it goes without saying that I became a pauper, and I couldn't carry out my part of the agreement. Not that I didn't wish to do my part, perish the thought, but simply because my hands are absolutely empty. And what did the groom say, that splendid lad? The groom said, "I want out. If the *main thing* is lacking, what do I want your daughter for?" He stood there and ripped up the prenuptial agreement. As a result my daughter wasn't married, and she's gone back to being a maiden as before. There she is, sitting in shame and disgrace, shedding tears and weeping, and my wife, may she live long, is shedding tears too, wailing and reproaching me, "Thief, why did you let the groom go! Thief, why don't you take pity on your daughter? All her friends are married already and giving suck to children, and she, you thief, is still a maid! Whither shall I take my disgrace?" Today is *Lag B'omer*, the wedding day according to the agreement, and her weeping is loudest of all, as on *Tish'a B'av*. The one cries, the other cries, they both cry, and as for me, my heart is perishing. Alas, if only a dog licked my heart and I went mad on the spot! What shall I do? What can I do? I'm prepared to go this far: let my wife and children go on their own to ask for help with all the others who were burned out, and I'll set forth by myself to beg for dowry money in Jewish towns. What do you think, Reb Mendele?'

'What can I tell you?' said I to Shloyme the windbag. 'Dowries are certainly good merchandise, a fine business, of even higher import-ance to the Jews than burned-out people.'

While the men of Beggarsburgh were talking to me, the women-folk added their own spice, seasoning their husbands' talk with lam-entations and groans, with oaths and curses, as is their way. Even the frogs raised their voices and croaked in the pond, and the cicadas and crickets chirped from among the stalks of grain. There was great noise and shouting, hubbub and wailing in the camp.

Nothing softens my heart and arouses a multitude of elevated senti-ments, feelings of love and pity, yearnings, and many more which can-not be defined or named, than the face of an innocent child asleep, especially when he drowses in weakness or scourged by the rod that smiteth him. One wretched child, a weak, frail boy, came up to me while I was engaged in conversation, laid his head upon my knees, and dozed off—and I did not know. After I stopped talking, I noticed him, and my mercy was aroused, and a powerful flood of emotions stirred within me. I looked at his sweet, thin face, which was with-out a drop of blood, and his parched lips, which were slightly open, and his thin, weak arms. One arm lay on his chest, which was swelling and rising, and the other hung loosely. His features were all imbued with a spirit of grace and pleading, and a note of sadness could be heard in them: lamentations and woe for suffering and pain, forgive-ness, pardon, and pleas for mercy, relief, and rescue. I looked, and my soul flowed out of me. I was filled with mercy and exalted feelings of sanctity. I wished to weep, to embrace that poor waif, all my suf-fering townsmen, and all my oppressed brethren, my fellow Jews, and to kiss them all with my lips. I looked from that innocent child to the Beggarsburghers, bitter in soul and full of anger, oppressed, down-trodden, and crushed, and I was crazed by what my eyes saw.

'Oh you heavens,' my heart cried out to the Lord, 'how afflicted are the Jews and how different the way they live, their food, and the satisfaction of their needs, from all the other nations of the earth! Who is like thee, O Israel, one nation in the world? Its people are like the limbs of a body, attached and dependent upon each other, influencing each other, supporting each other, maintaining each other, perishing and lost with one another. Misfortune comes to some of them, and many are in distress. Flames attack Beggarsburgh, houses are burned down, and all the children of Israel weep for the fire! All the people of Beggarsburgh cry out, even those who never had houses in their lives. The town's idlers and teachers, judges and clerics, cantors and slaughterers, marriage-brokers, grooms, and brides, storekeepers and hucksters, traders, and all its many beggars.

'My heart, my heart goes out to you, poor child!'

'Hannah, Hannah!' I heard the sleeping boy's father call to his wife, 'Go and pick up Chaim-Yankele. He's sleeping on Reb Mendele's knees, and he will be a burden to him.'

'Alas for the mother, and alas for her soul!' cried out Hannah, full of love and great pity, as she stretched out her arms to take her son. 'See how he's lying there, my precious one, the delight of my eyes. He is wrapped in the weariness of his soul, his left hand beneath his head, sleeping like a bird. He's hardly tasted life, yet how many troubles has he seen in this world!'

'Let him sleep! No matter, no matter, let him lie down and rest a little,' I told his parents, engaging the boy's father in conversation. He was a good, honest man, and learned in Torah. 'Tell me please, Reb Yehiel-Mordecai, how you found nourishment and sustenance in the bad times that rose up and beset you?'

'Blessed be our God, who has done miracles for us and sustained us, for in His goodness do we live,' answered Reb Yehiel-Mordecai, raising his eyes to the heavens in praise and thanksgiving. 'What does a Jew need for nourishment and to keep his soul alive? A bushel of potatoes from one sabbath eve to the next. We made do with little and trusted in His great name, may He be praised, and in the mercy of our Jewish brethren.'

'And did our Jewish brethren come to your assistance from their homes and dwellings?'

'From one city and from the nearby villages they sent a few wagons full of bread right after the fire, and from the rest of the cities came nothing except some personal contributions, and they were few.'

'Why were you not diligent in informing them of your troubles in writing, telling them you were in great distress?'

'We wrote, Reb Mendele, we wrote. We also sent special delegations to Jews all over, to gather contributions for us, and neither voice nor answer has come from them all! When we saw that no help came

from our brethren, and we could no longer sustain ourselves, we followed the maxim of our Rabbis, "Judge not thy friend till thou art
in his place," and now we are walking to our friends' place, with our
children and our old people, our sons and our daughters, and perhaps they will take pity on us. Perhaps they will have mercy. And
what is your opinion, Reb Mendele? Will our journey succeed?'

'Did you ever have a pain, Reb Yehiel-Mordecai, somewhere in your
body at any time?'

'What kind of question is that, Reb Mendele? I have pains. My hips
ache. May you be spared. Can't you see by looking at my face and
body that I am a man in pain, oppressed by agonies?'

'And how did you cure it, Reb Yehiel-Mordecai?'

'When my hips first began hurting me, when I could still do something for my own relief, I made an effort to distract myself from them.
I did nothing else, hoping silently that God would deliver me. Now
that the pains are very severe, I have nothing, even if I wished, and I
am even doubtful whether remedies would be effective. For now I
have pains not only in my hips but in every one of the 248 members
of my body. I am like a broken vessel, may such a thing never happen to you. But Reb Mendele, what does that have to do with what
we were talking about?'

'What does it have to do with it?' I asked bitterly. 'It's just like the
burned-out Beggarsburghers and all sorts of other wretched and destitute folk. They are all mortally ill, infected members of the body
of the Jews! If only our fellow Jews were wise and intelligent, they
would make every effort to find a remedy and cure their weakened
limbs, to strengthen and restore them in counsels and knowledge, to
keep the illness from becoming worse, so that the pain shall not be
eternal and the blow not mortal, refusing to be cured, spreading
and harming the entire body. If only our brethren took part in the
troubles of the Beggarsburghers, in their time of woe, and the men
of their city each gave a penny to help, the pennies would add up to
a great sum, so that in a short time they could rebuild their ruins
and return to their work as before. Then they would not be driven
from their homes into exile, wandering and lost in the world.

'Now listen, Reb Yehiel-Mordecai, and I shall tell you what will
befall you and those like you, the lost and rejected, and our brethren
from here too in the end of days. The Beggarsburghers, abandoned
and neglected, will be like other unfortunate and poverty-stricken folk,
shoved out of their homes. Once they have started to fall, they will

fall lower and lower, never to rise up and return to their former state. Along the way they'll eat whatever comes to hand, and in the end they'll be wandering beggars, penniless and a sore affliction on the house of Israel. That ulcer will spread through the whole body of our people, bringing rot to its bones and causing pains and grave suffering. Since our brethren did not support all those among them who fell, willingly and voluntarily giving a little right away when their feet stumbled, in the end they shall be forced to give a great deal more, but to no avail. The poor and destitute will beg forever from door to door, collecting from them no matter what. They will give and give again as to a bag with holes in it, whatever they can afford and more than they can afford. Against their will they will establish almshouses for poor and wayfaring guests; they will be obliged to scatter their money to miserable idlers, to the weak and downtrodden, both to the lazy and to the disabled. Against their will they will support widows and feed orphans; against their will, poor kinsmen and kinswomen will live with them, and they shall not turn away from their own flesh. Against their will they shall give charity and much else, without limit, until they can do no more. Then they'll consume less and spend less, they'll do less business, and their livelihood will suffer greatly. They too will become poor, and new indigents will be added to the first. The poor of that place will then go elsewhere and do what was done to them, and so the scab shall spread through Israel, and poverty, penury, and destitution will increase.

'Do you see, Reb Yehiel-Mordecai, what that frog does by hopping into the pond? When he leapt he made a circle of waves in the water, and those waves made more waves around them, and they produce more and more waves, spreading everywhere without cease. That tiny little cause had many effects, going on and on. A fire broke out in Beggarsburgh, bringing many evil consequences. In the end of days *all of the House of Israel will weep for the fire!*'

'Our Sages have said that before you,' said Reb Yehiel-Mordecai, shrugging his shoulder and waving his arm. His lip had that twist typical of those who frequent the House of Study when they disparage what someone else says. 'Since we find them in our rabbis, what's your new point? In the Midrash to the Song of Songs our Sages said: "Consider the walnut. If you take one away from the rest, they all fall down and roll away one after the after. So it is with the Jews. If you take one of them, they all feel it."'

'So what's to be done, Reb Yehiel-Mordecai?' I asked bitterly.

'In heaven's name, will the Jews always be behindhand in self-improvement and slow to better their lot, so that they won't fall down and roll away one after the other like so many walnuts?'

Reb Yehiel-Mordecai put his hands on his face, sighed and moaned, and made no answer. We sat wordless, keeping silence, each sunk in his own thoughts.

Presently the Beggarsburghers moved on in noise and confusion, setting forth on their way with their women and children, and Leyzril the madman trailed along behind them. I went with them on my horse and wagon to see them off. When we reached the crossroads I parted company with them tearfully and went my own way.

I never saw those miserable Beggarsburghers again in my life, and I don't know what happened to them in the end. Doubtless they rolled about like walnuts with the rest of the destitute Jews until they vanished from the face of the earth. I did run into Leyzril one day in Foolsville. He was walking through the street like the village idiot, and little boys ran after him, mocking him: 'Up the madman! Up the madman!'

Translated by Jeffrey M. Green.

Micha Yosef Berdyczewski (Bin Gorion)

WITHOUT HOPE

Beyond the River

(Memoirs of One Who Left)

Berdyczewski (1865–1921) was born in the Ukraine to a rabbinical family. His stories reflect the tensions of a traditional upbringing, an orphaned childhood, an early first marriage and a tradition-bound society. Some of his Hebrew stories are seen as marking the transition from the nineteenth-century narrative to a new mode of Hebrew fiction. They suggest an underlying ferment in the life of the Jewish intellectual in the shtetl. On the other hand, Berdyczewski's Yiddish works depict the shtetl with affection and nostalgia. The impact on Berdyczewski of Nietszche and Schopenhauer led to a series of influential pamphlets advocating a change of values in the Jews' spiritual life. He also argued for a broader, more European emphasis in Hebrew literature, and urged that its inspiration be drawn from life and nature. Berdyczewski wrote one novel, Miriam, *and a number of novellas, stories, essays, and works of criticism. His large collection of Jewish myth and folklore, upon which he had worked until his death, was published in 1924.*

I was a young bridegroom then, living under my rich father-in-law's roof in a small town in Russia.

It was a two-faced town: half of it sat upon a hill, where the Gentiles lived in comfort, and half lay below, in the valley, where the Jews huddled together in their houses, religious schools, and shops, all around a big market square to which all eyes were turned.

The market square was an open area littered with boxes and lumber and some canvas huts. Farmers passed through it in their laden or empty carts, the produce of the country lay spread upon the ground, women milled about, buying, and boys dawdled up and down the market itself in the centre, the place where things were weighed and measured.

The shops which clustered around the market square like chicken-coops bore no signs to announce the nature of their merchandise or the shopkeeper's name. Jews wearing cummerbunds around their waists stood in the doorways and called out:

'Come here! Come to me! Come into my shop!'

They stood thus day after day, always buying and selling, as they had always done, doing everything exactly as their fathers and grandfathers had done before them since time immemorial. It never occurred to any of them to stop and wonder and perhaps think a different thought ... Nor did any of them ever cross from the lower half of the town to the upper, which were separated by a river that could well have been a border between two nations.

When evening fell they counted the money they had made that day, a mere handful of coins, and a terror seized their bodies, and they exchanged anxious whispers with their wives, as if their ships had foundered ...

And at night, when studies and earthly labours alike were at an end, and evening prayers too were over, a kind of sorrow seemed to echo in the air.

I was not yet eighteen years old. I was a boy in a family of great men, and a different spirit moved me. Walking from my father-in-law's house to the religious school, I looked at the row of shops and the faces of the shopkeepers and my heart filled with strange emotions and my mind with longing.

Sometimes in the house of God, too, the men around me seemed to be strangers. I sat and read books, and gazed through the windows at the open air and the high heavens. In the mornings, when I walked to dawn prayers, having just got out of bed, everything seemed to move slowly, as if the world sensed that there was no need to hurry.

But where was I going? Where were we all going? What were all those dos and don'ts, and all our rushing about? What have we to offer the Lord of all deeds, the God of all the generations? Sometimes I closed my eyes and saw those generations, all of them, their countless eyes on me, blazing, pleading.

But I was nothing, a man of clay.

*

On Saturday evening, when the whole congregation gathered in the house of the Lord for evening prayers, each man absorbed in his own world while his lips whispered to the Lord of the sabbath and the profane, my heart would carry me far away and I would stand there bewildered and amazed.

Sometimes I pitied my people and felt sorry for them, and angry with their misguided teachers, who did not know the difference between darkness and light. But why did the Children of Israel not break their bonds, once and for all? Why did they not open the windows? Why did they bar them?

'Blessed be He who hath separated the sacred from the profane, Israel from the Gentiles'—but why did He separate? Why did He create boundaries between nations? I dreaded to seize the horns of the altar and ask outright, What is up there? But in my heart of hearts I never stopped asking.

Do they know? My townsmen, do they know that I am a doubter? Do they realize that I do not believe as they do, that I doubt everything? But the Lord is the One who knows all, and He is the One I must fear. He hath spoken—shall I not hear? He hath commanded—shall I not obey?

Come ye back, ye wayward children . . . I too shall come back. Not just yet, but after a while. Starting next week, next first-of-the-month, next New Year . . .

At noon, in the midday quiet, I sit on the soft divan in my father-in-law's house, and the beautiful girl, the wife of my bosom, sits beside me, sewing. She looks at me and I am far away, from her, from her father's house and her native land. I do not know what is happening to me, I cannot understand why the love of this dear soul does not satisfy me. My heart and my mind are borne away from here.

I pore over books, delve into works of religion and of science, perchance to find some hint of what I am seeking, but my mind labours in vain. My thoughts rise up to heaven, plunge into the abyss. Everyone seems mute. We are all far apart, we have nothing to do with one another. Why are we alive? Why was the world created? Why do we question and seek all our lives? What is our purpose and whither are we going? Fragments of thoughts and emotions rise up and swamp my soul, and I am always abstracted.

But I love the moon, the stars, the night and its sadness. Only then does my heart rest. I recall, too, the time of the flaming sword, when God drove out Adam, who became godlike . . .

I love my bride, but her parents are strangers to me. All the townsmen offend my eyes. I loathe these men who chase after the 'heavenly wisdom', and I feel nothing but enmity for our great luminaries, who have heaped these endless dos and don'ts upon our backs to oppress us.

After supper I go out to the porch of my father-in-law's house and sit on the bench. At once I am filled with an urge to drop everything and leave this place. Then my wife's soft voice calls, 'Come inside, Nathaniel, the air is chilly . . .' My heart pounds. Like a guilty man, I gaze intently at her face. The innocent knows nothing, and she kisses me on the forehead and says, 'Do not think too much, please don't . . .'

Sometimes at the beginning of the Sabbath, when I have bathed and changed my clothes, a new feeling awakens in me, and for a little while I forget my doubts, my perplexities and questions, and am once again a trusting child.

The hanging lamp brightens the parlour of my father-in-law's house. The table is covered with a white cloth, and the silver utensils upon it gleam in the light. My father-in-law, wearing a black silk caftan, walks up and down the room, saying, '*Shalom aleikhem!*' in a contented voice, and I echo him. My wife listens to our talk, and we speak her praises. My bride is a housewife, a housewife in that same house, that same street, town, world . . .

Through the windows we can see the flames of the Sabbath candles in the neighbouring houses. They move me inexplicably. At such a moment I am filled with warmth. My wife stands beside me, whispering in my ear. Tears of love fill my eyes, tears of joy.

But soon the sadness returns, the sense of loneliness. On Thursday nights at the religious school we stay up till all hours, poring over the dead books. My heart escapes from that company and wanders far away, to an unknown place. A strange desolation overwhelms my spirit. I do not know what it is. I cannot express what is in my heart. One thing only I do know: this place oppresses me.

The image of my wife, her blue eyes, her charm, are not enough to stifle my yearnings. My life is comfortable, but I lack the life of the mind and an atmosphere of thought. A moment after I embrace my wife, my mind returns to its secret quest, its search for God's mysteries. I am imprisoned in a circle of love and riches. They deny me nothing, but the desire for knowledge never leaves me.

Who are we and what is our life? What is the world and what is God? What are the Torah and the Jews? Tell me these things and take back all you have given me. Settle my doubts, solve my questions, and then my heart will rest and I shall be at peace. Are there really good and bad deeds? Does God watch us, and does he make covenants? Tell me. Give me books which will throw light upon these things.

Then I heard that on the other side of the river, in the neighbourhood of Gentiles, lives a Jew who has been ostracized by his brethren, Mahaviel the Brewer is his name. In his house food and drink are consumed without head-covering, his wife shows her hair out of doors, his sons went to school and his daughters play music. The man is a complete unbeliever, but accomplished and learned. Then I knew that one day I would cross the bridge and visit that house. My life depended upon it.

*

It happened one summer night. When evening prayers were over I slipped out of the religious school, circled the neighbourhood and reached the bridge. I crossed it slowly, feeling that the sky above and the water below were looking at me. When I reached the upper town on the hill I turned and looked at the lower town. From afar its houses looked like a cemetery.

A sense of power filled me, knowing that I was turning away from a dark graveyard to a place of light. But down there in the valley lived my bride, my beloved . . . I recovered and walked on. White houses stood in gardens all over the hill. Above them rose a placid house of worship with a tall steeple and stone steps leading up to it. I walked on slowly. At the end of the street lived Mahaviel.

Lights showed in his windows. My heart beat faster.

I stood before the door for several minutes. I could not bring myself to step on the strange threshold. Then I pulled the bell-rope. It was the first time in my life that I had rung a doorbell.

A handsome dark girl opened the door. I was inside. Before I could tell them my name they knew who I was, and said they had been expecting me to come for some time. They all extended their hands to me warmly, and received me like a friend and a brother.

I sit on the divan and my eyes wander. Fine furniture, fine pictures, beautiful books in a bookcase. My heart swells at the sight of this family and this life. They give me tea in a clear glass and I drink. For the first time in my life I drink with my head uncovered, and it inspires me with spiritual courage.

The mother's eyes rest on me with maternal compassion. Mahaviel, the head of the family, speaks. He speaks warmly, voicing his anger with the Israelites of this town, who walk in darkness.

I also speak, saying, I live among scorpions; I cannot bear the superstitions and the customs; I can stand no more . . . I shall go away, very far from here, and acquire knowledge and wisdom. The thought had never before entered my mind.

Mahaviel and his sons say, Leave your people and your father-in-law's house and go to a distant land. The girls say, Do stay here. We pity your bride.

There is much time yet. My heart is restless. It is ten o'clock. I must return home, and I stand up.

'I shall see you again soon.'

'Soon! Come back soon!'

I knock on the window of my room. 'Batshua, Batshua, let me in!'

'Here I am, here I am.'

I went in, embarrassed, stammering, 'I am late . . . I debated with my friends, it went on for a long time . . .'

'Why are you so late? I was worried about you.'

Her tenderness moved me to my soul, filling me with remorse.

'Why were you late?' she asked again. 'My parents were worried too, and they were angry with you.'

'Never mind,' I replied.

'Something is happening,' she blurted out. 'I see a strange spirit in you. I know that you love me, but something is pulling you away . . . You think too much, you read more than you should. I do not know what has come over you, but I know that you are not following the path of my parents and the rest of our townspeople . . . Why are you silent? Why do you not justify yourself? I wish you were again as you used to be with me. You cannot imagine how I suffer.'

'Do I make you suffer, my dearest?'

'Indeed you do. You are breaking my heart. I do not want those thoughts and books which take you away from me . . . Why is my love not enough for you? Why are you not with me? . . . Nathaniel, my beloved, come back to me, come back to us, to your people and to our Law. Leave those strange books. Do it for me.'

I can hear her heartbeat. I fall on her neck, crying, 'I cannot kill my thoughts! I cannot!'

'You could do so, if you wanted to,' she pleads, her hands on my neck and head touching mine. 'I shall always be with you. Tell me what you are hiding in your secret heart. I shall help you, light of mine.'

But I can tell her nothing.

*

Those were difficult times for me in my father-in-law's house. They all argued with me, my in-laws, my wife and our near neighbours, while the townsmen gossiped about me, the scion of rabbis who was straying from the path . . .

What have I to do with them? What good would it do them if I believed? But they feel responsible for my thoughts. Two thousand years of 'I believe', of generations who lived and died by their faith

—and I do not believe, I do not believe in anything. But they are many and I am all alone.

My father-in-law and my mother-in-law both quarrel with me, and when they abuse me my bride weeps and says, 'Why can you not leave him alone?' But they ask of me only to fear God and walk in the ways of our forefathers. They give me all the worldly goods—why can I not do this one thing for them, stop reading those alien books?

They regard me as a cruel man, one who does wrong wilfully. They try soft ways, too, pleading with me, 'Come back to our Lord! Be a Jew like all Jews, read the books that are sacred to our people!' But I remain silent and do not respond.

'A spirit of folly has entered him. Heresy is obstinate . . .'

*

My heart is not softened. My thoughts do not let up. Only once did I feel like turning back, and the occasion is with me still.

In the second watch of the night, at the end of the summer, a voice called to us from outside, waking us from sleep: 'Arise, Arise, to the worship of the Creator!'

It was the first night of *Selihot*, and time to go to the house of the Lord to pray. My wife awoke too and dressed and said, 'Get up, Nathaniel! Let us go! It is time.' My father-in-law and mother-in-law were ready. We went outside, groping our way in the dark streets. A chill wind blew. My bride walked beside me, leaning on me, her hand in mine. I felt love and compassion for her.

We reached the synagogue courtyard, which was flooded with light. My wife and her mother went to the women's gallery, and my father-in-law and I went inside the building to take our places. The synagogue was full of people praying in anguish. In front of the open ark, beside the lectern, stood a man wrapped in his prayer-shawl, addressing God Almighty, and the congregation echoed him: 'Hear our voice, Oh Lord our God! Spare us, have mercy upon us!' 'Cast me not off in the time of old age; forsake me not when my strength faileth.'

Old age is plainly etched on the men's faces, on the walls, the mute brass lamps, the ancient prayers, and the dripping candles. The hall is full of grief and sorrow. A sudden fear came upon me, a divine sigh. It seemed to me as though the congregation had just risen from the cemetery. We had all risen, and we were praying to a distant God who was also full of sorrow.

It was as though a mighty power hurled me out of my own world,

which had preoccupied me, into a world which was ancient and sacred.
I raised my head to the women's gallery and heard a broken sob.

Over there is my bride, I shall think of her. I shall return to her
and to the God of her forefathers . . .

*

I strove to do what was good and honest, and these aims helped to
cleanse the seeker and draw him closer. The eve of the New Year was
truly like a new beginning for us, a new year of peace. The wayward
children had come back . . .

My happy wife looks radiant in her yellow silk gown, worn in honour of the holy day. I myself, dressed in a black silk coat, sit beside
her at the white-clothed board, feeling the day's solemnity. Like a
brother and sister we sit side by side, holding hands under the table.
With one hand we give each other our love, our youth, and with the
other we accept from her parents a piece of pure white bread dipped
in honey.

Peace. The whole world was at peace.

*

That night my wife was again my bride, as when we were newly wed.
We were alone in our room with a candle burning on the night table
between the beds, spreading its dim light. Suddenly I was abashed by
the proximity. I was amazed that we, a youth and a maid, could be
alone together in a bed-chamber. How did they allow us to be alone,
without speaking ill of us, as is the Jewish custom? . . . Before we married, if I had so much as addressed a word to her it would have been
a scandal.

'Do you know,' I whisper to her, 'my love for you knows no words.'
I embrace her and try to kiss her mouth, but she moves away, saying, 'These are the Days of Awe . . .'

I want to say to her that the days are not awesome at all, but I pity
her innocence and desist.

'Nathaniel, do you believe in reward and punishment?' she asks.
'Do you believe that everything we do is recorded in a book?'

'Batshua, why do you ask?' I feign surprise. I take her in my arms,
embrace her and stifle our thoughts. A long kiss, the spring of life . . .

*

Peace reigns in my father-in-law's house, but it is the calm before the
storm. Even my wife's uncle, old Shmuel, no longer argues with me
to reform me, no longer tries to convince me that when our fore-
father, the Patriarch Jacob, and his wicked brother Esau fell out over
the right of the first-born, they were divided over two rabbinical schools

of thought . . . Before me lie open the great volumes, bound in red leather, printed by the sainted brothers Shapiro, whose very typesetters had been granted a vision of the prophet Elijah.

They believe that I have mended my ways, while I slide back to my doubts and dreams . . . The townspeople are preparing for the great day, and I with them, while my heart is elsewhere. In my inward soul I have no faith in the prayers, in the actions, I believe in none of it. Alien ideas fill my mind as I walk to the religious school, wrap myself in the prayer-shawl and look into the prayer-book. Apostate that I am, I wash my hands before the meal, though I do not believe in the ritual. I keep my head covered all day, while nursing the memory of the hours I spent bare-headed at the house of the enlightened family.

Away, thoughts! Get ye behind me!

*

I can no longer bear this community, I want no part of these customs, these actions. Why have they trammelled our minds? Why have they dictated our very ideas and thoughts, our beliefs and ways? Why do they forbid us life, and seek to kill our desire for pleasure? Books—that is all they have ever done, written countless books, generation upon generation. But I do not believe in them or in their books, not one jot! I do not believe in anything.

Such were the thoughts that stirred in my mind throughout the ten Days of Awe. I was angry with myself and with the others. I blamed them all for their superstitions, the barriers to sublime enlightenment. For it is a wise and sensible nation, yet it walks in utter darkness, in benighted ignorance down a tortuous path.

Turn, turn away! Wake up, my people!

On the eve of the Day of Atonement, when the entire community, from infants to old men, gathered in the synagogue, and everyone stood in prayer, wrapped in their prayer-shawls; when two ancients stood at the lectern with bibles in their hands, and in the name of God and the congregation gave leave to the sinners to participate, then a wild passion seized me to raise the prayer-shawl from my head and cry aloud in Yiddish, 'Wake up, my people!'

All that long night and the long day which followed I battled with my soul, struggling to rein in my stormy spirit. During prayers, morning, afternoon and evening, I looked at the worshippers and saw them as victims of delusion, long lost to reason . . . But when the closing prayer came I too trembled.

A twilight terror filled the hall, as though the very world shivered, and an oppressive darkness rose from the dense crowd, man next to man, bench next to bench. The women wept aloud. The travails, the suffering of the Jews, the sorrow of endless exile and the siege of the souls, all awoke as from sleep and clung together, as though they too feared the imminent end.

I am not the man I was. My heart questions, I long to weep, for my life, my youth.

The Lord is our God! The Lord is our God! The Lord is our God! ... Then came a long blast on the ram's horn.

*

I cannot keep on lying, I cannot! Let them walk in their ways, I shall follow my heart. Let them think what they will, I shall think my own thoughts. And mine are richer.

I resumed reading the alien books. And at the school, after prayers, when a little crowd gathered around me to discover what was in my mind, I told them. And before long disputes brokes out again at home. My mother-in-law often supported me, and tried to soothe her husband's rage. But he persisted: Those who stray do not return! One day he burst out before her and my wife: 'Do you see this innocent man? You see him so deep in thought? I wager my head that a time will come when he will leave his people and his native land, and go abroad to study at a school of science!'

At the words 'school of science' a terror fell upon the house. My mother-in-law fell silent. My wife almost swooned with fear, and I too was amazed.

*

That night I had a dream: I am in a strange country, wearing alien garments and speaking the language of Gentiles. I attend an academy and learn diverse kinds of knowledge and profound sciences. These alter the ways of life and the world, and I am a wholly different man, twice my present age ... And upon my forehead there is an indelible mark.

Bearing that mark, I grow great. I spread knowledge, I lecture about nations and men ... And then one day I am told that a young woman wishes to see me ... She comes and kneels at my feet ...

I woke up. It was broad daylight. The sun was shining bright and there was something strange about my room. My wife had risen and left. Then the Jewish maidservant came in and said that the coachman was asking about me.

'What coachman?' I asked, surprised.

'The one who goes through your father's town,' she replied.

I understood and my face fell . . . But I rallied and began to prepare my things for the journey. I spread a white cloth on the floor and placed my clothes and books upon it. Then I folded it over and stitched up the corners. The maid stood by the door, watching me crouched on the floor, stitching.

I sat on my bundle, feeling numb, until they informed me that the coachman was waiting outside. I rose, somewhat shaken, put on my overcoat and scarf, and went out of my room to the parlour. I found my father-in-law pacing up and down, his features grim, while my wife sat in a corner, saying nothing. I went up to my father-in-law and gave him my hand in parting, but he did not take it. I wished to say some words to my wife, but my throat thickened and the tears filled my eyes. The maidservant carried my bundle outside, and a few moments later I was seated in the coach, which was drawn by two unmatched horses.

The coach crossed the bridge, we passed the upper town. We reached the highway, and the wind blew in the trees alongside the road. My heart was desolate and heavy.

'Shlomo! Shlomo!' I heard a voice from a carriage behind us. 'Stop your horses! Wait, stop!'

I turned around and saw my father-in-law's horses approaching. The coachman pulled up his horses. The carriage behind us stopped too. Shlomo climbed down and walked back to the carriage, and exchanged whispers with the person inside. In a little while he returned, took my bundle and carried it to the other carriage, and told me to get off too. Before I knew it, I was seated beside my father-in-law, and the coach I had ridden in moved on. My father-in-law spoke to me gently. 'Are you not like a son to us? Do you not love Batshua? How can you go away? Where would you go? To your poor father and your stepmother? To quarrel with her and her children? You will soon be eighteen years old, you must think of your future . . .'

He went on to say, 'We have done so much for you, we have laboured so much since you married our daughter. Your mother was still alive then, and Batshua was the apple of her eye . . . Remember your mother, remember your sainted forefathers, remember who you are, and who those "enlightened" people are whose company you seek . . .'

I did not speak, but listened to his speech in a daze. He put his hand on my neck and I pulled away.

'What is the matter with you?' he asked. 'Do you see, over there lives the apostate, Mahaviel the Brewer.'

'Why do you all vilify that man?' I asked.

His face changed.

'I visited him and saw that it was unjust. Yes, it is an injustice.'

'You went there . . .'

'Yes,' I replied, trembling.

'If I had known that an hour ago,' he said aloud and turned away from me. At that moment we approached the house of Mahaviel the Brewer.

'If you please,' I said to my father-in-law, 'tell the coachman to stop here a moment.'

'What do you want here?'

'I must get off for a moment.'

The carriage stopped and I jumped out and ran to Mahaviel's house and disappeared inside. I did not heed the voice which called after me.

*

I was received with open arms at the brewer's house. They spoke to me kindly and gave me courage and resolution. They hoped that I would overcome the obstacles, that I would study and become an admirable man.

For three days I celebrated my freedom in that house. The daughter of the house liked me, but I thought of my wife on the other side of the river. On the last night I went out of the house and walked towards the bridge. Once more I looked down at the lower town, at its inhabitants, who were already generations removed from me. Only some dim lights flickered over there, in the dark domain . . . They filled me with both anger and sorrow.

I hate those people, them and their houses, their religious schools and their books. I cannot forgive, shall never forgive those fanatics, who barred my way. Down there, in the darkness, lives an innocent soul, my beloved. Tears filled my eyes. I looked at those old houses, filled to the brim with all those books, beliefs and ideas, which were my stumbling-blocks, which reared up in front of us both.

'O Lord God, to whom vengeance belongeth! O God, to whom vengeance belongeth!' I fell down and wept.

Translated by Yael Lotan.

Mordechai Ze'ev Feierberg

THE CALF

Feierberg (1874–99) was born in the Ukraine into a deeply pious Hasidic family and received a traditional education. The Haskalah, which penetrated some of the religious schools at the time, attracted him to contemporary secular Hebrew literature, which he read in secret. Soon he rebelled against his narrow-minded, traditional society, which in turn punished him severely. Nevertheless, he published his first story in 1896. He became active in organizing Hebrew and Zionist discussion groups. Because of his early death from consumption his literary contribution is slight, consisting of several largely autobiographical stories and one novella, Whither (1899). Despite his keen support of the Haskalah he preserved his affection for the spiritual world of the Orthodox Jews. The central theme of his stories is therefore the internal struggle of the post-Haskalah Jew, who is equally attracted and repulsed by the worlds of tradition and of Enlightenment.

It was summertime, and I wasn't yet nine years old.

The sun looking down from its station overhead bore into the gloomy *heder* with fiery eyes. As though to put our teacher to shame, it glanced scornfully off the protruding fringes of his dirty undershawl and ran teasing rays through his pointy beard. It poured playfully golden beams over the muddy morass by the open sewer that ran along the Street of the Poorhouse, which was also the Street of the Synagogue, as well as the Street of the Tutors, the Street of the Slaughterers, and the Street of the Marketplace, as if to say in so many laughing, magical words: 'You silly children! What makes you sit all cooped up like this with such an old fool of a rabbi?' How dearly we loved them then, those spinning sunbeams that twirled through the window with the fondest of ease. It was a clear, balmy day outside. What fun could be had there! The vapours rising from the sewer made a fine sight; a scrimmage of boys was having a jolly time wrestling on the ground and making mud pies to dry in the sun. But the hardhearted rabbi refused to reprieve us and sat droning on and on. Beads of sweat fell on the open Talmud. Our damp shirts clung to our skins. Our hands felt leaden; our heads ached; our throats were hoarse; but the rabbi droned on and on. . . .

Yet even he had his breaking-point. He finally shut his book, admonished us with a few brief words, and warned us to go straight to the synagogue for the afternoon and evening prayer. In a frenzy of impatience we tumbled outside—to be met by the town herd coming toward us. First came the billy goats, looking as stately and staid as a delegation of rabbis and town notables on their way with the common folk to attend some celebration, a wedding perhaps, or a circumcision or a funeral. Next came the she-goats, followed by the cows, calves, pigs, and colts, each in a formation of their own. The dust rose sky high. We slipped and scrambled in and out of the herd, here someone stealing a ride on a billy goat's back and there on a she-goat's, while yet someone else terrorized the animals by stampeding them wildly to let them know he was a man, a scion of that heroic race whose dominion was one with the world. Suddenly, at the herd's edge, I spied our own cow coming toward me by the side of the herdsman, who was carrying a lovely little calf on one shoulder. I put two and two together at once, for my mother had mentioned several times that our cow was 'expecting'. I couldn't contain my excitement, and I stared longingly at the herdsman as he strode toward my father's house with the pretty calf on his shoulder. I wanted desperately to run after him, to throw myself ardently on the calf and cover it with kisses, but what was I to do? What about the rabbi and the afternoon prayer? And what would my mother say if she were to see her son the Talmud student giving in to such unworthy impulses? And so I had no choice but to force myself to go to the synagogue to pray. As soon as the service was over, I rushed home to see the calf. My little sisters and brother ran out to greet me with news of the calf's birth when I came. 'Hofni,' they said all at once, 'you should see how pretty it is! You should see how big its head is, and how wide its nostrils are, and how long its tongue is, and how red and thick its lips are! You should see . . .' Unable to restrain myself any longer, I ran impatiently to the barn, where I knelt before the calf on my knees and ran both hands over each of its limbs; then I took it in my arms and carried it to the kitchen to see it better by candlelight. I salted a few crumbs of bread and laid them on its tongue; it lapped them up hungrily and looked at me with a satisfied, genial air. I knew right then that it liked me and wanted to make friends with me more than with any of the other children, my brother and sisters too. It had eyes for me only, which followed me fondly wherever I went. I fell madly, proudly in love with the pretty calf and pledged myself heart and soul to be good to it and to repay its devotion with my own.

'Well,' said my mother to my father when he came home that evening, 'we're in luck! The cow gave birth. We'll slaughter the calf next week and roast it the way you like it for the Sabbath.'

'Do you mean it, mama?' I asked in alarm. 'Do you really mean you'd kill such a nice, pretty calf?'

'You're still a child, son, and you're just being foolish. People would laugh at you if you talked that way in front of them.'

When I returned from the kitchen to visit my calf, my pride and my joy, and saw it lift its eyes to me as though suing for mercy, I burst into tears. I threw myself on it passionately and stroked its sides while the hot tears trickled down my throat. The more I kissed it, the harder I cried.

That night, I remember, I couldn't stop thinking.

For the first time I felt as though a little bird were hatching inside my brain and pecking away with its sharp bill. . . . 'Hofni!' I seemed to hear it say. 'Why was such a calf ever made? To be slaughtered? But what for? Why slaughter a sweet little calf? And if it really was made to be slaughtered, why was it made so pretty? Wouldn't it have been enough if it had been born just a piece of meat inside a leather bag? Why does your mother want to kill it? Who gave her the right to kill such a pretty calf?'

I vowed that night to give eighteen pennies to the alms box of Rabbi Meir Baal Haness if only he would make my mother change her mind. Then I fell asleep.

In my dreams I saw a bound calf, over which stood the slaughterer, knife in hand. Down it came . . . the calf went into convulsions, the blood spurted out. . . .

When I rose from bed in the morning, I ran straight to the barn to discover to my relief that my darling calf was alive and well and peacefully resting. Its mother stood lovingly over it, licking its back with her tongue and arranging its short hairs in rows.

When I came home the next evening, I found the slaughterer talking figures with my mother and fixing a price for the calf's hide. I said nothing, because I had already been told that I was a fool, but my temper flared and my heart beat like a gong. Was I really such a fool, I wondered? But why? Who said that I musn't have pity on the pretty calf? My mother? But I'd heard her say more than once that we were commanded to be merciful to animals and not treat them cruelly! Not treat them cruelly—but slaughter them? Be merciful—and slaughter them? So she said, but who said she was right? Could she be wrong, then? Could mothers be wrong too? Dear God, my mother and the calf are both in Your hands—why did You make the calf live and make my mother want to kill it? God! Why should this calf, which You created perfect in all its parts so that it should be able to live for years on the face of Your earth, have to be slaughtered? If You knew in advance, God, which calves were meant to be slaughtered and which were not, why did You create the ones meant for slaughter and give them the power to live and to bring more life into the world after them? And if You made them to live, why should you be disobeyed? And what about my little brother who died when he was eight days old? My mother said that even before he was a twinkle in her eye it was written down in a book in heaven how long he would live—but then why was he born with all the makings of a man? What did he need legs for if he wasn't going to walk on them? What did he need hands for if he wasn't going to use them? And what about his mouth? And his lips? What would have happened if the wet nurse hadn't choked him accidentally? And why should she be blamed if it was really the Angel of Death's fault? My mother told me that it was, but if it was the wet nurse who choked the baby, what was there left for the Angel of Death to do? Was it possible for someone, even a little child, to die without him?

'Mama, can someone die without the Angel of Death?'

'Are you out of your mind, Hofni?' my mother exclaimed in embarrassment before the slaughterer, who broke into a broad smile at my idiotic question. 'What's got into you? Do you already know the whole Talmud that you have nothing better to do than to worry about how people die?'

I was left feeling furious and crushed.

I couldn't sleep that night. Bitter, horrible thoughts kept crossing my mind. I hid my face in the blanket because they frightened me so terribly and made me ask such tormenting questions. I felt as if some structure inside of me were collapsing, as if something were being torn from its place and uprooted. . . . I felt that I was at war—with myself, or rather that my mind was at war with my heart, which was in full retreat. Now it made one last stand against the mind's assaults . . . it stumbled and was downed. . . . I felt wounded to the core. . . .

I vowed eighteen more pennies to the alms box. 'O God,' I

whispered the words of the night prayer intently and contritely like a penitent alone with his sinful heart, 'into Thy hand I commit my spirit'—and I slept.

'Minute follows minute, day pursues day.' The second day came and went, the third day, the fourth day, the fifth. . . . On the eighth day the calf would be killed. I went about in a daze.

The calf grew by leaps and bounds and skipped on its long, thin legs. It came running toward me whenever it saw me in the distance, prancing with giddy glee. I greeted it with an inaudible groan, laughing and crying at once.

The terrible eighth day arrived.

I watched the hideous moment come closer. The hours flew by. The sun climbed higher and higher . . . now it was already dipping to the west. How awful it was!

I knew that the calf would not, could not be slaughtered, yet my heart pounded within me. I knew that God would think of something . . . the angels would come to its rescue . . . the knife would explode or its throat turn to marble . . . there was no other way out. My mother was adamant—but a miracle was bound to take place. It was the only solution. The calf was so pretty, and I had promised so much to the alms box. All day long I'd kept raising the sum.

And yet—who knew?

My heart pounded. There were tears in my eyes. I was bursting with emotion. My thoughts raced out of control. It was too much to make sense of. Even the rabbi wouldn't know . . . no, I wouldn't even ask him. He would just laugh at me like my mother and call me a fool. . . .

They slaughtered the calf.

Translated by Hillel Halkin.

Uri Nissan Gnessin

UPROAR

*Gnessin (1879–1913) was born in Russia and received a traditional Jewish education.
Thereafter he led a life of wandering and poverty, like many Hebrew writers of his
time. He was one of the first Hebrew writers to make subjective feeling the primary
content of fiction and to describe it authentically. His minutely detailed approach
to the description of landscape exerted a powerful influence over the Israeli writer S.
Yizhar. Gnessin also introduced the stream-of-consciousness technique into Hebrew
literature, in his case an internal monologue reflecting on the landscape, people, and
ideas in general. He is best known for a series of four long, autobiographical stories
or novellas in which he describes the spiritual trials and psychological dilemmas of
the East European Jewish intellectual. In later years he developed a psychological
style of writing through which he continued to record his observations in detail, this
time of human interaction in the Jewish communities of his day.*

There by the long, plain, flour-dusty carts, which usually stood idly
in the middle of the spacious empty square, beside the pot-bellied
road which sprawled somewhat in the spring sun, with the scrawny
little horses which seemed from afar to be frozen in rigid dreams,
standing like a wall-painting, but for the occasional switch of their
lazy tails at the troublesome flies about them—by those distant carts
a multitude of loud voices suddenly erupted in ringing laughter, and
the rather desolate square, eternally strewn with wisps of loose hay
and sunk in flaccid sleep, suddenly shook feverishly and its immobile
space resounded with bright waves of:

'Oh ho ho ho!'

Along the low wires strung beside the broad road, from one pole
with its white lamp to the next, perched a flock of staid sparrows,
facing the brilliance; alarmed, the birds all took off at once, with a
frightened rustle.

Whrrr . . .

They flew off and began noisily to bathe and swirl in the tranquil

azure light under the vast and friendly sky. *Whrrr*— Come, let them
be, those floury, busy creatures down below! Let them fuss in their
rows of squat, dismal shops on this insignificant patch of ground.
Let the Duke's abandoned castles and clipped orchards serve them
for beauty, and the bright steeple with its proud, foolish neck serve
them for height. *Whrrr*— in truth, are all of these worth one deep
breath of this pure wide azure, and the sublime dreams of its distant
horizon?

Whrrr . . .

Down below there was clamour and the area was suddenly shaken
and full of voices. Dumb Yoli, a yellow, snub-nosed carter whose speech
was incoherent, was apparently one of those speakers, as he lolled in
his cart and excitedly emitted a strange yellowish roar, with a pointed
conclusion:

'The blagues of Egybt take im! Eh? Ho ho ho bull im, bull him,
the blind dog! Ho!'

And his comrades, the other carters, shouted from their carts with
voices like hammers:

'Ho! that cock, let him go to hell!'

'Ho ho! He's just a blind dog! Eh?'

'Ho ho ho! Throw him out! Out of here, Chicken!'

'Cover it up, my boy!'

'It's the truth, as I'm a Jew, ho ho!'

And suddenly the original loud outburst broke again and drowned
the voices.

'Ho ho ho ho!'

It being a partial Christian holiday, the doors of the shops were par-
tially closed. Soon the shopkeepers came out or peered through the
shutters. At the butcher's a little way off, the thumping of the cleaver
was suddenly stilled. A window-pane rattled in the notary's office on
the second floor and the casement was opened wide; at which the fat
chambermaid of the Central Inn, a low, many-windowed hostelry, who
regularly appeared with her skirt hitched up and her arms bared as
she meticulously emptied her pail into the rising black swamp opposite the shabby hallway, stood and rested her idle, longing gaze on the
gang around the distant carts. It was quiet and the square was still
again, the morning sun being sleepy, and nearby, in the apothecary's
yard, the young redhead Prokhor, who served as a coachman, was
grooming his master's horses and placidly chanting psalms in a strange,
churchy voice. Over there, by the long carts, where that ringing, extraordinary clamour had been raised, the wretched horses stood as if

lifeless, while the robust, floured men sprawled wordlessly in their carts. One of them, a stocky, broad-shouldered fellow in a floury apron, stood beside his horse, his whip tucked under his arm, tying on a nosebag full of hay. It was quiet, and in the blue space above them a single sparrow turned and then descended calmly and settled on the iron wires. Had it been an error? Or a delusion, a dream of the ears that ached with the agony of the frozen stillness? A cock began to crow beside the distant river.

But human hearts had been aroused and could not be quieted at once. A wave had broken over them, and even if it was a dream, they would have another in its place. An error, you say? Oh no—do you really want, my merciful Jews, to see human life as devoid of all interest, like a dusty breeze? What else can the more intelligent among you have to offer? A dream . . . The dream of a suffocating soul stuck in squalid idleness and dreaming of salvation? These are the vapid philosophizings of a professional idler. No. Those ears heard laughter —will you please tell me what that laughter signified? The gods are kind, and those voices were tremendous—what did they mean, eh? Now people began popping out of their holes, grasping at straws. Soon they began bringing out rickety benches. Empty crates were shaken and thumped, while the shopkeepers sat outside their shops, expectant. What were they waiting for?

See here—the gods are kind, but not as kind as good people. One of the carters, Kopei Bendit the Chicken by name, tall and robust, somewhat cross-eyed, with one hunched shoulder, suddenly stood up in his cart and pointed his whip at his stocky, broad-shouldered brother-in-law, Chaim Lemi the Orphan, the one who was tending his horse. This same Orphan was always running away from his stumpy, sickly wife, who resembled her tall robust brother in having a crooked shoulder and was even more cross-eyed. She used to go to the Rabbi and wail in a deep, incoherent voice, and get something in writing, then wipe her nose and travel to Starodob, where she would drag her husband from the circus and take him home. The Orphan had married her more than eight years before, moved partly by love, a lonesome orphan's love, instilled in him by the halfpenny stories he devoured in the travelling circus's filthy stable, where he had been employed in his youth, and partly because he had had enough of the circus. Kopei Bendit, the tall, robust, cross-eyed fellow, had slapped him affectionately on the shoulder and cried:

'Take my word for it, brother! After all, you're not a baby. You see that piebald and its cart? They're yours. Trrr! Trrr trrr! Wait a minute!

Pillows and featherbeds too. And that fat samovar, that's also hers—hey—spit, brother! We'll have a swig and be brothers—What more do we need? By my life, eh?'

Only when he took his place under the wedding canopy one clear, icy night, his hand tucked under his arm as the elders led in the bride, and the harps and flutes played, he saw his little woman weeping, a single drop trickling down till it reached the tip of her nose, where it winked at him like a star on the rim of those blue heavens. And when they began reciting the blessing for him to repeat, he stammered and stumbled at every word, the merciful Jews correcting him in unison; and he did not recover that night except when his tall brother-in-law came and sat beside him and gave him a hug, already fairly drunk, and chattered, nodding weakly:

'Mmm . . . Mmm . . . and so forth . . . You understand? Brothers—and so on . . . Don't talk too much with that witch . . . Don't! After all, you're not a baby—that's what it comes to . . .'

Suddenly he got up, struck his chest with his fist, and bellowed mournfully:

'Come to me! You understand? To me! I'll blunt her teeth I promise you, as I live! Mmm . . . Mmm . . . Let's have a drop, brother—and so forth!'

The Chicken was half out of his cart and apparently preaching, and floury caps began rising out of the other carts. Now and then someone laughed briefly, or a whip pierced the air like that of the Chicken, and voices began to rise. Ha! To hell with them. . . . Their wives must have been stingy with the beans today, or that crust of bread they're mourning about—aye! Carters, what do they know . . .

Then Reb Israel Leib Sweet, a prosperous shopkeeper who dealt in sweetmeats, rose and began strolling along his shop, the one under the notary's office, and slowly moved on, while his fingers clumsily rolled a cigarette. He wore his usual black coat and red neckerchief, with the worn cap on his head. Reaching the opposite corner of the road he stopped and carefully licked the edge of the cigarette-paper. He was observed from the further row of shops across the street by Reb Mordechai Ber Shchavil, another affluent shopkeeper who dealt in flour. He was a broad-shouldered, well-dressed person, with a full beard and red nose, and a black mole which sprouted hair. He too rose and left his shop with a loud triple groan: 'Ah,' he said, 'Reb Israel Leib . . . Would you please, just a minute, Reb Israel Leib . . . I would like to say, if you would be so kind . . . this afternoon they will open the mill, and I would like to reclaim my carts—maybe he could lend one a small sum?—I will pay it back tomorrow—eh? Those carters, why are they so noisy today?' Someone in another corner saw them and began yawning and got up for a walk, while on the edge of the square, behind the steeple, a different scene began taking shape, and soon the old square resembled one of those scenes of the resurrection, such as children imagine in their dreams, with figures moving about, tall and short, bent and straight—moving slowly, individuals and groups, grunting and sighing and even talking.

Meanwhile that gang was also changing. The carts were empty and people, some floury and some not, crowded about them.

The Chicken was there too, holding forth, but he was not alone. Many others talked in excited tones and ringing laughter, and the gang swelled. The Orphan was gloomy and ranting:

'You animals! Savage Tartars!'

That was the language he remembered from the circus and the half-penny stories he had read, and he always resorted to it, especially when he was angry.

'What did I say, what? I said you were all a pack of donkeys, all of you! Aye, as I am a Jew. What's your life worth? You're like dumb animals, savages, Asiatics, damn you! All you do is eat and drink and snore and . . . Shut up, Nosey! Human beings—you are human beings? Have you ever been to a show? Ever been to the *teatre*? You asses! Asiatics! Living with you! It's hell living with you. As I'm a Jew! How can anyone live with you? Pfui!'

'Hey, hey!' These words got up the nose of one of the gang and the commotion grew louder. The bystanders began joining in, even those who had not come to watch. Kopei Bendit was silent, his flushed face stilled in dull wonder, while his companions whispered in his ears. Suddenly it seemed that something pierced his feeble brain and he pounced like an animal on his brother-in-law, and his voice rang out:

'Whaa? That's what you want, you uncircumcised Antichrist? To go back to being a tramp? Starodob's calling you again?' He gritted his teeth: 'Shut up, you dunce! Hey? Or I'll squash you right here, like . . . like a flea—pfui!'

The gang fell silent and crowded closer. They were exercising self-control. But the Orphan started again from the beginning, in the same dark tone:

'You animal! You African Tartar! What do you want from me, eh? What . . .'

But he did not finish. At the end of the opposite lane stood Moishe

Butcher, a redheaded Jew who was always laughing and whose white
teeth always gleamed in the sun, together with his filthy apron. He
suddenly jerked forward with a resounding cry, with harsh tones which
sounded like the pounding of the smith's hammer:

'Aha! Shut him up, Chicken! So the fine lad has started again? Shut
him up, I say!'

The Orphan desisted. The blood rushed to his face, but he paled
at once, turned his shoulder to his brother-in-law and began to defy
him.

'And what if it is Starodob? So what, Starodob— What then? I'll
run off to Starodob, if I want to! Hey! So what?'

Suddenly a heavy sigh burst from all the listeners and the men took
a deep breath. Then the excited voices rose again and the uproar
increased:

'Oh ho ho! What a plague! With a wife and children! The nerve!
Oh ho ho ho . . .'

Dumb Yoli's dirty, burning face came forward and his angry bel-
low pierced the eardrums:

'The Antichrist! The horsh and cart, Topei! The horsh and cart, as
I'm a Jew—let him go to hell! Hey!'

Moishe Butcher's hammer resounded from the sidelines:

'A con, is he?' followed by: 'Flatten him, the crook, flatten him!'

The clamour grew and burst like a dam:

'Crush him! You, Chicken! Stick it to him! Squash the unclean
animal! Hit him! Oh ho ho!'

The heads began to move apart. Suddenly there was a crack of a
broken board in one of the carts, and a short, broad-shouldered figure
burst through the crowd, its shorn head uncovered and its shaven face
pale and bleeding on one side, its apron drooping, and it began to
leap and charge and scream wildly, flinging its whip about, shouting
and bellowing:

'You Tartars, the plague take you! Animals! Eat and drink and snore
. . . Animals!'

The group fell silent for a moment, somewhat stunned. Dumb Yoli,
who had marched in fury to the harnessed horse with the fodder-bag
and taken the reins, left the whip to dangle over his shoulder as he
stood with one foot on a wheel axle, remaining thus with his dirty
face flushed and rigid. The Chicken, standing immobile, his big mouth
wide open, breathed heavily like an overworked horse. The Butcher
suddenly groaned from the depths of his belly:

'Animals?! Hey? Finish him off!'

The gang shook. The heads came together again. The more respectable began to sidle away, while others, who were ready for a fight, fell into a commotion. The big Chicken closed his mouth and was the first to jerk forward with a strangled cry, waving a thick wooden board in the air and resembling, from a distance, one of those cheap prints showing Moses breaking the Tablets of the Law, while his hobnailed boots began stomping on the cobblestones. Moishe Butcher groaned and followed him, cleaver in hand, while the other carters swayed and moved on. The commotion swelled. First it was Yoli's roar that thundered:

'Hey, you bastard!'

But the roar was drowned in the great tumult of voices that filled and overflowed the boundaries of the square.

'Ho ho! Get him, Chicken! He wants Starodob, damn him to hell! The Antichrist! With a wife and children, plague take him! Get a move on, Chicken!'

Suddenly the runaway's cart began jolting down the road with a deafening clanging of metal, with Dumb Yoli standing up in it, his strong legs wide apart, whipping the wretched horse which swung from side to side between the shafts. His roars were jolted wildly amid the tumult and he growled like a beast:

'The horsh and cart, damn him to hell! The traitor! You rotter! You unclean shaushage! Damnation!' And more shrilly: 'Leave your wive and children to berish? Well, you vilthy beasht!'

A sudden wind swept over the spacious square, which had always been rather desolate, strewn with loose wisps of hay and sunk in languid sleep. Columns of dust rose and moved like waves, and through them could be discerned the rushing Jews, dogs scrambling from the butcher's shop, barking frantically, and women shouting in the yards, while here and there windows slammed shut, and Yoli and his cart made a deafening racket, and the heavy door of the post office creaked and banged, until the raging storm conquered the square.

But once Yoli and his cart were gone and the pillars of dust slowly began to settle and dark knots of Jews formed, women clustered at the windows and a bunch of clerks gathered beside the post office and the notary's bald pate shone in his second-floor window, not a trace of the storm remained. Silence fell, and the barking dogs vanished, and there was no more shouting. Far from the heart of the deserted square, at the end of the street, there appeared a dark crowd of men, swaying strangely, having apparently forgotten what they were about and fallen silent, the broad-shouldered Orphan at their head, his whip under his arm, followed by the tall Chicken with the wooden plank in his rigid hands, and then the rest of the carters, leaning forward as they trotted at a steady, lumbering pace, only concerned, apparently, not to spoil the formation. It was a strange parade, and the onlookers, who had not witnessed the start of the row, watched it in amazement, searching for an explanation. What was the meaning of the race run by these grown men, for their enjoyment, or perhaps not? What was its object? But even those who might have provided an explanation, in the secret smugness of the sober-minded, for which their arid hearts yearned, even they ignored the nudges and whispers of their companions who did not know the answer, ashamed to admit to them that they too had been carried away, beyond the usual limits. They preferred to remain silent and gaze at the wordless, moving throng so as to avoid looking at their inquisitive companions. The square must have been too spacious for the small gang to conquer, and the dusty low roofs of the shops suddenly began to complain: What a dreary life it is, this life of ours, oh good people . . .

From a distance the gang caught a glimpse of Prokhor's red shirt beside the apothecary's squat, white, proud little shop. He was standing, combed and bare-headed, on the slightly raised porch at the entrance, and his usual psalms were suddenly recalled in the true purpose of the race. Moishe Butcher shouted in a ringing voice: 'Prokhor, hey Prokhor!'

Prokhor shook like a hound at the hunter's whistle, and abandoned his verses. He vaulted over the railing of the porch and dropped down on the fugitive, who swerved like a cat and ran back to the square, beside his pursuers, who were unable to follow him because of Prokhor, who had misjudged his jump and to avoid falling hopped up and down in the street, his body leaning forward and his legs apart, kicking out. By the time he regained his balance he had reached the steeple on the other side of the street, and blurting out a curse he burst out laughing and resumed his tranquil recitation of verses. The gang found itself facing the market again, and continued its silent run in the same formation. Only when they reached Mordechai Ber Shchavil's shop, which was open at both ends and had a door on the street where the Rabbi lived, the Orphan suddenly stopped still. When he saw Mordechai Ber's sickly son sitting in the doorway with his hands on his cane, close to his chest, he gasped and growled, and for some reason shook his fist at him:

'Spoiled offspring of a rotten mother! Her atonement, are you? Pfui!' Having said this he ran through the shop with the gang at his heels.

The square was visibly relieved. A filthy apprentice, holding a shoe-tree in his black hand, shouted to one of the lower windows:

'To the Rabbi! As I'm a Jew—to the Rabbi, Mendel!'

Children broke into a run and women laughed and the Jews chatted and whistled. Mordechai Ber the shopkeeper turned up near the post office, to tell the gang of clerks all that had happened. His companion, Israel Leib, was enlightening the notary, whose head emerged from the second floor, with many Russian words and giggles. At the Central Inn the fat chambermaid was gleefully expounding to the guests who came out, and one traveller with a sleepy face and red blotches on his cheeks kept getting behind her to pinch her on her bare neck. She let out a shriek, which subsided softly:

'Och, my trials . . . Mr Rosilkroit!'

In Shchavil's passage shop the sickly young man, excited and pale, lips trembling, groaned and voiced his complaint to the crowd, which was dwindling as people went by the opposite exit to the street, which echoed with the laughter of women and the pranks of the children, with and without shoes on. The Rabbi's house stood wide open, its windows packed with children and adults, thick as flies, as were the dining-room and corridor, while the black tail of the crowd straggled into the street.

Inside everyone was talking at once, including the peepers in the windows, a noisy racket, in the midst of which a little cross-eyed woman stood beside the red curtain, holding two miserable, frightened girls by their hands. She was sobbing in a gruff masculine voice, blowing her nose and bellowing unintelligible phrases, while the Rabbi, who had come out of his private room with a great book in his hands and his spectacles on his nose, stood beside his great chair and listened with difficulty to the Chicken's roar:

'Hey! All of a sudden, the devil knows what goes on in his dirty mind. A man goes to sleep at night, healthy and sound—and then she says, Rabbi, he's got fire in his belly!'

Chaim Lemi stood by the wall, pale and crushed, the trickle of blood on his cheek now dry and his head covered with a sort of crushed silk cap which had been found for him in the Rabbi's house. He was silent, his pale face looking as if he had just broken the bonds of a strange dream and was wondering where he was. The Rabbi, still standing with a hand in his half-opened book, was saying something, it seemed, and asking several questions, but did not hear anything. The Chicken was close by, wiping his dirty, low brow with his filthy sleeve. It seemed that he had finished speaking. But suddenly the

Orphan's face flushed and he emerged from his corner, ploughed through the crowd to the Rabbi and shouted:

'Rabbi! No . . . Rabbi! I ask you . . . what I want to ask you. . . . For example, Rabbi . . . when I married the woman—doesn't it mean. . . . Doesn't it mean that I'm the man? Me? I'm the man, aren't I?'

He stopped and glanced at the Rabbi's face. Seeing the Rabbi's face turned to him he banged his fist on the table.

'The hell with her! When I say beans, that's what it should be, beans! Isn't that so, Rabbi? Should be beans, say!'

Suddenly he fell silent and his face turned pale again. The uproar began again. The Rabbi sat down and laughed, and his twitching shoulders revealed his growing anger. The woman continued to chatter unintelligibly, and the tall Chicken began to yell again. The crowd was aroused. Dumb Yoli's piercing scream resounded from the street as he approached, now on foot, scraping his hobnailed boots on the hard ground, and Chaim Lemi looked down and backed away to the wall in a daze. Suddenly the woman began howling again, and Chaim Lemi looked at her and saw her cross-eyed face, faded and wrinkled like an old boot, and from the swollen tip of her nose hung a trembling drop, and unable to restrain himself he charged at her, roaring:

'Home, you witch! This minute!'

One of the frightened girls began to cry, while peals of laughter filled the place and the racket started again. The woman was alarmed and her face fell even more. She put up a hand to shield her lowered head, as Chaim Lemi suddenly spat: 'Pfui!'

Rushing to the open door, he roared: 'That's enough, you animals!'

The onlookers, shocked, moved out of his way. In the corridor some tried to block his way, but he grunted and someone fell down with a curse. Once in the street he stopped and shouted up at the windows:

'You, witch! Hey, tell that witch of mine to go home now. Right now! I want something to eat!' He roared out in conclusion:

'You wild animals! You savage Tartars! The hell with you and your dirty hearts . . . pfui!'

That afternoon, when the doors of the flour-mill opened and the carters drove up their noisy carts, including Shchavil's two carts which he had reclaimed, Chaim Lemi stood by, urging on his lazy horse and lighting his cigarette with the burning end of his brother-in-law's, who was also whipping his horse forward. And when the Chicken saw the other's apron hanging loose, as it had that morning, he growled:

'That witch, the plague take her! Is she too sick to sew it up so it won't hang down?'

He sucked on his cigarette and handed it back to his brother-in-law, spitting with excitement.

But Chaim Lemi seized his brother-in-law's thick paw and touching the end of his cigarette to the other cigarette, exclaimed as he inhaled: 'To sew it? . . . And what about food? . . . Women—She made a Yom Kippur for me today!'

The Chicken recoiled as if bitten by a snake, and his neck swelled and reddened:

'What?! That's the sort of trick she's up to?— The idiot. I'll teach her a lesson!'

He fixed his cross-eyed gaze on his brother-in-law, who had lit his cigarette and was puffing on it to get it going. He seized his shoulder affectionately and straightened it. Then he promised him, beating his fist on his heart:

'You listen to me, brother—you'll see! Don't let anything stop you— just slap her down! One-two-three—slap her down! Hey hey, stop right there! Ah, that's the way!'

Translated by Yael Lotan.

Yitzhak Dov Berkowitz

CUT OFF

Berkowitz (1885–1967) was born in Belorussia and received a traditional educa-
tion. From 1905 his articles and stories appeared in most of the Hebrew and Yiddish
journals of his day. In 1913 he and his wife immigrated to the United States, where
he continued his editorship of Hebrew journals. He settled in Palestine in 1928 and
became one of the first editors of the Hebrew literary monthly Moznayim, which is
still published today. Berkowitz's short stories, which consider the general crises of
Jewish life at the time, are realistic and notable for their precise style. His novel,
Menahem Mendel in Palestine (1936), is a satirical work which reflects the
life of immigrants to Palestine. He was the author of a number of plays and he
translated into Hebrew the collected writings of Sholem Aleichem, the great Yiddish
writer, who was his father-in-law.

The journey from the quiet little Lithuanian town to faraway New York passed over old Dvorah like a dream. The days and nights in the fast train, the immense, crowded stations beyond the border, where the sounds of alien voices filled the air, the changing views and faces, lands and foreign languages, the hurried desperate rush of her fellow Jews—all these appeared like a fascinating vision from the ageless past, like a forgotten fairy tale from her distant childhood, miraculously revived. Her dim old memory recalled ancient visions from the tales of *Tsena Ur'ena*: the Tower of Babel, the cries of men and women who could not understand each other's speech, the journey of the sons of Jacob to Egypt and their entry through the gates of the alien city, the Judaean exiles in chains, with their hunger-stricken women and children, led in chains by the butcher Nebuzaradan . . . In the night, while the train rushed past darkened fields, she saw in the black window-pane the image of the weeping Rachel by the roadside—the image of her dead daughter, running in step with the rattling iron wheels, her hands outstretched and her wail blending with the shriek of the loco-motive. Then came days of darkness, without shape or form. In the dim cabin, under its low ceiling, amid the roar of the sea and the ceaseless creaking of the ship, the old woman turned on her narrow bunk in mute solitude, full of wonder, travelling upon the face of the dark abyss. Her seventy years in her little native town seemed like a remote and deserted island which she had left behind—like that wondrous island, its mountains and cliffs lit by the setting sun, that slowly shrank and disappeared from view when the ship set out from the shore in the evening mist. Her five sons and daughters who had died in childhood appeared before her in their true forms and features, and her husband, too, rose from his grave, and with them a multitude of dead friends and neighbours came up from oblivion, and they all gazed at her from the distant cemetery hill, with its low white tombstones, peering through the green foliage, shaking their heads at her: Where, where are you fleeing from us? . . . The sea growled fiercely outside the cabin wall, and in the dead of night the old woman raised her head dizzily from her pillow, awakened from another world, sat up and stared at the bunks of her sleeping fellow-travellers, unable to comprehend who they were, and what she was doing, or where inscrutable fate was leading her in her final days of life. In her confusion, the single image which flickered like a spark of light in the darkness—that of her one living son in America—was blurred out of recognition.

One morning they roused her from her hazy dreams and told her that the ship was approaching the shore. She was made to get up and walk through long, narrow corridors and stand before some uniformed officials, who asked questions about her and were assisted by good people who came to her rescue, and wrote everything in a book. Then she was led out into the open air. All at once a strange new world was revealed to her, with clamouring crowds of people, all hurrying to disembark, looking excited, frightened, or full of joy. The sun shone warm and bright, white ships with tall funnels gleamed in the clear air, glided over the water as if on parade, blew out smoke and uttered mighty shrieks against the heavens. The little old woman trembled on her unsteady legs, peered out from her black kerchief at the bustling passengers, utterly confused, and wondered if there was any mistake. While going down the ship's gangway, led by one of the stewards who was carrying her belongings, she noticed a man pushing his way towards her through the crowds below, who then climbed up the gangway, waving excitedly and laughing, flashing gold teeth. Her heart went out momentarily to this man, whose dark laughing eyes looked familiar, but the alien glitter of his teeth held her back. And while she wondered abut him and turned this way and that, the man embraced her in his strong, warm arms:

'Mama, it's you! Don't you recognize me, dear Mama?'

'Mr Rabinowitz?' asked the steward.

'Mister Rabinowitz, Mister Robbins, it's all the same, my friend!' the son replied joyfully. 'I am he, the man you're looking for!'

Bent and helpless, leaning on the arm of her tall, broad-shouldered son, the little old woman walked among the heaps of chests and bundles which cluttered the harbour station, blinking with tear-dimmed eyes at the strange, clean-shaven features of this son of hers, and her wrinkled lips alternately smiled and wept.

'I did not know you . . . Indeed, I didn't recognize you, my son! Such a very long time—it's been eighteen years since I last saw you . . . But I looked at you, and I said to myself, who is that strange man? And it was you, Reuveleh! . . . I always carry your picture with me, but your face looks different in it, like it was at home, with a moustache . . .'

'The moustache, Mama dear, has departed this world,' said the son, laughing gaily. 'What do I need a moustache for, now that I have money?'

'Ah, well, in that case, thank God . . . I am not saying anything, my son . . . Where is the chest? My head is going round and round, and my eyes, the Lord be praised, are not as good as they used to be . . . I have only one chest. I brought it for you, my son, your father's inheritance, God rest his soul—a chest full of books. And for your wife, may she live long, I have a different gift, some silver candlesticks, which belonged to your grandmother, may she rest in peace . . .'

When they reached the son's house they were met by a tall young woman with short-cropped blond hair, wearing gold-rimmed spectacles. Slowly and calmly she came forward to meet the guest, took off her spectacles and looked at her with cold, enquiring blue eyes. Her hard, chiselled features smiled briefly, politely, as she exclaimed, 'Oh hello, Mother!' and gave her a casual, fluttery kiss on the cheek. Then she put her spectacles back on and stood gazing at the newcomer with cool curiosity. The old woman recoiled a little in alarm.

'This is Florence, Mama,' the son said proudly. 'My wife.'

'I see, my son, I understand,' the old woman said in a low voice and looked uncertainly at her daughter-in-law.

'She's a good woman, but a terribly strict housewife, God help us all!' the son went on in the same tone and hugged his wife. 'Mama dear, did you expect to find such a fine daughter-in-law, with short hair and glasses? That's how it is out here, you know. If you like, you can call her by her Jewish name—Faigeh-Leah. That's what her grandmother called her.'

'Oh no, please, not Faigeh-Leah!' protested Mrs Robbins to her husband, in a language which was mostly English and a little Yiddish, slipping out of his embrace and wrinkling her nose. 'I don't like that sort of thing!'

Mr Robbins's two sons came out of another room to kiss their grandmother. The older boy, a lad of fourteen, blond-haired and blue-eyed like his mother, approached the old woman calmly, asking his father in a precise, matter-of-fact voice: 'Is this the grandmother?' He kissed her coolly and politely, as if doing his duty. But the younger boy, ten years old, with laughing black eyes like his father's, flushed with excitement when he felt on his neck the thin tremulous hands of his grandmother, newly arrived from across the ocean.

'A couple of *goyim*! Two complete *goyim*!' their father said happily. 'They don't know a single word of Yiddish. American boys, you know!'

The old woman sat, speechless and remote, in front of her new family in their splendid living-room, and glanced uncertainly at the strange opulence around her. Her stiff trembling fingers continued to grasp the bundle at her feet, as though for support and security in the alien surroundings. The others stood silently, gazing with curious anticipation at the little old woman with the wrinkled face, who looked so strange in her kerchief and the full, old-fashioned black dress. She looked as though she had only come in briefly, as though at any moment she would rise and take her bundle and go back as she had come. The first to break the silence was the older boy. He moved away, bored by the scene, walked around the room looking up at the ceiling, and suddenly went to the wall and slapped it hard.

'A fly!' he explained, looking reproachfully at the startled family.

When they were left alone in the room, the old woman looked up at her son and observed him dully for a moment, without saying a word. Then her mouth twitched and her eyes filled with tears:

'And what do you say, Reuveleh, to a pain like my pain? She died, she too died on me, Shifreleh . . . The one daughter left of all my darlings, and God took her too. They all left me, every one of them, and I'm alone, like a broken pot . . . And he, my son-in-law, God have mercy on my grey hair, he didn't even wait one year, but took a second wife, a stepmother for my daughter's orphans . . . How could I stand by and see it happen? . . . So I have come to you, my son. You invited me and I came. Who else have I got in this world, for my sins, who else? . . . I dragged my old bones to America, though God knows, it's hard for me to be a burden to you and your wife and children, the Lord give them many years, and I don't even understand their speech . . .'

'Oh don't, Mama, please! Don't, my dear!' Mr Robbins, agitated, sat down beside his mother and gently stroked her bent shoulders. 'You mustn't . . . On the contrary . . . We both, that is, me and Florence, we're happy and honoured! . . . You'll get used to us, you'll be pleased with us. Of course, America is not like Europe. Many things here don't look right at first . . . But that's why it's America! You know, Mama dear, America is worth everything, and she pays handsomely. America has everything in plenty!'

Mr Robbins rose, lit a cigarette, pushed his hands into his pockets, stretched to his full height and looked at his old mother with sparkling eyes.

'You know, Mama dear,' he said warmly, 'Here I am a wealthy man, thank God. How much do you think I'm worth now, Mama, eh? I can tell you the secret. I suspect a hundred thousand dollars would not buy me out today! Do you know how much that is in European money? And that's not including this house, with the garden and the furniture and the jewellery. It's all mine! I made it all, with these ten fingers . . . Not that it was easy, to get to where I am now!'

Mr Robbins began to tell his old mother about the trials and tribulations of his first years in America. Excitedly, he narrated everything that he had done from the time of his arrival until the present moment. The old woman sat hunched and attentive, her face alternately sad and smiling, listening not so much to what he was saying as to the sound of his voice, which seemed to grow clearer and more like the voice of her dead husband, until it became exactly like it in tone and intonation.

'Eighteen years!' the son repeated, deeply moved, blowing cigarette smoke at the ceiling. 'So many adventures since those days . . . You know, Mama dear . . . Just think how strange it is . . . I remember now . . . In the early days I lived on bread and salt herring, and was still dreaming of going back. I used to lie awake at night, thinking thoughts and imagining things, how I would go back to my mother and father, just to rest a little, how I would sit with you in the evenings beside the samovar, and tell you all sorts of things, all that I had seen and suffered here, in the alien country, in the days of my unhappiness . . . For many years I kept those thoughts to myself . . .

But much water has flowed since then, and everything has changed. Father died . . . And now, here you are today, you have come to me in America. I was able to send for you, thank God, travelling first-class, to this house, with its fine furniture, and the jewellery, and . . . everything of the best . . . and now when I want to remember the old things, my memory fails . . . well, nothing doing* . . . I've forgotten it all . . . the important things . . .'

Mrs Robbins was standing in the doorway, straightening her spectacles.

Her coolly pleasant voice addressed no one in particular:

'Would Mother care to eat? The table is laid.'

'Do you want to eat, Mama?' Mr Robbins echoed his wife's question.

'No, daughter, I am not hungry,' replied the old woman, turning to her daughter-in-law with obvious affection.

'If Mother wants to eat, she needn't be afraid,' the lady of the house said in a softened tone. 'We've made everything in the house kosher.'

The old woman stared at her in amazement.

'Florence says,' the son hurriedly explained, throwing his wife a pleading look, 'that is, what Florence means is that here in our house everything is . . . of course it is . . . we are regular Jews here . . . that is, our food is kosher . . . strictly* kosher . . . You needn't be afraid . . .'

'God forbid!' the old woman said, horrified.

II

They put the book chest in the old woman's little room, which was set aside for her in a corner of the house, near the boys' room. Humbly, wordlessly, she opened it in the presence of her two grandsons, rummaged among the big old volumes and brought out two small, new prayer-books, which she gave to the boys with a mute gesture. The older boy opened the strange little book, glanced at it dubiously, and replaced it in the chest with a shrug, as if to say, What use is it to me? But the younger boy was pleased with his grandmother's gift. He took it to his room and returned a few moments later, and without a word showed the old woman that he cherished the gift—he had covered the book in yellow paper to protect it. He smiled at her with his bright, good-natured eyes. The old woman patted his bare head with a wistful smile, as one pats a nice Gentile child.

Mrs Robbins accepted her mother-in-law's gift of silver candlesticks with a little nod, and said, 'Oh fine!' The next day the old woman

* An asterisk indicates that the preceding word or phrase appears in English in the original.

found them standing on the table in her own room, brightly polished, with fresh wax candles in them. Later Mr Robbins explained to his mother, with an apologetic smile, that candlesticks from Europe did not go with American furniture. He himself would not have noticed it, but she, that is to say, Florence, was very finicky about her house. And, after all, she was the housewife, and she was a native of this country and knew better than any of us . . . Nothing doing!*

During the first few days the son led his mother all over his house. He took her down to the basement, showed her all the fine objects above and the marvellous furnaces below, showed her how coal was used for heating the house and the water, and as he went along he quoted the price of everything and converted it to 'European' money. Then he led her out into the garden, showed her the bushes and shrubs one by one and the surrounding hedge—all of which he had cultivated with his own hands. It was the end of summer, the days were overcast, and by then not much was left in the little garden but a few young trees which were already shedding their leaves, and some unsuccessful lettuces sticking up here and there in the parched beds. Mr Robbins realized that there was not, as yet, much to boast about in his garden, but he assured his mother that in ten or twenty years the garden would be like a splendid orchard, and when the subway reached the neighbourhood, why then, the value of the house with the garden would be multiplied ten times . . . In European money that would really be a princely sum! . . . The old woman listened to all these strange statements, nodded with a wistful, resigned smile at her triumphant and happy son, and looked around her very sadly. Mr Robbins's house was in one of the new suburbs on the outskirts of the city, a quiet, desolate area, and behind the garden, through the fine mist, there were only bare fields and dusty roads, leading to dark woods—a vast, foreign land to her lonely, troubled heart.

Mr Robbins began to go to the city every day, to look after his business, and the old woman wandered about the opulent rooms, bent and worried, as though searching for something she had lost. Or else she sat for hours at the table in her room, blinking dimly at the shining silver candlesticks, which gleamed with great age. Now and then she could hear, coming from the quiet adjacent rooms, the voice of Mrs Robbins speaking to the cook—the strict, imperious tones of the mistress of the house. From time to time young neighbours came to visit, and then the house rang with lively voices and loud, alien laughter, which startled the old woman from her mournful dreams and confused the visions and illusions floating about her.

One day, as she wandered aimlessly from room to room, she found herself in the kitchen with the black cook, and stopped hesitantly in the doorway, as though in strange and uncertain terrain. The black woman smiled at her good-naturedly with brilliant white teeth, pulled out a chair and offered it to her respectfully. The old woman gazed curiously for a few minutes at the fat cook's shiny dark face. Then she remained to watch her work. Suddenly she saw something strange and terrible which shook her to the core. Confused and shocked, she stumbled out of the kitchen, and rushing to her room with unseeing eyes, she accidentally opened another door. Inside stood her daughter-in-law, her face painted, half-naked, fastening her corset. She stared at her with cold eyes and exclaimed harshly:

'What do you want here, Mother?'

That evening, at the dinner table, the old woman did not touch anything, putting her son off with the excuse that her head ached. But after she had not touched her food for two days, Mr Robbins became alarmed and went to her room to discover what was wrong. She began to weep and plead with him to let her eat only dairy dishes at his house, or else to take pity on her and send her back across the water to her native country and town.

'I cannot, my son, I cannot stand it . . .', the old woman wept feebly. 'How much more time have I got to live? I cannot change my nature, my son . . .'

'But what did you see in there?' asked Mr Robbins awkwardly. 'I thought we'd made everything kosher . . . We even bought new dishes . . . Strictly kosher . . .'

'Of course kosher, my son . . . What am I saying, God forbid? But I can't change my nature, Reuveleh, I can't . . .'

Later that night two voices came from the master bedroom, arguing until late, Mrs Robbins's forceful soprano and Mr Robbins's soft, pleading baritone. In the morning Mr Robbins came to his mother's room, his face as always clean-shaven, fresh and cheerful.

'Well, Mama dear, everything is all right!* Did you think you came to America to starve, God forbid? That would be a fine state of affairs, I swear! . . . In short, Mama dear, everything has been settled in the best possible way, thank God. From now on you can prepare your own meals, just as you like them. We'll get you the very best kosher meat, with the kosher stamp on it, and you can prepare it any way you like—salt it, wash it, cook it and eat it to your heart's content!'

Thereafter the old woman cooked her own meals. Abject and ashamed, she would stand in an unobtrusive corner of the kitchen, shrinking into herself while she furtively prepared her daily meal. Then she would sit in her room, miserable and alone, gazing distractedly at her plate for a long time.

On the eve of Rosh Hashanah, the New Year, Mr Robbins put on a new hat, which he had bought in his mother's honour, called his two sons, and they took the old woman to the synagogue.

'What do you think, Mama, isn't it like the synagogue in our town?' the son boasted as they walked. 'You'll see what kind of synagogues Columbus builds for his Jews in America. I swear, you couldn't get a synagogue like this for less than half a million dollars! . . .'

Pressed on all sides by the gorgeously dressed congregation, the little old woman sat beside her son. She wore her ample, orange-white holiday dress, with a knitted silk scarf over her wig, her ancient earrings dangling from her ears. She turned her tremulous head this way and that, and gazed wonderingly at the massive, big-bellied men with their fat, worldly, smug faces, and the fleshy women, bare-throated and bejewelled, their gold teeth gleaming. She heard loud talking, a merry clamour, the loud laughter of well-fed, secure and satisfied souls. From afar, high above the crowd, appeared the cantor, dressed in white, and a chorus of singers in black hats stood in a row, like soldiers on parade, and broke into a strange, chill song, which seemed to flow far from the heart. She felt as though an icy profane wind was blowing through the dense warm atmosphere, and the bright electric lights seemed to dim. Glumly, mutely, she looked down at her old prayer-book with its worn pages. The sacred emotion which had filled her heart at the start of the ten Days of Awe, stronger than ever in her solitary exile, was dispelled there and then. Her soul felt bare and empty. She closed her eyes and sank into a stupor.

'There is no God here . . .', a chill, terrifying thought passed through her desolate mind. 'He is not here, not here . . .'

Later, when they sat down to the festive dinner at Mr Robbins's house, amid the jingling silver spoons, the old woman slipped out of the dining-room, repelled by the warm, fatty smell of the food, which was making her feel ill. She went to her little room and stood in front of the window, which faced the dark empty fields and skies. Like a prisoner in her forgotten cell, she stood unmoving in wordless prayer, longing for the lost and distant God across the ocean, in her town far away.

III

Autumn came, dark and wet, with long, desolate nights, and the old woman's gloomy solitude intensified. The window of her room overlooked a narrow, fenced back yard, where laundered underclothes always hung in rows on tightly stretched lines. The old woman would sit at the window for hours, gazing at the rows of white garments flapping in the dark air, and musing about her remaining days, which were passing in this strange and incomprehensible place, far from God and from people, without warmth or solace for her grieving heart. Sometimes she slipped into a doze, and the darkness around her filled with a multitude of long-lost forms and shadows from bygone years, among them her husband, upright and black-bearded, who went to the water-bowl in the passage to wash his hands, returned and walked about in the dark, humming a prayer in a sweet, low voice, familiar and wistful, suggesting eternal rest.

Then something happened in the Robbins house: Mr Robbins bought an automobile, and the family was all agog. Everyone learned to drive the automobile: husband and wife, Mrs Robbins's two brothers, who lived nearby, and Mr Robbins' partner, who came up from the city several times to see the novelty with his own eyes. Mr Robbins walked around with his shirtsleeves rolled up, his face streaked and shiny, entirely absorbed in his new pleasure, like a man to whom fortune has opened the horn of plenty, who can't take it all in. One day he strode into his mother's room, his face beaming triumphantly:

'Today I almost killed a man with my car . . . And you, Mama dear, still sitting all alone in your room, thinking that nothing grows in America but women's petticoats and stockings and men's underwear . . . Just you wait a little—I'll learn this coachman's trade properly and then I'll take you with me and show you this country's marvels!'

In the evenings there were guests, mostly neighbours, young couples who would sit around the table, drinking tea and playing cards until late. Mrs Robbins presided over these activities, her face changed beyond recognition, flushed red. A blue flame burned in her eyes, and her spectacles became fogged. When they stopped for tea they asked the old woman to join them. To cheer his mother up, Mr Robbins opened the gramophone and played Jewish records. Out of the hissing machine came the songs of Yiddish comedians, wedding tunes played by traditional fiddlers, music from the Yiddish theatre, and in the midst of it all, the *Kol Nidrei* prayer. Reticent and shy, the old woman sat among the strangers, listening in speechless wonder to the familiar voices and melodies which emerged from the gramophone's rasping throat, and imagined the wretched Jew hidden inside the magic box, who had sold his soul to Satan for a silver coin and turned the sacred prayer into a rowdy song . . .

At night the old woman tossed and turned, gripped alternately by insomnia and nightmares. Once she saw her little native town in a new guise: it was built of strange new houses, stretching to the horizon. She was stumbling wearily down a long, narrow street, looking for her house, where her husband was awaiting her, but on either side there were wet clothes flapping on laundry lines, blocking her view. When it grew dark, her daughter came from the back of the garden and waved and beckoned her to follow. There, only there, would she be able to rest her aching legs! But then she was rushing past in an automobile, rushing and shouting to her daughter to stop, to stand still for a moment, before she lost sight of her among the petticoats and stockings. Then the car slipped away from under her and she fell hard on an iron-bound chest which had been thrown out. 'The book chest!' cried a skull which hovered in the darkness, the skull of the Jewish wizard who had sung *Kol Nidrei*, and his menacing voice filled her with horror and foreboding.

She would wake with a start from these dreams, and in the still darkness she perceived with awful clarity the vast distance which separated her from her lost town, and the deep void which gaped in her final years of life.

One cloudy morning her son came into her room, freshly shaved, to tell her that one of his acquaintances, who lived nearby, had just lost his aged father, and the neighbours were arranging a magnificent funeral. Twelve automobiles had been ordered! Since Mrs Robbins did not care for such things, he suggested that his mother might like to accompany him in his car when he went to the funeral. In the first place, it would be a pious act, since the deceased had been a truly righteous man. It was said of him that from the moment he came to America he ate nothing but bread and onions. Secondly, he, her son, wanted very much to take her in his car. And while they were about it, she would see what a Jewish graveyard in America looked like.

'A Jewish graveyard?' the old woman asked, agitated. She was amazed that in all that time she had never given a thought to this important matter. The most important thing, and she had forgotten it!

'They call it a cemetery* here,' her son continued contentedly. 'You really should see the tombstones the Jews in America put on their graves. Some of them look like palaces, and believe me, they cost tens of thousands of dollars!'

The old woman put on her ample dress, tied her black kerchief on her head, and unsteadily followed her son. When they were seated in the car to go to the funeral, Mr Robbins turned to his mother and said:

'Don't worry and don't be afraid, Mama. You can trust me, nothing will happen to you. I have become a first-rate coachman, thank God!'

In front of the deceased's house stood a long row of shiny black limousines. On the wide porch and in the open entrance hall stood groups of men, chatting calmly, laughing, smoking thick cigars. Mr Robbins greeted his friends and heartily slapped them on their shoulders. The old woman shrank beside the door, hunched and observant, watching the people who milled about with their ordinary expressions, the same round, well-fed, smug faces. The women among them were painted and bejewelled, as if it were a holiday. The man of the house, the son of the deceased, stood leaning against the wall, one hand in his trouser pocket, and talked at length on the telephone in a calm, confident voice. There was no weeping and mourning, not a sign of bereavement. A strange funeral!

When the man finished speaking into the telephone, Mr Robbins slapped him on the back. 'Hullo, Marcuse!' he said. 'So the old man died, eh? I'm so sorry, believe me . . . Still, as they say, may no one die any younger . . . Listen, Marcus, if you want to sit comfortably in a new car, I'll take you and Mrs Marcus with me. My car is empty— only me and my old mother.'

'What, you want to bury him together with his father? Leave him alone, he's still young!' joked one of the men, and everybody laughed aloud. The bereaved son also grinned, showing his gold teeth. But remembering that it was unseemly for him to be laughing on this day, his face assumed a grave expression.

The door of the adjoining room was opened, revealing a long, narrow coffin, wrapped in black cloth and covered with a worn old ark curtain with a white Star of David on it. A man peered out, wearing a big hat which came down to his ears, and his eyes, above his stiff, clipped yellow beard, looked hard and angry.

'Well? What are you waiting for, eh?' he snapped at them in a hoarse commanding voice, making the most of his momentary importance. 'Where is the son? They should bring the *tallit*, bring the *tallit* here!'

The funeral was a hurried affair. The long line of automobiles sped past empty streets and bare fields, looking like a flock of black demons chasing the dead man fleeing before them. The old woman swayed alone in her son's car, gazing with a heavy heart through the little window at bleak and alien buildings, iron bridges suspended in the cloudy air, factory smokestacks looming black through the mist. Then the funeral passed through seedy alleys, among dilapidated old houses, and encountered a long row of freight cars loaded with coal, timber, rags for paper pulp. The automobiles rushed past, bumping on the uneven cobblestones. Here and there between the houses tombstones could be seen, Jewish as well as Gentile ones with crosses on top. Finally they emerged among bare autumn fields surrounded by desolate hills and valleys, with a scattering of trees which seemed to be in mourning.

The funeral procession stopped. The mourners emerged from their automobiles and slowly followed the coffin-bearers through the wide open iron gates. Large and small tombstones with English inscriptions stood on either side of the white gravelled path. Among them rose some magnificent marble structures.

'You see, Mama, what it's like here?' said Mr Robbins to his mother, leading her by the arm, as he had done when showing her around his property. 'It's not bad here, not bad at all!'

A fine drizzle began to fall and everyone hurried. Beside the open grave stood two Polish Gentiles holding spades, their smooth, predatory faces expressing a cool contempt for the outlandish activity before them.

'You take the head, Yuzesh,' one of them called to the other, pointing to the top end of the coffin with his spade.

The grave was quickly filled, and the Jew in the big hat with the clipped yellow beard began to sway and chant the prayer of submission in a hoarse voice and with a strange melody that sounded as if he had borrowed it from the Pentecost prayers. Then he turned his stiff beard to the assembled company, who were standing, looking sad and curious, around the fresh mound of earth.

'Well? Where's the son?' he demanded angrily. 'Kaddish! Kaddish! . . .'

The rain intensified and became a downpour. Through the dark mist which was blowing in from the bare fields, the hummocks and tombstones looked like silent witnesses from another world. The company hastened back to their automobiles, running past each other. Mr Robbins called some of his friends to his car, and with a wet, smiling face held the door open for them. Once again the car rocked on the bumpy road, while the rain streamed down on it. The old woman, pressed into her corner by the strange, clean-shaven men, shut her eyes and sank into a tumult of obscure images. She saw huge freight cars loaded with coal, desolate fields stretching to the heavens, alien tombstones glistening in the autumn rain, and herself abandoned and alone in a deep, dark hollow, cut off from God and from memories of family, sinking and lost in a great void.

Upon their return from the funeral Mr Robbins invited his friends into the house for a light meal. In their honour, and because of the rain, Mrs Robbins produced a strong cherry liqueur. They drank and felt warmer, talked about the funeral, joked about the bereaved son's mangled reading of the *Kaddish*, and laughed heartily. In the midst of the jollity, Mr Robbins remembered that his mother had not had time to prepare her kosher meal, and went to her room to see her. When he reached her door he thought he heard an unusual sound from within, like the thin wail of a baby. He opened the door carefully and recoiled in astonishment.

His old mother was sitting on the book chest, looking smaller and more bent than ever, clutching her shaking head and weeping feebly, bereft of hope and comfort, like a tiny, abandoned orphan, forsaken by God and man.

Translated by Yael Lotan.

Yosef Hayyim Brenner

TRAVEL NOTES

Brenner (1881–1921) was born in the Ukraine into a pious home, and he studied at the same yeshivah as Gnessin. After two years in the Russian army he fled to London in 1904. After some months back in Lemberg he immigrated to Palestine in 1909, where, after having suffered through the First World War, he was killed in the Arab riots of 1921. Brenner was a novelist, a short-story writer, a literary scholar, and an editor. His stories and novels reflect the grim realities of Jewish life in the countries in which he lived. His writings mirror his own experience in graphic detail. His major novel, Breakdown and Bereavement (1920), represents an autobiographical journey into the difficulties and dilemmas of Jewish life in Palestine during the period of the Second Aliyah. His principal characters are anti-heroes, uprooted and despairing intellectuals trapped in the poverty and physical degradation of diaspora life. Or they wander from place to place, hoping that a change of abode will also change their destiny. Brenner wrote six novels, a play, and many short stories and articles.

I

We arrived at that little town from the nearest railway station at about ten o'clock at night. This was, as I have told you, in the early days of the month of *Nisan*, when late winter and early spring are mingled. The distance from the station to the town was scarcely thirty miles, but it took us the better part of a day. We were, of course, riding in a carriage, and so broken ice as well as mud served to slow us down. I must say that our coachman did his very best to get us there on time, but he struggled in vain. His mares were most patient and submitted meekly to the whip, and if now and then it roused them into a trot, it was a purely Jewish arousal, meaning that it lasted no more than a minute. The road, moreover, twisted and writhed over hills and gulleys, streams and valleys, like all the roads in that border province.

When I say 'we all', I am referring, gentlemen, to four people: three 'souls', namely passengers, and one 'messenger' or guide. At this time he was guiding us to the border town, there to hand us over to the 'leader', namely, the man who was to lead us secretly across the border.

I ought to tell you that the one who was now our guide was a regular fellow: tall and sturdy, sure of his strength and contemptuous of danger, cold of speech and stolid of manner, haughty, externally off-putting and distant but with a fire in his belly . . . In brief, my friends, he was first-rate . . . But he is not our subject here. Our subject is us, the passengers: your humble servant, myself, obliged to exile myself at that time, and my two companions; the one scrawny, with sick, gummy eyes and spectacles, the other well-fed, jowly, and pot-bellied. They were both the sons of solid burghers, maintained by their broker or shopkeeper fathers, both single, educated, and involved in the kind of activities that get you arrested. The first had already been caught and imprisoned, and freed on bail until his trial. He was about to jump bail, abandoning his father, who had sold his house and belongings to set him free, and fleeing the country. The other one had not yet been caught, and who knows what great deeds he might yet have done, but for the fact that he was about to be conscripted the following autumn, and his own parents urged him to hurry and escape from that unwholesome fate . . . So, where were we?

Yes. We arrived in the town at about ten o'clock at night. Whoa . . . Our coachman, a man accustomed to such journeys, halted his mares with a special call as soon as we reached the outskirts, and there the four of us, the three passengers and the guide, got out. Shhh . . . The coachman received his pay, whipped up his fleet steeds and disappeared into the night. Then the four of us began walking into town, but not together. Two by two: myself with the guide making up the first pair, my two companions behind, as the second pair.

A strange hush hung over the streets, a suppressed sort of quiet, humming, it seemed, deep in its throat, like the stifled silence of a besieged city. Whoever has not experienced the silence of those border towns cannot imagine what it is like . . . would not know or understand. The very air was charged with suspicion . . . hush! . . . no one passes . . . Who goes there?

Our stalwart guide took the long way around, going down byways and avoiding the highway. We passed through gardens, slunk through gaps. Shhh . . . If anyone found out that we were there, it would be all up with us. Every step we took was taken by stealth. The ice under our cautious feet crunched and filled our shivering bones with dread . . .

At last—a courtyard with a lodge. Shhh . . . 'You stay here and I'll go across to the house opposite. You see it? The house across the street. If I find that it's empty, I'll take you there.' So said the guide, and vanished. We pressed ourselves soundlessly against the wall, holding our breath. We stood thus for a little while until we heard a voice: 'Come on—shhh.' Then we sneaked across the street, climbed the stairs to the porch, opened a door into a dark passage, felt our way, opened another door—and there was the house . . .

A little wrinkled grandmother of some sixty years returned our greeting—Good evening to you—but did not look at us. She sat and looked in front of her, in a sort of detachment and apathy, like that of a person who has been going over the same thing for many days, in a sort of frozen amazement, like an infant seeing its reflection in a mirror and wondering at it . . . She was tending to something in a corner, where stood a big, rough bowl and beside it some *matzos* covered with a cloth.

Our guide, or, as he preferred to designate himself, the messenger, who had to hurry back to his own town before the night was over, did not stop but hurried away to the 'leader', to conclude the business with him without delay, to wit, deliver the three of us into his hands. The scrawny bespectacled one tried to hold him back—he was afraid to stay where we were—but he was overruled. Indeed, the fat jowly one scolded him, and the guide went away after warning us to stay quietly and not utter a word. 'Cover your mouths, men. Silence! Do you hear?'

The old woman rose and led us to another room, in case a stranger came into the front room and saw us. Our presence in that place was to remain unknown, a deadly secret. For it was an established fact—surely we knew it—that certain agents and smugglers turned in anyone who was not their customer and had not greased their palm. Their pig-snouts sniffed out, damn them, any new arrival in the town . . .

I need not tell you, gentlemen, that the old woman's words did not set our minds at ease. Even without her dire warnings, we knew how great the danger was, how terrible that place, and hearing it from her mouth . . . ! In brief, we scuttled, terrified and speechless, into the small chamber, a sort of bedroom, into which she showed us, and there we sat in the dark—too fearful to light a candle—sat and listened to every worrying little sound that reached our ears. When we heard the door of the front room open my two companions buried their faces in the featherbeds, until the old woman came in and assured them that it was only her old husband, none other but her old husband, who had come in, and there was nothing for us to fear . . .

At last our guide returned with fresh tidings, to wit, that the 'leader' had said it would be impossible to cross that night. We had to wait. And so, after bestowing on us further commands, instructions, counsels and warnings, our guide took his leave and went away. We remained where we were . . . Oh yes, we remained right there, to pass the night . . .

At once we were overwhelmed by a spirit of deathly danger, which stifles every sigh and silences every voice. Food repelled us . . . Every slight movement shook our souls, every faint rustle at the door made our hearts pound, every creature that entered the front-room all but finished us. We were afraid to walk, afraid to sit, afraid to step out; we were also afraid to sleep and afraid to wake up, afraid of the cat's wail, of the crunching of the matzos in the bowl, the soughing of the wind, the glimmers in the window . . .

We spent the night in that place.

II

The next morning we rose early, but did not wash ourselves or drink a hot drink. Our longed-for deliverance had not come. We sat on the beds, or lay down, or walked about the room slowly and quietly. Once the glance of the bespectacled one happened to light on the old man, our host, who was busy in the courtyard. He straightened his eye-glasses and peered through the window-pane, to assure himself that his eyes had not deceived him and that it was indeed the house-holder and not a stranger. At once his jowly friend roused himself and chastised him for his wickedness: How dare the man go near the window? The air itself has eyes, you criminal! And the wretched criminal retreated from the window, shamefaced, and humbly admitted his guilt.

Well then. Once again we sat in silence, holding our breath, terrified by every creak of the front door, our tension and anticipation rising to a filthy degree . . . At long last the jowly one could stand the rule of silence no longer and began softly to effervesce.

'Consider this,' he argued, 'just think about it—here are three intelligent men, fit in body and soul, confined to a room, and what is more, of their own volition. Think about it. No guard, no iron bars, but the prisoners dare not leave their cell . . . That really is something! Don't you know? I can stand no more of this. For the past hour I have had to go outside . . . I must . . . You understand? I can't hold out any longer . . .'

At this point his friend could not contain himself either, and declared that it was a disgrace, a great disgrace and eternal humiliation, for a

young man to be so very craven and cowardly. A man must ever be—
a Man!

The first sufferer, on hearing this homily, grew very warm and
began to prove to his accuser, citing chapter and verse, that he had
never in his life been craven and cowardly. On the contrary—who
knew better than the bespectacled one that he, the sufferer, had been
one of the first 'companions' to go to every forbidden gathering and
venture into the firing-line . . . But what of it? This was a different
kettle of fish! . . . What must he risk his life for? . . . He could see no
need for it whatever, except his own personal need, and he was at liberty to postpone that for as long as possible . . .

Meantime the door in the passage uttered its little shriek, and a
great terror fell upon us. The brave sufferer turned pale as a sheet and
his last words froze on his tongue. His reproachful friend cowered
in a corner, trembling all over, and I laid my ear against the wall, to
hear who the newcomer was. We need not have trembled: it was
only a neighbour come to borrow a pot. We resumed our whispered
argument, but the sufferer did not recover until after the neighbour
left and her voice was heard no more. But not many minutes later
another person came in, and this newcomer was of the inquisitive
sort, who needed to know what was in the second room, namely, the
chamber we were hiding in. Without much ado he opened the door,
thrust his nose and beard into the opening, and peeped. And when
he peeped our hearts died inside us and turned to stone. We almost
gave up the ghost. Had it not been for the old housewife, who at
once came in to reassure us, there is no telling what would have
happened. However, the old woman calmed us down, saying there
was nothing to worry about. It was only a *yeshivah* student—she was
keeping his matzos for him, and he had come to see that they were
well. Moreover, the old woman went on, why were we so frightened?
Were we babies, small children? So help her, she thought it a shame
for grown men to be so cowardly. To be sure, it was best to be careful, but within reason. In her house, thanks be to God, no harm could
come to us. Why had we tasted nothing since morning? Was it a fast
we were observing? Nor had we eaten a morsel the night before.
What man can live without food? . . . Come now, the sky had not
fallen down on our heads, had it? We were neither the first nor the
last, but, by your leave, she had never seen such cowards as we . . .

'And what is there to eat at your house, for example?' the fat-cheeked
one challenged her in a dubious voice, like one who expects to be
disappointed.

The bespectacled one was at first abashed by his companion's greedi-
ness on such a fateful day, and tried to pierce him with a scornful
look, but his anger lacked conviction . . . And when the old woman
began to enumerate, by way of an answer, a variety of light meals,
such as boiled eggs, buttermilk or hard cheese, and the like, he too,
the bespectacled one, gave in and consented to share our breakfast.

We had got no further than the first mouthful, when—shhh . . .
The door squealed . . . Gasps, groans . . . 'Good morning to ye!' A
hoarse, tired voice, which had once been deep and harsh . . . Who
was it? Who had come in? Shhh . . . Our mouths were full, we could
neither spit nor swallow. Shhh . . .

The voice is speaking . . . The heavy gasps and drawn-out groans
which muffle the voice make it sound as though the speaker's tongue
was hanging out thirstily, like the tongue of a mad dog, and his words
were clinging and wriggling about it, suffocated by it . . .

'Eh?' The old woman put in a question.

'Total devotion, I tell you, Breinah-Brakha!'—the smothered voice
rose—'Total devotion. Oh yes! Such times, oy, such times we are living in. Everything's in their hands. No one else makes a living. People
are fearful, rushing around, chucking their money and belongings all
over the place, and they take everything. Not a creature can stand up
to them . . . Agents—phew!—oh yes. That's what I'm talking about.
Only the day before yesterday I stood to make a little profit on some
hats which were brought in. God is my witness—it was total devotion that brought those hats in . . . a whole company . . . villains, stool-
pigeons. Oh yes!'

We in the inner chamber had not yet recovered, but the quality of
the voice, the gasps and the groans, relieved our terror.

'True, true, everything is in the hands of those agents, damn their
eyes,' the old woman added with sighs of her own. 'The robbers have
taken over . . . there's no one but them . . . oy . . . no one . . .'

'No one,' agreed the newcomer, 'and the gates of mercy are shut
tight. That's what I'm talking about. Oh yes. It's the same over there,
in the matzo baking in my house—not a moment to bless yourself.
Working like bullocks . . . Raiseh, Rachel, Gruneh—like bullocks . . .
and nothing! And those . . . —are they here?' Suddenly he lowered his
voice.

'Who?'

'The passengers . . .'

'Passengers?'

'Right . . . yesterday . . .'

'Here.'

'That's him, our man . . . ,' we whispered to one another.

Our prison door opened and a middle-aged Jew, broad-shouldered and bowed, with a big black beard, entered the room, huffing and blowing with weariness and from habit. His big black beard and his big black boots were thickly dusted with flour. Around his waist he wore a filthy porter's cummerbund, and his thick form, broken and bent, looked as if he was carrying a mountain of sand on his back. The creases under his eyes spoke of horse-like patience, but the eyes themselves were extinguished. And yet, it seemed to me that I saw in them . . . how shall I put it? . . . a sort of sublime yearning to cross borders and carry others across them . . .

This was our 'leader', a private one, not an agent, one entirely to ourselves. And at once, of course, my two companions pounced on him: When? How? In what way? Was there no danger?

'With God's help!' the smothered voice replied to all the questions. 'Nothing is known in advance . . . And it does not depend on me . . . Beyond my powers . . . What powers have I got? Oh yes . . . But I've already spoken with the army man. I shan't abandon you. I'll be going with you. I have to go across with you. Oh yes. You are not my first. That's what I'm talking about. And I'm no agent . . . After supper, that's when I'll call for you . . . Be ready . . .'

And he left.

He left, and my companions' spirits plummeted. Our saviour made them doubt that he was capable of saving us. Their grievances against the 'guide', the fellow who had brought us to this little tightly sealed border town and put us into such incompetent hands, grew apace. Think about it, what did the man mean by being so cool? Such coolness has laid many people low. To be sure, we were sent out with an extremely chilly sort of man, a regular lump of ice, and what did he care about the danger to others? Had anyone ever seen such hard-heartedness?

The boiled eggs were pushed aside and left uneaten.

'What do you mean, "able"?' our landlady replied when we questioned the strength and ability of our 'leader', and whether he could be relied on. 'Everything's in the hands of fate . . . When everything goes well, everyone is "able" . . . On the contrary, you should be pleased. He will go across with you . . . That doesn't happen every day. And especially if he takes you from this side—why, it will be nothing, like drawing a hair out of the milk . . . Just a few steps . . . But if he takes you through the river . . . What do I know? Sometimes it goes well on that side, too . . . And the agents, do you think they are better than he?'

Now the old woman began to tell us about something which had happened 'maybe a week ago': a dreadful story about a young man whom the agents had sent across the border, and who was already on the other side, but the devil confounded him and he missed the road, wandered about in circles all night, until he found himself right back at the border post . . .

We stood listening to her, our faces growing paler, the hair on our heads standing on end, our three hearts hammering . . . The word 'border' kept rattling our nerves . . . The word 'disaster' kept buzzing in our minds . . . We lay down to rest, hoping for relief—perhaps the day would pass after all. But we could not rest. We could not leave the room, and it had no room for us. Only a few more hours to the great and dreadful moment, the moment of crossing the border . . . Border, border, border . . . Like a rattling cart: border, border, border . . . Oh, who would take us across the border?

III

Evening came. The old woman lit a candle on the other side of the wall, and once again we sat in darkness, with strange sensations, weird notions, endless ideas and some terrifying images arising together, like a column of smoke, swirling and dispiriting . . .

And then, thank God! Heavy gasps broke into the house . . .

'Well, ready?'

'What? Are we going? . . .'

'Yes. Come on, let us go to Freissen!'

That thread which all that day had stretched expectantly in our hearts, snapped. The time had come, at long last. In a little while we should know if we were fated to live or to die.

On the way the man told us that he thought we were a little late. We should have set out half an hour earlier. That was his agreement with the 'army man'. But at the right moment some housewife brought her flour to be baked, causing the delay. It was matzo-baking time at his house.

The man who was leading us looked much as he had that noon, except that his face was even wearier, his back more bent, and his big boots more encrusted with flour and mud. Yet he walked astonishingly fast, almost at a run; not like a confident athlete running for the joy of it, but like a desperate man risking his life insanely, as if to say: I fear nothing, because nothing can be worse than what surrounds me now . . .

He ran ahead of us, and the spring mud made *chup-chup-chup* noises. Night fell, a cold dark night. We saw few people on our way, but they all stared at us keenly. The man brought us to the edge of the town: a railway to the right, a fence to the left, and an open field before us. Then he turned around and walked back the way we had come. We, of course, followed. His face expressed no confidence, only a forlorn hope seemed to flicker inside him. He seemed not to know the way, seemed to be wandering like a blind man. And we in our hearts rebelled against him, cursed him, cursed too the 'guide', the evil traitor, who had delivered us into the hands of an incompetent, of a man who was willing, for a few miserable coins, to cause innocent people to perish, who did not even know how to tread carefully, but made those ghastly *chup-chup* noises with his filthy boots . . . Nevertheless, we followed him, willy-nilly . . . He led us into some opening, through a gap in a wooden shed, and then through two or three courtyards. In one of them a Gentile woman came out to draw water, but he ignored her. Finally he led us into a vegetable field. Beyond it spread a vast plain. That? . . . That was—the border? We saw some men on horseback passing nearby . . . Oh-oh, our 'leader' groaned . . . We fell flat on our faces . . . Crunch went the icy surface and our hearts with it . . . Shhh . . . We roused ourselves . . . Bent quite double we moved forward, crawled as far as a reed fence which rose before us, climbed over it to the other side . . . A gulley . . . To our right a barn, to our left a railway . . . We must have been wandering along that railway for the past hour . . .

'Well, then, you . . . Hide here, lie around the barn . . . I'll go to the border-post and speak to the soldier . . . If possible . . .'

The heart of a murderer raising his axe to kill a fellow mortal could pound as loudly as ours did at that moment. Nevertheless, wonder of wonders, my companions could not forbear from passing remarks and whispering:

'Is he gone?'

'What happened to him?'

'What will happen to us?'

'Where are we?'

Every minute was an eternity. What was that? Nightmares. He was gone. Really! . . . Moments of eternity—and not a sound . . . But who was this, walking on our left? Who appeared to be slinking along the

railway? Here he comes . . . walring this way—stopped . . . Imagination?
. . . Oh, keep quiet, at least . . . Lie flat on the ground . . . Hold your
breath . . .

'Aha . . . You there! What are you doing here?'

Before us stood a tall soldier, an officer, in strong high boots and
a short woollen cape, with a rifle over his shoulder. Ah . . . So it was
all up with us . . . Or perhaps not? Perhaps he had been sent to meet
us? No, he had come from the left. . . . He was joking . . . We were
lost, lost . . . Our worst fears were coming true . . . What we had anticipated was about to happen . . .

We pressed ourselves to the damp ground we were lying on: perhaps the frightful dream would pass . . .

When the soldier saw who was lying at his feet, he grew very merry
and arrogant, and began to taunt us, ordering us to lie still until he
fired his rifle to summon others to come and arrest us . . .

Our tongues clove to our palates, but our lips mumbled discon-
nected words: Let us alone! . . . We were just leaving . . . We lost our
way . . .

'Lie still!' the soldier commanded, and slipped the rifle from his
shoulder.

At this point I rose, leaving the others lying down, and broke into
run . . . 'You'll be shot!' someone shouted, I know not who. I shouted
'Eh!' in reply—and fled. I ran and ran, my ears awaiting the sound of
a shot, but all was silent. A silent world. Here was the railway. I would
follow it back to town . . . I saw myself as a lost child in a faraway
land . . . For a moment, only one brief moment, the idea flickered
through my mind that, in effect, I was better off thus, that in effect
the danger was not so very great . . . But at once the terror returned,
a dark terror, and spread through my body and soul—and I fled as
fast as my legs could carry me . . .

Only when I reached the town and entered it did I perceive my
true situation. I was afraid to be recognized by the passers-by . . . And
when I found that house and ran into it, I burst into bitter tears!

The old woman was making supper. She shook her head and sucked
her teeth while I told my story. When I finished talking she took the
peeled onion, sliced it thinly over pieces of salt herring in a platter,
and sprinkled it with vinegar.

'So I am lost . . . Oh, clearly, I am lost . . . Now I am lost forever . . .
I shall never cross that border . . . Where am I to go now?'

Then the old woman promised to send her old man, when he came
back from evening prayer, to see what had befallen our 'leader' . . .

'But no matter what, I am not going with him again . . . I am lost . . .'

'No, it seems the *goy* did not shoot'—the old woman insisted—'We heard no shots . . .'

As we were talking, the heavy gasps, the frequent heavy gasps, heavier and more frequent than before, broke into the house, and the muddy boots squelched *chup-chup* . . .

'It's my fault! . . . I was late . . . That bushel of matzos of Baileh the grocer put it clear out of my mind . . . We should have left before dark . . . Before the guards come out . . . Total devotion . . .'

The sweat broke out all over his body, from his forehead, his hair, his clothes, his entire form, like a horse which had been working at the mill for three days on end. He was gasping and could not speak, but did not cease to speak and apologize and exclaim that he ought to be chopped in pieces for being late, and that he too deserved some pity, that he had not abandoned us, and had risked his life like us . . . The story of his miraculous escape was truly dreadful: he had run downhill, that is, to the border, where a guard found him and wanted to arrest him, but his sainted ancestors must have protected him, because the soldiers believed him when he said he had come from the nearby wood . . . And what a miracle it was, he said, that we did not go with him then, or we would surely have been caught by those riders whom we had seen when we lay on the ice in that vegetable field . . . But oy, oy . . . He had already been fined twice for smuggling, and what would have befallen his family if he had been caught again? Total devotion!

'But, *gevald*, what is to happen now?'

'Now I've come for you. We shall go together.'

'Where?'

'To look for the others . . . I have no idea what happened to them. As soon as I was set free I ran to the barn, but they were gone . . .'

'They must have been arrested!'

'No, not arrested. The soldier did not fire. Let's go and look for them . . .'

There was much force in that incompetent, and I almost succumbed and went with him, but managed to resist him and refused to go. Let him go alone. A few hours later he returned with good news: my two companions were at his house. They were saved by their madness! When they saw that the soldier was about to shoot me, the runaway, their minds became completely addled and they gave him all the money they had, and he let them go. They broke cover and

began to wander about the town, and if he had not found them—
who knows what might not have befallen them. Thank the Lord,
thank the Lord . . .

His face betrayed no joy. That face was incapable of it. Only his
great unkempt beard took on an even weirder, twisted shape . . .

'But what will happen now?'

'What will happen? Nothing. In the morning we will go to Freissen.'

'I shall not go.'

I had made up my mind about that, and would not change it. It
had become quite plain to me, that I must not go with him. But I
could not and would not remain, even 'for the time being', in the old
woman's house, and after some heart-searching and inner strugle I
was compelled, eventually, to move to his house—at least for an hour
or so. I went with him.

No sooner did I enter the 'leader's' house than my two companions fell on my neck. 'Oy, oy!' They almost swooned as they embraced
me, the survivor. Then they sat down to discuss in what way they
would return to their native city: the one to face trial and the other
to be conscripted. But even more than the future, they were preoccupied with the miracles and and deliverance which they had experienced that night. They vied with each other in recounting in great
detail the frenzy which seized them when they saw the soldier prepare to fire, how they clutched his arm and said: *Na tebya denghi*,
which means 'Here is some money for you', how they circled the
barn and returned to town, and began to wander about, until a man
showed them the way, but they got lost again, until our 'leader' found
them . . .

From time to time our 'leader' burst into the room and declared
that he was to blame, that he and he alone ought to be chopped up
alive, but as we had seen, he had not abandoned us, but had gone
with us into the firing-line . . .

IV

It was after midnight, but still in the outer rooms the sound of matzos being rolled, tins banging and the shouts of the bakers went on
. . . Yet over all the noises and voices hung an air of sleepiness. The
three of us sat in darkness, as we had the night before. This time,
too, in a bedchamber, which was so full of various household objects,
quite out of their place, that there was room for a cat to squeeze
through. The matzo-baking in the other rooms had caused all those
objects, which had not been made kosher for Passover, to be exiled

to this room. It was a strange agglomeration: tables, benches, barrels, beds, featherbeds, chairs, table-tops, a dresser, a mirror and the like. Our fingers felt the layer of dust and flour which covered everything. My comrades in adversity sat and whispered together about the 'conditions and obligations' which they would impose on our 'leader', and I sat nearby, speechless and incapable of thinking. I felt as if all the world's griefs and disasters had clumped together and invaded this chamber, and here were crumbled into fine dust which spread over the walls and the objects, and all over me, who was stuck in the middle and unable to move, never to be let out and set free. An eternal darkness . . . The horror of the barn invaded me again, that barn out there in the field, and with it fear of the 'agents' and the 'stool-pigeons' here in the town, and of the matzo-baking in the house, and of that man, our 'leader', whose life had run its course, whose strength was gone and whose vital spirit had evaporated, who had consumed his own life and become a doormat to his own troubles and was willing to carry any and every load . . .

'The soldier himself will come to fetch us at two,' the man informed us an hour later. 'Now lie down somewhere, and I shall wake you in time . . . Be ready . . .'

I searched for something to lie on. I put two chairs together and stuck my hat under my head for a pillow. But no sooner did we lie down, and the clock rang one hour, than the chamber door began to open, and each time it opened it let in a beam of light from the tin lamp in the hallway, and with it, one of the daughters of the house. They were young women—Raiseh, Rachel, Gruneh, I recalled their names from their father's conversation the previous noon—tall and handsome, tired and filthy. All three had thick plaits of glossy black hair, were preceded by their ample breasts, and their long eyelashes were dusty with Passover flour. They burst into the room, one after the other, groaning wordlessly, and collapsed where they stood—one on a flour-sack, another on a bed full of sleeping infants, and the third on chairs joined together. Finally the houswife herself also came in, a big and nimble woman. She tore off her white smock and in the dim light we saw her bare shoulders. We, the strange men, were like grasshoppers in her eyes, utterly beneath her notice . . . Before lying down she muttered, instead of the bedtime blessing, a brief remark:

'Oy, the scum . . . The plagues of Egypt on him and all his doings . . .'

But the 'scum' himself did not appear until the last moment. He never lay down at all, and we could hear him labouring in the outer room; huffing, worrying, doing business. Everything was laborious,

worrisome, and a business. The very air in the room became tainted
with aggravation. A note of futile effort hummed ceaselessly, zzzzzzzzzz
. . . A soft, sibilant snore . . . A cart drew up near the window . . . No,
the cart rolled on . . . zzzzzzz.

I fell asleep.

'Well, ready? Get up and let us go . . . The soldier has already been
. . . The main thing now is to get across the town . . . Mustn't make
a sound . . . I've taken off my boots . . . carry them in my hand . . .
walk in socks . . .'

'He's mad,' one of the daughters grunted sleepily. 'On such a night,
in socks . . .'

'Let the scum alone,' the housewife scolded, just as sleepily. 'What
is it to you? Let him walk in socks . . . No great loss if he catches
cold . . . Let him go without his head . . . go about his business . . . the
scum . . .'

The scum went, and we followed.

V

And when we had crossed the border, my honourable friends, I was
so tired, so exhausted and dispirited, that I lost all relish for the freedom on the other side. The danger had passed, and I survived . . . But
this life is so inferior, evil, wearisome that . . . I am ashamed to say it,
but—what is it for?

My companions were as broken and sickened and bruised as I was.
But they knew it to be the way of the world: that after sneaking across
a frontier people begin a new life, shake off the dust of the past and
look forward to the future. Therefore, when the jowly one stopped
moaning wearily, 'Oy, we're saved', and recovered somewhat from the
trials of our journey, he began to philosophize about the questions of
borders in general, and said: 'Only consider—such a short stretch of
land, after all; a short stretch of land.' And who knows where this
line of reasoning would have led him, if the bespectacled one had not
interrupted him? Not at all, he commented, the jowly one was mistaken. The border that we had crossed was not at all a short stretch
of land. In reality it was a frozen river, almost three miles wide, to
be precise, and most dangerous to cross over the ice, which moved
as you walked on it. Moreover, the bespectacled one remembered
exactly how many times he had slipped and fallen on it.

In the meantime our 'leader' sat on a hillock wringing out his socks
. . . His face bore the same miserable expression and his back was as
bent as ever . . . Then he began to speak. He talked fluently but in

broken sentences, making a kind of confession. He was not afraid of the cold, as you could witness for yourselves. He generally feared nothing. Already his strength had left him and he had nothing to fear. It was not his strength which kept him alive, but his total devotion, his 'impetus'. This 'impetus' kept him on his feet, it alone carried him, took away his weakness and made him forget his age. That was how he risked his life getting us across. With the roubles we paid him he would buy some merchandise, and the following night he would risk his life again to take it across. We had seen his family? He had to support them, was obliged to feed them, to carry the load, for everyone must live . . . Take, for instance, this race across three miles of frozen river, in his socks—that really was beyond his strength . . . Nevertheless, he ran, even faster than we, younger men, did . . . And so, if need be, he would run twice that distance, three times . . . What was he to look at? A crock, an old crock . . . But he had to live, had to support, and his troubles drove him on, and above all, the 'impetus', the force of total devotion . . .

A glowing streak appeared in the east. The bespectacled one raised his spectacles skywards and said he thought he could see a figure of a man approaching. Which, he said, served to illustrate what our 'leader' had said about troubles and devotion, 'impetus' and darkness: yes, darkness . . . How powerful they were! His own eyesight was notoriously weak, yet now, now of all times, he could see so well . . . There was darkness for you, if you will!

His fat friend said nothing. He was preoccupied with his accounts and paid no mind to his friend's brightened spectacles. And to be sure, in a little while we saw an old German walking towards us from the ridge. Our hearts went out to that German, the first man we met on the other side . . .

The east was not yet light, and our 'leader' hurriedly pulled his wrung-out socks on his frozen feet, stuffed them into his great muddy boots and stood up. The old German had hardly reached us, when he greeted him in a singsong voice: 'Good morning, man. Here we are, bright and early, ready to meet the day.'

Translated by Yael Lotan.

Dvora Baron

SUNBEAMS

Baron (1887–1956) was born near Minsk in Belorussia and settled in Palestine in 1910. While still very young she began publishing stories in local Hebrew newspapers, and after her arrival in Palestine she wrote for the literary journal Hapo'el Hatza'ir. She published her first collection in 1927. Most of her stories incorporate some form of human drama related to or arising from the Jewish milieu, predominantly within the small East European Jewish communities. Many of the stories reveal a sense of personal and social disintegration. Baron identifies most with the alienated individual, whom she portrays with compassion. The shtetl described in her stories is permeated by a deep sense of loneliness and insecurity caused by poverty and anti-Semitism. Later she described Palestine during the Second World War as well as encounters with the survivors of European Jewry. Baron was the recipient of many literary prizes.

She was brought to our town from the village of Bikhov, after both her parents had died there. Her sole belongings were a bundle of bedding and a little warmth from her mother's last caress, which was soon dissipated in the alien chill.

The villager who brought her placed her in the care of the Valley Quarter women, and for several days she was passed from hand to hand like an unwanted object.

Those who did agree to take her in grudgingly allotted her a corner near the stove, but first they wanted to make sure she had no skin disease and that her bundle of bedding was quite clean.

Her eyes round with astonishment—her name was Haya-Fruma and she was five at the time—she watched her pillows being divested of their pillow-cases and beaten out by the disdainful hands of strangers. Her own hand, missing the one she was accustomed to clutching, hung limply at her side, and she trembled in the chill blast of orphanhood like a leaf whose sheltering parent-tree has been felled.

Moved by pity, an old woman from the uptown hillside quarter took her in; but alarmed by the child's ravenous appetite, she very soon returned her to the Valley Quarter slum. Here she roamed about in her peasant smock, her faded hair tangled and unkempt, her face devoid of a single endearing feature. Thus she was denied even that grain of sympathy which people are wont to impart to a strange creature if it but pleases the eye.

When she was eight, she slipped and broke her leg one winter morning as she was on her way to a house where she had been promised a meal. The frantic cries she uttered as she lay on the ice in the cold sunrise brought the early congregants rushing out of the nearby synagogue. They carried her into the nearest house and called the doctor. For some time, various families, with the eager willingness of do-gooders, took turns in looking after her, procured a bed for her in the local inn and kept bringing her bread and soup. But no sooner was she up and about than she was again left to her own devices. Again she became a street urchin, eking out her existence, as before, by doing chores for the local housewives. She had lost much of her former nimbleness: her leg had not been set properly, leaving her with a bad limp, and besides, the unaccustomed plenitude of food had made her put on a great deal of weight. But her strong muscles compensated for her slowness, and these she used to the satisfaction of all who employed her.

By the time she was twelve she was able to scour a samovar, lay firewood, kindle a stove, and fetch water from the well, and her bear-like paws scrubbed the laundry a dazzling white. On Sabbath eve she cleaned out the hovels of the poor in the Valley Quarter, whose single living-room served also as a workshop or grocery store during the week. The gleaming window-panes, after she had washed them, reflected the splendour of the world, and people removed their shoes before treading on her newly scrubbed floors. With a few deft strokes she would restore to wooden benches their original colour, as yellow as the yolk of an egg, make the brass candlesticks glitter like gold, beat out the feather pillows till they billowed and reared up like towers at the head of the bedsteads. Emboldened by her strength and her handiwork, amidst the warm, tempting smells given off by the Sabbath delicacies cooking on the stove, and encouraged by the kindly expression of the housewife who was working alongside her, she might for a moment abandon herself to the hope of sharing in the pleasant homely atmosphere that was being engendered here. But no sooner had she finished her work than she would be given her pay in unmistakable dismissal. Letting down her tucked-up skirt, she would pick up her basket and leave.

'There goes crooked Haya-Fruma!' children at play in the street would call after her; but the grown-ups, who appear to ostracize those of unlovely appearance, would not so much as look at her. They seemed to have reeled in the line of contact that usually forms a bond between people. And she, the world empty about her, would go her lame, hobbling way.

The beadle of the synagogue, in whose house Haya-Fruma sometimes washed the dishes, had a daughter whose appearance aroused in her an emotion akin to that dimly evoked by the memory of her mother. She was a good-natured girl of clear complexion, with a gay, sunny sparkle dancing in her eyes whenever she smiled.

One Friday, Haya-Fruma watched her washing her hair—a golden cloud that lit up the dingy kitchen. On an impulse, with a feeling akin to awe, she stretched out a hesitant hand and touched the glittering locks with trembling fingers. Somewhat taken aback, the beadle's daughter without a word pushed back her hair with a gesture of mild distaste. But her mother, who was standing near the oven, advanced on Haya-Fruma in a towering rage, brandishing her baker's shovel.

'How dare you crawl all over her with your clumsy paws!' she screamed.

Haya-Fruma glanced sadly at her large wet palms, then looked up at a neighbour, who happened to be present, as if asking for her support. But the latter, like all the others to whom she looked with longing, pleading eyes, refused to meet her glance—like a blank wall one encounters where one had expected to see a mirror.

She left the beadle's house and never returned there. In the other houses where she went to work she now kept her eyes lowered and she stayed as far away from the people as possible.

She preferred to be alone with the inanimate objects at the far edge of the yard or in a corner of the kitchen; for the kettle she was polishing would send back a kindly gleam, and the firewood she kindled in the stove would respond with a gay, dancing flame. By dint of her constant silence her speech became slow and blurred. Over the years, steeped in soap suds, laundry steam and slops, she herself gradually mouldered, like a dark, dank cell that has long been kept shut.

In time, she got a steady job as a drudge at the bakery in the uptown Hill Quarter. It was there that she caught the eye of a vegetable-gardener from the village of Kaminka, a lonely old widower whose children had all married and left home. Impressed by her strength—she was kneading a huge mass of dough in the kneading-trough—he asked the baker's wife, who was a relative of his, to act as go-between. The woman, who approved of the match, agreed.

She did not put it to the girl during the week, however, so as not to fill her head with idle, time-wasting thoughts; but on the following Saturday afternoon, as they were sitting out on the porch—it was springtime—she broached the matter to her.

'You'll be able to bake your own bread there,' she explained, and some other women who were present, and who had on occasion taken some interest in the girl's welfare, added, 'Surely you can't go on grubbing on other people's dung-heaps all your life!'

With the little money she had saved up out of her wages they made her a woollen dress and a flowered apron, and bought her some new pillow-cases and chequered inlays for her pillows. When the vegetable-gardener turned up the next market day, they fixed the date of the wedding. It was arranged that this would be held at the house of the baker, who would have the food prepared in his ovens and supply the drinks.

The villager rather embarrassed his relatives when he turned up on the day of the wedding with a cartload of vegetables; but the marriage was later solemnized with due ceremony. The velvet *huppa* was set up in the open, as prescribed by custom, and the girl was led under it, dressed in white and faint from fasting.* After the ceremony the children, also according to custom, accompanied her with loud hurrahs, which were this time possibly longer and more significant than their usual jeers.

The next morning, her head covered by a married-woman's kerchief, she was seated next to the villager on his cart and driven along the bumpy road to Kaminka. She gazed around her with wide-open eyes, as if seeing some distant reflection of her native village: the same green glow of the luxuriant fields, the same song of birds merging with the blue stillness, seemingly charged with far-away undertones of her mother's voice. Now and then the old man seated next to her would turn his head to glance at her, his white beard fluttering in the dense smoke of his pipe. Her kerchief, into which she had secretly wept after the ceremony the night before, fluttered back at him.

Arriving at his house, she roamed about for some time, unable to find a place for her chest of belongings. Finally she removed her laced shoes, which, she decided, were the cause of her inner discomfort. Seeing how neglected the house looked, and the day still being young, she changed into her workday clothes and got down to giving the place a thorough cleaning.

The dankness inside her very soon permeated her whole being,

---

* The bride and groom usually fast until after the ceremony, then immediately go into a separate room where they have their first meal together.

filling her with the dark desolation of a long-forgotten dungeon. It was not that her husband was unkind to her: most of the time he was too busy even to acknowledge her presence. He would leave for his fields early in the morning after a hurried prayer, return at noon to snatch a meal, and in the evening after his supper he would light his pipe and sit down to his accounts. And she, after pottering about aimlessly for a while, would lie down unobtrusively on a bench to one side of the stove, feeling rootless and without support—the same stray waif that used to be taken in for the night in the Valley Quarter.

The dining-table in the living room stood on a kind of hummock in the centre, the floor around it sloping down to the walls. Every time she came in from the kitchen with some dish or utensil she would look up there hopefully, like someone climbing out of a dark pit towards the light, as if expecting a kindly look or gesture. But the man seated at the table would go on staring out of the window— now spotlessly clean—at his fields. After he had left she would go outside, only to be confronted by the same indifference there. The houses all along the street turned blank, windowless walls to her, just as their occupants cold-shouldered her. Sick at heart, she would go indoors again and look about her for something she hadn't polished brightly enough. Again she would scour and buff the copper pots and bowls, or scrub the wooden benches till they looked as if they had been newly planed. This done, she would let down her tucked-up apron, as she used to do after finishing her day's work in one of the Valley Quarter houses, and unconsciously reach for her basket as if to leave the house.

After about a year had gone by like this and springtime had come again, her husband told her that he had just bought a milch cow at a neighbouring farm. A few days later he led a young reddish cow into the yard; she had just calved for the first time and was struggling to break loose and get back to the calf she had left behind at the farm. The old man, after tying the cow to a post in the lean-to which was to serve as a cowshed, warned his wife not to go near the excited, skittish animal, and went back to his fields. The cow kept on lowing plaintively—to Haya-Fruma it sounded like weeping, and she could not resist the urge to peep into the cowshed. The cow did not seem in the least enraged or violent. On the contrary, as Haya-Fruma entered, the animal turned to gaze at her as if seeking sympathy, mooing piteously all the time in the direction of its native farm. Gently she stroked its flank and spoke to it soothingly, using the few words of

endearment that came back to her from the mists of her early childhood. Then she fetched some grass from the meadow, made a bed
of fresh straw, and later led the cow out into the yard, where she
would be able to keep an eye on her as she worked in the kitchen.

During the first few days, when it was still too soon to send the
cow out to the common pasture in case she should bolt, Haya-Fruma
led her every day to a little meadow beyond the bridge where the
grass was rich and plentiful. The cow—she was called Rizhka—seemed
to have calmed down and no longer looked sad, and Haya-Fruma,
too, began to feel a sense of release as though the warmth of the
sun and the freshness of the spring breezes were dispelling the long-
accumulated dankness inside her. And when one evening, as she sat
alone in the doorway of the cowshed, the cow turned to her and
affectionately licked her hand with its rough tongue, she—who
had never known laughter—felt as though her inner being were pervaded by a broad smile, and the dark dungeon was suddenly filled
with dancing sunbeams.

One day, her husband—still a vigorous man despite his age—
suddenly fell ill and died. The rainy weather had kept him home in
enforced idleness that day. Feeling strangely tired, he had lain down
to a rest from which he never arose.

His three sons, who had farms in the vicinity, and his daughter,
who lived in a nearby village, came to spend the *shiva* at the house,
and the miller from across the river came over with his sons every
day to make up the *minyan*. Haya-Fruma prepared dishes of vegetables, which she picked in the garden, and respectfully served meals
to the mourners in between prayers. She moved about silently, having removed her shoes in mourning, like them.

She particularly earned their gratitude by the way she behaved over
the division of the inheritance. Whenever their arguments became
heated she would slip silently out of the house, and she even looked
the other way when one or other of the heirs slipped some object of
value into his travelling-bag. When her turn came to state her claims
and she was asked to produce her *ketuba*, she did so, but timidly asked
whether she could keep Rizhka the cow instead of getting the money
due to her. The heirs agreed.

She stayed on at the house until it was sold and its new owners
came to occupy it. Then she sent her belongings by the greengro-
cer's cart to the township, and followed on foot with her cow. That
same day, she rented a wooden shack (long-abandoned for fear of

floods) down by the river, near the flour-mill, and partitioned off part
of its single room for a cowshed.

She easily readjusted to the old life. Every morning she placed
the cow in the charge of the common cowherd and went to work
in one of the houses in the long Valley Quarter street, or up on the
hillside. Again she scrubbed floors, washed dishes, kneaded dough at
the bakery. Wherever she went she would pick up crusts of bread
and vegetable peelings and put them in her basket. Returning home
in the late afternoon, she would mix them in a tub with bran, salt
and hot water and stand in the doorway to await the cow's return
from the pasture. Then she would place the tempting mash in front
of her and sit down beside her with the milking pail.

For both of them this was an hour of silent communion, as it were,
a reciprocal bond between them, wondrously precious, such as only
those who are doomed to silence can savour in their hearts.

Very soon the neighbours would come over with their jugs and
pots to buy their milk, and the sweet stillness would be broken. Haya-
Fruma would ladle out each one's portion, then go for a short stroll
with the cow down to the river bank, or up the hillside. Her reddish
coat gleaming gold in the rays of the setting sun, the cow would
round off her evening meal by cropping the grasses along the hedges.
Passers-by would stop to admire her.

'Did you bring her from Kaminka?' they would ask.

'Yes, from the village,' she would reply. 'But she was born on the
Gräfin's farm.'

'A fine animal,' they would say—words of approval for which the
woman had yearned all her life.

There were all sorts of worries and anxieties, too, of course: the
summer rainstorms when the herd was out at pasture, the danger of
floods when the river grew swollen, and the fear of cattle diseases
which sometimes ravaged the herds. And one morning, when she
went out to the yard, she found Mottie the butcher sizing up her cow
speculatively. It was a festival, and the butcher merely happened to
be passing on his way to synagogue; nevertheless a shudder ran through
her and her heart almost stopped beating.

Then there were the anxious days when the cow was 'expecting',
and the yearly calving in spring, and the sad ordeal of having to separate her from her young, the tiny cowstall being too small to house
more than one animal.

On no account could Haya-Fruma be induced to hand over the

calves to the butchers. Instead, she sold them to be raised on neigh-bouring farms. With the money she bought a churn and vats to make butter and cheese, for the cow was giving an abundant yield, which could not always be sold the same day. She also installed her own oven in the shack and there—instead of slaving for others—she baked rye bread and millet cakes, which were eagerly bought up by the chil-dren when they came out of *heder* and by the peasants who came into town on fair-days.

The patch of ground around her shack became green with beds of sprouting radish and onion, and the whole yard was filled with the fragrance of a village farm. On Sabbath, this blended with the singing of Sabbath hymns, for on that day a blind old scholar, who had no family, came to take his meals at her table. A man of deep learning and wisdom, despite his blindness, he was able to pave a path of light to the dark recesses of the woman's soul. It was due to him that she started attending synagogue services and doing acts of charity among the needy.

She now went about dressed in a wide, pleated apron, which gave her a matronly look; and her face, framed in her coloured kerchief, beamed with the light of the deprived who have at long last come into their own—like a long-empty lantern in which a lighted candle has been placed. All who saw her going down to the Valley Quarter on some errand of mercy, wrapped in a fine shawl like a well-to-do housewife, her limp barely noticeable any more, would stare after her in wonder, as if to say: 'Can this be Haya-Fruma?'

What they did not realize was that even the salty, arid soil of the desert, if only it be watered from living springs and fertilized, will eventually become enriched and burst into bloom.

Eight years had now passed since she had come back to live in the Bridge Quarter. She now owned the shack and the plot of ground around it, and her cow had brought forth its seventh calf. One day she was racked by a sudden stabbing pain, but never having known what it was to be ill, she paid it no heed. Very soon the pains became more frequent, however, and she began losing her appetite and grew thin and emaciated. It was then that she realized that a malignant ill-ness, like a cankerous worm at the core of a fruit, was gradually con-suming her. Calmly, with the same provident husbandry with which she had managed her affairs all these years, she took stock of her situ-ation and started setting her affairs in order.

She handed over her bakery to a neighbour and stopped churning butter and making cheese, selling all the milk fresh. This gave her far more leisure to engage in charity, or listen to the blind old savant, whose wise words opened up new worlds to her.

She had a banister made for the steps of the Valley Quarter synagogue and bought a candelabrum for the women's gallery, so that they should no longer be obliged to pray in the dim light that filtered up from the men's section. When the month of *Ellul* came round and the blast of the *shofar* reverberated through the township, she heard it as a kind of warning, for the pain was now lacerating her chest, like a saw cutting through a tree-trunk.

This made her decide to do what she felt could no longer be put off.

She sent word to the city contractor's family (she had heard they had a proper cowshed built of bricks) informing them that she was prepared to sell them her cow. The fame of this animal having reached them, they readily agreed, particularly as their own cow had died some time before. The contractor's elegant wife came over in person and concluded the deal with hardly any haggling. She placed her diamond-ringed hand on the cow's reddish-gold flank, as though to finalize the purchase, and the intelligent animal, seeming to understand what was going on, turned its head to her and mooed contentedly.

'You'll be very pleased with her,' was all Haya-Fruma could say, gasping weakly.

That same day she put on her best clothes and led the cow down the path that ran beyond the pastureland to the back gate of the contractor's yard, where a stout peasant girl—she had a kind face, Haya-Fruma was pleased to note—was already waiting for them. She went over to peep into the cowshed, which really was built of brick and had a stamped-down floor like a human dwelling, looked back at the footprints on the path, along which she and the cow had taken their last walk together, then crossed the yard and left by the front gate.

She stayed in bed the next morning—there was no milking to be done—and drank down the analgesic drug the doctor had prescribed. Her pain vanished instantly. As she sank into slumber, she felt as though she were becoming enveloped in the golden haze of an unseen sunrise. This radiance that dawned on her—as the blind old man had predicted—awaits all those who have been refined and burnished by suffering in this world.

Translated by Joseph Schachter.

Hayyim Hazaz

RAHAMIM

Hazaz (1898–1973) was born in Russia and spent much of his youth in the Ukraine. An early story, 'Shmuel Frankfurter' (1925), prefigures his fascination with thwarted messianism and the story of Jesus. After he settled in Palestine he began to romanticize the East European shtetl environment. Later he used the short story for the presentation of ideas. The most renowned of these stories is 'The Sermon', in which he critically examines the philosophy of Zionism. In 'Rahamim' (1933) he pits the cynical, life-weary intellectual against the simpler, regenerative, life-affirming principles of a Kurdish porter. Later the drama of messianism and Zionism in European and Oriental Judaism became Hazaz's central preoccupation. He was fascinated with the Yemenite community, about which he wrote a great deal, including the novel Mori Sa'id *(1944).*

One sunny day Menashke Bezprozvani, lean as a pole, wandered through the streets of Jerusalem, his face seamed and sickly-looking, his mouth unusually fleshy and red, his eyes discontented and disparaging.

Bitterness gnawed at his heart, piercing through him like some venom—a bitterness of heart which was unconscious rather than clearly expressed, resulting from the years he had spent without achieving anything, neither contentment for himself, nor property, nor a family; the bitter, gloomy quintessence of fever and hunger, of unsettled wandering from one agricultural commune to another, of vexations and suffering and troubles enough to drive a man out of his mind and make him lose his strength, and all the other effects of his past experiences, his lack of employment, and his present sickness.

His despair set him in a fury. All sorts of evil thoughts possessed him, recriminations and accusations directed against the Labour Federation and Zionism, against 'the domination of the Zionist Imperialism'; against everything in the world, it seemed. As though one might claim that everything was fine and bright, he would have had a job, his spirit would be refreshed, he might have everything he desired

and the whole of life could be brilliant, were it not for the worthless
leaders and the Zionist imperialism that hindered things.

All these were the complaints of a dejected, despairing person who,
more than he wanted comfort, wished to torture himself, to cry out
aloud and rebel and remonstrate against the whole state of affairs.
But his complaining was only half-hearted. Like it or not, he possessed
a great love for the land and a great love of the Hebrew language; a
strong, deep, irrational, obstinate love that went past all theories and
views, and led beyond all personal advantage. And since his complaints
were no more than half-hearted, he complained all the more, denying
everything and destroying everything in thought without getting anywhere, and just making himself uncomfortable.

Apart from all his bitterness, the excessive heat was tiring him. It
was the middle of July. The heat was like that of an oven stoked with
glowing coals, and the white light dazzled to blindness and distraction. The roadway quivered uncertainly in the light as though in a
dream; it might have been so much barren soil or else a field left fal-
low because of drought; or it might have been anything you like in
the world. The sun quarrelled with the stones and the windows. The
slopes of the mountains on the horizon shone yellow-brown through
the dryness, while the skies in their purity of blue called eternity and
worlds-without-end to mind.

A yell stopped him as he walked. A dozen or so Arabs dashed
excitedly among the crowd in the street, yelling at the top of their
voices as though attacked by robbers:

'Barud! Barud!' (Blasting going on!)

Menashke Bezprozvani stood among the group of stationary folk
pressed together, until the road echoed to a loud explosion and stones
flung aloft scattered around and fell here and there in confusion. When
he began to resume his walk he found himself accompanied by a man
riding a donkey.

'Noise, eh!' said this stranger, turning his face to him with a smile
of satisfaction and wonder.

He was a short fellow with thick black eyebrows, a beard like a
thicket, his face bright as a copper pot and his chest uncommonly
virile and broad. He was dressed in rags and tatters, rent upon rent
and patch upon patch, a rope girded round his loins, and a basket of
reeds in front of him on the donkey's back.

Menashke Bezprozvani glanced at him and made no answer, but
the stranger entered into conversation and drew him to reply.

'Got a missus?' he turned on the donkey's back to ask.

'What do you want to know for?'

'Ain't got one, a missus?' wondered the man on the donkey.

'No, I haven't, I haven't!'

'Not good,' the owner of the donkey commiserated with him, as though he saw something strange and impossible before his eyes. 'Take you a missus!'

'I'm poor and I have nothing. How shall I keep a wife?' Menashke Bezprozvani answered, half-mocking, half-protesting.

'His Name is merciful!'

'How's His Name merciful? I'm an old bachelor already and so far He hasn't shown me any mercy!'

'His Name is merciful!' maintained the owner of the donkey. 'Him, everything He knows. Me, got nothing, and His Name never forsook me.'

'That's you and this is me.'

'What's a matter, huh? Must be everything all right. I had sense and got missus! Plenty all right.'

He lowered his head between his two shoulders and closed his eyes tight with satisfaction and contentment.

'Plenty all right, His Name be blessed!' He opened his eyes and went on speaking. 'Plenty all right . . . one day was in shop, I brought boxes. I saw there's one missus there . . . first, long, long before men gave me a missus and wasn't luck. His Name never give . . . I heard they told me, it is a missus come from Babylon wants to marry. Goes to Kiryat Shaul—and that's the missus from the shop. . . . From heaven, eh! No money I had—not got money what'll you do! Look, look, took six pound in bank and did business. At Muharram I made five pound also—and married! His Name be blessed, plenty all right . . . take you a missus, a worker, a fat one, be all right. His Name is merciful . . .'

He rapped his two soft sandals on the belly of the donkey which was plodding slowly under him, while his face expanded and broadened till it beamed like two copper pans.

'Never get on, no man, without a missus!' He moved from where he was sitting toward the donkey's crupper, speaking in a tone of absolute and assured finality. 'No mountain without top, no belly without belly button, no man get on without a missus!'

'And how many wives have you?' asked Menashke Bezprozvani, looking at him from the corner of his eye. 'Two? Three?'

'Two is two.' He raised his outstretched palms aloft as though saying, Come and see, I have no more than two . . .

'Do they live at peace?'

'Eh! Mountain looks at mountain and valley between them.' He turned a mouthful of strong white teeth toward him. 'If a young one in house, old one always brrr, brrr. . . .'

'And how much do you earn? Are you a porter or what?'

'Yes, mister.'

And having found himself a comfortable part of the donkey's back to sit on and having settled himself firmly there, he began telling him all his affairs. To begin with, he said, he had been a plain porter, and now he was porter with a donkey! This donkey under him was already his eighth, and from now on, nobody swindles him anymore. He was already a big expert on donkeys, an experienced and well-versed donkey-doctor! Through a bad donkey and a bad wife, said he, old age comes leaping on a man, but a good donkey and a good wife, nothing better than they in the world. Like a fat pilaf to eat, or the hot pot on the Sabbath! And His Name be blessed, he earned his daily bread. His Name is merciful! Sometimes one shilling a day, sometimes two shilling a day, and sometimes one mil. . . . There were these and those, all sorts of days!

'Then was all right, long before,' he passed his hand over the back of his neck as he spoke, 'earned four shilling a day also! Then was all right.'

He put his hand into the reed basket before him and took out a few dirty eggs.

'Take the ecks.' He held them out to his companion. 'Take, mister. Fresh as the Co-operative!'

Menashke Bezprozvani did not wish to take them.

'Have you a chicken run?' he asked, in a better humour.

'His Name be blessed! Got seven hens!' replied the other contentedly and with pride. 'All make ecks, eck a day, eck a day . . . take, mister! Please, like the Co-operative . . . chickens all right, His Name be blessed!'

Were it not, said he, for the money he needed, he himself would eat the eggs his hens laid, so all right were those eggs! But his little daughter lay sick in Hadassah and not a farthing did he have. Yesterday he had bought her bananas for half a piastre and she ate. . . .

'Eating already!' he said as one who announces great tidings, while his face lit up in a smile of good nature and happiness. 'Eating already, blessed be His Name!'

While he put the eggs back in the basket, Menashke Bezprozvani noticed that he wore two rings on his fingers, two copper rings set with thick projecting coloured stones. He asked:

'What are these?'

'This? Rings. And you haven't got?'

'Haven't got.'

'That's it,' he smiled into his beard. 'I'll tell you saying they tell by us in Babylon . . .'

And he began telling him the story of a certain man who loved a beautiful woman. 'Once it happened he had to go a long journey. He said to her, to that beauty: Lady! because that I love you much, you give me your ring, and as long as I see it on my finger I remember you and long for you. And that beauty who was sharp, never wish to give him her ring but said to him: Not so, only every time you look at your finger and see my ring not there, you remember me because I never give you ring, and you long for me . . .'

Ending his tale, he burst into a peal of laughter.

'Ha-ha-ha!' He threw his head back and filled the whole road with his powerful, noisy laughter. 'And so you also, ha-ha-ha!'

His laughter and the yarn he had spun turned Menashke Bezprozvani's mind in a different direction. Despite himself, he began to think of his own girl—her merits, her strangeness and the whole of that chapter.

The donkey, left to its own devices, was proceeding lazily and heavily while the porter sat shaking on its back, his face ruddy as copper and glinting, his beard spread in his satisfied smile, and his mood good as though he found everything in the whole world satisfactory. Menashke Bezprozvani turned his eyes to him and observed the way in which he sat on the donkey's back among his wooden vessels and ropes and pieces of metal; short and broad a sort of doubled-over and redoubled-over man. It looked almost as though his height had been doubled over into breadth, his backbone was double, and the teeth in his mouth were double echoing from one end of the road to the other, his laugh with childhood in it scattered itself throughout the universe; and the Holy and Blessed One was with him, near him, at home with him among his children and his wives, his chickens and his donkey . . .

Menashke walked slowly beside him and pictured the other at home. Here, his thoughts gradually emerged in clear pictures: the porter sits at the entrance to his home of an evening in the closed courtyard beside the cistern built over with stones. The children—a mixed heap of children—hang round him and tumble over him from every side, squalling and yelling. The womenfolk are busy at the fire. They cook the evening meal and quarrel between themselves on his account with vituperations and curses. Both are heavy and solid as two blossoming garden plots, and he makes peace between them, looking at one with affection and at the other with even more; every glance of his falls like rain upon thirsty soil. At the side lies his sick father, a heap of rags in a corner—an old man, his days drawn near to die. The fire crackles cheerfully and brightly, the pot boils, and one of the wives begins singing, rolling her voice toward the stars and drawing out her song . . .

'How did you come to the land of Israel?' he interrupted his reverie to ask.

'With the help of His Name!'

And before a moment had elapsed he was telling him all his wanderings. Thus and thus, he was a Kurd from Zacho. Did he know Zacho? . . . One day he heard there's a legion in the land of Israel, warriors of the Children of Israel. He said: wish to be a Jewish warrior —what is! He rose and went from Zacho to Mosul and from Mosul to Baghdad and from Baghdad to Basra. And already in Basra he is a servant to a Jew who has a shop to wear clothes, a rich man, plenty blessing he has, His Name be blessed. He made bread, he made food, everything, everything . . . because a man is better fit for work than a missus, fit much more . . . and then from Basra he went to Bombay, as the way to Damascus was then—long, long before—closed because of the war with the Turk. He stayed in Bombay two months, and every day, every day walked in the garden of Señor Sassoon, eating and drinking and walking . . . until at last he went to the land of Israel. Did he know Haifa? . . . As yet then in Haifa the Commercial Centre wasn't, eh! The lads told him there in Haifa: stay with us, Rahamim! But he didn't want—to Jerusalem, to the Jewish Legion! So he came to Jerusalem and the Legion wasn't. . . .

'None there!' He clapped his hands together, speaking in a downcast, long drawn-out voice.

For a while he was silent, shifting on his saddle. He turned his eyes and casually glanced at Menashke Bezprozvani, and his face changed. It was as though something astonishing had occurred to him just then.

'What for you're so sad?' he asked in a slow, soft voice.

Since Menashke Bezprozvani did not answer, he scratched the back of his neck two or three times and stirred himself.

'Late already,' he said, raising his head aloft.

He kicked his heels into the donkey's belly and tugged at the reins in his hand. The donkey tossed its head, put its feet one here and one there, and began kicking up its heels and galloping.

'Take a missus! His Name is merciful!' he turned his head and shouted back to Menashke. 'Peace! Peace to Israel!'

The donkey changed its gait, began to move precisely, and its tiny hoofs tapped in the roadway like castanets.

Menashke Bezprozvani remained alone and walked on, his body heavy and his spirit worn-down and weary. Strange feelings were pricking at his heart, chop and change, piecemeal, in turn, then all tossing within him in confusion; half-recollections of his childhood, the affairs and misadventures of his girl, and all his suffering and distractions. For some reason he remembered the days at Migdal, the baths at Tiberias, Ras al Ain and Kfar Gileadi; and the rhythm of a tune which was still indistinct to himself began to trouble him, half-remembered, half-forgotten—half-forgotten, half-remembered; he could not bring it fully to mind . . .

Until he heard the sound of a donkey's hoofs clacking on the roadway like castanets. He raised his eyes and saw that the porter had turned back toward him. He stood in surprise, blinking his eyes in the sun, and stared.

When the porter reached him, he pulled up his donkey, and stopped.

'Mister! Mister! . . . Listen!' He lowered his head to him with a wayward smile, his face strangely affectionate and humble. 'Mister! . . . Don't be sad! By my life! . . . Be all right! By my life! His Name is merciful!

'His Name's merciful . . .' he explained again, with a modest, almost maternal, smile. 'Don't be sad! My life! On my head and eyes! Be all right!'

Menashke Brezprozvani stood astonished with nothing to say. His heart leaped within him, and the beginnings of a confused smile were caught frozen at the corners of his mouth. The other had already left him and vanished along the road, but he still stood where he was as though fixed in the ground, his heart leaping and his spirit in a protracted, dark turmoil, like a distant echo caught and hanging all but still of an evening. And he could not understand it. It was as though something had happened within him, something big, but he did not know what. As though—as though—the guilty and soothing smile of that porter and his face which had been bright with love and humility did not disappear from his thoughts, but soothed him, comforting him and raising his spirits above all the errors and mistakes and recriminations and bitterness.

After a while he moved and turned and stirred to go. He descended into an open space covered with dry thorns, with many sunken stones in it, and a few twisted old olive trees. Under one of the trees stood five or six sheep pushing their heads one under the other and standing as though bewitched.

Menashke Bezprozvani sat himself down on a stone. He looked
up at the Mountains of Moab—desolate in their blue, indistinct in
outline—as though they had been swallowed by the sky or, perhaps,
as though the sky had been swallowed by them. Before his eyes stood
the likeness of the porter with his smile; his spirits rising within him,
his thoughts divided, he sighed, almost tearful, then began to hum to
himself the words of the song which the children had been accustomed to sing at Kfar Gileadi in those days of hardship and hunger:

> In Kfar Gileadi, in the upper court,
> Next to the runnel, within the big butt
> There's never a drop of water . . .

Translated by I. M. Lask.

S. Yizhar (Yizhar Smilanski)

HABAKUK

Yizhar was born in Palestine in 1916 and was a member of the Israeli parliament from 1948 until his retirement in 1967. His father was a pioneer and his great-uncle was one of the founders of the towns of Rehovot and Hadera. His major work is the enormous novel The Days of Ziklag *(1958), which minutely dissects Israeli culture and society of the 1940s and 1950s. More accessible, however, are his many short stories which depict the landscape of his youth and the milieu of the War of Independence. Yizhar was influenced by Gnessin, an influence that is evident in the stories which contain inner monologues and detailed descriptions of objects, and particularly of the landscape. He is a master of the delineation of childhood and early maturity and his stories, taken as a whole, suggest a kind of* Bildung. *The central concern of his writing is the conflict of the individual when confronted by the possible compromise of moral values.*

I

Well, I have been meaning to tell the story of Habakuk for a long time, and always kept putting it off for one reason or another. But today I'll begin without more ado.

The beginning of Habakuk is rather well known, and it's very simple too. Like this—

Ah, but it seems I must stop here, even before I've begun, and give warning to any of you boys who cannot bear sad stories, for I'm not at all certain this story won't be sad. Its beginning is bound to be a little bit sad, and so is its end—inescapably so—and only in the middle, maybe, it'll be a bit different and not just sad. Anyone who has reservations about sadness, therefore, well, he's been warned here and now, so let him leave off before we've begun and go in search of something that'll make him happy, and more power to him.

Well now, Habakuk. Though of course not the Habakuk of: 'O Lord, how long shall I cry and thou wilt not hear! Even cry out unto thee of violence and thou wilt not save!' or of: 'Wherefore lookest thou upon them that deal treacherously, and holdest thy tongue when the wicked devoureth the man that is more righteous than he'; not that righteous man whom God heard and to whom he even answered at last.

The one I am going to tell you about today—as indeed it's time his story were told, after all this delay—his name wasn't Habakuk at all. His name was Jedidiah. Why then do I call him Habakuk? I call him that because that's what he was called. By whom? Well, naturally, by the gang, those young scamps of whom I was one; those who, never content with the name bestowed upon a tender infant on the day of his circumcision, must needs drop the old name, that empty shell of a name, and find him a new one, a more becoming name as far as they are concerned, more to the point, better expressing the essence of his being—well, don't you know? Weren't you ever called names?

Now then, he was called Habakuk. A thin man he was, of middling height, going a bit bald in front and a bit on top too; a very big nose he had and a very nasal twang and very mobile eyebrows above brown eyes, eyes that had a singular expression in them and that perhaps—and let the comparison not be counted against me—that perhaps were brown as a dog's, the eyes of an Alsatian, say, if you know what I mean.

And what did those young 'uns I mentioned before have to do with this man, this man balding a bit in front and on top and older than they were by ten, twelve years? Ah, here now comes this abandoned beginning at last, the one I embarked on before, and it's a very simple beginning too. Like this:

One day I came to Jerusalem. I was coming to Jerusalem to study, and my mother had come along because this was my first time away from home and she wanted to see all the arrangements for herself, everything that I had arranged on my own and that others had arranged for me, and she still had a great deal of advice to bestow upon such a novice in the matter of arrangements as I. And behold, by the bus stop, walking towards us there came a man, a big-nosed man, going bald a bit on top and a bit in front, with a broad smile and a big hello on his face. My mother returned his greeting, then pointed at me, the young resident-scholar-to-be, and said, not meaning anything: 'Here I've brought you something of a friend . . .'—the conventional and commonplace thing to say—never imagining how far-sighted she was and how, from there on, that 'something' she had so uncompromisingly offered would take its course and wax and grow and become what it did, what it so unforeseeably and against all expectation did become.

And indeed, as early as the next morning and by the same bus stop, whom did I meet, big-nosed and balding, corn-on-the-cob teeth showing large in a smile, bobbing a bit in his walk, body and shoulders thrown forwards in a kind of rhythmic bowing, who but this acquaintance of my mother's from yesterday, and what did he have in his hand but a violin case containing, presumably, a violin.

'I didn't know you played!' I told him with undisguised admiration, even before the greetings were over and done with.

'Didn't know you cared for music!' he countered.

'Oh, but I do!' thus I, enthusiastically overstating the case because, to tell you the truth, I knew next to nothing about music at that time. All the music that I could be said to know then was of two kinds: the music that I'd read about, and the music that I'd heard about. As for the music itself, I'd neither heard nor knew any. Think back and you'll know what kind of music was available to us then—except for the ditties bawled out at the top of one's voice that went for singing among us boys, and except for my father's occasional melancholy yah-bim-bam-boom rendition of a Hassidic tune—what other music could I possibly have heard? Well, you know the little village I come from—what else was there except dim orange groves, acacia hedges, the thud-thud of water pumps, the rustle of eucalyptus leaves, the screech of crows in autumn before the first rains, the babel of Arabs hawking their wares, in Arabic, and Jews bidding for them, in Yiddish, donkeys braying before dawn—what else would you hear there, where I lived? The little I did know of music I had gleaned, awed and enraptured and with an intimation of sacredness in my heart, from Jean Christophe and Uncle Moshe's.

As far as Jean Christophe is concerned, you can read it and see for yourself. But at Uncle Moshe's they had a gramophone. A wonder box, highly polished and with an outlandish air about it, did my Uncle Moshe have, and it had a peculiar kind of smell, foreign like the fragrance of an English pipe or a rare wine. And it shut with a kind of latticed lid, and it had its place on a special stand in which the records, too, were kept; and if you'd go and turn the handle stuck in its side and put the pick-up arm gently on the record—then its notes would break over you; and if on top of that you'd bend down and place your ear against those lattices—then the notes would swell and reverberate and make you forget the whole world and create another whole world for you, a new and unknown one. All you had to do from there on was to change needles for each new side (as, indeed, was printed there explicitly: Use each needle once only!—a warning we adopted for our own use and applied to various occasions), and turn the handle some more, and pick a time when Uncle Moshe was not having his siesta—then oh then you could listen, endlessly ('Hast thou found honey? Eat so much as is sufficient for thee lest thou be filled therewith.' Uncle Moshe once quoted Proverbs at me when, coming home, he found me still by the gramophone just as he had left me; I smiled noncommittally, though, and told myself: 'Hast thou found honey? Eat it all up!'). I just couldn't listen, couldn't tear myself away, and even the paucity of Uncle Moshe's records did not hold me back. On the contrary, I could listen to the same record over and over again, till everything, every last detail, had sunk down deep and been embedded in the core of my being, fused there with the swaying of the eucalyptus branches beyond the window, merged with the flickering dots of light, tied up inextricably with the smell of the smooth box and rippling with the stillness in the large room (empty except for Kadya, the maid, padding about barefoot), and with the splashes of scarlet shimmering on the red tiles where the sunlight fell.

As a matter of fact, Uncle Moshe had plenty of records, but nearly all of them, alas, were of cantors. Those he loved and would listen to when overcome by a homesickness for times and places I knew little about; all kind of drawn-out prayers and psalms and litanies which would elicit nothing but a mocking smile from me and from my friend Jishai. Yet besides this disdained treasure of cantors there was the smaller and the more wonderful treasure that I was at liberty to cherish. There were fragments of Tchaikovsky there to wring your heart, and scraps of this and that opera, Caruso and Chaliapin and Galli-Curci, and in addition there was Sarasate's 'Andalusian Romance', which I could whistle, so high and shrill as to frighten the ravens in the topmost branches and make them complain loudly, and so as to astonish the gang, who would stop what they were doing and give me a scandalized look—me walking by whistling with my gaze on the clouds and my hands in my pockets, my shoulders hunched and the sound coming from between my pursed lips like a violin in my ears, and like a rusty kerosene pump in theirs—so they would point a finger to their head as a plain mark of their opinion, or even pick up a clod of earth or a pine-cone and throw it at me to help bring me to my senses and make me behave like a normal being: *Uskot, inte el thani*, they would shout at me the cry of an Arab carter scolding his horse—Shut up, you there!

But Uncle Moshe's treasure included Beethoven's Violin Concerto. Ah, what do you know! And to that I would listen with my finger stuck between the pages of Jean Christophe. Yes. In those days I had never yet seen either an orchestra or a conductor, nor was I familiar with the various instruments and I could only guess what they were and what they looked like. Not that this prevented me in any way from being enraptured, of course, and from finding a thousand thrilling and wonderful things in the music which no one would ever have imagined were there; nor did it prevent me from taking it upon myself to conduct—with two hands and ten fingers and stormy tossings of my head and flourishes of my whole body—fervently leading the great Beethoven and his magical musicians from glory to glory, up to the exultant moment of triumph—and on, humming short phrases and tiddle-dumming others with one foot beating the rhythm like a dozen drums, and being moved to tears, and to joy, and to great and colour-ful flights of fancy beyond anything their creator and begetter could have imagined or thought possible, beyond any time or place, and beyond supper-time—till somebody in the household would weary of me and the noise of my music and my odd caperings, and would scold me and pack me off with a 'Come, that'll do for now!'—and I would rise as in a trance and trudge home through the sand, between houses framed in casuarina and tall eucalyptus trees, singing, blissful, unaffected by being sent home, dreaming, romancing, gesturing, and there would be no containing my heart that yearned for faraway places and marvels and secrets, for the not-here, not-thus, and for beyond all this, beyond all and any of this here, beyond every given thing, now, like this. No.

Do not be surprised, therefore, at what I asked Habakuk (I believe I still politely called him Mister So-and-So then, and he grinned and said, 'My name is Jedidiah', with an emphasis on the name as though he were quoting it straight from the Bible, and as though it were some unfamiliar Adaniah, Jozabad, or Jediael!), while still exchanging my first words with him I already asked: 'And Beethoven's concerto, can you play that?' and I whistled the famous theme to make sure he'd know what I meant, and also to make him realize that I was an old hand and knew what I was asking, even if at the same time my expression must have shown an awareness that I was asking the impossible, asking for rain from a clear sky, asking with such plain and obvi-ous doubt in my voice—the which he, nevertheless, ignored, to say with astounding simplicity:

'Yes.'

'Yes?'

'Yes. That is, I'm no Heifetz, but I play,' said this balding, big-nosed fellow with his nasal twang, as though he hadn't said anything extraordinary.

'Oh!' I said and fell silent.

'Really?' I said when I could speak once more.

'Would you like to hear it?'

'Would you play?'

'Why not?'

'When?'

'Why not now?'

'Now? You mean right away! Do you mean now?'

There and then casting to the wind everything that that same 'now' had initially been meant to contain, my going that had been aimed at some task, some necessary thing to do, necessary beyond all doubt—forgetting all about it without a moment's hesitation.

'Come on, then!' I cried, ready to grab his hand and sweep him along. But he started out with his odd lurching gait, his bob and bow with each step, smiling broadly, making me forget that he, too, was turning back from wherever he had been going, altering his course for my sake and abandoning some worthy and necessary purpose which he had been pursuing prior to our meeting, leaving it unaccomplished—everything was cancelled and abandoned, his pursuits and mine, and we walked off together to hear Beethoven on the as yet unproven violin of Habakuk, whom I called Jedidiah then with some hesitation on my part but with obvious pleasure on his, as though I were calling him, say, Adaniah the Priest!

We did not have far to walk. In fact, we didn't have to walk any distance at all, only to turn around and enter a yard through a battered wooden wicket hanging on its last hinges, skip down the two high stone steps, cross the yard and then, instead of climbing to the wide portico and walking through to the front door, veer off to the right—not for us the main entrance—and along the wall and, yes, to the left again and across the path hugging the house, over worn, wobbling flagstones, turn left once more and down a flight of stairs to the low entrance.

I stopped at the door.

'Down here?' I asked.

'In the vast depths,' he confirmed, 'Yes, down here I live,' and smiled at me.

And we went through the door, which wasn't locked, and were inside a room whose small windows floated just above ground level.

So this then was the room which I'd soon be at home in, an *habitué* familiar with all its nooks and crannies and all its accessories. Not that there was much of those latter. In fact, there was hardly anything inside that room. This new friend of mine had nothing. He was not weighed down by anything. Such was Jedidiah, or rather, Habakuk —he had nothing. At any rate, nothing but what his room contained. And the room contained nothing. A table and chair, a bed, a few packing-cases (serving various purposes: cupboard, bookcase, pantry), all of it pushed up against the wall, into corners and out of the way, so that there was a large clear space left, bare except for the music stand jutting out in the centre of the room like a raised hand waving pages of music. In addition there was a tin container crouching in a corner and adapted to contain a paraffin lamp, when it turned into a stove, or a 'furnace', as Habakuk called it ('Whose fire is in Zion and whose furnace in Jerusalem!' he grinned one wintry morning, proud of his ability to find apt quotations from the Bible for every last thing). A kettle would be put over the holes punched in the top of the tin, and slowly the water would come to the boil, and tea would be made when tea would be called for, between one thing and another.

But all this emerged only later, of course. There was none of it that first morning but: 'Sit down,' said Jedidiah and pointed at the bed covered with a grey army blanket. He opened his violin case and, moreover, took out a violin (for there is a story about a man who opened such a case and came out with a hatchet!), and he took the neck of the violin in his hand, and it transpired that his hand was white, with long fingers, tapering, nails like nut-shells, and he took out the bow and strung it, and swung his violin in place under his chin and tuned it.

'Beethoven: Violin Concerto in D Major,' he announced ceremoniously (pronouncing the 'Beethoven' differently from the way I used to in Jean Christophe) and, tapping his foot one, two, three, he began to play. His fingers quivered on the strings, his hand flourished the bow, his eyebrows worked their way up, way up the height of his forehead, and his forehead contracted, and his brown eyes looked straight in front of him and his chin bulged atop the wedged violin.

But the sounds emitted by his violin's belly did really and truly bear a faithful resemblance to those produced by Uncle Moshe's gramophone in the red-tiled room, though it would be wrong not to mention right at the start, without detracting from the man or his beloved memory, that there was something pale in the playing of this new-found friend of mine, and not only for the lack of an orchestra but also, I am afraid, due to a creaking here and there and a jarring now and then and a note gone a little wrong, so that the particular brilliance that would dazzle you when you put the record on inside the polished box was wanting here. And yet it didn't matter. For I was absorbed, lost in this man and his playing, fascinated by the very reality of notes being produced before my eyes—a man standing here and making his violin sing; not some hidden mechanical device but the product of these hands belonging to this man here, these hands bringing the wonder to pass; and despite the fact that the man was big-nosed and balding and brown-eyed like a dog, here he was singing fervently in this basement of his that contained nothing, nothing but him.

II

And so his foot tapped out the four drum-beats, and at the fifth the woodwinds joined in and sang two phrases, and the drums came back and from there on the violins' strumming kept their beat, and then the second theme broke forth (so there were two themes, were there, and not just a flow of countless melodies following one upon the other . . .). And apparently there was a transitional passage too, between one theme and the next—like this, and then the violin made its entrance. Majestically. It came and climbed and surged and soared rapidly to its towering heights. And staying with that theme, the famous one, and then on and away, passionately—Habakuk drew his bow back and forth over the strings, the fingers of his left hand flying and flickering on the strings. And then, suddenly, the musician made a sideways gesture with his chin and wrinkled his brow at me, as a sign for me to turn the page—but I did not know what to make of his sign, and he was obliged to interrupt his playing and turn the page himself quickly with his bow-holding hand. I did not yet know the meaning of that sign, just as I knew nothing about the notes on his pages, and just as I marvelled at the words introducing a new movement, never thinking that 'allegro ma non troppo' wasn't some sort of inscrutable incantation to be understood by none but the initiated, but meant, simply: 'fast, but not too fast', 'fluent but not hurried', or some such thing. A little later he had to stop again and explain to me, ignorant me, such a rudimentary thing as the meaning of that obscure 'D Major'. And it wasn't at all easy to get to the bottom of it and walk this valley between major and minor, or to look and

listen and make out all the minutiae of the scale, and place the finger
on each ascending 'sharp' and trace each 'flat' down to its precise
spot—and move on and deeper into this wondrous valley and actually feel the spirit expand and grow richer and everything around get
clearer and brighter as it opened up wider and wider, and we go on
and up and down, from low D to high D and back, and we fetch
paper and draw sweeping scales on it, and beat out a rhythm with
one foot and hum and sing a phrase, high and happy. And we pick
up the violin again and he fiddles a snatch, bits from here and from
there, by heart and from the heart and in plenty, the greatest and
purest, the most simple and glorious of music.

Oh, how dreadfully ignorant I was of all this. I am ashamed to
tell—such utter ignorance. I knew nothing, nothing. I was nothing
but a lad from down there, from the plains. A lad loving the almond
trees in bloom in winter, hankering after the hum of the water-pumps
in the summer orange groves, forever daydreaming, in and out of season, simple and naïve as a bird on a bough, a cone on its pine, and
knowing nothing, not even that he does not know—a sort of plain,
white, simple circle.

And thus several great and weighty matters were explained to me,
and we arrived at the *larghetto* and went on from there to the *rondo
allegro*—and we enquired briefly into the construction of the concerto
in general, and Beethoven's concerto in particular, and such novelties
as the innovators had introduced—taking exception to all those triflers
and new-fangled tricksters of the present day—and what, as against
these, those others, the geniuses—had written in their diaries, and
what he himself had written in his diary, so that meanwhile I found
out that indeed, people do write things in diaries, day by day, and we
could open the exercise book and see—and on such and such a day
we found an entry written there, and it was just exactly what we were
looking for: a neat and complete phrase, complete, too, with allusions
of the kind that make you crave for an explanation: 'The world is full
of gods!'—such and no less was written there on one page, in carefully drawn letters deserving equally careful study and, more than
that, unlimited admiration, which I proceeded to bestow upon him
liberally, and with all my heart.

And in due time it was noon, and then it was afternoon already
and he, with his violin in one hand and bow in the other, smoothed
the wrinkles of his mobile brow, and asked would I do him the honour of sharing his meal with him, a plain and simple meal, a mere
appeasing of hunger with a bowl of soup, which he could prepare in

a twinkle, a soup made of nothing but vegetables, yet thick and tasty and good and containing, what not?—tomatoes and onions and carrots and pumpkin and peas and pods and greens and golds and lapis lazuli, nourishing as anything when dished up with lots of bread and good cheer, one heart, one plate, one spoon—so how about it?

Said and done. And while the soup stood simmering on the makeshift stove, light and joy trickling through its holes, we drifted back to Beethoven in his heyday, from Opus (q.v.!) 55, which is the 'Eroica', to 57, which is the 'Appassionata', and to 59, which is three famed quartets—up to Opus (ditto) 73, which is the celebrated piano concerto, the 'Emperor', and including Opus 68, which is the 'Pastoral' Symphony, which is the Sixth; and these are happy matters and inspiring, and they open up wells of emotion, and they make for bright eyes and induce an urgent need to hum snatches from here and from there, and a wish to do things in this world, great and burning and sky-high things, heart-conquering things that bring tears of joy and gratitude to the eyes.

Yes. Ah yes, of course. And afterwards we sat down in peace and brotherhood and ate that soup, as promised, with soft fresh bread, and its flavour was thick and buttery, even though rather oddish—and yet, if there had been a piano in that room we would have left everything then and there and gone over and played it, played one after the other two great, two stupendous, thrilling works filled with the fierce rapture of youthful love, like Orion on a bright winter night—the 'Appassionata' for one, and the 'Waldstein' for another—and until then, and for lack of a piano, that big-nosed fellow blowing and breathing through the steam of his thick soup, sat and sang the principal themes at the top of his weak voice, trusting to me and my lively imagination, and gesturing with his narrow-jointed, thin-fingered, long white hand to indicate how one thing proceeds from another and how passion mounts and scales summits, up, up to the god-like heights.

III

And it was well into the afternoon when we suddenly discovered that the time had come, or had perhaps even gone by, when we must stop and rush out and apply ourselves to various urgent affairs, postponed and forgotten and now coming back to mind like a horde of impatient, clamorous creditors. 'Time's passing!' I said close to despair, though still unable to tear myself away.

'Time is always passing. Space is fixed but time passes,' said he, lofty but obscure, gently laying his violin in the case and returning the bow to its place.

'I didn't manage to do a thing,' I complained, getting up to go.

'One manages to do what one has to,' he told me then. 'One can't do more, just as one can't do less than one has to.' Weighty words he uttered, words like these, without my having any idea how to apply them. 'And you are young still,' he added with a toss of his high forehead, 'There's everything you can manage to do before you yet. You've only just begun,' he said, and smiled at me. 'How old are you anyway?' he asked, and I became aware of the approach of something new and unknown, something very special and very strange, beyond our sphere, as it were.

I told him. But he wasn't satisfied. On what day, he demanded, and what hour was I born?

Why the hour? What did it matter? By the way, I have an idea that my mother used to say, when telling us her once-when-you-were-a-little-boy stories, that I was born at sunrise, I think it was, though...

The words weren't out of my mouth before this friend of mine, this odd Jedidiah—whose face suddenly took on a new expression, lit up as of a man crouching over a fire—this odd one stretched out a hand and picked up a sheet of paper and deftly drew a circle on it with one swift stroke of his hand; a curious-looking booklet filled with figures appeared out of nowhere upon the small table, and he began leafing through it at incredible speed, found what he had been looking for and hastily marked a few dots inside the circle he had drawn—a blank space as yet, a breathlessly blank space seeming to await events; and he started mumbling and muttering incomprehensible phrases, obscure expressions among which I seemed, however, to catch the names of the better-known stars, without being able to catch their significance or present purpose—names like Venus, Mars, Saturn, and Jupiter, as well as the lesser-known ones like Uranus, Neptune, and Pluto, and maybe some more names or terms or god-knows-what that appeared to surround his diligently bent head like a halo—and he was completely absorbed, joining dots with a sure stroke, never wavering, as though no doubt could exist, adding here and there some extraordinary mark the like of which I had never seen before, in or out of a book, nor ever heard of, like some secret language; and he was creating all manner of curves and angles with the touch of his pencil and then making some of them run to squares and triangles, and all the while he ignored my questioning face as well as my actual questions,

only making sounds of surprise and admiration like someone who
has suddenly come upon a magnificent view from the top of a hill;
he blurted out exclamations, and from time to time he looked up as
though great and wonderful things were being unveiled for him.
'Really?'—'Is that so!'—'But that's marvellous!'—'Incredible!'—and
more of the kind, not to mention his 'Terrific!' and 'Fantastic!' and a
host of other superlatives; add to that his eyes which, time and again,
would be raised with a faraway look, far beyond the here and now,
then would come back for a minute to rest upon my puzzled self
(standing there somewhat apprehensive, and hiding in self-defence
behind a forced smile), then back again to their encounter with the
unseen and unknown. And I had already reached a point where I was
wondering whether I hadn't better take myself quietly off, when the
man waved a long white finger in the air as though calling for attention, as though on the point of speaking out, revealing great things—
and I could almost feel my flesh creep, and stood transfixed, spellbound
and fascinated by him, him gazing now toward his faraway distances,
now at me, and as it were comparing what he saw there with this
one before him here, or as though surprised perhaps to find that whatever he was seeing there was actually identical with this one here or
with what he would turn out to be—the moment thickened and
condensed, soon, very soon now it would burst, here now, it was
coming—and the man lifted his finger, the magician's finger, and his
face lit up: 'See?' he addressed me suddenly in a somewhat stifled
voice—'Look here: d'you see it?'—and his long white finger seemed
to sprout out and point at a section his pencil had cut in that circle
of his, and at another section, which later he entitled: 'Here, this
"house" here'—he said with inexplicable excitement—'A beauty!'—he
said and raised his eyes—'But this "house" over here is rather dangerous, or it would be but for this angle here,' he said and burst out
laughing—at the frustration of the Arch Fiend's attempt, apparently—
'This is an excellent angle. You can put your trust in it, never fear!'—
he said and looked at me like a doctor reassuring a frightened
patient.—'The only thing that's still in doubt is this square here . . .'
—he said, and his whole forehead wrinkled in a frown. And once
more he arched his crooked eyebrows at me, peered at me, or through
me, and I was an open book, plainly, there for him to read.

'What is all this?' I quavered.

'It's you,' he said, 'and these are your stars. Everything's written
here!' he solemnly declared. And I didn't know whether to put on a

disparaging smile or a worried frown, whether I should come out with the first witticism that would occur to me or swallow it all and keep my mouth shut. Fate itself seemed to hover in the air over our heads. And anyway, it was obviously impossible to laugh it off. I shrugged a shoulder. I must have looked rather wretched.

'Venus and Sun!' he sang out, for me to appreciate the achievement to the full. 'Here they are playing now!'

I glanced over his shoulder, cautiously, to see for myself, as though peering into an abyss:

'Where? What's all this?' I said reluctantly, feeling like a naked man among the clothed.

'Your horoscope!' he threw me a magic formula. 'Written in the stars,' he added with a big, friendly smile. 'It's all written in the book of heaven. A man is born under his stars, inescapably. Man is, and the world is.'

Thus he explained the matter to me, only obscuring it the more. And it all remained very vague and not a little frightening, even though extremely tempting to jump up, if that was the way it was, and take a peep through that window giving on to the terrible place, where one would fain look though it is forbidden, and where if one does look one will pay for it heavily. I did not know what to do or say. And perhaps, I thought, I had better put on my man-of-the-world face now, and scoff at all this as silly nonsense and childish games, a world removed from two-and-two-are-four.

'So you read the stars?' I said, not knowing what else to say.

And at once felt as though, for some reason, I were tottering on a brink, or as though something that I had always held in a firm grasp were slipping now, and I must pull myself together and hold on fast. And I wriggled and squirmed and put a finger inside my collar.

'An astrologer,' the man said and smiled at me.

'And soothsayer? . . .' I whispered, not without respect, and perhaps with even an edge of terror.

But to this he did not reply, only spread his hands and inclined his head a little as though to say: Have it your way.

'Or prophet . . .' I let fall, half-question, half-pronouncement—and then of a sudden felt that I would do better to get up and go away from here, and the sooner the better, rush out and see and feel and touch the things that would be there, out there, that existed, yes, them and others, things substantial, things under the sun—and lo, there they were outside as they had always been, thank God, and always are.

IV

That was the beginning. And the rest followed soon after. I grew to be a regular visitor in the man's basement—the kingdom of music and stars. And I yielded to the sway of the one and resisted the reign of those others. I did not keep this great discovery, with its splendours and its dreads, to myself, however, but shared my secret—and my cellar—with first one, then two and three of my best friends and, notwithstanding test papers and examinations, we would linger there for hours on end, completely at home, behaving as though the place were ours by right and as though he, its owner, were there only for our benefit. And the man would accept it all without demur, and he was at home with us boys as we were at home with him and within that empty lair of his—empty of all but himself, his being, his fiddle and his stars, and of our excited flourishes.

We would come, arriving each by himself in a free hour, or all of us together, to the never-locked room, would throw ourselves into some corner, leave all the outside and beyond-this-room beyond and outside, sprawl so or thus, light a fire under the stove for our pleasure, joke a bit, gossip—and an instant later it would all have blown away: our chatter carried on from the street, our affairs and preoccupations with this and with that, our noise and our laughter, everything would leave us and nothing remain but ourselves, with the great Beethoven on our right and God's stars on our left and us basking in their light, carried away, excited, conducting from our respective corners the fullest imaginable orchestra, conducting with both our hands and a tossing of our young heads and a flinging of our hair, so that, had a stranger come upon us from without he would have been scared out of his wits: a bunch of epileptics in a fit. Luckily, however, there was no one there but us, reverentially pronouncing upon the greatest and most vital of matters, holding forth with passion, with enthusiasm, eyes sparkling, never fearing or faltering, not hesitating either to exalt the great or to deny an axiom, drawing back in the face of neither the sinful nor the sacred, and rising to great heights of enthusiasm and inspiration, rising to God and all his angels and higher yet—

'Woe to the land shadowing with wings, woe to the nation scattered and torn, a nation meted out and downtrodden, whose lands the rivers have spoiled . . .' O wonderful inexplicit words, words full of Biblical splendour and magic, words that excite the imagination, O all ye inhabitants of the world and dwellers on the earth—when

he bloweth a trumpet, hear ye—O noble and declamable words, O
cloud of dew in the heat of harvest, O pure breathless heat, O purity and O, no breath left but so much eagerness still, O—

It needs no saying that, as long as they had come across a prophet,
they were all eager to find out right away what the future might have
in store for them—nor did our friend and benefactor hold back. On
the contrary, he would happily take a sheet of paper and draw a circle
with practised hand, leaf through his booklet of figures and signs and
determine the position of the stars on that particular birthday, trace
each star to its house and home, and go on to create triangles and
squares, curves and angles, just as there had been in the sky on that
fateful day, and he would let fall a word here and there, mumble his
spells and incantations, and all of us would be listening and our ears
would go pink with youthful expectation and curiosity (the fact that
we were in a group lessened the tension a little and drew some smiles
of mockery), a merry, all-embracing curiosity aimed at nothing in
particular, but containing, nevertheless, a momentary tremor at this
contact with an alien magic, as at an actual contact with the future,
a confrontation of its veiled secrets which no human eye may behold,
and whose misty distances only the sharp glance of this man could
pierce—now he would fetch it from afar and place it on our palm,
here was this as yet unhatched chicken of the future, here it sat chirping on our agitated hand . . .

How far could he see? That isn't the question at all. At least, it is
not a question we ever thought of asking then. There was nothing but faith in our hearts. He did see and he knew and we never
doubted him. Although it may be that he saw but did not tell it all,
saw and kept it to himself. For towards us he always turned a
smiling face, and the heavens smiled upon us with him. He would
always find us someone to protect us against the unfavourable stars,
the bad, harmful ones, and against the harsh, perfidious, ill-omened
angles. Moreover, he had apparently unravelled his own destiny too,
but he kept his lips firmly closed and never let fall a hint about that
shell hitting him out of a clear sky, there beside the kibbutz dining-
hall, on the lawn . . . Oh no, he never foretold anything but growing
and blooming and flowering for us, nothing but drinking the cupful
and taking the world by its mane as you take a wild mare by its mane
and gallop forth to freedom.

And inasmuch as he was a seer we needs must crown him with a
fitting prophetical name, and without the least difficulty, without giving it another thought, we pronounced him Habakuk. Why Habakuk

of all names? There you are—why not? For that precisely was the point: Habakuk of all names, and Habakuk alone. He did not object and we were delighted. And from then on he was Habakuk to us. Habakuk the Prophet, as we said, looking up at him. And sometimes, in a less reverent mood, it would turn into 'good old Habakuk'. And more than once you could have heard us among ourselves: 'Four o'clock at Habakuk's!'—Or perhaps: 'Let's hop it—to the prophet!' —or again: 'Arise ye and let us go up unto our seer!' and the like exuberant banter and biblical flourish.

Some of us would sit, arms clasped about our knees, on the steps leading from the door down into the room, others, a distant look in their eyes, would recline on the bed in the corner, one would sit nodding his head in rhythm, his back against the wall, another sprawl on a chair with his legs up on the window-sill, tapping out that selfsame rhythm—and only our prophet Habakuk would be standing, violin under chin, bow in hand, eyebrows arched, forehead wrinkled, and all of him aglow, interrupting his playing for a minute just to breathe and utter a 'Glorious, isn't it? Just glorious!'—and everybody, one after the other, would nod his head to the look in his brown eyes (brown Alsatian eyes) and go one better on him: 'Great!'—'Super!'—'Terrific!'

And now what? Now we come to Mozart. To one particular sonata, for violin and piano (sad to say, I have forgotten its number). And as a piano is not available, our prophet doesn't give in but takes it upon himself to sing the main parts and highlights that would have fallen to the piano's lot had there been one (never mind the fact that, as Habakuk himself remarked, Mozart had had the piano mainly in mind and had meant the violin only as accompaniment)—but we catch on quickly and fill in the missing parts without the least difficulty and with the aid of our generous imagination, fired by him, and we are always ready to admire, always full of enthusiasm, giving vent to it, aloud or in deep whispers, and ever ready to encourage and reassure him when he runs into difficulties, and to go back with him to the beginning of the passage, and discover its substance and essence, and go on to carve out the next passage with him, and ask him to play that again too, and he will always comply and play it again. And we ask him to repeat all of it and then compare with what we had yesterday, and he will always comply and compare. And we say very, very clever things, and are open-minded and generous, and we talk and talk and are wise and speak three thousand proverbs about every subject under the sun and sing a hundred and one songs on every topic, and are always excited and our hands fly hither and thither.

And once in a while Naomi will burst into the room to join us for a while and listen too. And she is always in a hurry, Naomi, always between a hustle and a bustle, between the giving of a lesson and the taking of one, always flushed with excitement and with running and with the cold outside, afire within and without, burning heart and the touch of winter—and we vacate the sole chair and offer it up to her, as is due to a girl alone among men, but she squats down upon the edge of the blanket spread out on the floor in order to be in the shadows, less seen, less obvious, not to draw attention to her cheeks burning like fresh roses—even though everybody beams at her and bathes her in the warmth of his eyes, and Habakuk the Seer tosses his head and waits no longer and says: 'Second movement, the *Adagio*.'—And everyone holds his breath and prepares his spirit for the soaring journey, eyes awash with emotion; yet two pairs of eyes edge away stealthily and meet—eyes meet in a shy glance, show surprise, linger, and dart away, aside and up, always upwards, very excited, to the ceiling and beyond, oh, far beyond, always, oh, dear God!

The *Adagio* has ended and no one dares breathe. And our gentle Habakuk makes deep furrows in his brow and, never lifting his chin off the violin, he tries at the same time to pull his mouth into a crooked, soothing smile, while his hands busy themselves tightening the bow and plucking the strings to test them for tautness; then he announces: '*Rondo Presto*'—and away off with a flourish of his sword to conquer that land unknown, land of summits swept by wind and rain, and lit up with glimmers of sunshine too, brief, clear flashes shining like rain-washed tufts of grass, insisting joyfully that it isn't over and done with yet, that even the hardest of all has its song of hope, and everything is still before us, oh, very much so.

Finish. The bow is lowered with a round sweep of the arm. A full great moment's silence, a withholding silence. Then the flame leaps up. Everyone, all of us together. What each of us felt, what thought, what fancied, what was struck with, what it seemed to him as though, and where the core was, the emphasis, the song, and that transition between the first theme and the second, how did it go, and how did the one grow out of the other, and the structure, and the construction, and the planes, and lines, and contrasts, and resolutions, and the lilting and the stresses—yes, and what we had learnt from history too, and what was found written in the diary of that great one, and in his letters from the same year, and what is it he mentions there that we could apply here, and why was this particular scale chosen out of all others, and how high this scale and how vast and who can scale it, man and angel, and where can you find in the Bible something exactly like, and where did we read a poem that says just that, and when was it you suddenly felt this was pure prayer, the prayer of a man weary unto death, a stricken man empty of everything, of all faith, all but: Out of the depths I cry unto thee, O Lord, hear me, O Lord, hear me—shine thy face upon me and give me peace.

And once in a while the door might open and the Prophet Isaiah come down the steps. We drop back and clear a space for him in our midst, that he may stand in the light, look at us and tell us fiery things. We listen, heed, our hearts swell, and before long he has vanished. And the room reverberates with the echoes still. Or else Jeremiah, the Prophet of Anathoth, or Amos the Herdsman from Tekoah. And at times Habakuk would close his eyes and recite for us—none of us understanding a word of German—from his beloved Goethe, the giant, the unique. And once, with soft and gentle tread, crown of thorns on his head, even the Nazarene came into our room, gave us a silent look and returned to his cross. Yes, but need it be said that there was one who never left us, never loosened his hold upon us, not before, not during and not after all, not in the long evenings, not during the many afternoon hours, nor on the free Saturdays—those we stayed home and did not spend on cycling trips over the Hills of Ephraim—he never left us coming or going, roaming the streets or lying in our beds at night—the one and only, the greatest of them all, burning-eyed, wild-haired, hand in waistcoat, chin stuck out, stormy and restrained—oh Ludwig, oh Beethoven, oh God of Youth!

Ah, here now we are at his Seventh, its finale (with the record-player discovered and dragged by someone to our lair), with might, with majesty, with a leap, with a cry to end all cries, with an—Oh come and gather ye together, a day of trumpet and alarm, the day is coming, don't ye tarry, oh you there, come from here and beyond, come up and be not slack, all ye who desire, all ye who have faith, all ye who love—come hasten ye, come ye hosts, ye armies, come marching, all of ye, here, now—my God, my dear God—here we are all of us before you, here we are, ready. When I grow up, when I am I, if I shall be granted to become what there is in me, if indeed it is there within me, when I shall know things, shall be able, shall stand on my own legs, then I shall call out, hands spread, shall call out with all my power—to be attentive, alert, to be ready for anything, ready to leave everything and go, responsive to the slightest gesture as players to a conductor, spellbound, bewitched but awake, so as to rise and go, to his kingdom, the kingdom of beauty—and he shall reign triumphant, sole ruler, and we shall come to him, there, don't know where, stand there transported, our bodies humble but our eyes raised high . . .

V

And one day, when our little group had once more gathered, and it was raining outside and the stove, that 'furnace in Zion', was dripping gold from its pores, and each of us curled up in his corner, huddled in his coat, and the room bare as ever, containing nothing but the few odds and ends pushed aside, and us—Habakuk the Prophet placed some pages of music on the stand, turned over a few and found the title and pointed at it with the tip of his bow and said nothing but: 'Sonata for Unaccompanied Violin, by Johann Sebastian Bach'. And he lifted his bow with a sweep and drew it over the strings once, harshly, and began playing and did not stop till he had played it through to the end, the whole Sonata, movement by movement. And no one opened his mouth or dared speak. Only afterwards did one of us take courage to beg in a whisper: More, once again, Habakuk, once more, please!—But Habakuk hung back, this once. Tired, perhaps. His brow was furrowed and his lips were tight with thought; his eyes were not upon us.

'It all begins peacefully,' Habakuk said into the silence around him, 'Like this'—and he picked up his violin and played to show us how.— 'And soon the terror sets in . . .' he muttered and played to show us how. 'Everything is tossed. Nothing keeps still, keeps fast. A fearful wind . . .' he whispered and played to show us. 'What will remain of all this?' he whispered, his eyes closed, not turning to us. And nobody tried to answer. Very silent we were. And the room filled with our silence and his words. There was nothing in the room except the beating of hearts and the listening to his voice.

'Now what do we have here?' said Habakuk over his violin. 'In the Book of Isaiah, Chapter 19, we have its like: "Behold, the Lord rideth upon the light cloud . . .",' he said, not to us, not opening his eyes, and played that phrase about the Lord riding upon a light cloud. Everything is right. Everything is meet, calm, before any test, before the trial. A light cloud in a clear sky.

Who can imagine the gravity of what is coming, of what is contained there within the light cloud, how suddenly the darkest of all should issue forth from it.

'And He shall come into Egypt . . .' said Habakuk, his arm raised as in dread, 'and the idols of Egypt shall be moved at his presence . . .'

Rising and descending scales. Chords running, pursuing each other. Wave upon black wave.

'And they shall fight every one against his brother, and every one against his neighbour; city against city and kingdom against kingdom . . . ' The holocaust grows and spreads. Even the most stable topples. Wilting, as a flower discarded or as a ravaged feast. What now? Is there no sign of salvation on the forehead of the Seer?

'And the waters shall fail from the sea, and the river shall be wasted and dried up. And they shall turn the rivers far away, and the brooks of defence shall be emptied and dried up: the reeds and flags shall wither . . . '

No. No sign. Even Nature is relentless. There is no escape. Where, what then? The bow twists and plunges, the strings lament.

'Where are they? Where are thy wise men and let them tell thee now . . . ' Ah, what taunting mockery. Swept by the fearful current, losing all foothold, their last defences shattered, and what was even yesterday the image of everything good and pure and valiant is now exposed in all its vanity and meanness, powerless to withstand the great test, the day of trial. And what is left you then? What is there for you under this overflowing scourge, in this perverse spirit, this fear and horror? What star of deliverance? Oh, who shall tell, who shall know, who shall see that far? You, Habakuk?

(Did Bach really write all this at the time? Just like this, the way Habakuk is reading and playing it for us now, with unusual force, sweeping and pulling us after him relentlessly and heeding neither a squeak here and there nor an occasional shortcoming in his performance? Or is Bach only in brackets and is it Habakuk come to prophesy on his own and as he played, lo, the Spirit of God was upon him? . . .)

'In that day . . .'— — What day? Whose day are we reading of and in whose book of fate? Whose fate will it be to be killed beside the bridge in his twenty-eighth year? And whose to perish of a malignant disease with half his life unspent? And whose to live a humdrum, mediocre life till ripe old age, whose to become entangled in a plot and whose to be tripped by a snare, who is destined to climb the mountain and who to fall at the foot of the mountain, hit by a stray shell? Oh, leave off and don't ask questions now. This is no time for questions.

'And it shall be afraid and fear because of the shaking of the hand of the Lord of hosts which he shaketh over us . . .'— —And how long, how much longer? Will the land mourn for ever? And shall every thing sown wither, be driven away and be no more? . . .

Whither, Habakuk? Oh, do not be so hard with us, so inexorable? Give us a sign. Prophesy and tell us about after the great and terrible wrath. Do you know? Can you tell? Do you see an omen in your stars? What is it that a man must be? What is it that we must be so as to make the world good, and make us care? Look down at us sitting at your feet—have you no message for us?

'And the Lord shall smite Egypt,' plays Habakuk, 'He shall smite and heal it . . .'— —rising and descending (not always without some unpleasant squeaking, from sheer inability to play better). Perhaps that is it: ebb and flow. That it is never just one level line but that it flows, all of it, rising and sinking, being drowned and saved. Is that it? Look up, children, look round you, isn't that it? (producing a jarring dissonance at times, bracing himself and then continuing onwards). Look, then, and see whether the light of day does not always follow the dark of night, be it even the darkest of nights—and after winter, is there not the spring? Evil is not eternal. No, but back and forth, wave upon wave. Remember that and don't forget. Oh. Please, Naomi, please try and smile at us here, with our bent heads and drooping hands. Yehiam will be killed, Ya'acov will die, that stray shell is still waiting for Habakuk too, others will stay alive, will live this way or that, as best they can, for good or for ill, becoming shopkeepers, becoming teachers or clerks, becoming successful, building a home and begetting children. Or is there perhaps another way? Not theirs? The way he is playing now—in awe. Raise your eyes to us, Naomi, your eyes that shine like Sabbath candles, look at us, take each one of us; draw us into the goodness of your light, you who guard the house and gather its four corners together: will you forge us a dam? And will you set us on the way? And already it changes, no more just prayer, but prayer and first glimmer of light, prayer and first hint of change, and now its sounds clearly: 'And they shall return even to the Lord, and he shall be entreated of them, and shall heal them.'—Oh, let us return. Who knows what is awaiting us at the next corner. Who knows if not another such fearful journey. But 'In that day shall there be a highway' . . . There will be. There must be. And the light cloud will be nothing but an ornament in the sky from now on, an ornament and not an omen. And nothing ill will be borne upon it. No evil will be lurking behind the light smile. A cloud will come and vanish. That is all. Come and go. And there will be a blessing in the midst of the land. Amen. Amen and Amen.

And why are all eyes staring at the floor? And Habakuk, what does he say? No, he says nothing. He has finished playing, lowered his violin, placed his bow on the stand. He does not move. His face is tilted upwards, as of one who has seen far things. Everyone is silent. Bach and Isaiah and everyone. An infinite echoing, reaching no shore. As within a large bell that has just stopped ringing. For a long time no one speaks. It is cold in the empty room.

At last Habakuk says—not to anyone but straight before him and scarcely audible:

'Naked and barefoot
And freezing with cold
And awaiting him
Always
Amen.'

And, drawn together over this, no one dares breathe. A slight shiver passes down one's back. Someone wipes the corner of an eye. None of us can find anything to say that will be right, that will live up to this moment. We must away. Let's go, boys, let's go home. Those of us who have a home. This one here, Habakuk, has none. No home, no possessions, no family, not anything. We shall go away and he —in this bareness of his, always. A violin he has, though. And the distant, evasive stars—they speak to him. And boys come to him, boys in their blossoming. And one shining-eyed girl too. What else? What else is there? What else is given man? In addition to music, to stars, and to the beauty of boys with one girl among them? And who doesn't love her? Everyone does. Whether they tell her so or keep it in their heart and do not, yet. She is our hope. She is our light. My light. My soul.

Rising and leaving. One by one. Good night, Habakuk. Good night, each. A tentative smile. He does not respond. Upright beside his music stand. Beside certain pages crossed by the violin's bow. And outside, pine trees rustling in the wind, and the smell of pines. Buttoning coats. Clouds come and go. Heavy clouds. A great rain is going to fall. Run boys, run. Come, let us run, you and I. Will you give me your hand and shall we run together through the wind and the rain?

VI

Well . . . And then afterwards . . . But now I have lost the desire to tell what happened afterwards. A sadness has come over me. Indeed, I warned you boys at the start this was going to be sad, remember? In fact, I had an entirely different opening in mind, but it turned out this way. So let it stand. I shall not begin to make changes now.

But you, my friend, will want to know what happened afterwards

to this man Habakuk—he of the violin and stars—and how his story
ends. Well, the truth is that I do not know. We drifted apart, after a
time. We lost sight of each other and there was nothing except an
occasional sending of regards through a chance acquaintance. Like
stars whose orbits cross once and part again, who knows if ever in
eternity to meet again. But I did hear of his end. Hard and bitter it
was, his end. And I have hinted at it more than once throughout my
story. And I have hinted, too, that perhaps alone among us he was
not surprised by it. He could see over and beyond the stature of ordinary things, those among which the rest of us dwell.

Though it is just as possible that he did not, that this particular
secret was not told him by the stars. It is possible that they preferred
to conceal it from him, for some reason, to hold back any sign, and
that his end came upon him like a sudden blow, like an eagle swoop-
ing down upon its prey. And that it caught him unprepared, like us,
like all men, and unasked—terribly unasked. Who can tell now whether
it happened this way or that. If I knew where those diaries of Habakuk
were now, then perhaps I would find out more. And perhaps it is written there even, if indeed it was revealed to him from above, perhaps
it is there—the hidden purpose of a man's dying in mid-life. Yet if we
were to look in vain, what then is left but that a man may die without purpose, that one evil thrust will suffice. Who can tell? Ah, the
angels fly high but man unto trouble is born.

As far as we were concerned, at any rate, it would never have
entered our minds that it would be he—that among all of us it would
be he for whom the shell came. He, who would not hurt a fly—
and we, members of the *Haganah* underground to a man, and commanders in the *Palmah* storm troops in the not so distant future, we
who spent nights secretly learning to use weapons—we did not consider the shadow of any such possibility. We did not, but the powers
of doom, those that the stars know all about, they acted the way they
did and placed their messengers in such positions that it all became
inevitable. And it all was, and it happened.

I have no idea at all where, for instance, on the afternoon of that
fateful Friday, the stars were.

Apparently they broke up and they stood at hard, stiff angles, and
in one corner of the earth a war broke out. And it happened that
there was sent a number of labourers to an embattled kibbutz in order
to dig trenches, and among them was Habakuk. He was not a fighter,
nor could have been one. He had never in his life borne arms nor
learnt to hold a weapon and, since he was rather too old for it as

well, they made him a digger of trenches. And on that day, at noon-break, the labourers lay down to rest on the lawn in front of the communal dining-hall, talking, one imagines, about the impending cease-fire which was to go into force that very evening, a cease-fire between the two warring sides. Only a few hours divided them still from the haven of peace when there suddenly came a brief little last-minute shelling, completely insignificant were it not that one shell, suddenly, found its way and chose to come, to fall, to hit that lawn by the dining-hall and to explode amidst the labourers resting there. Habakuk was among the killed (Habakuk—though no doubt they didn't call him that, nor knew that he was he). They picked him up and buried him on the slope of the hill, in the shade of the pine grove. And there, along with all the other *Palmah* lads, he rests in peace.

And that is all. Or maybe just this. You know that there is a Memorial Day, when all the comrades of the fallen make a pilgrimage to the graves of their dead. There is a ceremony, things are said, and then people scatter and each seeks out the little mound where his friend lies buried—silent with thoughts of 'Where are you now, and we, where are we?' and listening to the strange quiet, to the rustling of the pines on the slope and to things unsaid, things that were and things that might have been were it not that. And mothers sob, and girls draw shawls over their heads and young men pluck at their moustaches, ill at ease. One lingers a bit still, one leaves behind a flower or a green branch, and turns to go, parting again, each to his own, back to the land of the living and all its hubbub.

And that, to tell you the truth, was how I had wanted to begin this story, with some kind of melancholy opening, like this: Among all those at the cemetery dedicated to the war dead, among all those graves of young lives mown down in their very blossoming, on that pine-covered slope—one grave, I fear, remained unvisited, unasked for, and that is the grave of Habakuk (who wasn't one of the boys—though he loved and cherished them most truly). Who and what this Habakuk was—thus I had intended to say in that opening—that is what my story is going to be about. And may this story—thus had I intended to add—be as a candle to the memory of an unusual man. Such and suchlike sad words had I meant to say at the beginning, but then things turned out otherwise and I didn't.

But the way things have fallen out, I feel that I cannot now leave off and go my way before I, too, have stood there by this mound, head bent, silent and listening. And afterwards, perhaps, I shall gather courage, and lift my eyes to question my strange and wondrous friend.

My heart is sombre. My heaven seems empty. But still my eyes are raised, truly they are. Ah, Habakuk, you who can see so far and so much higher than any of us, you who can look the stars in their eyes— can you hear my voice? You, wherever you are, say if you have found out there, beyond, tell us now, at this hour, when we are drained, when all our wonted wisdom is spent, is useless, and we are sick and weary and unable to bear this dull, flat, compromising nothingness, and in our agony we steal a look, sidewards and up and even unto the stars, so high and so very unspeaking—let them tell, then, if they know better: What is it? What is demanded of us here? What must we do? Where must we go?

Habakuk, Habakuk, oh where then must we go? What should, what must we be? We who are left here, above, in the land of the living, having the sun, and our soul left us for prey—where must we now? Oh, what? What do you say? What do your stars say? Where?

Say, speak to us, be not silent, not now, speak. Thou that seest in the stars, thy companions hearken to thy voice.

Translated by Miriam Arad.

Benjamin Tammuz

THE SWIMMING CONTEST

Tammuz (1919–89) was born in the Ukraine and emigrated to Palestine with his family in 1924. He became a columnist on the Israeli daily newspaper Ha'aretz. Under the influence of one of the founders of the Canaanite movement, Yonatan Ratosh, Tammuz became one of its active members. His contact with the Canaanites, who aimed to create a Hebrew nation as opposed to a Jewish one, provided the inspiration for Tammuz', utopian early stories. One of the best-known of these, 'The Swimming Contest' (1952), considers the elusive dream of peace between Arab and Jew in all its tragic complexity. Similar in intention is his celebrated novel The Orchard, 1973, *an allegory that traces the fate of two half-brothers, one a Jew, the other an Arab, in their battle for a single piece of land. Tammuz was the author of numerous novels and short stories.*

One hot summer's day many years ago I was sitting in the kitchen at home, staring out of the window. The chill of the red floor tiles seeped into my bare feet. With my elbows leaning on the oilcloth-covered table, I let my eyes stray outside. The rooms were pervaded by the afternoon stillness and I felt dreamily at peace.

Suddenly, galloping hoofbeats sounded down the road and a black Arab horse-cab—the kind that plied the roads before cars took over—came into view; it was like those cabs we used to hire to drive us to the Jaffa railway station when we travelled up to Jerusalem to spend Passover with Grandmother.

The horses drew nearer and were reined in outside our house, and the Arab cabman alighted and knocked at our door. I jumped up to open it, and a musty smell filled the kitchen—a smell of horses and far-off places. The cabman's shoulders blocked out the light and prevented the sultry heat from forcing its way inside.

He handed me a letter. I glanced at it and saw it was in French, which I could not read. My mother entered and took the letter, and her face lit up. She asked the cabman in and placed a slice of cold watermelon and a fresh *pita* on the table before him. Leaning his whip against the wall, the Arab thanked her for her kindness, sat down at the table, and began taking large bites out of the watermelon, filling the air with the smacking of his lips. My mother told me that the letter was from the old Arab woman who lived in the orange grove. She wrote that she was well again and her pains had left her, and that she had been cured by my mother's hands, which she kissed from afar. She also wrote that now that summer had come and she had heard our holidays would soon be coming round, she hoped my mother would be able to get away from her other patients and come with her son to stay at her house in the orange grove.

The sun was about to sink into the sea as we left the house and climbed into the cab. The cabman folded back the rounded leather hood, and as we sank into the deep, soft seat I was instantly overwhelmed by a sensation of travelling to distant parts. The Arab climbed onto his high perch, whistled to his horses, and flicked his whip in the air. The springs creaked, the seat sank and surged up again beneath us like an ocean swell, and a farewell whinny rose on the air. With a wrench of wheels the cab moved off, its rumble over the pitted road sounding like a joyful melody.

Before long we had left the Hassan-Beq Mosque behind and were plunging through the alleyways of the Manshieh quarter. Smells of cooking assailed our nostrils: waves of *za'tr*, of roast mutton, of fried aubergine and mint-spiced salad washed over us in turn. The cabman's voice filled the air, sounding warnings right and left, coaxing street-hawkers to move out of our path, bawling at the urchins who squatted in the middle of the road. The horses trotted in a lively, unbroken rhythm, their brown shiny rumps swaying from side to side. The horse on the right, without breaking his stride, pricked up his tail and dropped his dung. Turning around on his lofty seat, the cabman threw us an apologetic smile and remarked that horses were shameless ill-bred creatures and we must excuse them.

We jogged along pleasurably and restfully in our seats till the city lay behind us and the horses were drawing the cab laboriously along a track of reddish sand lined with hedgerows of cactus and acacia. Waves of heat rose from the sand, settling beside us onto the cool seat. The sun must already have dipped into the sea, for beyond the orange groves the skies glowed crimson and a chilly dusk descended all around. Suddenly the horses stopped and made water on the sand in unison.

Again the cab lurched forward. A quiver rippled the horses' hides

as their hooves struck a stretch of limestone-paved road, lined by
cypresses on either side. Before us stood an archway of whitewashed
stone, enclosing a large, closed wooden gate with a small wicket set
in it. Near the wicket stood a girl of about my age, wearing a white
frock and a pink ribbon in her hair. As the cab drew up at the gate
she bolted inside, and the cabman said, 'We're there!'

You don't see such courtyards any more. And if you should happen
to come to a place where there once was such a courtyard, you will
only find a scene of wartime destruction: heaps of rubble and rafters,
with cobwebs trying to impart an air of antiquity to what only yesterday still breathed and laughed.

But in those days the courtyard was in good repair and throbbing
with life. It was square-shaped and enclosed on three sides by a two-
storey building, with stables and barns occupying the lower storey.
Black and red hens roamed about the yard, their clucking mingling
with the neighing of horses. On the second floor was a pump-house,
and next to it a pool-like reservoir into which water splashed from a
pipe leading from the pump. Goldfish gathered near the outlet, darting among the bubbles created by the jet of water. A wooden parapet railed in a long veranda that always lay in the shade. A coloured
glass door led from the veranda into a central reception room, from
which numerous doors opened onto the living rooms, the kitchen
and the pantries.

In the centre of the room stood a long table surrounded by uphol-
stered armchairs. In anticipation of our arrival that day, their white
linen dust-covers had been removed and lay folded in neat piles in a
corner. Earthenware vases painted red and gold were arranged about
the room; they contained large paper roses and lilies, some of them
fashioned into strange, unflowerlike shapes. One vase, its paint long
faded, had been brought there on the wedding day of the elderly mistress of the house.

From gilt wooden frames on the walls stared the portraits of sword-
bearing men in fezes. The old lady led my mother up to one of the
pictures and said, 'My husband, may he rest in peace! His father built
this house. Now we live here during the summer and go back to Jaffa
for the winter.'

With a sigh my mother replied, 'My husband's no longer alive,
either. But his house and his father's house aren't here; everything
remained over there, abroad, and I live in a rented apartment summer and winter.'

'That's because you are newcomers, immigrants,' the old lady said. 'But with the help of God you'll thrive and build yourselves houses. You're hard-working people and your hands are blessed.'

My mother caught the hint and threw her a grateful look, but I blurted out: 'But it's not true that we're driving the Arabs out. We are out for peace, not war.'

Placing her hand on my head, the old lady said, 'It all depends on the individual; everyone who wants peace will live in peace.'

At that moment the young girl appeared in the doorway.

'Come over here, Nahida,' the old lady said, 'and kiss the hand of the *hakima* who cured your grandmother. And this is her son.'

Nahida came hesitantly into the room and stood in front of my mother. My mother embraced her and kissed her on the cheek, and a flush suffused the girl's dark complexion. She hung her head and remained silent.

'Our Nahida is shy,' the old lady said, 'but her heart is kind.'

Hitching up her white skirt, Nahida sat down in an armchair. The rest of us sat down, too, as though permitted to do so now that the most honoured person among us was seated.

The old lady made a remark in French and my mother laughed. Again Nahida blushed and I noticed her eyeing me to see whether I understood French.

'I don't understand a word,' I told her. 'What are they saying?'

'My grandmother says you and I would make a fine couple.'

'Rubbish!' I answered and stared at the floor.

'You can go and play,' the old woman said. 'We're not keeping you.'

I got up and followed Nahida out onto the veranda. We went and sat down at the edge of the pool.

'Do you believe in God?' I asked her. 'Because I don't, not at all.'

'I do, and I have a place in the grove where I go and pray. If we become friends I'll take you there and I'll show you there's a God.'

'Then you fast in the month of Ramadan?' I asked. 'I eat even on Yom Kippur.'

'I don't fast because I'm still too young. Do you rest on the Sabbath?'

'That depends,' I answered. 'I rest if I've got nothing else to do. Not because there's a God, but just if I feel like it.'

'But I love God,' Nahida said.

'Then we certainly won't make a couple unless you stop believing.'

Nahida was about to make some retort when we heard the gate open, and two men entered the yard. Nahida leapt up and rushed over to them, throwing her arms around the neck of the older man, who wore a fez and European clothes.

'Daddy, we have visitors!' she cried.

'I know,' her father replied. 'The *hakima* has come to see us.'

I stood up and waited for them to mount the steps to the pool. The second man, who wore a *keffiyeh* and *agal* and looked about eighteen, was Nahida's uncle, her father's brother. He came up first and held out his hand to greet me. Nahida's father patted my cheek and ushered me into the house.

We had supper out on the veranda. We were served large dishes of fried potatoes, sliced aubergine in tomato sauce and diced salted cheese, and a bowl of pomegranates and watermelons. There was a heap of hot *pitas* in the centre of the table.

Nahida's uncle—his name was Abdul-Karim—asked me if I was in the Haganah. When I told him that was a secret, he laughed and said it was an open secret which the whole country knew about.

'Abdul-Karim is studying at the College of the Mufti,' Nahida's father told us. 'And he's in constant fear of your Haganah.'

Abdul-Karim's face darkened and he kept silent; but the old lady, his mother, laid her hand on his arm and said, 'My Abdul-Karim is a fine, loyal man. Don't you tease him.'

Abdul-Karim kissed his mother's hand and said nothing. Just then, a shaggy sheepdog appeared on the veranda and wriggled under the table, butting against the tangle of legs as it looked for a spot to lie down. Finally it came to rest with its head on Nahida's feet and its tail on mine; it kept licking Nahida's feet, and its wagging tail tickled mine. The tickling made me smile and I turned to explain to Nahida why I was smiling, but when I saw she was taking my smile as a mark of friendship, I kept quiet.

When supper was over, Nahida's father said to his brother:

'Abdul-Karim my brother, go and show the children what you've brought from town.'

Motioning to Nahida and myself to follow him, Abdul-Karim went into a toolshed in the orange grove and came out with a brand-new shotgun.

'We'll go hunting rabbits tomorrow,' he said. 'Know how to fire a gun?'

'A little,' I told him. 'We can have a shooting match if you like.'

'We had a swimming match here in the pool last week,' Nahida said, 'and my uncle beat them all.'

'I'll take you on at swimming too, if you like,' I said.

'*Ahlan usahlan!*' Abdul-Karim agreed. 'Tomorrow morning, then. Now let's get back to the house and listen to some songs. We have a gramophone.'

Back in the house, Abdul-Karim put on a record, wound the handle and adjusted the soundbox. The sound of a *kamanji* and drum and cymbals issued forth, immediately followed by an Arab song, sung in a sweet plaintive voice, with delicate, floating trills. Abdul-Karim sprawled back contentedly in his armchair, his face beaming. When the record ended he put on another, though to me it seemed as though the same song was being played over again. This went on again and again till I got bored and slipped out to another room where my mother was chatting with the old lady. But that bored me too, so I went out to the veranda and gazed at the pool and the orange grove beyond. A large moon hung just above the treetops and a chill rose from the water in the pool. Some night bird was calling nearby, but stopped whenever the gramophone fell silent. As a yawn escaped me, I thought regretfully of my pals at home who were probably roasting potatoes on a fire under the electricity pylon, having pilfered the wood from the nearby sausage factory. What had made me come here, I asked myself.

Nahida found a queer way of waking me up next morning. They had a fat, lazy cat in the house, which Nahida dropped onto my face while I was asleep. I leapt out of bed and flung the cat back into her lap. That was how we started our second day in the house in the orange grove. I was still brushing my teeth when Abdul-Karim came into the kitchen and said, 'What about our swimming race?' 'I'm ready,' I told him.

We hurried through breakfast, got into bathing trunks and went outside. My mother, the old lady, and Nahida's father had already drawn up chairs at the side of the pool to watch the race.

'Ready, steady . . . go!' Nahida called out, and Abdul-Karim and I dived in. Either because I was over-excited or I wasn't used to fresh water, I sank to the bottom like a stone, and by the time I had recovered sufficiently to surface Abdul-Karim was already halfway across. I saw my mother bending over the parapet and heard her calling out to me, 'Don't be afraid! Swim fast!' I started swimming, but it was no use. By the time I reached the pipe leading from the pump-house, Abdul-Karim was already sitting on the parapet on the far side, squeezing the water out of his hair.

'You beat me in the pool,' I told him. 'But I'll take you on at anything else, if you want.'

'At what?' he asked.

'Let's say at arithmetic.'

'Why not?' he answered, and told Nahida to fetch some paper and pencils. When Nahida came back with them, I tore a sheet of paper into two halves, and on each I wrote down seven million, nine hundred and eighty-four thousand, six hundred and ninety-eight multiplied by four million, nine hundred and eighty-six thousand, seven hundred and fifty-nine.

'Let's see who figures that out first,' I said.

Taking a pencil, Abdul-Karim started jotting down figures, and so did I. I was through before he was and handed my sheet to Nahida's father to check. It turned out I had made a mistake. Then Abdul-Karim handed over his paper and it turned out that he had gone wrong, too.

'Then let's have a general knowledge competition,' I challenged Abdul-Karim. 'For instance: who discovered America?'

'Columbus,' Abdul-Karim answered.

'Wrong!' I said. 'It was Amerigo Vespucci, and that's why it's called America!'

'He beat you!' Nahida called to her uncle. 'You see, he beat you!'

'He beat me in America,' Abdul-Karim said, 'but I beat him *right here*, in the pool.'

'You wait till I'm grown up and then I'll beat you right here in the pool,' I told him.

Nahida seemed about to nod her agreement, but thought better of it and looked at her uncle to see what he was going to answer to that.

'If he ever manages to beat me here in the pool,' Abdul-Karim said, 'it will be very bad indeed. It will be bad for you too, Nahida. Bad for all of us.'

We didn't get his meaning and I wanted to tell him to cut out his philosophizing; but I didn't know how to say that in Arabic, so I kept quiet.

Later we went hunting rabbits in the orange grove.

II

Many years had gone by and summer had come round once again. Tired out after the year's work, I was looking for some place where I could take a fortnight's rest. Packing a small valise, I traveled up to Jerusalem, only to find all the boarding houses full. Finally, wearied by rushing about the city, I boarded a bus bound for the Arab village of Ein Karem. As I took my seat, I started wondering what I would do there and what had made me go there of all places.

At the end of the main street stood a domed building, with a fountain gushing out from under its floor. Opposite, on a hillside that sloped up to the Russian monastery on its summit, in the shade of a clump of sycamores, some men sat on low wooden stools, sipping coffee and puffing at their *narghiles*. I walked over and sat down on one of the stools, and when the waiter came over to take my order, I asked him if he knew of a family that would be willing to put me up for a couple of weeks.

'I don't know of one,' the lad answered. 'But maybe the owner does.'

The café proprietor came over to have a look at me. 'A family to put you up?' he said. 'What for?'

'To take a rest,' I answered. 'I'm tired and I'm looking for somewhere to rest.'

'And how much are you willing to pay?' he asked.

'As much as I have to,' I replied.

The proprietor sent the lad to the house of a certain Abu-Nimr. Before long he came back and said:

'Go up that way. Abu-Nimr is willing.'

Picking up my valise, I trudged up the hillside, wondering all the time what had made me come to this place. I entered a courtyard and knocked at the door of the house indicated. A tall, bald Arab of about forty-five came out and said, 'Welcome! Come right in.'

I let him precede me down a long, cool passage and into a small room, almost entirely taken up by a tall, wide bed.

'If you like it, you're very welcome,' Abu-Nimr said.

'It's very nice,' I said. 'How much will it cost?'

'I don't know. My wife will tell you that,' he said and left the room.

I unpacked my valise and sat down on the bed, instantly sinking into the soft bedding, which billowed up to my elbows. There was a deep stillness all around, pervaded by the familiar smells of frying oil, mint leaves, black coffee, rosewater and cardamom seeds. I felt my face break into a smile as my ears strained to catch a sound that was missing in order to complete a dim, distant memory.

Suddenly I heard a tap turned on in the kitchen and the sound of gushing water made me hold my breath: water gushing from a pipe into a pool!

I got up and went out to the yard. There was no pool, not even orange trees; but there was something about the apple and plum trees, some quality of strangeness peculiar to an Arab homestead. It was obvious that the courtyard had not evolved all at once, that each generation had added something of its own. One man had planted the apple tree by the water tap, another the mulberry tree near the dog kennel, and in time the garden had sprouted up to tell its masters' life stories. I stood listening, my fantasy peopling the courtyard with Nahida and her grandmother, with Abdul-Karim, with the horse-cab that would suddenly draw to a halt outside the gate and the horses that would stand and urinate.

That evening I was invited to join the family at supper, and Abu-Nimr introduced me to the people who sat round the table: his round-faced, bustling wife, who smiled into space without resting her eyes on me; his two sons, aged thirteen and fifteen, who attended high school in the city; his plump, white-skinned daughter, married to a policeman who was away from home all week, and who came home loaded with a wicker basket containing a trussed pigeon, apples from Betar, and a dozen eggs commandeered from some villager who happened to call at the police station.

The food that was served was no more than a continuation of that faraway supper in the orange grove. At that moment I realized what I had come there for.

After supper the strains of an Arab song rose from the gramophone. Abu-Nimr asked me whether I would care to show his boys how to operate the English typewriter he had bought in the city the day before. I sat down to instruct the lads, who set about their task with tremendous awe while their parents looked on, their hearts overflowing with pride. After a while their mother brought me a glass of cocoa and urged me to take a little rest. The gramophone was still playing, and as I sipped my drink Nahida's voice came back to me and Abdul-Karim's features formed themselves before my eyes, and out of the gloom in the passage there rose the sounds of my mother chatting with the old lady. It was then that I knew that I had been waiting all these years for just this moment, that I would relive our stay at the house in the orange grove.

Again the years went by. We were in the grip of war with the Arabs. I was serving in a company that was lined up to storm Tel Arish, an Arab stronghold in the Jaffa dunes, east of the city.

We had launched an abortive attack there several weeks before which had cost us twenty-six men. This time we felt sure of success and looked forward to the battle as a fierce retaliation.

We set out from Holon at midnight, and soon began crawling in the direction of the Tel Arish buildings. The sand dunes afforded excellent cover, and we slipped across them effortlessly and soundlessly. A west wind carried the Jaffa smells over to us, but later the wind veered round behind us, from the new estates going up in Holon, breathing the smell of new, white houses on our backs. The sand beneath us surrendered the sun's warmth it had absorbed during the day, telling of the days of light we had known among the white houses, and auguring the liberty and joy that would again be ours once victory had been gained.

When the Arabs spotted us it was too late for them to do anything about it. We were already within grenade-range of their position, and we stormed it from three sides. One of our first grenades burst inside their forward machine gun nest, putting all its crew out of action. We charged inside and raked the village with the German machine gun. The Arabs there panicked and rushed out of the houses, only to be cut down by our riflemen, who lay in ambush on our two flanks to the north and south. This left the Arabs only one escape route, westwards, and it appeared that some of them managed to slip through in that direction and escape into the cover of the nearby orange grove— the same grove where, about twenty years before, I had spent a few days with the old lady's family.

I had been expecting things to turn out like that, for that was how it had been planned. The house in the orange grove was our second objective that night. We didn't know whether there were any soldiers there, but we were quite sure that any we failed to destroy at the Tel Arish position would easily be able to reorganize and entrench themselves in the stone building and courtyard. It seemed that they had kept a reserve force in the house in the orange grove, for heavy fire was opened upon us from that direction, and there were other indications that fortified positions there were ready to go into action in the event that Tel Arish should fall.

Our luck didn't hold out there, however: the battle continued till dawn and we lost six men. This only heightened our desire for revenge, and besides, we still outnumbered them. Soon the defence of the house showed signs of weakening and the fire gradually slackened off. At dawn we rushed the courtyard, got through as far as the stables and laid a charge of high explosives, then withdrew. A few moments later there was a violent clap of thunder and the wing of the house next to the pool collapsed into a heap of rubble. This was immediately followed by the groans of the wounded and cries of surrender. We re-mustered in the courtyard and shouted to the Arabs to come out and surrender.

I was not surprised to see Abdul-Karim. He seemed to have expected this, too, though that was something I had never dared to imagine. I recognized him straight away. I went up to him and called his name. When I explained who I was, he gave a weary smile of recollection.

'Nahida . . . is she here too?' I asked him.

'No,' he said. 'The family has left Jaffa.'

Some of the boys listened to our conversation in surprise.

'D'you know him?' our officer asked me.

'I know him,' I said.

'Can he give us any important information?'

'Maybe,' I said. 'But let me settle an old score with him first.'

'Want to finish him off?' the officer asked me.

'No,' I told him. 'I just want to talk to him.'

The boys burst out laughing at this. Abdul-Karim, who hadn't understood what we were saying, must have taken offence, for his hands trembled with suppressed fury.

I hastened to explain to him that I wanted to talk to him alone.

'You're the victors,' he said. 'We do as we're told.'

'As long as I haven't beaten you in the pool,' I told him, 'there's no telling who is the victor.'

Abdul-Karim smiled. He seemed to have got my meaning.

Our officer didn't seem to get it, however, for he ordered Abdul-Karim to be taken into the orange grove, where the prisoners were being rounded up. I went up to the pool and sat down on the parapet. Our reinforcements from Bat-Yam and Holon began to appear and the orderlies set about attending to the wounded in the courtyard. I stripped and entered the water. It was warm and dirty: it must have been a long time since the pipe overhead had jetted water from the well pump.

Stretching out my arms, I swam across the pool, then back again. I closed my eyes and waited to hear my mother's voice, urging me on: 'Don't be scared! Swim fast!' But instead, I heard Abdul-Karim say: 'You beat me in America, but I beat you *right here*, in the pool.'

Just then I heard a shot from the orange grove. My heart missed a beat. I knew Abdul-Karim had been killed. Leaping out of the water, I pulled on my trousers and rushed into the grove. There was some commotion and the officer was yelling:

'Who the hell fired that shot?'

'My gun went off,' one of the boys said.

When he saw me coming up the officer said, 'We've lost that information, damn it! They've killed that Arab of yours.'

'We've lost it,' I said.

I went over to Abdul-Karim's body and turned it over. He looked as though he had seen me swimming in the pool a few moments ago. His was not the expression of a man who had lost.

There, in the courtyard, it was I, all of us, who were the losers.

Translated by Joseph Schachter.

Aharon Megged

TEARS

Megged was born in Poland in 1920 and emigrated to Palestine in 1926. He was a kibbutz member from 1939 to 1950, and his early stories and plays depict the kibbutz environment. He is regarded as being typical of the so-called Palmah generation (the generation of 1948), although problems of identity, emotional strength, and individual responsibility in a collectivist society pervade his work. Another interesting theme in his work is the gap between reality and the work of fictional characters who represent ideological stereotypes. Megged excels at descriptions of the lives of intellectuals and men of letters, writers, critics, and academics, a subject close to his heart. He has written over twenty books including fifteen novels, and he is well known as a playwright. His novel-length satire, The Golden-Humped Camel on the Roof, *has recently been translated into English. In addition, he has published numerous short stories, novellas, and collections of essays.*

Mirtel lived in a small shed, behind a hedgerow, on the outskirts of the settlement. He treated his home with the same slovenliness with which he treated himself and his attire. There was a bed there that was never made, a lame table with a faded top that he had appropriated from the public domain, a chair, and several boxes used for odds and ends. In the corners, on the dusty floor, there were always old socks, leather straps, and sometimes a work shirt or a towel caked with days-old grime. The smell of cigarette smoke never left the room.

He was a short man, but with a sturdy build. His legs were muscular and his hands were like spades. He had the hazy, somewhat baffled expression of one who awakes in the morning from bad dreams. There was also a haziness in his watery eyes that made it difficult to see in them either joy or sadness, or even indifference. He spoke little, and when he did, his words were jumbled, his sentences chopped and scrambled, and words like 'fine', 'that's it', or 'might as well' would often be substituted for the things he could not or would not say. Since he treated himself with deprecation in his behaviour, his ways, and all his dealings with others, his fellow men did not feel sorry for him, nor did they bother to make fun of him. They were used to his presence as one gets used to assorted tools left lying about the kibbutz yard; no one bothering to discard them or to put them to good use.

For most of the day he was the cartman. When evening came he distributed the small provisions to the members of the kibbutz, as he had done for several years. He performed both tasks with meticulous care. No hint of his slovenliness was to be found here. He looked after his donkey with a devotion bordering on fanaticism. He was particular about its cleanliness and its harness, and he cushioned its manger with whatever scraps he found in the chicken coop, the stables, and the rubbish-heap. He never forgot to prepare its evening ration, to arrange its straw bed, and to clean the pen and inspect it; often, when it rained or the night was stormy, he would get up in the dark and rush over to the pen to see if all was well. No one dared touch the donkey without his permission, for fear he might break their bones. Nothing was likely to stir up his wrath more than an injury to his beast.

The supply room, the domain over which he reigned supreme, resembled a museum more than it did a tool-shed. All the items were arranged upon shelves, row upon row, cubicle by cubicle. A tag was attached to each compartment, indicating the number of units and the date as well as the item's name. The walls and the floor were spotless. Mirtel would distribute the supplies through a hatch, and forbade anyone to set foot beyond the threshold. This chamber was his holy of holies and everyone treated it as such. He kept a strict ledger wherein no evidence of partiality could be found. All the same, if someone in need came knocking at his door in the evening or on the Sabbath—he never refused. He would take the keys and wordlessly walk over to the storeroom, indicating that the fellow should stand in front of the hatch. He would go inside and give him what he wanted.

When Heddi left the kibbutz, there was no evident change in Mirtel, nor could anyone tell whether he was overcome with grief or not. That summer morning he even carried her belongings from their room to the gate, and loaded them onto the truck. Some saw him bid her an ordinary farewell, as if he would be seeing her again within a short while. And when the truck pulled away, Heddi stuck her head out the window and called back at him: 'And take good care of the child, Mirtel.' 'Okay,' he said. This scene brought a smile to the faces of those who chanced to witness it. When he walked back to his donkey-cart, one of the members addressed him with a nod, as one would when comforting a mourner 'She left, eh?' Mirtel shrugged his shoulders and said, as if in jest: 'That's how it goes, what can you do. Women, you know.'

*

Six years before, when Mirtel and Heddi had moved into a family room, the match caused great astonishment. Mirtel would shirk the company of women, and was so shy in their presence that he would blush, stammer and say silly things when one of them turned to him with some trivial question. It was hard to picture him being intimate. Heddi was a little wild animal, a voracious she-cat in heat who knew no shame in her flirtations with men. This little creature, golden-haired and fire-eyed, would lay claim to all she desired, and assertively so, giving much publicity to her claims. When she worked in the clothing warehouse, she would speak of her love affairs with no modesty whatsoever, as one would talk of guzzling and boozing. She was vociferous in her love, vociferous in her hatred, and vociferous in her jealousy. Yet whatever she said, she said out of innocence, and it was this trait of hers that muddled all conventional notions of morality. One could not be angry with her, just as one cannot be angry at a child's sweet tooth, even if he is caught stealing candy from the pantry, or smashing the dishes. It seems that our view of the sinner is determined by his own view of his deed. Heddi did not know what a sin was; hence the inclination to be forgiving towards her, even when it came to the most pious of moralists. Her stories, like her actions, never gave rise to anger or contempt. They were amusing and generated laughter that was not without sympathy, even affection. At times it seemed that she would sweep the other girls along with her; to love her 'lovers', hate her enemies, and burn with vengeance for her 'betrayers'. Funniest of all was when she would gnash her teeth and moan about these 'betrayers', or shoot her arrows at them. Then she appeared in all her wildness, in all her animal cruelty that knew no mercy. It seemed that she was meant to scratch, pull, bite, and slay. And still, it was nothing more than a good laugh.

What did Heddi see in Mirtel, whom she chose out of all her 'lovers'? It soon became clear that this madness was not without method. New pleasures, like cosiness, sitting side by side, and a seemingly more respected status in society, did not cancel the old ones, those of a carefree existence. For the first two or three months Heddi was as devoted to him as a maidservant, and saw to the upkeep of their new room with such dedication it seemed their house would remain standing longer than any other. And indeed, her behaviour was moderate and reasonable, and all the women commented on how she had settled down, at last. Many learned a lesson from this miraculous change and said, this is what permanence does, blessed be He who transforms His creatures. Yet once the few honeymoon months were over Heddi went back to her old ways and proved wrong all those know-it-alls who hasten to pass judgment. Once again she would fall upon the necks of young men and chance upon the night-watchmen as they patrolled the settlement. Yet even now no sense of wrong doing seemed to influence her conduct. She would scurry after strangers and remain faithful to her spouse, and saw no contradiction between the two. She was meticulous in her conjugal duties; and not only that, but she would vehemently defend Mirtel against anyone who insulted him, and she fought his battles whenever she felt he was being derided. 'My Mirtel,' she called him at all times.

It was unclear whether Mirtel was aware of her escapades or whether he just pretended to see nothing. In any event, he let her run riot to her heart's content. There was no indication of any breach in their domestic harmony, nor of any disruption to his peace of mind. He would do his work as usual, return to his room early in the evening, and sink into sleep. He probably never saw her coming or going. When their son, Yossi, was born, there were those who gossiped that he was from the seed of another; yet this slander certainly never reached his ears.

Their life together lasted for six years, growing neither stronger nor weaker, yet it ceased to arouse wonder and malediction, until the day Heddi told Mirtel she was leaving for the city. Some said she was following her lover, a fine-looking Sephardi, a driver in a taxi depot. After she had left, Mirtel felt it improper for him to stay in a room designated for families and moved to the shed that had once been the shoemaker's workshop.

*

Indeed, there was no visible change in him thereafter, but from the day Heddi left, it seemed his love for his four-year-old son grew sevenfold.

Yossi resembled his mother in appearance, but inherited his social standing from his father. In the children's house he was insulted but did not insult, and, being withdrawn, was a target for the bullies in the group. While his peers played their games, he would stand in the corner, thumb in mouth, his other hand supporting his elbow, and watch them sadly from the side. He, too, was slovenly in his attire;

his trousers were always loose and soiled, the hem of his shirt trailing behind him; and always, come rain or shine, he had a runny nose. He would burst into tears at the slightest provocation and seek refuge under the nurse's apron. Out in the yard he would occupy himself with solitary pastimes.

His father was his sole consolation. On seeing him cross the settlement on his donkey-cart piled high with garbage or pitchers of milk, Yossi would run to the gate in the yard, call out to him and ask to be taken along. And when Mirtel refused, Yossi would stand at the fence, his mournful look following the donkey-cart until it disappeared. When the children were let out to visit their parents it was Yossi's hour of deliverance. He would fly from the yard like a bird from its cage and run with all his might to meet his father. There was no sight more pitiful than Yossi looking for his father and being unable to find him. At night, after bedtime, Yossi's cries could still be heard in the settlement, Daddy, Daddy! He would stand on his bed and shake its iron posts, like a prisoner trying to break the bars of his cell. Eventually he would lose heart and fall asleep, exhausted.

Mirtel treated his son as his equal. He spoke to him with the same matter-of-fact gravity he used when distributing supplies, and with the same confounded and stammering tongue as well. On occasion one could hear them arguing over some issue as they walked through the settlement, and Mirtel would pause, stretch out his hands, as he would in his quarrels with the work co-ordinator and say: 'But Yossi, you must understand that I can't . . . it cannot be helped . . . that's the way it is . . . I'm only human after all . . . I can't . . . believe me . . .' And at times Yossi would defeat his father in arguments and then Mirtel could be heard saying to him: 'Okay . . . you were right . . . no need to go on like that . . . you were right . . . that's that.' And there was nothing in this to diminish in any way whatsoever Yossi's admiration for his father.

In his games with his father Yossi found compensation for all the insults he suffered in the company of his peers. He and his father would find a secluded place on a small lawn at the edge of the settlement and amuse themselves undisturbed. Mirtel would kneel on all fours and Yossi would ride on his back, waving a stick in his hands and prodding his backside to spur him on. At times they would crawl on the ground and with their hands dig ditches that became streams, lakes, and oceans. But what really made Yossi's day was when Mirtel took the donkey out of its pen—the donkey he would not let anyone touch—and let him ride it before sundown. Yossi would sit atop the donkey while Mirtel held the reins and led the way. Then Yossi would be adorned in majesty. He would order his father to lead him along the paths of the settlement for the children to see him in all his glory, and from the height of his seat he would look down haughtily at his friends and enjoy their envy. All the way back to the pen, the son would be silent and the father would be silent: it was Mirtel and Yossi's muted victory march through the enemy camp. They passed through the streets of the conquered town and its inhabitants bowed before them.

Not far from Mirtel's shed, near the mechanic's garage, stood the frame of an old jeep, sunk to its headlights in the sand. It was in ruins, rusted, scorched and dented, nothing more than a piece of junk; yet by some miracle the steering-wheel had remained intact. Mirtel and Yossi took possession of this jeep and made it their private domain. Every Saturday they would go there, where silence prevailed and no children were to be found, seat themselves on the rusting seat and embark on their journeys.

'Where to today?' Yossi would ask.

'To Haifa,' his father suggests.

'No. To mummy,' Yossi says.

'Okay, then go.' Mirtel says.

And Yossi holds onto the steering-wheel, turning it from side to side, screeching and honking like a horn as he sets out on his voyage. When he reaches his destination he stops and says, 'Hello, mummy, we're here.'

'Okay,' Mirtel says, 'Now to Haifa.'

'Okay, now to Haifa,' Yossi agrees with his father.

And in Haifa Mirtel shows him all the fine places worth visiting. The harbour, the oil factory, the oil pools, Mount Carmel, and the groves. And even though Yossi knows Mirtel's stories by heart, he listens to them as if hearing them for the first time, and even helps him along with questions.

'That's it,' Mirtel ends their trip. 'Now we're going home.' Yet the journey back is somewhat gloomy, for leaving faraway places is always a hard thing to do.

*

It happened one Saturday afternoon, a time when the entire settlement was asleep. Mirtel and Yossi had just returned from their journey. Mirtel was tired and had a headache, so he left his son in the jeep and went to the shed to rest. He lay down in his clothes and shoes and in a short while was fast asleep. He was woken suddenly by a scream—'Daddy! Daddy!'

Mirtel leapt out of bed, and from the doorway saw Yossi being dragged from the jeep by Eitan, a boy of almost eight years old, son of Peretz the dairyman.

'Stop that!' he yelled at the top of his voice.

Eitan held onto Yossi's feet and Mirtel ran to him, grabbed his hand, and pale with anger, shouted in his hoarse voice: 'Whadda you doing to him, whadda you think you're doing?'

Eitan went blue in the face from the pain of Mirtel's large hand clamped around his arm.

'Let go . . .' he said, gasping for air.

'I won't let go,' Mirtel still clasped his arm 'What do you wanted of him?'

'I said let go!' Eitan shouted.

'Shut up!' Mirtel muttered in exasperation, thrusting his finger at the boy. 'I said shut up . . .' and suddenly he felt the blood rising to his head, flooding his skull, and his vision became dim. 'I'll show you what it means to drag him by his feet,' he said and slapped him across the face, 'I'll show you what it means to pull him off this jeep,' and slapped him again, 'I'll teach you a lesson . . .'

The boy coiled up from the force of the blow and tried to protect his body, but Mirtel could not control his anger, and with one swipe threw the boy to the ground. He rolled in the sand like a slaughtered chicken.

'Come,' he took Yossi's hand and lifted him off the ground. Yossi sat there wailing, stunned by what he had seen. 'Come,' he pulled Yossi behind him, as if fleeing the scene of a murder.

He collapsed onto his bed and felt no regret. He savoured the sweet taste of revenge on his palate, a taste he had never known.

It took fifteen minutes, or maybe more, before there was a loud knock on the door and Peretz stood in the doorway, holding his son by the hand.

'What have you done to him?' he said, his voice choked.

Mirtel looked at the boy and saw his bruised face and the large swelling on his forehead. He stared at him and said nothing.

'I feel sorry for you,' Peretz said after a long silence, 'Otherwise I'd finish you off. But you won't be staying here much longer.' And he left, slamming the door behind him.

*

In the evening, after lights out, Mirtel went back to the shed, closed the door, and, gathering his few belongings into a pile, wrapped them up in a blanket. Then he went to the pen and put straw and barley in the donkey's trough and bedded the ground with hay. From there he went to the supply-room and stuck the bunch of keys into the key-hole. He returned to his room, threw himself onto the bed and slept.

The following morning, the grey light of dawn still outside, and no one yet risen for work, Mirtel walked over to the children's house, woke his son, dressed him, and said, 'Come, we're going.'

'To mummy?' Yossi asked.

'No, not to mummy,' Mirtel said and pulled him along.

'Where then?' he asked.

'Never mind. You'll see.'

Yossi sensed something out of the ordinary had happened, some-thing terrifying and ominous. And when they walked into the shed, and he saw the bundle in the corner, he burst into tears and cringed down onto the floor.

Mirtel grasped the bundle in one hand and held the other out to Yossi, 'Enough crying. Enough. Come. Let's go.'

Yossi wept and would not budge.

'Come,' Mirtel pulled him by the hand.

But Yossi would not move.

'Come on. We're going. Everything will be all right,' Mirtel tried to lift him.

But he was stuck to the floor. Mirtel did not understand how the boy could suddenly have become too heavy for him to lift. Yossi fell back each time Mirtel eased his grip.

'Don't be a baby,' Mirtel tried to persuade him, 'We have to go and that's that.'

Yossi wept bitterly.

Mirtel did not know what to do with him. He sat down on the bed, helpless. The morning chill sent a shudder through his body. Outside it was dim, quiet, and moist with dew. And the boy's tears trickled on and on, as though they would never end.

Translated by Shaun Levin.

Moshe Shamir

DOCTOR SCHMIDT

Born in Safed in 1921, Shamir was raised in Tel Aviv. From 1941 to 1947 he was a member of kibbutz Mishmar Ha'emek and from 1944 served in the Palmah. He was a member of the Israeli Parliament, the Knesset, from 1977 to 1981. Shamir is a leading member of the first generation of native Israeli writers and is best known for his novels, although he is also a playwright. In his first novel, He Walked in the Fields, Shamir proposed the idealized stereotype of the sabra (native-born Israeli), and he refined this portrait in his novel of 1951, With His Own Hands. Shamir is one of the few Israeli writers who have written historical novels (notably The King of Flesh and Blood), which allowed him scope for an indirect critique of modern Israel. His novel of the Russian Revolution of 1905, The Bridal Veil (1985), attracted universally positive reviews.

I

A small lemon-coloured Morris car crossed the Yarkon bridge between Ramatayim and Petach Tikvah. The criss-cross shadows of the high, steel girders were woven into the asphalt bridge. The river ran slow and green under it, and aged eucalyptus trees cast their shadows from both banks.

As soon as the car had crossed the bridge, it moved to the right side of the road and picked up speed. The driver, his unlit pipe between his teeth, was Dr Schmidt, whose eyes, like the pipe, showed not a flicker of light. They were half-closed, partly from the glare of the sun setting on the horizon, but mainly because of the sense of weariness which never left him.

In the rich complex of his personality—compounded of deft fingers, an active brain, a wealth of knowledge, stubbornness, amiability, and physical vigour—his eyes were always the first to tire. You would never succeed in revealing the Doctor's fatigue judging only by his movements, by the humour in his conversation, by the strength of his will or his mental alertness. All these had a tremendous staying power and could never be overcome by weariness. Only his eyes would close, and because of this he would often baffle people with whom he was talking by a sad, tranquil look which was difficult to interpret—even while he would be participating fully in some activity.

Now, after a day of hard work and travel, he held the steering-wheel lightly, his eyes half-closed. In a few minutes he would pull up at the office in Petach Tikvah and would ring home once more. 'This will be the fifth time,' he said to himself. The first had been when he had set out from Tiberias in the morning. Miriam had answered the telephone and said that No, there had been no word although one couldn't tell, but nevertheless it would be best if he could hurry home. From the Jordan Valley he range twice. He sat in the bustling, stifling offices, swallowed grapefruit juice and waited for his call—while giving final instructions to the local cowhands for coping with the epidemic.

Once again Miriam had answered. Her voice was overcome with dejection, and he imagined her standing there in her blue housecoat, her orderly hair tied in a bun on top of her head, her large eyes full of suffering. 'No dearest, not yet. There has been no message, no phone call, no telegram. Perhaps he will contact us before three. You know . . . how stubborn he is. He may leave without coming home at all . . .'

He could see the tears silently filling her eyes, her mouth straining, forcibly controlling her throat to speak calmly so that he should not be aware of her grief, lest he hear the cry welling up within her, lest the aching shame be conveyed to him.

From Haifa he had phoned a fourth time. He sat in the Department's district office, which was buzzing with clerks, typewriters and telephones—and waited for the call to come through. There was a steaming cup of black coffee in front of him. An Arab youth kept going out, returning, and thumbing noisily through his papers. Doors were opened and closed by busy clerks—and the eternal smell of lysol and shaving soap and khaki clothes dominated everything. When the call came, he trembled. It wasn't Miriam who answered the phone, but one of the neighbours, who had to shout over the bad connection. 'Your wife received a telegram from your son. It looks as though he is coming home for a short while—before he leaves. I don't know. But Dr Schmidt—I don't know . . . He may arrive any moment, you can't tell. I will tell her, of course. Mrs Schmidt left the key with us. Yes, Yes. *Shalom*, Dr Schmidt. Goodbye . . .'

II

They were waiting for him now at Petach Tikvah. He would have to check the reports of the local clerks and of course they would add their usual complaints and all sorts of suggestions. He would have to stop there, investigate and work, since the epidemic had also struck in this district, no doubt about that. Perhaps this would require serious attention, his full attention. This cursed plague had spread over the country like a storm, penetrated every nook and cranny and deposited its poison in every crevice. In reality it was not one epidemic, but two or three.

The fatal chicken pest had begun in the Arab villages and struck down their thin, neglected chickens. It had then penetrated to the Jewish settlements and destroyed even the strongest birds in their coops—those strong white Leghorns which cackled during the day and scratched at night. Then there was the dread foot-and-mouth disease, which had attacked nearly all the farms in the Jordan Valley and was still spreading. You would look at the heavy Friesian cows and the tall Damascus breed, and to see them suffering in their animal dumbness was heartbreaking. And, last but not least, there was that cursed horse plague. They didn't know exactly what it was yet, but it had already managed to strike fatally in many stables at various places throughout the country, and this had happened just at the time of the autumn ploughing.

Two weeks ago the little Morris had begun to bump along the roads and narrow paths, raising clouds of dust and sounding its horn, passing through farms and Arab villages, panic-stricken district offices and gas stations. First and foremost, the epidemic had to be isolated. Those places already affected were segregated, and a strict quarantine was imposed on all farms throughout the country, as well as on the roads. British and Arab police stationed on the main highway received strange orders which they did not understand. Drivers of the huge red trucks coming from Damascus and Beirut loudly cursed the thorough examination, but the foreign cigarettes they offered were of no avail. The gates of the Jewish farms were locked, their soil covered with lime; drums of lysol were placed on both sides of them bearing large signs: 'Disinfectant.'

All this activity was due to the efforts of that little Morris which had rushed everywhere, conscripting people, explaining, threatening, placing some on guard and spurring others to activity. The Arab *fellaheen* were overcome by fear of the accompanying policeman, of the official documents, of the syringes and veterinary instruments. Only one policy was effective in their villages: to frighten and isolate them, burn the stricken animals and dead birds, forbid all communication with neighbouring villages, and promise reward and punishment. But in the Jewish settlements, the cowhands and poultrymen were quiet, understanding people who penetrated to the heart of the problem. They would listen attentively, accept advice with thanks, and carry out the instructions fully. They would accompany the car to the road, gravely shake hands with the vet, and, at his departure, immediately lock the gates.

Those had been dark days for the cowhands of the Jordan Valley. One by one the big cows fell. First they would begin to drool yellow saliva between their teeth, in their black, sore-scarred mouths; then they would sway on their legs, hooves covered with festering sores. The sight of those tottering animals was heart-rending. Although whole cowsheds lost their milk, their health, their very sustenance, the cowhands were restrained and comprehending, and through the car window Dr Schmidt would jokingly declare: 'I'm not worrying about you. Whatever you've lost is lost, but if you bring the epidemic down to the Emek there'll be the devil to pay! Don't you dare to go anywhere near there. Don't even stick your noses out. Do you hear? Well, don't despair.'

Don't despair—God! They had received a telegram from his wife Miriam saying:—'The troops are going overseas. No word from Shlomo. Return home immediately . . .'

III

That had been yesterday. The telegram had awaited him in the Department's office in Tiberias. The troops were leaving—perhaps for the firing line. Shlomo had not been home since the winter, December— nearly a whole year. The roads were teeming with soldiers going home to snatch a farewell leave of a few hours. One short order could transport thousands to infinite distances. Perhaps—to the firing-line . . .

But today there had been six, eight, ten farms waiting for him along the road taking him south. Were they supposed to know that there was a certain Shlomo, that he had not been home an entire year— and that now he was being taken away? Were they supposed to visualize his high, pale brow, his sad eyes, his incredible stubbornness? Unwillingly, Dr Schmidt had made his visits to the farms—farm after farm, hour after hour. But at some station a railway engine is already getting up steam, darkened carriages are waiting; on some distant horizon guns are reaping their grim harvest of death. There is a lot of mud in the world, epidemics, horse carcasses lying along the roads and soldiers climbing over their warm bodies.

Yes, this horse plague. What would they say at Petach Tikvah? What if this epidemic had not yet struck there, and he wasn't required? What if Shlomo is sitting in his uniform on the sofa opposite his mother, finding it difficult to make conversation, fiddling with the radio and then turning it down, glancing idly at the daily newspapers? Mother is silent—from time to time making some prosaic comment: 'I think Father will be here soon, they told him you were coming.' He is answering with a growl, or with a smile, or looking into her eyes . . . standing by the window, hands in his pockets . . . smoking and staring into the ashtray with narrowed eyes: 'You know Dad. He's probably operating at this very moment on some cow, or drawing blood from a donkey, or talking to the man in charge of the sheep-pen . . .' His laugh sounds unnatural and awkward, and Miriam is gazing at him with a prayer in her eyes.

Here is Petach Tikvah. The Morris pulls up in front of the office with a jerk, Dr Schmidt jumps out and, coat-tails flying, sweeps into the outer room.

'Shalom. Good evening. How are things? Bring the papers into the other room. Get me Tel Aviv on the phone. My home. Thanks.'

In his office, he sits down at the desk, takes off his coat and hat, tosses them aside, and pulling the telephone towards him, leans back in his chair.

Shlomo's high, pale forehead . . . well, a father's soft spot! Only yesterday he was still an infant in swaddling clothes . . . they had to raise him in cotton wool—he was so weak and soft. And then, then one day he swaggered into the study smoking. 'Dad,' came from behind a cloud of smoke, 'Dad, I have a driving licence.' He had literally jumped out of his baby clothes. Then he'd come home in the early hours of the morning, sprawl on the bed in his smart suit and sleep with his shoes on until dawn, when he'd get up and walk about the house like a shadow. He was constantly complaining about the food, the furniture, the books, and his clothes. Evenings he'd sit, lighting his cigarettes one after the other. Then: 'Dad, give me the keys to the car. Don't wait up for me. As usual.'

Mother and father would wait wordlessly in their easy-chairs. Even when he had closed the door behind him, and stolen out like a burglar, silence would reign between them. Each lost in his own thoughts, they would seek refuge in books, letting the lowered radio continue to disturb the stillness. But they could still see him: pale, elegant, hair slicked back, the white silk scarf round his neck emphasizing the deep-blue weave of his suit. They'd hear the car as it noisily left the yard—and even then, for a long while, they wouldn't dare to look at one another . . .

The telephone buzzed. Dr Schmidt seized it nervously. 'Hallo. Who's calling? From the farm? Which farm? No, tell them that I'm not in. I won't go, and that's all there is to it!' He hung up. To hell with them. Someone else can do it. We'll send someone tomorrow.

Gutterman entered unexpectedly, unbidden. He had never looked so stupid, superfluous, and dilapidated. Files in hand, he stood in front of the desk. The two gazed at each other silently a while, until suddenly the phone sprang to life again. Seizing the receiver nervously, the doctor shouted into it: 'Hallo. Dr Schmidt. Petach Tikvah.'

As he waited for the line to stop crackling, he went back to that evening when Shlomo, dressed in grey flannels, white shirt neatly pressed, had stood by the door, the moment when he could stand it no longer.

'Shlomo, don't go out tonight. Mother is ill. We'll need you.'

'Me? Since when am I needed here?'

'But Mother is ill.'

'She'll get well without me.'

'Shlomo, a minute . . . (but Shlomo had grabbed the door-handle and leaned on it slightly)—You know how long I've kept quiet. I've wanted to talk to you, *to talk* to you! But it seems that I can't. If you go . . .'

'I'm going.'

He had run forward and thrown open the door for his son, and as he did so their hands touched. Then he bowed deeply: 'Get—out!' Shlomo smiled, went out—and was swallowed up by the night . . .

Suddenly, Miriam's voice came through the receiver. He couldn't catch the first few words. Her voice was trembling, her strength and courage drained from her. 'He hasn't come yet. Some of his friends I met said he may still come. They have to be back at Lydda by seven-thirty . . .'

The doctor glanced at the watch on his wrist—fourteen minutes past six. He shouted into the telephone: 'What do you mean "he may"? Didn't he get leave like all the others? Has something happened?'

'I've been sitting here waiting for him. I switched on all the lights in the house, prepared supper, packed a parcel . . .' Her voice choked with the tears she couldn't control. But she continued: 'Sorry . . . don't worry. But come immediately. For my sake. If Shlomo won't come— then you come. Right away. They'll understand, they'll manage without you for once. Will you come?'

'Of course I will. And dry those tears—because Shlomo is standing outside and looking through the window.'

'How I wish he were! Come—right away.'

'Don't worry, I'll manage. *L'hitraot* . . .'

'*Shalom.*'

He replaced the receiver . . . A week after that evening which had left its bitter taste of folly, Shlomo had knocked at the door and come in dressed in the uniform of the British Army, the Jewish Brigade. Miriam was still ill, and night after night she would wake him as she sobbed into her pillow. He would get up, light his pipe and sit by the dark windows until morning. Shlomo had come in uniform, his pale forehead hidden under a silly pointed cap, his slender body clothed in greenish khaki, and dragging his heavy black shoes as he walked. Schmidt didn't talk much, as if he were being faithful to what he had said then: It seems I don't know how to talk to you. Shlomo would keep vigil at the foot of his mother's bed whenever he came home, and would reply quietly to all her questions, shutting him out. But even with her he was apathetic. Then they had been transferred from place to place and Miriam had risen from her sickbed. And then winter had come, December weather, and he had not been home since. But now in Lydda, at seven-thirty exactly, the engine would whistle and set out on its journey, and a steel helmet would cover the pale forehead . . .

Dr Schmidt looked up at Gutterman, who had not moved all this while: 'Take those papers back. I'm going.' He stood up, gathering his briefcase and coat, and added: 'You sign the monthly report yourself. I'm not going to do any more today. If anyone rings, tell them I've been in and left. Don't ring me at home. Well, it doesn't matter —you can ring me if you need me. Open the door, please.'

IV

Coat, hat, and briefcase in hand, he went into the outer room, nodded to the telephone operator, and opened the door. Coming up towards him on the steps outside were a Yemenite couple. In her arms the woman carried a baby wrapped in swaddling clothes. There could be no doubt as to their origin or class, from their clothes. On his thin body the man wore ragged, borrowed khaki trousers, obviously not made for him, and a badly worn coat. The woman's bones were covered with black trousers, above which hung some rags, and she wore a filthy shawl on her head.

Doctor Schmidt took in the whole of their plight at a glance. He saw them without pity, but he was unable to escape without saying anything. Unwillingly, he asked: 'Where are you going? Whom do you want?'

The Yemenite was startled, and his wife also stopped at his side.— 'Doctor Schmider. They tell me here . . .'

'What's wrong? What do you want him for?'

The Yemenite paused two steps below and looked up at him. His wife lowered her head and hugged the baby tighter. As though aware of the identity of the man standing before him, the haggard, balding farmer began talking rapidly, swallowing as he blurted out his story: 'The horses, Doctor. Two horses—they sick all of a sudden. The Lord knows—both not moving. Sweating something terrible. One more than the other, and he swollen too. They tell me, wait, the Doctor he come. They not die yet, they only sick. They say they not die from that there sickness. They not die—but I got to work. They say, Schmider he come and see what to do . . .'

The Doctor let him talk on, but it was absolutely clear to him that he would have to go and look at the animals. Within three days the plague could spread and destroy the entire district. It was essential that he investigate this case, even though—what was the time? In one hour the train leaves Lydda—damn those horses! He turned round, shouting 'Wait here!'—and flung open the door. Inside, Gutterman was leisurely drinking the tea in front of him. His elongated head, narrow eyes, big hands, and enlarged jawbones were all completely engrossed in this task. The Doctor thundered at him: 'Gutterman, get the instrument case . . . and bring the certificates, and the pistol . . . and please give me an overall, any one will do. Immediately, Gutterman, and hurry!'

Going outside again, he found the man and woman exactly where he had left them. 'I'm going to your place,' he shouted to the terrified pair, who followed him with their eyes, and threw his coat and hat into the Morris. In the meantime Gutterman had appeared at the head of the stairs, and stood waiting in confusion.

'What are you standing there for? Come on, you're coming with us.' And opening the back door for the couple he commanded: 'Get in!' The frightened Yemenite, suspicious of this offer, timidly suggested: 'Never mind, Doctor. I show the way. No need. We go like this.'

'Do as I say, and don't be a fool. I'm in a hurry—get in!'

Gutterman bent his huge body and, groaning loudly, forced himself into the seat next to the driver, holding the instrument case in his lap. Painstakingly, the Yemenite climbed in and sat in the back. His wife stood silent and motionless, the child in her arms. Dr Schmidt felt his blood coursing to his head, but, clenching his teeth, he regained control of himself with a tremendous effort. 'Get in, damn it!—Are you a human being or not?'

She was finally persuaded by her husband's entreaties and increasing shouts: 'Get in, Miriam—come on, *yallah*, we go in the car, so what . . . ?'

The doctor set the car in motion as soon as the woman had got in and crouched on the back seat. They moved off before the door was closed, and for a short while it swung on its hinges until Gutterman turned around and slammed it shut. As they glided through the streets of the town, a smile broke out on the doctor's face at the sudden realization: Fancy that—there was a Miriam in both places. They soon turned into a dirt road bordered on both sides by trees and houses at irregular intervals. In winter these empty fields would become lakes of stagnant water, and in spring they would be covered by carpets of anemones, groundsel and poppies. Now, only dust rose from the desolate, grey fields. The car swayed slowly between wheel-tracks and puddles. 'There, Doctor, behind huts, in Yemenite quarter. Turn right here, this here side . . .'

The Morris turned right between two rows of closely crowded wooden huts and came to a quick stop. Puddles of sewage water, stacks of bricks, and scattered piles of rubble and garbage blocked the road completely. 'We'll get out here.' The doctor announced his decision with a finality which left no room for objection. 'We'll walk from here. The car can't pass. Come on, *yallah*, no time to waste!'

Gutterman got out last, straightened his weary body, gathered his heavy overcoat about him, and tucked the instrument-case away under his arm. The mother and child trailed along behind, but the Yemenite's spindly legs carried him quickly over the familiar ground. 'Here sir. Behind that there hut. Then another one . . . Then my house. You see the horses. It not so bad. A son I have, and he go in the army. He run away from home. I say to him, You dog, you do this your father, what'll we eat. Then he spit on me, not give a damn, and go in the army, and I not hear from him nothing. I not know where he be now, where they sent him. Now I alone myself with horses. I work for Koblosky, but he's a swine, he not give enough even for bread. I think we get work building, I harness horses—they start—they not going. They sweat something terrible, one swollen. My heart jump. If they die . . . I die. Now the Doctor see . . .'

V

It seemed as though he had seen this self-same yard many a time before: the small, one-roomed hut, the filthy area, the wagon thrown together from rickety boards. The Yemenite ran ahead leading the way, but his wife had entered the hut immediately, leaving the door wide open. Inside could be seen a bare table standing by the windows, and the clay floor. A boy, skinny and with close-cropped hair, stood in the doorway staring at the newcomers.

The Yemenite led the way to the horses standing in a corner of the yard. A number of twisted boards over their heads formed a kind of shelter, and a makeshift manger—two crates propped up on poles—was absolutely empty. 'They not eat nothing. Not this much. Nothing,' explained the owner of the two miserable animals, raising a finger. Dr Schmidt approached the two drab, emaciated male nags. One was shaking all over, sweating, his bloodshot eyes protruding from their sockets. A thread of yellow saliva drooled from his drooping lower lip. The other horse was also covered with sweat, shaking, nodding its head sadly, and its swollen veins looked like black cables.

The doctor stood before them in silence. There was no need to examine them. 'Peste Angina,' he mumbled to himself, not intending that his voice reach the mystified Gutterman who was standing close by. Peste Angina, African Horse Plague. Shaking off the weary distress which had overcome him momentarily, he turned round and spoke to the two waiting men. 'Nothing can be done. You will receive ten pounds for each of them. Did you bring the pistol, Gutterman? Give me the certificates. And you, mister, dig a big hole immediately and bury the two carcasses as deep as you can. Tomorrow someone will come to see whether you have done it . . .'

The Yemenite stood silent staring in bewilderment. 'No understand, Doctor. They no good? Not get well? Why they die? Not get well? Not so bad. Look, they standing.'

He hadn't the strength to argue. The doctor continued as though he had not heard: 'Come inside with me, please. I'll sign the certificate. You can take this to the district office tomorrow and you will receive twenty pounds . . .'

'Why twenty pounds? What they do to the horses?' he mumbled as he went over to them. Gutterman had not yet done a thing.

'Gutterman!' Dr Schmidt startled his assistant out of his reverie. 'Do as I told you. And you, mister, if you don't want the money—I won't sign the certificate. I have no more time to waste . . .'

From his inside coat pocket, Gutterman brought out a long-barreled pistol and strode towards the horses. The Yemenite backed towards them and joined the unfortunate beasts.

'No!' he burst out suddenly, screaming wildly, 'you not kill them . . . kill me first . . . you not got to kill, they still good. They work. Come, kill me! . . .' Finding his path blocked by the raving Yemenite, Gutterman stopped short and turned helplessly to the doctor. The Yemenite also was gazing at him with madly pleading eyes. Hearing the cries, the wife rushed out to join them with the baby in her arms. 'Take him,' she sobbed. 'Take him and kill him. Kill me. Kill the woman.' Helplessly she raged at Dr Schmidt: 'I swear, by your father's life . . . Where we get food, where? These here horses, they all we got. They go, work a bit, not work. Eat a bit, then not eat. So what. Look at the house. Look at the baby. Look at me.'

Dr Schmidt looked at his watch. Seven o'clock. Well—good luck, Shlomo. And that whole quarrel . . . see how your eyes are laughing again. They leave Lydda at seven-thirty. But there is no need at all to shoot healthy men through the head. Such a fate is only for sick horses, no one else but sick horses.

VI

He went quietly up to the thin, excited man, and with a slight gesture prevented his unconscious retreat. Of itself, his hand came to rest on the farmer's shoulder, and only a ragged sleeve was between them. He said: 'Your horses are suffering from a terrible sickness. It is a plague which comes from Africa. It will infect other horses, donkeys, and mules. Even if your horses get well—and I don't think there's a chance of their recovery, just look at them—in any case, they are now threatening the lives of hundreds of horses in the district. Do you understand? All the horses of all the carters, the co-operative settlements, and the private farmers would be affected. The same thing would happen to all their horses. They will shake all over, they won't eat, won't work—they will die. Understand?'

Greeted by a dense, stubborn silence, the doctor turned to Gutterman and said drily: 'Take him inside and give him a certificate for two horses. Afterwards see to it that he buries them. Give me the pistol.' The owner of the horses stood between his two beasts, not uttering a word, as though he had neither heard nor understood what had been said. Gutterman approached and motioned him to move, but when he did not stir—he put his long arm around his shoulder and began to lead him in the direction of the house. The Yemenite now began to resist. He screamed, lashed out with his fists—but he was dragged on. 'You rats, you cut my throat . . . kill me . . . come, burn the house. You go way, you. Let go me. I not thief, you dog. You not shut my mouth. Leegggoooooo!!!'

An excited group of neighbours stood in the street by the broken fence. Many of them seemed like brothers of the screaming man, in stature, dress, and features. They looked at the horses, listened to the shouts, and shook their heads. They shook their heads in pity, but not one of them climbed over the fence.

Although Gutterman did not succeed in closing the door, he kept his prisoners inside the hut. Dr Schmidt went up to the horses. One of them drooled saliva and would have died in two or three hours' time. We will have to send policemen to dig a grave, this man is out of his mind and won't do anything. The horse's head sagged loosely, its scraggy mane full of straw. The doctor placed the pistol barrel to its ear, a quiver passed over the half-paralysed beast, and he pressed the trigger. The shot was not frightening, and yet the horse staggered immediately and fell on its side. At that moment the shouts from the house became louder, the woman wailed, the children cried, and Gutterman's solid form blocked the doorway.

The other horse shook its head nervously. Dr Schmidt stroked it and patted its wet swollen muzzle. While doing this he grabbed its nostrils and squeezed them. At first the horse was surprised and resisted a little, but soon it yielded and was quiet. Its large head remained steady, turned upwards and back. With his free hand Dr Schmidt put the pistol to its ear. At that very moment the Yemenite managed to force his way through the door, but the shot re-echoed and the horse sank immediately without a tremor, and with no loss of blood.

The bereaved carter clutched the doorpost of his hut at the sight before him. He groaned, and his sobs chocked within him as his shoulders shook convulsively.

'Did you make out a certificate? You had better send policemen over to bury the horses immediately. If only one mosquito lights on the carcasses it will spread the plague like wildfire.' He glanced at his watch again. Seven-fifteen. The group of spectators stood quietly by the fence, and the thin Yemenite, sobbing silently in the doorway and leaning his head on the post, did not move. 'Come on, let's go.'

When they reached the road, the heavy puffing of someone run-ning suddenly reached their ears. 'Schmider, Schmider!' The doctor stopped, and turning saw the Yemenite lean on the fence with both hands, and gasp: 'I swear, now I take everything. My wife and chil-dren. Lock the door. Spill kerosene. Let fire take us to Hell. You destroy my house. May that eat you till you die. You destroy my house . . . Your house be destroyed too. I hope the Lord destroy your house. Your sons die like my horses you kill. Die, die . . .'

They walked on, crossed the road, avoided the scrap-heaps and puddles. Black wondering eyes stared at them from the doorways, and at the end of the street the car stood like something from another world.

'You come over here yourself tonight to supervise the burying of the horses. And see if you can help him with something . . .'

'Yes, sir.'

The entered the car. Dr Schmidt started the motor, and his glance fell on the hands of his watch. Seven-thirty. The engine is blowing its whistle and letting off steam, the carriages are beginning to roll—and the boys are off to the firing-line. The Morris began to move forward, and suddenly splinters were flying: a window-pane was shattered and the stone landed on the back seat. The doctor accelerated the car as it jolted along the furrowed road. A shout pursued him, once, twice, thrice:

'Your house be destroyed, murderer—your house be destroyed!'

Translated by Shlomo Ketko.

Yehuda Amichai

THE SNOW

Amichai was born in Würzburg, Bavaria in 1924, to an Orthodox family and arrived in Palestine in 1936. He was educated in religious schools both in Germany and in Jerusalem. During the Second World War he served in the Jewish Brigade and then in the Palmah. Though known primarily as a poet of international eminence, translated into twenty-nine languages, Amichai has written two novels and a collection of short stories entitled In This Terrible Wind *(1961, 1975). His novel* Not of This Time, Not of This Place *(1963) refers to the dislocation of Jewish life after the Holocaust. The novel and the short stories are written in a confessional prose style, embellished with the lavish figuration that characterizes his verse. While conveying a portrait of life in modern Israel, Amichai is also able to explore the human problems specific to life in any modern Western society which has deviated from defined cultural and spiritual paths.*

The snow began in the blind and moved outward. For years the white snow had settled in the blind. Now it was out, and white: blindness lodged everywhere, covering everything.

The world stood like railway cars during a strike, the smoke dead. A different smoke entered the young women, and they warmed themselves, and voices rose above the hopes of ashes, and the night went on white and undisturbed.

Yaakov and Tirzah prepared to visit me, and I didn't know it yet. The wind tapped at the doors of my apartment and at the doors of my spirit with a big blind man's cane. Yaakov and Tirzah arrived and rescued me for the bath.

My house is at the bottom of a slope, and Yaakov rolled his woman all the way to me, so that she arrived in an avalanche of snow—then leaped from inside it, her face red with the air of summer and of roses. Her breath was white when she spoke. My love too is not always visible: Only when I am cold or anguished can you see it, like Tirzah's vaporous breath.

The wind knocked at the door, and we pushed the furniture aside; I extended a hand to the wind to guide it, but it hit Tirzah's face, and her black hat was blown askew. She was wearing those black pants fastened up, the kind that girls wear on cold days of merry loving. Now black is no longer the colour of mourning, and there can be no other colour to mourning: it is transparent; through it you can see cities and people—everything.

The electricity was out and wires jumped on all sides, curling on the white forehead of the snow that had no thoughts beneath it.

The moon was cold, extinguished, like the monarch of a country become a republic. The letters were cold in the red mailboxes. Some tried to flap their wings, but couldn't.

The electricity stopped, and all of it entered Tirzah.

'You can write on it like a piece of paper.'

'People can make love anywhere.'

'It's wonderful loving in the snow.'

'Sex in the snow!'

'We ran all evening.'

'I rolled her.'

'A snowman with no telephone.'

'My warm oven-man who loves me.'

That evening the steps up to my house led only down; so how did the two climb to my door? From the rooftops! The window rattled us its commentary; the bath water got cold, and the coffee deepened in seriousness in the cups.

Yaakov and Tirzah slid down; he wanted to roll her all the way to their house in the heights of Jerusalem. But they never made it. Instead they got as far as the Valley of the Cross and remained there: In the morning people found two black, fallen telephone poles, their wires so entangled that only God knew how to unknot them. The nearest house was too far away. Another house faced the mountains where it was forbidden to go.

All night the snow lay on my sleep. And so it was when I was born. Flesh came like white snow covering my red blood, in which swam that hungry shark, my heart. My mother's cords were cut in a storm; my ears were the cups of a telephone receiver; my nose was hope setting forth; my mouth the black wound in snow when it is stepped on. And my fingers were silent, and my legs were like the beating of hammers.

A black dog of conscience barked near the field where one goes astray. The snow that lay on my sleep melted, penetrating it. I woke up and lit the snow in my room, and saw that the world was immense and inconsolable.

The snow settled heavily where the archaeologists had excavated. But that grave was accustomed to the weight of many strata. The wire fence that had been put up to protect it had rusted out some time ago. No one cuts through there except to reach the adjacent grocery store, to get to the colourful cartons. The cartons thrown into the garbage still bear illustrations of what they once contained. That's good.

I went outside and stood under a balcony near where my close friend used to live. One day he raised a sail on his violin and put out to sea. The water seeped into his violin and he cried; but he was already too far out, participant in the world like a biblical chapter, his violin filing up. Why did he go? What was he looking for? Perhaps he set out to find the horse from whose tail the bow of his fiddle had been made. He went out very far, and the horse was swift.

When he went away, they threw him a party. His eyes were heavy, having fallen to him from distant generations. He stood by the stairs and said goodbye to us. Sometimes I feel a pull in my heart; he is tied to me as mountain climbers are tied to each other. By the tug I must surmise his movements. And sometimes the tug is painful, especially during the spring. Sometimes the rope is pulled and sounds a bell, as on a bus requested to stop.

I would have liked to continue standing there, but the snow sent me under the balcony; it had turned to hail. And then, like someone who at first has difficulty speaking and says difficult things, whose words gradually soften, the hail turned again to snow. One window in the house was blocked up with rocks. One vertical pipe stopped short of the roof; there was no longer blood in it. Other red pipes entered the ground, all standing against the wall of the house like vessels bulging on the hand of an old man. I was holding onto my dead thoughts like slaughtered chickens, their heads drooped to the ground on the way home from market. A young woman lived in the old house—lived there alone. At first it was dark, then light leapt from window to window. I stood under the balcony that had been extended into the world, like someone superfluous, someone without inception.

Sisters with necklaces bustled around in the house. Brothers with bubbling hopes sang in the tub, as I had done when Yaakov and Tirzah rolled down the slope to visit me. A car pulled up, its snow chains jangling. Dr Gordon got out, his bag in hand. His voice said, 'She's

a student.' The driver said, 'I'll wait. I'll leave the motor running.'
The doctor took the bag and went into the house. All the pipes filled
with new blood and smoke began to rise from the house and lights
flicked on like fingered piano keys. I sat in the taxi. The doctor returned
and showed me his hand: 'I performed an operation in that old house.'
His hair was curly and his eyes looked off across the Old City, and
the Old City in turn looked off toward the mountains beyond the
Jordan, and the mountains looked off still further. I got out of the
taxi and it drove away. The now-healthy student—who wore a man's
coat . . . she draped it on a chair . . . by now she has forgotten me—
was like a trumpet call in that old house. The balcony remained thrust
out like the palm of a pauper.

Sated with white, I went to look at pictures in the gallery. There
was no one there but me. The gatekeeper was not at the gate, and I
went in free. In one painting there was a woman combing the hair
of a woman combing the hair of still another woman. Where would
it all end?

I heard the guard walking through the rooms. They would be closing soon; it was almost dark. My heart lay like a carpet on the vast
quietness. A carpet that's been well trampled. The sound of a typewriter came from some hidden room. Surely they were making a list
of those who didn't attend. Policemen in plain clothes watched me
so that I wouldn't steal. I asked: 'When did you acquire these paintings?' They said: 'They are ours and you are ours.' I wanted to know
where the typewriter was. I wanted to know what was behind the
paintings. I took down a picture, and saw that a bright rectangle
remained on the wall, like my heart that hasn't loved in a long time
and remains clear—for the sun hasn't touched it, and it's been hidden under a picture.

I looked at the inscriptions: A painting's name did not always suit
it. That's how it was with the name written on my identity card, and
with the snow that was inappropriate to Jerusalem.

I took in the names of the painters. A date of birth, a date of death,
and between them a short line. Some of the paintings showed only
a date of birth and a blank space waiting on the other side for the
second date. The hail beat on the glass roof; others of the plagues
of Egypt were still to follow. The paintings turned themselves to the
wall, and I went out to the courtyard, and saw only snow. I paid the
gatekeeper, who had returned in the meantime.

The smell of pines and other trees was in the air. Many trees were
broken. Every leaf was freighted with snow. So it is with me: All the

words I speak are leaves, and fate, like snow, rides heavy on them. The great danger is that I will break, so I sometimes stop speaking. If I don't produce words, I won't crack with the cargo. If I am silent, the weight of the snow can't break me. If I am unloving, I am unburdened. If I have no handles, they can't catch me; I can slip from their hands, left with myself. If I refuse colour, then they can't see me.

The trees were broken and their fragrance filled the air. Only now, after their breaking, is their smell good in the world, and strong.

New hail started to strafe the earth. I found shelter in the voluminous robes of a nun. There was room in her habit for another two or three people. At first she didn't feel me. Then she objected. She accepted her situation, and we walked on together in her capacious gown. She went up the steps of the old building with me and said, 'Now get out. Get out of there. Why did you come to me?' I entered her room with her. Her collar was white as snow. Her room was patched up, a shell having exploded a hole in it. I asked, 'Did you cause the snow? It seems to me that a nun like you made all the snow.' Suddenly I knew how to speak Swedish. I told her that Swedish was a beautiful language, and so was the shell-hole through which prayers in all languages had made their exit, until the room was repaired.

On the table stood roses in a vase. They were from before the snow and had already begun to wilt. One rose was like a heart in surgery; another like a dog run over in the street. One rose was made of paper; another rose was like a bed left unmade after sleep. I saw that the nun's eyes were sad. I saw that her eyes retained in reflection the numbers she had seen in the street; they remained and her eyes saddened.

'I've learned nothing but how to die,' she said. 'I still wear my father's smile like a bib tied around an infant so it won't dirty itself.'

'I stand before my life like a small boy at a kiosk. The coin in my hand held out to the shopkeeper, I see only what has been laid at the edge of the counter—and not the wonderful shelves behind him.'

We went over to the small window and saw that Jerusalem was entirely white. My life speeded up. Episodes ran by and I didn't know what to say; the plot of the film advanced in a foreign language and the Hebrew translation lagged behind at the bottom of the screen.

Jews passed by with foxes on their heads, foxes from distant forests. The face of my nun was like a country with many small gardens in it. I told her that there were two seats of tiredness in my body—the soles of my feet and my eyes. They both roam a great deal without rest.

She said, 'There are two seats of sadness in my body—my feet and my eyes. My little nephew Yigal once said that everything beautiful is sad.'

Sometimes she spoke to me in a faraway archaic language, from some distant Bible of snow:

'Good man.'

'You were pleasant to me.'

'Until when will you stay with me?'

Sometimes she sang and sometimes she turned from the window. The snow was laid on the heart of Jerusalem to slow the city's death by fire. Jerusalem is always burning. Things come along to delay her death, like the snow that fell this year.

After dinner we shared a smile, insufficient for both of us; when she smiled, my mouth narrowed and contracted. Her robes were scattered around the room. She was as skinny as a chicken. My nun's brother lived at the edge of the village. He was a heavyset farmer who had settled behind a heavyset wooden door in the northern part of the world. It was difficult to reach his place in the snow.

We went out for a walk. I hid myself in her robes because I was cold, and I didn't want anyone to see me walking with a nun.

Black-haired young men passed wearing shiny moon-jackets with fur collars.

The triumphal stones of the Roman Tenth Legion were covered with snow; other stones were like human hearts, scattered and silent.

The thoughts of Tel Aviv didn't arrive; red postal-thoughts stood en route. I saw Dr Gordon's car and knew that the student in the old house was sick again.

I sat down opposite my nun. All my thoughts were on my brow, like boats pulled onto the sand when not out fishing. I looked at her head against the waning light, as if assessing a negative: It was a good picture. We couldn't keep sitting because fresh snow began to fall on us. The houses of Jerusalem stood to the side. Some of the houses would outlive their occupants, and some of the occupants would continue living after the houses—like a man who has nothing to drink, who then finds a drink but has eaten the bread, who then gets some bread. . . . People, superfluous, needing new houses, then superfluous houses needing new people, without end, without equilibrium, without respite.

We stood beside the gate of Dr Miller, who fixes broken limbs. The world had shattered and the snow had set as a false plaster cast. When the snow melts, the fractures will again be visible. I left her then, and went down the street.

My students came sliding down the hill. Tomorrow I'll assign

them the task of finding every mention of 'snow' in a concordance.
As the rain and snow come down from heaven and do not return
there. . . . But everyone returns. A bear was killed on a snowy day. All
will be silent. Sins will become white as snow, and in my mind
I'll be looking in all the snowbound places. When I was a boy, there
were conventional essays in honour of snow, with conventional rhetoric. 'The snow sits like little white domes on the fences.' 'Snow covers
everything like a sheet.' The rhetoric sucked out all the life. Only the
tears, which it was meant to absorb, it did not absorb. The world is
covered with those killed—the dead, like torn socks my mother never
finished mending. I almost went back to the nun.

The car with a loudspeaker attached to its engine came by and said
'Everyone aside!' I made it. 'Beware of the power lines!' Employees of
the Electric Company tried to repair the damage. Employees of the
Post Office stood down below next to poles and telephoned heaven.
I saw one smiling in the middle of his conversation, as a man might
smile when phoning angels. A snowman had been built around a post
at the bus station, with the upright for a soul. Children had stuck eyes
in it. One boy had eaten the carrot that was the golem's nose.

Cars brought aged parents. Children tumbled in the air. Students
promenaded up and down the streets. The snow fell from giant text-
books. Young women were wide open with snow and shrieked as at
the seashore in the summertime.

It started to rain. I stood under a tree that protected me. The rain
stopped and the tree was no longer my protector, but itself dripped
on me. Quiet people are a lot like that: sometimes after everyone has
gone away they will start speaking. Sometimes no one hears them.
Sometimes a small boy carrying letters of a deaf man are their only
witnesses. Anyone just happening by hears them. I went to a friend's.
He wiped the lenses of his eyeglasses but they clouded over again.
Behind the curtain of branches of a pepper tree that bowed across the
street, children were playing. We didn't dare approach them because
they were living in another world. Cars separated from their owners.
All the words of junction were wrong, and I didn't know how to
speak. In everything there was death without forgetfulness.

But I was hungry. I went into a restaurant. The waiter took my
order, and then went to the far little window and repeated my order
over into that concealed and distant world. I was glad because now
they knew my desire over there—in that other cosmos, beyond the
mountains, above the clouds. Who was out there? Solitary pilots; lost
voices and prayers that returned like boomerangs to the worshipper.

I went into the university building to look at the clock. I hadn't come to learn but to observe the passing time and look over the list of those who had got through the tests. There is no other place in Jerusalem. Professors continued teaching under the snow, unaware that their students had gone out to play.

In came the Three Workmen of the Apocalypse. The first carried a broom, the second a spade, and the third carried his past. They walked by me and went further on, not knowing where my nun was, even though I asked them nothing. I threw a party: My eyes celebrated before all the sad people—my spirit made my body happy with dreams and my feet danced in the snow—I came back from there and the streets were smooth with ice—walking with small steps I finally arrived at sleep. All the time it snowed I hadn't slept. The snow, like white eyelids, slept for me. The earth slept for me beneath it.

The following day, the fog came in. The snow slowly returned to the blind; it retreated under a curtain of fog, concealing the ugliness, the black wounds, the polluted streams, the corpses of trees. On the bulletin boards many death notices had been tacked up. People usually restrained themselves, and didn't die. Now, under cover of snow, they all died at once, and there was no room on the bulletin boards. I hung a sign on myself, as on a driving-school car, and they let me pass. I learned how to walk all over again, and to love and to see and to think after the snow. Thoughts seated themselves in my mind, which they took for a dining room; and they ate in an uproar.

The Three Workmen of the Apocalypse came out of the fog, looked at me and disappeared. I never saw them working. They were always wandering around looking for a good place for their fulfilment.

A young woman got off a bus. She entered the fog. She stepped out of it, closing the door of the fog, and went into a cosmetics shop. She made her purchase and stood among the fragrances; that was her place. She never left there but I heard her voice when I fell to forgetting the nun.

The tree in front of my house that we thought would break rose again, but not to its full height. It stayed halfway to its death; or rather like a mother's neck inclined to her daughter, while her son has taken off a long time ago. The children stayed in the yard, absorbed in their games. Toward evening they hollered, 'Hey, Ma, throw me a sweater!' And that was just the attitude of those at prayer, who yelled up to God to throw them His blessing so they wouldn't have to go home to get it.

Many trees were in pieces on the ground. If it were *Sukkot*, it would have been convenient. If only we could bend down the year, like branches, so that it would touch us. This summer there will be

many bonfires in the Valley of the Cross. And perhaps Yaakov and
Tirzah will rise—the two who went down there after visiting me and
never came back.

In one place people were moving out of their apartment. The snow
surely drove them to it, the white carpet having dizzied them. The
voices of the movers were hard among the remains of the soft snow:

'Now the big chest.'

'Watch out! The door.'

'You there, watch out!'

'Hey lady!'

There were piles of snow melting like an unmade bed. I set up
a competition: Where would the last bit of snow be left? In the
back yard near the trash-cans among the terrible shadows where it's
deserted.

The melting snow stole the little warmth for its thaw; just as all
the lovers in the world expropriate the warmth of humanity around
them in order to soften each other. The others are left cold.

In a distant neighbourhood, nearer to the moon than my neighbourhood, a little boy drowned in a pit of water covered by snow.
The boy went down to collect meteorites. His shoes floated up like
water lilies. At first the pit had been full of snow. Then the snow
turned to water, and the water to astonishment, and astonishment
became a cry—and over it all rested a layer of snow. The soles of his
shoes were like two private clouds over the earth, already far away,
belonging to the rest of his body way below.

He was in the pit, having perished in the final plague, the slaying
of the first-born. The hail had already come and the blood was wonderful in Tirzah's cheeks, who had been rolled over and over by her
lover; the blood was in her cheeks.

The Three Workmen came and put down their three tools near
the side of the pit, and spoke quietly among themselves. Then they
lay down on their stomachs to pull the boy out. The shoes came
out in their hands, and light flickered on in their eyes like memorial
candles. Another man came by, carrying a portable stove in his buf-
falo horns, the stove belly a dazzling sun. The instrument was set in
the snow, which melted, but it did not save the boy. Tirzah's black
pants are draped on a stick, as are the rest of her clothes, cast like
thoughts on a chair—thoughts a person would like to quiet. Tomorrow
she'll be wearing a dress with flowers on it.

Ropes groaned, ships sailed out of the place; ships that were beside
the boy's cheek set out to sea. The world was a worldful of ships,

and the boy lay like an empty pier along the snow, all the ships gone. Anchors flew away like birds.

The mother came and threw cries like bombs at the boy and at the city to wake him. The Three Workmen picked up their tools and went away. A first train went by and screamed between the mountains constricting it. Anywhere in Jerusalem you can hear the train coming.

Not far from there they again took up construction work that had been suspended. The great mixer turned, setting cadence to death. The gravel and cement and sand bonded together; but we, drifting, never bond to one another. Instead we are sent off to the farthest extremities. The house was eventually built: At first only an empty space had been there, flooded with air, and light, and from time to time birds. Then they closed it up, turned it into cubicles, chambers, in which destinies were at once constructed. Where there had been air and expanse and the rush of wings, now was the fatedness of walls—women and men, books, and illumination after midnight.

There were sales again in the shops. In the shoe store was a sign: 'Single Pairs.' Is there a greater contradiction than the one between 'single' and 'pairs'? My thoughts were as tired and closed as the solitary passengers on a last bus: one here, two there, all bundled up and silent, and the cold wind like water already breaking into the sinking ship.

So I went to a coffee-house. The owners' crazy son sat flipping through illustrated newspapers as God must flip through the torn pages of His heart—without understanding. There was no room for me because a meeting of Hungarians was just getting under way. Hungarian words were laid out on the table. One man shed tears; a little boy played a game of marbles with them between the table legs and the legs of the Hungarians. The orations were balanced like scales, were cyclical like the seasons: an old man's spare words were followed by the blossoming eloquence of a girl. Someone came in and they all shouted 'Jarousz! Jarousz!' He brandished a rolled paper like a stick, struck the table, and joy burst forth. After a while they all left. The quiet was made up of many conversations between couples. In the houses and everywhere else I saw people.

In my eyes I cleared away the big building and another building and another building, and saw the last strips of snow near the border, outside the bars of children's dreams.

Translated by Elinor Grumet.

Natan Shaham

SPEAK TO THE WIND

*Shaham was born in Tel Aviv in 1925. After serving in the Palmah he joined kib-
butz Beit Alpha in 1945. Despite its air of social realism, Shaham's writing has an
idealistic orientation. It focuses on problematical areas of Israeli society but without
the pessimism and disillusionment encountered in the works of his contemporary S.
Yizhar. His portraits of Jewish life in the diaspora, particularly in the United States,
add a dialectical component to his fiction. Shaham has written eight novels and nine
collections of stories, in addition to plays and travel-books. One of his most celebrated novels,* The Rosendorff Quartet *(1987), is an exercise in documentary fiction
and an authentic evocation of the yishuv of the 1930s. It also displays his prodigious
musical knowledge.*

When the news of his father's illness came Amos Nehushtan remembered Wartman. And he felt a little guilty. Before leaving for New
York he had promised his father to visit his friend, but he had been
busy with the Defence Ministry's purchasing mission and the promise
had been forgotten. Even though his father never failed to mention
Wartman and enquire after his health in his letters. After a few weeks
Wartman's name became a reminder of his own dereliction.

As soon as he had read the telegram he made up his mind to do
his duty to his father, who made so few demands. That same day he
called Wartman on the phone. The visit to Wartman, he knew, would
be a chapter in the history of his father's life, which was now coming to an end.

Perhaps for this reason the visit was so difficult for him. There was
no lack of excuses. His days and nights were dedicated to the work
whose importance was beyond question. But even the best excuse
was still an excuse. His refusal to meet Wartman stemmed from a
deeper source. He didn't like writers.

His father was a Hebrew writer. And Wartman wrote in Yiddish.

Ever since childhood he was used to writers and meeting them depressed him. They reminded him of what upset him about his father: vulnerability, sensitivity, and the sad humour of cripples.

He didn't know Wartman. But the fact that he was an obscure writer in an obscure language was reason enough for him not to want to see him. He imagined that he could guess his appearance and his smell: a sad little old man with the smell of carpenter's glue that came from the covers of old books clinging to him.

And there was something else which deterred him too: he guessed that the meeting with Wartman was supposed to serve as a kind of landmark. A final, clinching argument in a bitter debate which had gone on for fifty years: the historical debate between Hebrew and Yiddish. Between the Zionist movement and the *Bund*.

In the twenty-fifth year of Israel's existence he—an electronics engineer whose mother tongue was Hebrew, a healthy spirit in a healthy body, a New Jew, buying sophisticated components for state-of-the-art control systems—was the irrefutable, living proof that his father, and not Wartman, had chosen the right road. Tel Aviv, and not New York. Hebrew and not Yiddish.

Nobody said this. But he felt that his father expected Wartman to take one look at his strong, handsome face and admit that he was wrong. He probably wouldn't actually say anything. But his stoop would proclaim submission, the abandoning of his previous position, and the admission of defeat. The victory of the young builders. And he was supposed to look at Wartman with his father's eyes, which would not gloat, but forgive the old man for the error of his ways. A touching moment, summing up an entire historical epoch.

Something of their emotion infected him too.

Wartman lived in Manhattan, not far from downtown Greenwich Village. Amos Nehushtan took a cab. He was afraid that he wouldn't find parking. To his suprise there was no traffic in the street. It was like an abandoned city. After he got out of the cab he was obliged to return to the main street in order to phone Wartman from a public phone. The door to the building was locked and the intercom wasn't working.

Wartman stood at the head of the stairs on the third storey of the disintegrating building—the lift wasn't working either—and shouted 'Is it you?' in a voice tremulous with fear. Amos Nehushtan didn't know Yiddish but he could infer the meaning. He spoke Hebrew, loudly, to quieten the old man's fears. But until Wartman saw him standing in front of him he wasn't reassured. He was afraid of a trick. In the doorway he told him that the day before an armed robbery had taken place in the building. Only then did he smile at him and say: 'Your father's eyes, no question about it.'

Wartman was astonishingly like the man he had seen in his imagination: a little old man, tired to death; a sad, shrunken piece of humanity. Only his big reddened eyes preserved a certain curiosity, which flickered on and off. Wartman knew six or seven languages perfectly, but the only one he could speak fluently was Yiddish. Even his English came out broken: every sentence included a few words in another language.

His wife didn't even know that much. She was a tall woman, ten years younger, who must have been good-looking once. She had arrived from Poland after the Second World War, and she hadn't succeeded in learning English at all. The irony of fate: ignorance of Yiddish was to her an important mark of aristocracy. In the country of her origin she had spoken only Polish. She was proud of it. She stayed with them for a while, after setting out a dish of dried fruit, but the attempt to conduct a conversation in English wore her out and she retired to the next room. The sound of a sewing-machine soon followed.

The conversation—peppered with words in Hebrew and Yiddish—was about literature and writers. Amos Nehushtan hardly understood half of Wartman's words, and much of what he was talking about passed him by, but he didn't mind being bored. He was resigned to playing the part of an attentive audience, to fulfil a debt of honour to his father, and he had no regrets about the wasted evening. He was glad he hadn't brought his wife with him. The meeting with Wartman would have depressed her. She hated New York. He didn't want to give her an opportunity to complain: he could have been managing a small plant in Israel instead of living in this dreadful city.

Wartman launched a furious attack on the Yiddish writers in America and the younger generation who wrote in English. He accused them of acting like 'informers', 'telling tales' on the Jewish community, as if they were all degenerate perverts who hated their mothers. He said that the way they wrote fed the flames of anti-Semitism. He was especially vehement in his denunciations of one well-known writer who 'sold the Jews to the goyim like a kind of demonology'. Amos Nehushtan, who had never read a single line of Wartman's writing, was unable to judge the extent to which the nobility of Judaism was expressed in his works, as he claimed it was.

Although he was amused most of the time, because he couldn't understand what the old man was getting so excited about, he soon began to feel a delicate undercurrent of melancholy, obscure and not

entirely disagreeable, impinging upon him. He thought sympathetically of the two childless old people, imprisoned in their disintegrating building and afraid of anyone who happened to climb the stairs.
He thought of their loneliness growing more absolute as the members of their generation died off, and he wondered at Wartman's
strange optimism, a writer, writing in a language that was disappearing
from the world. He listened with growing compassion to Wartman's
story about some young woman in Israel who wrote in Yiddish, the
living proof that the future of Yiddish literature was 'still before it'.
These thoughts put him in a philosophical mood, the kind of thing
he had always tried to avoid, the reason he had chosen to go into the
exact sciences. He believed that with the help of science he would be
able to put an end 'once and for all' to the oppressive burden of his
inheritance. His sadness grew intense when Wartman suddenly said,
'Your father should have come to America, this is the only place where
they're capable of appreciating him.' He stared in surprise at the old
man in the outmoded striped suit, sitting like a prisoner serving a life
sentence in the faded, peeling old armchair. Then he raised his eyes
to the glass cabinet full of unusable silver utensils and tasteless china
animals, scanned the books and dusty old journals stacked in hopeless disarray on the bookshelves, glanced without interest at the cheap
landscape in the ornate gold frame and the photographs of two old
people in glass frames, and he was filled with pity for his father.
Presumably the old man wouldn't live to see the defeat of Wartman.
The obstinate old Yiddishist dismissed all the achievements of Israel
as if they were nothing. And presumably his father, too, would not
value them at their full worth as long as Wartman failed to concede
that he had been right. His pity for his father suddenly became too
hard to bear. He wondered where he was hospitalized and whether
there was anyone there who would be tolerant of his extreme fasti-
diousness. He saw his father in his imagination in New York, in a
room like this one, surrounded by Wartmans, who knew how to
appreciate him at his true worth, each more pathetic than the other,
living monuments to sharp-witted Jewish melancholy, and they were
all complimenting him to his face and praising him to the skies, while
he responded with an exhausted but rejuvenated spirit, and his beautiful, astonishingly youthful eyes filled with a radiant, heartbreaking
joy.

Yes, something of their sensitivity infected him too.

Wartman's wife came back into the room and stood behind her
husband. For a while she looked at Amos Nehushtan with glazed eyes,

as if remembering something, and as soon as her husband's spate of words died down she began formulating a sentence in English, whose meaning escaped him until Wartman flung at him rapidly, in Hebrew: 'Don't agree to more than tea.' And even though he had no intention of eating anything at Wartman's he found himself drinking tea and eating crumbly, over-sweet biscuits and listening to a new spate of malicious gossip about Jewish writers he had never heard of, a fact which caused Wartman grave displeasure. After tea he thought that the visit had reached its end, but he couldn't get out of accepting the invitation to dinner at a restaurant. He sensed that a refusal would hurt their feelings. Wartman said that he would be glad to go out for once with a young man, who could protect him from the 'Negroes, hooligans, lunatics, junkies and anti-Semites hanging around on every street-corner'; from them and from the 'violent, half-crazy, drunken landlord who has no more memory than a cat, and forgets on the second of every month that he's already been paid on the first, and demands the rent for thirty days every month'. Wartman said this with a peculiar kind of solemnity, like a man counting his treasures. When he said 'Negroes, hooligans, . . .', he ticked the list off on his fingers.

Even though the restaurant was not far from Wartman's apartment, as he had been assured, only two blocks away, Wartman called a cab, on the phone, his only means of communication with the outside world, which he also used with a peculiar solemnity, like the proud possessor of some outstanding American achievement. They left the building only when the cab stopped right opposite the door. And then Wartman jumped into it after scrutinizing the cab-driver's face from a safe distance.

Wartman insisted that he was the host and that he would pay for everything, the cab and the meal, 'and no unnecessary arguments, please'. He gave the cabbie a dollar tip, with the extravagant flourish of a man of means who need not count his pennies. To Amos Nehushtan's surprise, the cabbie accepted the extravagant tip without any sign of gratitude; on the contrary, he looked at Wartman mockingly, like a shrewd customer seeing through an impostor, as if he too understood that Wartman was putting on an act of success and prosperity intended to impress a sick Hebrew writer who was in hospital in Israel, and therefore unable to see for himself that Wartman was right and that America was the true fatherland of Jewish writers, not the Jewish State, which did not require their clever scepticism and 'morbid destructiveness'.

In the restaurant, which was open to the street, Wartman revealed a surprising virtue: he knew how to keep quiet and enjoy to the full the delicious food and the girls who served it. Perhaps he also derived a certain provocative, albeit benign enjoyment from the impatience which Amos Nehushtan tried in vain to hide from his patient host while they waited interminably for the first course to appear.

Their silence was not only a matter of choice. It was a hot, humid evening and half the world seemed to have come out into the street. While the side-streets were dark and empty, a stream of people flowed into the avenue like a muddy, foaming river. Conversation was a lost cause in the garden which the restaurant had carved out of the side-walk. The noise all around them was so deafening that any attempt at dialogue was an effort. Amos Nehushtan was glad that Wartman did not force him to talk, and that he was content with his company and with getting out of the house.

The narrow streets of downtown Manhattan were incapable of absorbing all the traffic streaming into them from the broad avenues uptown. Cars waiting interminably at the build-up opposite the traffic lights hooted at each other's tails with savage despair. Magnificent, broad-beamed limousines were stuck in the crush like tanks in the Mitla pass after the Six-Day War. They were piled up in the street like a light-and-sound spectacle documenting the death of the metropolis. Motorbikes with sawn-off exhausts, ridden by leather-jacketed youths, weaved through the cars with triumphant blasts. From time to time the muffled roar of the subway broke from the bowels of the earth, like a groan breaking the body of New York in half. Once a minute a huge passenger-plane flew overhead with a loud, buzzing noise. The noise was as deafening as a buzz saw and it never stopped. In a minute it would grind the steel skyscrapers to dust. In the middle of all this commotion the hysterical wail of a police car or a fire engine would occasionally make itself heard, trying to assert its grim right of way, but succeeding only in adding its own nervous note to the general mayhem.

To Amos Nehushtan's suprise his ear isolated a human voice in the awful din. From time to time the commotion of the street was penetrated by a shrill, sudden, very brief voice, which seemed to wait for a momentary lull in the action of the giant bellows creating the deafening noise and then threaded itself deftly into the general racket, to be heard for an instant, before being covered up again in the mighty torrent and vanishing without a trace. For some time he was unable to locate the source of the sound—a hoarse shriek, heartbreaking in its despair, a brief cry exhausting the power of its owner's lungs. The screamer uttered meaningless syllables, never more than one syllable at a time, and Amos Nehushtan couldn't understand why nobody leaped up to go to his help. Perhaps he had been run over? Perhaps he had gone mad? Or perhaps he required urgent medical attention? Nothing happened in the street, which went indifferently on its way. As if nobody were screaming at the top of his lungs in the middle of the crowded street.

A city which has gone insane, he said to himself; and then he immediately dismissed the thought, partly because it was akin to his father's thinking which he wanted altogether to avoid, and partly because a moment later he solved the puzzle of the screaming.

Its source was soon revealed as the strained throat of a man standing very close to their table, leaning on the low wall marking off the area of the restaurant. The man, tall and thin, about forty, and decently dressed, did not look in the least like someone in need of help. And his face showed no sign of insanity. On the contrary, he looked like a serious man absorbed in a job which demanded concentration. What surprised Amos Nehushtan more than anything else was that the man was screaming from notes! He held a piece of paper with large letters written on it in his hand. After a number of cries, he would lay the paper down on the wall and rub out one of the letters. In preparation for the next scream he would take a step away from the wall, fill his lungs with air, raise his eyes to the sky, and shoot out his shrieks as if he were taking aim at some invisible target. Sometimes the air confined in his lungs would choke him, since no opening appeared in the din, and he would let it out in a kind of inaudible sigh. His shoulders would suddenly slump, but he would soon fill his lungs with air again like an athlete ready to take off.

Wartman too watched the screaming man, but his expression showed that his actions were intelligible to him. The faintest of smiles hovered on his lips. Amos Nehushtan tried in vain to guess what the man was looking up at. On the other side of the street was a building which looked like a factory whose windows were boarded up, leaving only narrow air shafts under their upper arches. Occasionally he saw something like a firefly glowing at the top of the building, but he imagined that it was only a spark from an overheated engine which had flown up into the air. However, when the firefly appeared again and again, he saw that Wartman's eyes were fixed on it too. He gave his companion an inquiring look, and Wartman leaned over the table and shouted into his ear: 'The woman! On the eighth floor!'

He went on to explain, in a series of shouts into his ear, that the building opposite was a women's prison. The windows were boarded up to prevent the inmates enjoying the commotion of the noisy streets and their crowds. If one woman stood on another woman's shoulders, she could signal down to the street with a lighted cigarette. Which was what the woman on the eighth floor did whenever the man's yells reached her ears. And then he would rub out the syllable that had served its purpose and proceed to the next one, until the firefly on the eighth floor announced that the message had reached its destination. 'The power of love,' shouted Wartman. 'Here's Romeo, and up there is Juliet. Selkinzon, of course, would say Ram and Yael.'

Amos Nehushtan had no idea who Selkinzon was, nor did he understand what there was to be so happy about. But something on Wartman's face, an expression which reminded him of the look which accompanied 'Your father should have come to America, this is the only place where people are capable of appreciating him', aroused his suspicious. These were verified when Wartman roared, with a kind of smile that possessed more than an iota of triumph: 'Look which side of the paper he's rubbing out from, the *mamzer!*'

What he succeeded in understanding was that the man was conveying to his wife, or his girlfriend, or his hooker, a piece of legal advice, and the cigarette verified that the message had been received. Wartman's happiness stemmed from the fact that 'it's all in Yiddish! And the *goyishe* policeman stands there at his wit's end . . .'

A strange expression of joy was reflected in the eyes of the old writer as he shouted these things into his young companion's ear. As if the scene being played out in front of their eyes was a proof of the vitality still possessed by the language whose speakers were dwindling so rapidly.

'*Men darf kannen redden,*' yelled Wartman and sent a warm look, full of affection and fatherly pride, at the back of the screaming man. His elation increased by leaps and bounds when the red face of the policeman on the beat suddenly loomed over their table, and gave them a shrewd, friendly wink. In a resonant bass voice, which instantly overcame all the other voices in the street, he said in an unmistakable Irish brogue: 'Who does he think he's kidding, the *gonif?*'

And Wartman's joy was complete.

Translated by Dalya Bilu.

David Shahar

THE DEATH OF THE LITTLE GOD

A fifth-generation Jerusalemite, Shahar was born in 1926 and grew up among the ultra-Orthodox but attended a secular high school and later fought in the War of Independence. He has been awarded the French Prix Médicis Étranger, in addition to major Israeli prizes. His works have been widely translated and are extremely popular in France, where he has been greatly honoured. Shahar sets most of his stories in the heart of Jerusalem, a city which for him is both physical and mystical and which is inhabited by a varied cast of idiosyncratic characters, mystics, madmen, artists, prostitutes, and idealists. His epic, eight-volume novel series, The Palace of Shattered Vessels, *published between 1969 and 1994, is his life's work, which attempts to create—through personal memory—a new mythology of human, Jewish and Israeli existence. Shahar has been compared, particularly in his philosophy of memory, with Marcel Proust.*

At ten to seven the beadle of the hospital, a bearded Jew with side-curls, knocked on my window. I don't know why he knocked on the window and not at the door. Perhaps he wanted to see whether I was in, or perhaps it was a habit that he had carried over from his days as a beadle at the Central Synagogue when he had had to summon the 'good Jews' (as he called them) to midnight prayers. At all events his knocking shattered my dream. The moment I opened my eyes and saw his big head pressed close to the window-pane I knew that the meaning of his visit was that the Little God was dead, but looking at his abundant, untidy beard and at his blinking eyes I refused to believe it.

Startled, I jumped out of my bed and hurriedly opened the door. He came in without uttering a word and, nonchalantly sitting down on a chair, he smoothed his beard with both his hands and placed its tip in his mouth, chewing it with his false teeth. At the same time his eyes roamed over the room till they rested on a picture of a naked woman reclining on her elbow and staring indifferently at the world. The expression on his face hardened and he quickly looked away from the picture to the bookcase. Next to the gaudy pocket-books there stood six heavy, old, calf-bound volumes worn at the edges with years and use. For a minute he hesitated, but then he got up and looked at the volumes. I glanced at him sideways, ready to see on his face an expression of wonder mixed with disappointment, for the six calf-bound volumes were neither talmudic commentaries nor prayer books but the first edition of Hugo's *Les Misérables*, which appeared about one hundred years ago in Brussels.

He pulled out the middle volume, wiped the dust off the cover with his sleeve, sniffed at the smell of old books which it gave off, and glanced at me to see whether I was ready to go or whether he had time to look at the book. I prepared two cups of coffee, one for him and one for myself. He opened the book in the middle, frowned at the sight of the Latin characters, shut it, and returned it to its place with a dry and bored face, like one accustomed to all sorts of oddities. He recited *shehakol* over the coffee and drank it slowly and deliberately. After I too had finished my cup it suddenly occurred to me to sweep the floor, but I did not do so because I did not want to delay him too long.

We went out and only after we had started walking was I seized by a hot and cold fever and by the need to hurry. I had to make haste lest I should be too late. I walked quickly, taking big strides, till we reached the bus stop. We both jumped onto the bus without paying attention to the people who were standing in the queue. Perhaps they did not protest or shout at us because they could see that we were agitated and pressed for time. If there had been any young people in the queue, people who stand up for their rights and who are quick to get angry, they would doubtless have tried to prevent us from boarding the bus, but in fact there were only some old and weak Jews, experts in suffering and accustomed to being deprived of their due, and they did not say a word. They looked at us with their sad eyes and murmured, 'Ay, ay.' Perhaps they even understood that we were hurrying to the chamber of the dead, on the floor of which the Little God was lying cold and silent, covered with a white sheet and with candles burning all around him.

In the bus the beadle took out a tin box which had once been ornamented with coloured pictures but which now showed a white, worn-away, tinny nakedness. He opened it and took out half a cigarette—all the cigarettes in the box had been cut in half. He put the cigarette in an amber holder and lit it. Looking at him, I wondered what was going on in the head of the old Jew. He was wearing a black hat, his face was wrinkled and brown like old parchment, and his red, flattened nose dipped into the sea of his moustache and beard. The holes in his socks peeped above his heavy boots and even from afar he gave off a smell of stale sweat mixed with Turkish tobacco. All in all he looked old and calm amid sorrow and disasters and many funerals— the funerals of my generation and of the generation which preceded mine. It was he who had seen my grandfather to his grave, and now he would accompany the Little God, who had died in his very prime if not in the bloom of his youth.

On the way to the hospital we passed many people and they all looked strange and distant and absorbed in their own business. Only a few of them walked calmly; mostly they had tense and worried faces and the children alone seemed happy.

I ran into the hospital and the beadle hurried after me. I wanted to go up into the ward where the Little God had been lying and to ask the chief nurse, 'How's the Little God? Is he any better? I am here, ready to do everything that's necessary.' But he drew me to the chamber of the dead. Before I entered it he held me and tore the lapel of my jacket and then took out of his pocket a small black skull-cap, which he put on my head. I knew that he would do everything that was necessary—that he would conclude the business with the *Chevra Kedisha*, decide on the site of the grave, and handle all the other funeral arrangements. He was the only solid basis in the void and formlessness, around which the darkness was in flux on the face of the deep.

When I went into the chamber of the dead I saw the long body of the Little God, enshrouded in white sheets, stretched out full length on the floor. My tremulousness vanished completely and one great wish took hold of me—to run out and to escape from the place as quickly as possible. Most of the candles around the corpse had already burned out and only a few were still flickering in the stench of the room. In a corner an old blind man was sitting and reciting psalms— a task which had occupied him for the last forty years, ever since he had been hired for the job. The beadle put an end to the silence in which he had been immersed since he knocked on my window at ten to seven, leaned toward me, whispered in Yiddish, 'A *finever*', and then went out to collect the ten men needed for the *minyan*.

'That means that this *minyan* is going to cost me a fiver,' I said to myself. 'Half a pound each.' I went to the corpse, lifted the white sheet a bit, and saw a thin cold arm on which death had spread a greenish yellowness. 'That's forbidden, that's forbidden,' somebody suddenly called out. The man who had stuck his red face into the chamber nodded at me as if I were a naughty child. I hurriedly covered the arm and went outside.

'You,' he said to me, 'are you a relative of the deceased?'

I did not know how to answer him satisfactorily so I started to fumble in my pockets, looking for my cigarettes. The man stuck the red, swollen fingers of his left hand into the packet and nimbly extracted a cigarette. He jingled the collection box which he was holding in his right hand. I remembered him from my early childhood. He always followed funerals with a sad face, rattling his collection box and calling out, 'Charity wards off death, charity wards off death.' It was said that he owned two buildings in the Mahne-Yehudah quarter and one in Nachlat Shivah. His daughter was a nice buxom girl and all the boys used to talk about her reverently till she married an English policeman and went with him to England when the British left the country.

'I was a lodger in his apartment,' I answered him.

'Ah?' He threw out the syllable like a question mark while he lit the cigarette.

'I lived in his apartment,' I repeated.

'He was a good man,' he declared, after blowing out a cloud of smoke through the nostrils of his big red nose, which was pitted like a sieve. He looked around and, seeing no one nearby, put his face close to mine and whispered confidentially, as if we were two old friends, 'A good man, but a bit touched . . . too much thinking.'

Only after the second cigarette did it occur to me to put a coin in his box. Since the coin was safely in the box, and since none of the deceased's family—or anyone else, for that matter—had come, as people say, to pay their last respects, and since the *minyan* of beggars whom the beadle had gathered were the only people in sight, he fluttered his eyes, made a curtsy in the French fashion of all things, and went on his way. After he had gone one of the *minyan* of beggars approached me, inspected me from head to foot, and finally murmured sympathetically and compassionately, 'A small family, eh?' Then as a consolatory afterthought of a more philosophical order he added, 'It is not good that a man should be alone.'

'I am not one of his family,' I answered him. 'I live in his apartment. He had a two-room apartment and I live in one of the rooms.'

'So . . . so . . . And what did he die of?'

'A brick fell on his head,' I told him.

He rolled his eyes in wonder, as if I had told a joke in bad taste, turned his back, and rejoined his companions.

'It really is like an odd joke,' I reflected. 'He was walking along harmlessly enough past the scaffolding of a seven-storey apartment house under construction when a brick fell on his head; he instantly lost consciousness and died two days later. And that's that. All over. And indeed he once told me in a moment of confidence that his whole life was nothing but a joke. "All in all," he said, "I am nothing but a practical joke of somebody else's making." '

And who was that somebody? He certainly meant his Little God. He had a sort of theory that God was small. Once he had gathered a couple of students around him and for two hours he had expounded his views about the divinity—ever since, he had been nicknamed 'The Little God'. In his big, lucid, somewhat childish handwriting he had even left a paper entitled 'Reflections on Man's Concept of the Dimensions of God in Time and Space'. Several days before the brick fell on his head he had started to translate the paper into English. 'It seems', he told me, 'that not until the gentiles accept my views will Jewish scholars listen to my system.' He was a physicist by profession, and until he dedicated himself to his idea about the dimensions of God, which are, according to him, much smaller than we can imagine— indeed so small that our minds cannot grasp their smallness—up to the time he sank into big thoughts about the smallness of God, he was, one might say, like everybody else, or at any rate like any other man of science. He was tall and thin and stooped, his eyes were grey and slanting, deep wrinkles ran down from his longish nose to the sides of his mouth, flaxen tufts flapped from the sides of his bald head, and all in all he looked as if he were constantly apologizing for his long figure and big arms and awkward hands and, in general, for occu- pying space in the world. One could not tell how old he was. Sometimes, when he smiled, he looked like a giant baby. But usually he did not smile and sadness flowed down his face, an ancient sadness.

It's strange that he was happy—when he wasn't sad. He would sing and even dance and drink heavily—but it's perhaps as well not to go into the details of his behaviour when he was happy, for at the end of each attack of happiness he would fall into the hands of a Greek prostitute and talk lovingly to her, in Yiddish of all languages, till he fell asleep on her lap. On such occasions he would also wave his fists and shout at the top of his voice that he hated humanity. 'I love men, and better still, women, but humanity, dear God, I hate humanity. I can love Yankil or Shmeril or Beril'—he would hit the table with his fists—'but giwald, geschrien, I hate Jewry.' Even when he sobered up and was in control of all his faculties he would avoid any human contact, and things came to such a pass that he was often attacked by a fear of crowds. Then he would shut himself up in his room, close the shutters, draw the curtains, plug his ears with cotton wool, and cringe on the edge of his couch, praying silently to his Little God to save him from humanity.

When I came to rent the room in his apartment about a year before he died, his condition was already pretty serious—or so his colleagues and other people who knew him thought. He himself was sure he had climbed as high, in spirit, as a man could. By then he had already abandoned his work in the Physics Department 'in order to dedicate myself to philosophical contemplation,' as he said. His colleagues nodded sagely and talked of the 'attacks' which more and more often laid him low. For a long time he had gone out of his way to avoid people and disdained to enter buses or restaurants or cinemas. Apart from going out in the early morning or late in the evening to do his daily shopping, with which even he could not dispense, apart from these excursions which he undertook as if compelled by the devil, he would sit shut up in his room sailing on his thoughts about the concepts of God. He would sit for two or three weeks, or sometimes even for a month, until happiness started to ferment in his limbs. The hummings and whisperings that emanated from his room at an ever increasing tempo gave me advance notice of such happiness. Like a volcano on the verge of bursting out, he would walk up and down in his room, turn on the radio, open the curtains, and lift the shutters to let in the sunshine and noise of the street like an overflowing river. Finally he would wash, shave his month-old beard, put on a white shirt, don his Sabbath suit—the only one in his cupboard—and run out like a prisoner escaping from jail.

During the last year of his life his whole income consisted only of the rent he received from me and of a small allowance made to him by one of the Zionist institutions. Throughout the time I lived in his apartment he only once told me about his life in the past and about his family—and that was when he was brought home by the fat, ageing Greek prostitute. I learned from him that his father had been a Zionist of some standing, important enough to have a settlement named after him. He had two sisters, one a communist who had married a gentile and the other, who had remained single, a doctor who had specialized in tropical diseases and had gone to care for the natives in Central Africa. Had he told more, perhaps I could have found some clue to the way of life of the daughters of the Zionist who had not had the good fortune to immigrate to Israel and who had been murdered by the Nazis, but the Little God was not communicative and I had to content myself with what he divulged.

And so during the last months of his life he was driven from seclusion to the most dubious and strange friendships, and from elation and belief in his original thinking, a belief bordering on a strange boastfulness, to the depths of despair. Then one night, some two weeks before that brick fell on his head, he gave me a terrible fright.

From eleven o'clock that night a wintry cold had prevailed over the sleeping world and a silent wind had brought layers of low cloud which completely covered the sky and the sickle of moon. I had closed the window and made my bed. I had fallen asleep a few minutes after I had gone to bed and would have gone on sleeping happily till morning had I not been woken by a muffled cry of fright which set my nerves on edge.

The Little God was groaning in his room like a wounded jackal. Then suddenly he came and knocked faintly at my door. I braced myself, overcame my fear, and even remembered to arm myself with a ruler before I slowly opened the door, ready to strike him over the head if he jumped at me in his madness. His long body was clad in pyjamas which were too short for him and his feet were bare. As soon as he appeared in all his shame and awkwardness I let the ruler drop and pushed it under the bed with my foot. He stood in the middle of my room like a man fleeing a catastrophe and urgently in need of shelter who suddenly finds that the anticipated shelter is illusory.

'Excuse me,' he muttered, 'please excuse me. I shouted in my sleep. I must have given you a real fright. I myself was frightened to death— otherwise I would not have shouted. But now it's all over and I must go back to bed. Yes, I must go back to sleep, but really I'd prefer to remain here with you a little while, a little longer, for I'm afraid to go back to sleep. These nightmares are worse than hell. Perhaps you'd like to come to my room and I'll make you tea? Till I calm down?'

'No,' I said to him, 'I'll make some tea. You just sit down here.'

He obeyed me and sat down on a chair. He knew he could not have made tea, for his hands were still trembling. He held his cup with both hands but it shook and tea dripped onto his hands and knees.

In his dream his father had come to him. He was wearing only a sleeveless vest and short underpants, and the Little God burst out laughing and his heart wept and his teeth chattered and his eyes shed tears. 'How is it, Father,' he said, and he pointed at him, but his laughter and the chattering of his teeth choked his voice, 'how is it that all of a sudden you decided to put on short underpants like a modern dandy? All your life you have worn long woollen underpants because of the chronic cold you have had since your youth.'

'Here in *Eretz Israel*,' said his father, 'one does not need woollen underpants.'

'What are you saying, Father? This is not *Eretz Israel*! Look, the fields around us are covered with snow and the trees are standing naked and a frosty wind penetrates to the marrow.'

'Stuff and nonsense, my boy, you're talking nonsense.'

While the Little God was talking to his father the scene changed to the father's study. A blue *Keren Kayemet* collection box was standing on the table with the carved legs. A map of Palestine, with all the *Keren Kayemet* land coloured green, was hanging on the eastern wall. Opposite the map, on the western wall, the faces of Herzl and Nordau stared down from within their golden frames. When the Little God approached the pictures in order to examine them more closely he was confronted by the faces of his two sisters. The sisters, he saw, looked as they had when they were in their first year at high school. His father went to the table and spread out on it an issue of the *Welt*, the Zionist organ, which grew and grew till it covered the whole table. Then his father sat on the table, crossed his arms over his chest, which was covered only by the thin vest, and said, 'Now tell me what's going on in the world.'

'The world is growing bigger, Father, and God is growing smaller.' His father jerked his head back and laughed heartily in the way he used to laugh when he was in a good humour. Protruding veins twined on his forehead and his belly heaved as he laughed and laughed until tears came to his eyes and his voice choked and one could not tell whether he was laughing or crying.

'God is growing smaller, Father, and now, already, compared to an ant, God looks like a flea compared to an elephant. He is still alive, wriggling and writhing under the weight of the world He created, but it is only a matter of time before His death agonies cease.'

'And how long will it take before He disappears?' asked his father, his face becoming serious.

'Two or three weeks, perhaps less.'

'Then this is the end.'

'Yes, this is the end.'

On hearing this his father jumped off the table and started to knock his head against the map of Israel. He knocked his head and cried out with pain, knocked and cried, and with each knock his body became smaller, and his son knew that only he could save him but his whole body became stiff and numb and he could not move a limb. He froze with cold and fright and saw how his father was becoming smaller and smaller, knocking his head against the wall and vanishing, till nothing remained of him but the reverberations of the knocking.

Translated by H. M. Daleski.

Amalia Kahana-Carmon

BRIDAL VEIL

Kahana-Carmon was born in 1926 on kibbutz Ein Harod and grew up in Tel Aviv. Her first collection of stories, Under One Roof, *appeared in 1966 to great critical acclaim. She has subsequently published three novels, novellas, and short stories, and she has lectured widely. She was writer-in-residence at Tel Aviv University and at the Oxford Centre for Hebrew and Jewish Studies in the United Kingdom. She has avoided political themes, as well as any narrative expansion that assists the reader's orientation. Her stories plunge the reader directly into an unmediated world of subjective feeling. Usually the subjects of her novels and stories are young women facing the problems of growing up and contending with romantic attachments. In a later novel,* With Her on Her Way Home *(1991), she deals with the problems of growing old. Kahana-Carmon's language is carefully shaped and unadorned, but possessing an idiosyncratic subtlety that makes translation difficult.*

Father accompanied her and sat with her on the Egged inter-city bus. Until the journey began. It was the bus before last. Because Father had taken her to the pictures. Now he was impatient. Irritable for some reason.

A group of UN soldiers were getting on the bus. One got on and Father said: 'Looks like Anthony Perkins, that one.' Another one got on. Looks even more like Anthony Perkins, reflected Shoshana but did not say.

For many hours she had waited for Father. An evening in another town. The park. Empty playground. Through branches and leaves, lights: dwellings. Residences, windows. Strangers' homes.

Since the early afternoon she had waited there. The gardeners were still having a rest in the shrubs' shade. Two long-haired vagabond tourists, one with hair like the sun in a poster, equal and matching tongues of flame in a blazing circle, with intense concentration measured and cut in two a single cigarette with a razor blade. Little boys and girls began arriving. Some of the little boys had their hair held to one side by a hair-clip. Some of the girls had tiny toy handbags.

Some little white woollies folded over the arm. Chilly in the evening in the mountain town.

Later on, deaf-mute children were brought to the park. With them two teachers. Or minders. Very young, dressed like sluts.

The minders went and sat on a bench. The mute children invaded the playground, swarming over every seat. Or, blank-eyed, violently spinning roundabouts, making swings and their sitters fly. The nice children scattered, scurried for mothers' or child-minders' laps. The mute children, like pirates, snatched at the vacated seats. Signalling to each other pleasure and delight; voicelessly, with gestures and grotesque faces only. Among them fully grown girls riding the infants' seats of the seesaws, on their faces the expression of mental retardation. One lanky boy, sombre, most obstinate, his shirt torn at the shoulder, kept on disturbing them. Trying to grab their rubber flipflops, rising and falling, while they draw back their feet and kick out at him lazily. Under his chin, in his stomach, his ribs, wherever the seesaw takes them. And whenever he, with his eyes shut, gapes in soundless pain, one can see, his teeth are false.

The park emptied. Soon it will be completely dark. And now it is. The recorded voice of a woman trails past. Clear and vivid as though a singing siren were sitting on the bonnet of the passing car. Silence again. Then the trail of the familiar voice of an announcer, reading the evening news. From a first-floor balcony, across the trunks of the pine trees, once or twice, questions are asked aloud. Of members of a family, settling for the night. Then the vertical slats of the blinds were turned slightly, their backs inwards, their insides outwards, just enough to seal off.

Shoshana took out and started eating the food her mother had given her for the journey. Brown bread. A little smoked mackerel. One or two apricots. A little halva.

A man—an Ashkenazi, bald and pot-bellied in too-wide khaki shorts, once everyone sported clothes like that, with a shabby briefcase, like a middle-aged clerk—went in and out, in and out of the park. Earlier, when he had passed by her, she could still make out the grooved buckle, held in the last hole of his belt. Beads of sweat on his forehead and the front of his bald head. Also his eye, fixed on her sideways, like a rooster's. Fixed on her all the time. Later on, one could hardly make out the features of his haggard face. The darkness deepened more and more. Shoshana made up her mind and went to wait on the pavement, under the street lamp. She was worrying that Father might not find her, as he had told her to wait in the park, in the playground, like all the children. And what if Father should come in through the other gate? What if he went away. But that's how it is. In another town. A strange town.

She stood on the street corner, peering furtively at the section of the main street, there beyond the alley. People were passing there. True, fewer people. But people were passing there. And cars. All along there had been some mistake, it was revealed to her now. She hadn't thought about it, but must have assumed that life outside came to an end when one went to bed, after supper. Except on special occasions. And here's something new, secret: there's the ordinary life of day. And there's the ordinary life of night. Life carries on at night. Differently though. At night everything is different. Houses, people, thoughts.

The bus lingered. Father started to grumble.

Since when do UN soldiers travel by bus, Shoshana reflected. Two were sitting in front. A third one stood over them, chatting.

Ice-blue eyes they had. And though they certainly had broad shoulders, something about them was seemingly narrow. They were as though made of drier stuff. As though we ourselves, our end is to shrink, leaking a spreading puddle. And later on, when all but shrunk to thin skin, to get all wrinkled, to evaporate and be no more. But they, their end is to crumble, turn into dust, and be no more. They were all similar, but each in his own way. Like guavas. They all taste good, but each tastes also slightly different, giving its own interpretation of the taste of the guava.

A man carrying a high cardboard box entered. On it, in big red scrawl, like a finger smear, it read: Parts—Incubators. He blocked the exit with it.

Again Shoshana was reminded of the story called 'Excerpt' in the 'Paths Reader Part Four'. A chick hatches out of its egg in the incubator. To whom will the chick turn its inborn human need for attachment? Will it turn to the electric incubator, it was written there, will it turn to the poulterer who breeds it in order to have it transferred to the electric poultry abattoir, to whom? The inborn human need, it was written. The human need of he who is not human.

From one of the seats could be heard the voice of a young man, of Oriental Sephardi stock, excited, even though whispering. 'Give it to me, let me be the secretary of the committee. No, not because you like me. Because I've got the hang of it. And you'll see if, within four years, I don't turn this place into a political springboard. First rate. If each one of them wouldn't need me, look for me, come to me for favours. Here's Ben-Dov. Who's Ben-Dov. Alright, he's head

and shoulders above. Today. Fifteen, twenty years ago, what was he.
A seaman. And today, you can see for yourself. And I, I'll get you the
whole of the construction lot going. Think of it: power. True, true.
But Anaby got demolished politically because he doesn't have the makings of a public figure. Just not a strong man. True, he was seen all
over the place. Ran around. But he doesn't have the makings. It's a
question of having an influence over people. You have to know how
to get them going. How? Work at the source. Besides, you know that
with me you'll get the works. Balance sheets, reports, deals, the lot.'
    The bus lingered on. Father got up, parted abruptly, and left.
    As soon as Father got off the bus, the UN soldier who had been
standing up came over and sat down beside her. Perched on his seat,
craning his neck forward, he picked up his chatting with his friends.
    Freckled, young, good-looking. But the light went out and he
stopped talking. Shoshana wondered about his sitting next to her.
Moreover, she had noticed that before he sat down he had considered
her, then the empty seat across the aisle, and making a quick decision
chose to sit by her. As soon as he sat down, it was as if a prize had
fallen her way.
    Even in the dark it was possible to see, his lips were finely drawn.
The fleshy hand, grasping the rail of the seat before them, firm. And
he's one of the boys. Very much one of the boys.
    The bus started moving off. Outside, a tall woman passed, crossed
its path walking very upright, and the driver cried out furiously: 'Greta
Garbo.' Shoshana peeped at the UN soldier, saw him smiling in surprise. Unaware, she too smiled inwardly. But now the strap of the
flight bag—the blue El Al bag, with Father's laundry, that Father had
placed on the shelf above—slipped down, swung about and almost
touched the beret of the soldier sitting in front of her. Meaning to
put it back, Shoshana struggled to get up, tried to stand on the curve
of the wheel at her feet. Trouble: the UN soldier was sitting on the
edge of her skirt, Mother's wide skirt given for the trip. As the bus
swerved to leave its bay by the platform side, Shoshana slipped, found
herself in the dark waist up across a hard and alien knee.
    'Sorry,' she cried out in Hebrew, reaching out with both hands, as
if for a raft, to the rail of the seat in front, whilst the embarrassed
UN soldier was saying in English: 'I'm sorry. I'm sorry. It's alright.'
    Trying to stand up again, the UN soldier still sitting on the edge
of her skirt, the bus swerving the other way, she flew to his knees
once more. This time he hastened to help, to raise her like a package in order to put her back in her place. But with the bus jolting

and straightening itself, he put his hand in the wrong place. 'Sorry,' he let go at once, alarmed. Straining to rise, Shoshana said: 'It's alright,' echoing his English, 'sorry.' And she tried a word from her school-days: 'Dress.' 'Dress? Oh, dress. I'm sorry,' his alarm increased and he rose. 'It's alright,' she mouthed in shame. The shadow of a smile was wiped off her face now. With it, her self-assurance.

Once, when Father still worked in Tiberias. A waitress, with a wink to her friend, volunteered to display her skills in making small talk. She announced, she'd ask a soldier if he was married. She couldn't find the word. Then she did: 'You, papa?' 'Perhaps I am and I don't know it,' the soldier laughed, very much taken by surprise. All the waitresses shrieked. What did he mean? Married or single. He invited the waitress to go out with him. 'Where to?' she asked. 'Dancing cheek-to-cheek,' translated Father, for all to hear the soldier's reply. What did the soldier mean. 'UN soldiers, they are like sailors of a ship,' Father had explained to her at the time. Father had a song in French, and once on a weekend, he translated it for us like this, with feeling: 'I see the harbour lights / Only they told me we were parting / The same old harbour lights / That once brought you to me / I watch the harbour lights / How could I help if tears were starting / Goodbye to tender nights / Beside the silvery sea.' And throatily: 'I long to hold you near / And kiss you just once more / But you are on that ship / And I am on the shore.' And again, as before: 'Now I know lonely nights / For all the while my heart is whispering / Some other har-bour lights / Will steal your love from me.'

Along the nocturnal road were trees, nodding heads like people. The light of the speeding bus falls on them, withdraws from them. And the vapour-veiled moon crescent is getting blurred. But why is her throat so dry? Shoshana gazed through the window for a long time.

Once, while she was travelling home with Father's laundry, a nice young man, maybe a student at the Polytechnic, sat next to her read-ing a paperback. Entitled *It Was Murder By Moonlight*. When it got dark, the young man put the book in his pocket and turned to touch her nape so artfully that until they reached the junction she couldn't make out whether he had, or she had imagined it. Then as now, at the first moment, the same panic. A blind panic. Like a wild animal's. Only this time there was no room for error. The UN soldier beside her is, he is, pressing his elbow on to her arm. This time she did not rise to leave her place and did not move to another seat. She sat on like a statue. Doing nothing. Gazing through the window.

Now, with his other hand he is seeking hers. And just as it's not for exercising their throat-muscles that people utter sounds. But for saying things with words, the things the matter. So it is here. He is seeking to say something, only in another way. What is he asking. Yes, I know. But it's not clear what he is asking right now about it. And what does he expect from her. Hard to know, let alone when one is confused.

She stole a look at him. And learned that he was already sitting very close, much closer than she had realized. Deadpan faced, as though he had nothing to do with her. Passing his arm behind to surround her. UN soldiers in front of us, UN soldiers behind us. How does he have the nerve?

At the junction the lights came on. The UN soldier hurried, moved away abruptly.

Cheerful girl-soldiers boarded the bus. 'Smadar, Smadar,' they cried out to another who was still outside, buying something from a young vendor. Good-looking, grown-up, laughing. Here goes, reflected Shoshana, this will put an end to me. Besides, there's no escape: I know what he must think of me now—she didn't dare look his way. As he sat staring straight ahead, so did she. As he folds his arms, so she folds hers.

The girl-soldiers spread out boisterously over the vacant seats. The ticket inspector got on. And the UN soldier beside her smiled to himself, privately, tilting his chin a little, as a UN soldier seated distantly threw a side-comment in a loud voice, probably a joke. Shoshana took out the two tickets from the pocket of her plaid blouse. The return ticket and the late-night surcharge one, holding them both in her hand.

And she saw: the UN soldier who was sitting still grinned at her. As if asking permission. Before she could know what he wanted, he took her tickets from her hand. Holding them with his ticket, entirely together, he handed them to the inspector.

As ever and always she, the eldest daughter, has had to manage on her own—what is it that passed through her now, piercing through the bark, penetrating the sapwood, making it ooze. She felt herself shattered, knowing nothing.

Returning her tickets, he attempted to strike up a conversation with her:

'Israel?' he pointed at her.

Shoshana nodded.

He pointed at himself:

'Riff-raff.'

Where is Riffraffia? she tried to remember.

'Canada,' he smiled as if in confirmation, raising a shoulder to push his ticket into his pocket.

All she knew about Canada, she reflected, was what Father had once told them. A Canadian walked into the hotel kitchen. He sat down and said, to Father and the rest of the assistant chefs, that where he came from, normally, they entertained in the parlour. But a specially welcome guest was always received in the kitchen. This was what the man had said, and dropped off. Totally drunk. Only later they found out he'd fallen asleep on the spice mill, which they had been looking for all that time.

The UN soldier pointed backwards with his thumb. To know whether she is a resident of the city they had left. Shoshana pointed ahead. The city they were heading for. He got it and laughed, as if by this she had proved herself sharp-witted. He pointed back again, shaking his other hand, as if enquiring. Shoshana pointed at Father's bag. 'Papa,' she said. The UN soldier's face became respectful, and Shoshana felt pleased. Very.

Then she remembered. Tried her hand at making small talk:

'You. Papa?'

He didn't understand. But pointed at himself, and smiled: 'No papa. No mama. No brother. No sister. No wife. No children. Nobody,' he said. And he took off his beret. Put it on her bag. On her bag he put it. Now, with his red hair, he was better looking sevenfold. And as soon as the light went out he returned to her. Once the bus danced. And he, using the inside of his arm which was on her back, pressed it on her hard then, deliberately. As if to protect her, to spare her the bumps.

In the vicinity of the city boundaries, but a good way from the station yet, the road was blocked with buses and cars. 'A traffic jam?' people said, 'an accident?'

For a long time they waited there. More cars drove up, stopped. People began to get off the bus. Got tired and boarded it again. A man wearing the bus company hat appeared. A real veteran. There had been a road accident, he explained. They would have to proceed on foot. Passengers going further would be provided with transport. Saying this, he left. The driver translated it into English, and picking up his satchel indifferently, left too.

The UN soldier got Shoshana's bag down from the shelf, but

people were shoving between them. Especially one woman, her fleshy bulk quivering, who continued her conversation whilst alighting, as if incapable of stopping: 'Twenty years later I saw her, the one he left me for,' it was unbelievable that she was saying. 'Quite my look-alike. And he did the same thing to her too. The bastard, the worthless bastard,' she said. 'How do I know? He did it with me,' she spoke ordinarily. The ordinary life of night.

Almost the last one to get off, down there waiting for her was the UN soldier.

'Goodbye,' Shoshana was glad to have found the word. She took her bag from him, whilst here too was a novelty: the language not her own language in her mouth. A man-made, contrived automaton. Look, as if at the press of a button it suddenly works, alive, performing: another secret new thing is revealed. Suddenly the world is full of questions and surprises. Meanwhile, she was overhearing a passing Israeli youth, who, casting a glance at the UN soldier, was saying about him in Hebrew: 'Some body.' And it was as if it were she who had been paid a compliment.

The UN soldier did not go. He was standing, hands in the belt of his narrow trousers, and waiting. Shoshana pointed at his friends, the UN soldiers who were walking away, after they had set themselves apart and crossed to the other side of the road. He shook his head signalling no, and took her bag from her. Smiling and saying, 'Little girl', he pointed at his watch. Meaning, it's late and it won't do for little girls to be on their own.

They were the last ones there now. And as she turned to follow the crowd, which was making its way along the stalled vehicles, he stopped her. Catching her lightly by the edge of her sleeve. Tacitly, as if conspiring. Now that she had stopped with him, Shoshana felt that he had her consigned to his charge entirely. Under his patronage. Now she was his. All she had to do was to rely on him. For his part, his contribution or guarantees, were in evidence by the quality of the skin of his arms, for instance. Fine, sand-coloured, strewn with freckles and as if brave, very appropriate. Or his watch, his square wrist-watch, this too was sort of appropriate, and by that an attested proof. Also his vest, like a white gym shirt, peeping out of his open collar. And so forth.

When there were no more passengers, the UN soldier pulled her to him, moved her to his other side, and led her with him down a path—many paths were here—leading toward the city. All went over there, whereas they go on a way that is theirs only. That too was right. She joined him unquestioningly.

From time to time he stopped her, hugged and fondled her. Once, kneading and kneading her, he said into her hair, slowly, so she would understand, 'You'll see. I'll be good,' and kissed her on her hair.

The words astounded her. Another secret new thing is revealed: this is what the grown-up girls are privileged to. Canadian girls. Blissful girls. Mysterious, haughty, and deserving. Is it they who got them instructed, trained them. On evenings of paths through boughs in leaf, and lanterns hanging from branches amid twigs, foliage and tendrils. His chest in uniform, to which he held her when he spoke, belonged there too. His surprising chest, close, straight, all vacant and free; and how is this, a safe haven. But what had he said. As though she had been asked, in astonishment: 'All these years, and you didn't know? Did you really not know that there is, there is a Mediterranean Sea in the east as well?' Of course. A sea, and a beach. And why the scary relief. 'I didn't know,' I answer, and already am not sure: did or didn't I. But what did he say? Did he propose to her? A little girl. Does it mean he intends to wait until she grows up? To take her with him, in the fullness of time, to Riffraffia? Run along, days, run. The only thing unclear yet is how, without ever knowing me, he recognized immediately that I am Shoshana more than any Shoshana, and that is why I should be singled out.

In the floral skirt too large for her, made to fit her waist with a safety pin. In the plaid blouse too short for her, the sleeve not quite hiding the slipping bra strap. The same Shoshana. And another Shoshana. Mysterious, deserving. Beautiful girls, beautiful women, like beautiful fans. Always, whenever she perceives the beautiful, it's a pleasure. As if she partakes of their beauty, from a distance. And now, there she is, a proper partner herself, deserving. And at a threshold.

Like then, in the dream? I stand in a large public square. Daylight fades. A very beautiful African lady, an ambassador's wife, stands spellbound before one of the flower beds in the square. A corner of tall, giant funnel-like arum lilies. Gaudy. Striped, streaked and spotted, in supernatural hues. 'Harare-Horse,' she says in a low voice, 'Harare-Horse.' I too fall under the spell. 'Harare-Horse?' I ask. 'Harare-Horse: the piles of sweets in our marketplaces.' And someone comes to call her. To the airliner. To the night sky. Already studded with stars like jasmine flowers. Run along, days, run.

Holding her hand in his all the time, at the end of the path they came to a very tall wire-mesh fence. Looking new. They turned back. Over and over, at the end of every path, was the same fence. Impossible to walk along it. Tall thorns, impassably tangled. No choice, the fence has to be climbed.

He threw her bundle over to the other side. Helped her climb the fence. Then joined her. He swung his legs over to the other side and jumped down. But she, she couldn't get down! Putting up his arms to catch her, she let herself go, fell into his arms.

Having received her, why didn't he allow her to go, steadily enfolding all of her, tightly against him? And why has he changed so? Why don't they keep on walking? And why is she suddenly again in the panic of a wild animal—she tried to free herself. But how very strong men are, it dawned on her. And he breathes as if he has a fit of shivers. Why did he abruptly fling her to the ground. And isn't it wrong to force down a person's head backward into the dust. Wriggling to set herself free, half of her trapped between his legs, and he keeps her legs clasped together, her top half locked in one of his arms, he only sprawled on her, hard, in his clothes and shoes, that's all, with his other hand, forcing her face towards his, seeking her mouth, as if looking for closeness and consent. Himself, giving, offering, donating his only pair of lips, the ones that matter to him, it must be, of lips that seem so well cared for. Yet, at the same time, he cruelly prevents her from freeing herself, as if forbidding her to make a move, what sort of a plan is all this, and he is sighing and is so worked up. Suddenly he lets go. Everything isn't clear, isn't good. Haven't we been friends? And I, for his sake, I am no longer of Israel. I am of the UN.

Sitting beside her he asked, slowly, so she could make it out:
'How old are you?'
Shoshana showed with her fingers: thirteen.
He laughed. Buried his face in her shoulder.
'God,' he said, laughing, 'forgive me.' Now he tapped the top of his head, meaning: he had thought. To explain, he stuck out his fist three times, opening and closing it, and added fingers, meaning: eighteen. He twisted his left hand, meaning: maybe. He stuck out his fist again and added with his right hand fingers, meaning: seventeen. Stuck out again and with one finger: sixteen. Thought it over, and only stuck out: fifteen. Shoshana was watching it all earnestly, patiently, trying to comprehend the sign language. But now he laughed, tapped her nose with his finger. Shoshana raised her head towards him, and he hugged her with one arm, drawing her to him. The private fair skin

of his arms is nevertheless very appropriate. His chest in uniform, a
safe haven.

'Mosquitoes,' he said. Of course, mosquitoes. He patted his back
pocket, as if to check, brought out a crushed packet of foreign cigarettes.
And matches, their heads a lighter colour than their bodies, attached
in rows to a small book. He lit a cigarette. He pointed to the cigarette
smoke and clarified: 'The mosquitoes,' making with his palm as if he
is dispersing them. Smoke drives mosquitoes away, she learnt. He's a
learned man.

He kept on smoking. Looking ahead. Turned and offered her the
cigarette. Shoshana took the cigarette. He laughed and corrected her
hold of the cigarette, encouraging her to smoke. But Shoshana gave
him the cigarette back. And so, making a move to lean on her fore-
arm, she gave out a small cry: she had laid the inside of her wrist on
a piece of glass, and cut herself. She searched, picked up the piece of
glass, clear glass of a bottle neck. He took it from her hand, hurled
it away. 'Let me,' he asked to see the cut.

Shoshana hesitated. Put her hand behind her back, smiling at him
shamefully. He resumed smoking, looking ahead. Shoshana brought
out her hurt hand gingerly, sucked it covertly. He saw, laughed. Turning
to her, he took the whole arm in his free hand. Could see nothing in
the dark. Pressed her arm as if promising, and returned it to her.
Having finished his cigarette, he stuck the butt in the ground. Rose
up, almost without using his hands, she noticed. Went to fetch her
bag, slinging it effortlessly over his shoulder.

He came over and pulled her up. 'Little girl,' he said tapping his
watch smiling.

Shoshana rose up, yielding. He said something, speaking slowly, so
she could make it out. And she couldn't. He repeated it, again and
again, and she couldn't make it out. 'Never mind,' he laughed lightly.

Now houses could be picked out clearly. Everything seemingly colour-
less. And the street lamps' lights over there going out all by themselves. Is it so that, in an ordered way, day after day, the sky is rinsed
white by the steadily increasing pure light, without hindrance, simply
and in silence day slips out of night? A neat, uncomplicated solution.
So very right. All the earth is full of heaven's glory. No need for witnesses. But the eyes see. Raising his hand, the UN soldier wiped off
dust from each of her eyebrows with his thumb. In her heart it was
as if he had sworn her in.

They were walking between the road and the line of trees along it. To the north-east, among the trees and across the flat roofs of the houses, she saw a reddening mark overlaying a suggestion of blue. And the clouds of reverence. The dwarfed cylinders of the solar tanks and their sloping panels, the ladders and spindly matchsticks of the television aerials, all blacker than black, against the background of incandescent sea, gradually igniting. It is of the revelations made visible, an inheritance in the possession of the sworn in, the initiated ones, to whom the mysteries of the world are everyday affairs.

Earlier, when they were looking for the way, they heard a gang of boys passing far away. Probably trainees at the vocational school. One was strumming the guitar, others singing indistinctly. She remembered that it had been the last day of school. The UN soldier even did a 'Bang-bang' in the direction of the sounds, as if holding a rifle in his hands. Now, in the light of daybreak, the boys were seen coming back. A reminiscence of colours: tight trousers, reminiscent of light blue; a belt, reminiscent of stripes of black and red; a shirt, reminiscent of yellow. Still singing, stopping to sniff each other's mouths, they were crossing the road, marching down towards the houses: the time is four o'clock in the morning, they'll wake up the whole street. 'I have no idea what I wrote in the exam. But what I wrote was the right thing.'

The UN soldier turned quickly, fixed her nimbly to one of the eucalyptus trees. Leaning against the tree with his arms held above her, he stood hiding her. She was astonished. By herself, it would never have occurred to her. She attempted to say something, but he put his hand promptly over her mouth, and she was breathing the fresh pungent tobacco smell on his fingers. Then he lowered his gaze to her, smiling amiably. UN-Soldier!—her heart clung to him. UN-Soldier!— thus she stood watching him all the time, her head tilted up to him, her eyes staring wide-open at him, his hand on her mouth. Until, when the boys were not there anymore, and bending his knees, he held her by the shoulders, jokingly attached his cheek to hers. Remembering, he rubbed his hand against his cheek to show the reddish stubble which had started growing, grimaced to make her laugh, and released her. 'Little girl, good girl,' he said.

UN-Soldier!—Shoshana plucked up courage, put out her hands, took hold of his waist, did not wish to walk on. Then joined him, continuing to walk.

Free of any dependence known to me. Unknown dependences have lent here character and grit, without which you are not a person— he strides as though without moving his head. Regards everything before him as though all, and this means all, is equal and the same. And speech is not a must for him, with or without it will do. This, you can tell, is his natural state. There's a kind of admirable quality here, like a sort of luxury. Serenity arising from a reservoir of strength— Shoshana tried to match her footsteps to his. And all the while his face, arms, uniform—all of his familiar self, is both old and new in the new light.

A lorry, still nocturnal, its lights still on, passed them with a great clatter. Full of Arab labourers, stooping. On the other side of the road, the football pitch. The two goals, and the hard ground cleared of scrub, surrounded by a stand consisting of two rows of stadium benches, one above the other, like scaffolding. And a bus stop. The billboard. From here, whoever is not in the know couldn't have guessed that the dark rectangle on the billboard is the big illustrated poster of the Indian film. The girl has a red pea in her forehead, above her nose, and an amber necklace; the beads thick and squarish. While the man has an inclination towards a double chin.

The UN soldier scanned the highway, looking lost, passing his palm over his ruddy neck. Inspecting her as if he's uncertain of her ability to lead the way. Perhaps he thought she kept looking at him all the time with great interest, waiting for his resourcefulness. But she keeps looking on at him as she walks only because she cannot take her eyes off him: I could not imagine him with a moustache, for instance, or with sideburns, or a beard. Now, that he is need of a shave, I can. Or, here. Despite the peeling nose owing to this country's sun, here are the azure shards of ice-mountains. Shards from the faraway country where his home is, the keepsake embedded in his face instead of eyes. His face, permanently wearing the sudden foreignness that a woman of ours has on her face, for a fleeting moment, when she first puts on her earrings. Like a foreign perfume. A foreignness that has a touch of class. Like fastidious sinisterness. Sinisterness that is the product of your own imagination, the product of your own effacement. Or his colours, for example. The colours of another earth, different—as far as the eye can see, other fields, different. With different electricity pylons, vanishing into them. With different tractors and combine harvesters, looking minute when they pass through them. The men who drive them wear different overalls. Perhaps dungarees? Are their hats straw hats frayed at the edges? In the heat of the day in the field they all drink whisky out of jerry-cans.

Shoshana stopped. To shake a bit of gravel out of her shoe. She tried to indicate that she was stopping.

He halted, smiled comprehension.

Shoshana resumed walking. The shards of faraway, they come complete with an arrangement of golden lashes. The colours, all the colours of a different, freckled earth, in the land across the ice-mountains: if you break with your axe a little ice in the valley, you'd be able to draw out with a hook a fish that is about man-size. And look, lo and behold, they have arrived, fallen right here. Striding right here. With our very own football pitch behind us, and in front, our neighbourhood. All the birds in the boughs of the eucalyptus trees welcome the future sunrise in concert, but I know: it is also in our honour, also in our honour. Is there anyone like you in the world, that like you is just right?

And here's the neighbourhood.

A cat could be seen passing from a house roof to a shed roof. All the houses are deep in slumber. The end of the wooden cart is showing, laden high with watermelons. Of the first ones this season. But it seems, none of the Ezra brothers is asleep on the mattress over there. Even the hanging hurricane lamp is out of sight. In a slow death, devoid of any noble fortitude, the two abandoned houses crumble away. Cracks on the wall, the yards are thorn bushes. They say, among their foundations' low cement stilts there are snakes.

At the back fence of the house she stopped. Pointed at the house. But the UN soldier bent back his thumb and stucked it pointedly between his teeth, as he tilted his head backward, demonstrating to Shoshana, with eyes surveying around, that he wished to drink. She understood. Pointed at the tap beside the dustbin.

He rode the fence, then was over. The shoulder-line straight as a coat-hanger, the big shirt hanging down his back like a scarecrow's, he turned on the tap. Leaned forward above it, legs apart, and drank. A cat, probably lurking there the whole time, suddenly made up its mind, leapt out of the dustbin and fled to the neighbours' yard, hid behind the old icebox that lies there, its side on the ground. The UN soldier wiped his mouth with his wrist.

He came. Stood before her. Lifted the bag, hung it over her shoulder laughing, saying something in his language. Shoshana did not leave. He looked at her. Shoshana did not leave. With his finger he moved his beret from the back of his head too far forward. From his forehead too far back. As if mimicking someone, good-naturedly. Shoshana did not leave.

He started rummaging in his pockets. Took out the Egged bus ticket. Examined the Egged bus ticket. Folded it correctly, and folded it up again. Put the ticket in her palm and closed her fingers over it, grouping them together into a brown fist enclosing the ticket. 'Souvenir,' he smiled. Shoshana did not leave. He stroked her cheek lightly, and left. Turned once, waved to her with his hand, and left.

When he could no longer be seen, Shoshana looked at the ticket. I don't know his name, it occurred to her now. He doesn't know mine, she looked at the ticket. Buried her face in the ticket. Then steadied the burden on her shoulder.

She entered home on tiptoe. Skirting the baby pram at the inside of the front door, she passed her sleeping brothers. Solemn, to the point of fear-inspiring, as if they are crucified. She changed in silence. And cautiously got into bed, together with her little sister, who was snuggled all curled up, and with her arms as if sheltering her head and face.

Her mother, her hair dishevelled, the eternal red dressing-gown now thrown hastily over her nightgown, came in from the other room. Pushing aside the yellow striped curtain, she stood in the entrance: Shoshana looked her mother in the eye. Her mother looked Shoshana in the eye. Didn't say anything. Left. And Shoshana could hear how her mother was suppressing her sobs, over there, in her creaking bed in the other room. Then how the baby woke up. And fell asleep again.

She wiped one last dust-grain, or two, off her thin eyebrows, off the base of her neck. From behind her earlobe. Rosita is my name, I would have told him. A name to conjure with in the world. My birthright name, until it was changed into a Hebrew one by Teacher Hephzibah's decree. Little-Girl my name will now remain. I've indeed shrunk to a small-finger size, yet have grown simultaneously by an arm's length: surrounded by the familiar, that at the same time is different. As with the girl Alice, in the show they sent us. For the adoption ceremony, when they adopted us on 'Love Thy Brother as Thyself Day'. There were all those misfortunes. The loudspeakers went dead on us. Then the lorry broke down. And the guests fated to wait were irate: they were given tea, said thank you, but hardly touched it. Teacher Hephzibah even organized us, the 'Clowns' choir, to start a sing-song, for them to join in. None of them did. Zvi performed for them his 'Dancing with The Lady Zvia' dance. In a lady's hat, a borrowed dress, a handbag and unshaven cheeks, he danced in ballroom style, embracing and stroking his imaginary partner. But some nervous ones whispered amongst themselves all the time: lorry—tow vehicle—a disgrace. Who's interested in these ones? Go on Mama, go on washing the laundry. Maybe in two weeks time, maybe in three:

over there, where all of them are good-looking, all are kind-hearted, all loving, in their dashing greenish fatigues, in the barracks yard, in front of the grey pillared arches, taking pleasure and in no hurry, all of them will be watering with buckets, scrubbing or combing, each his own pet horse. One by one they'll stand still, their work at a halt. They'll be restored into motion again as I'll go on, passing along the fence, set on searching. 'Hail to my cousin / All ruddy and fair / Is he doing well / Our King David?': the last in the row he'll be. Doing his work. Lovingly. Unaware. There I shall stand. Shall wait. Until he sees me. Recognized me. He will put down his brush. Will come out to me. Bring me in. And everyone will laugh, but be glad, the Regiment's Sweetheart. In two weeks time perhaps, perhaps in three, on an Egged inter-city bus. With a blue El Al bag. To my destiny.

'But my name is Little-Girl / The Regiment's Sweetheart / And UN-Soldier is thy name / I see the harbour lights... ' And maybe, even in another twenty years. And even if I see those for whom they'd give me up. Those will be quite my look-alike. And they will be cheated on too. How will I know? for they will cheat on them with me!—she buried her face in the bus ticket. With a sinking heart. Sensing herself as one who is brought to court, and at the end the clerks hand him a formidable paper to sign. And he signs. Among other things, also with a touch of satisfaction. A satisfaction which is not unlike a destruction wish, at once alluring and frightening. But the chick hatching out of its egg in the incubator, the one with problems, what about the chick—she was beginning to doze off. Prevented herself from falling asleep: as if without any restraints, how is it, suddenly a person is compelled to draw close. Extends attention, tokens of good-will, of affection, pampers without reservations. Unafraid. Giving, getting exposed in front of a stranger. He ought to be fond of that stranger. Must be. Surely he needn't have anything to do with all this otherwise. Moreover, to do it willingly. Out of himself. He's fond, yes, fond. And sinking into sleep, like one striving labouriously, who towards the end of his journey is shedding any superfluous load, this is what she was left with: a person wants. Wants to receive, to give. A person extends, attention, care, is fond, makes one take part, as if they are not strangers. And then he leaves. Does not come back. She fell asleep.

She heard her mother getting up, passing into the kitchen. Mixing the feed for the chickens. In the heat that already filled the world, like laundry air, was all the humdrum of the drudgery of the

newborn day. Born without a mask: no blessing, no chance, no reconciliation, no change, no novelty. No stir in the leaves of the creeper;
this calabash-like, gourd-like plant, it decks out only the yards of the
poor, as she had observed long ago. Twining over there, raising its
yellow flowers, clinging to the posts of the pergola in the yard, its
end can be seen from her corner in the bed. She heard her mother
attaching the hose to the kitchen tap, to fill the two large galvanized
laundry tubs and the pail for the baby nappies outside, under the
kitchen window. The way she had told us once. Told us of a story
that had taken place in their homeland. A story about a brother who
strangled his adulterous sister and threw her body into a well. 'Blessed
are the hands,' his mother had blessed him—she told us full of sacred
awe.

But me, I am never more of this place. Ever more of the UN.

And the backlash swept her over. Like a forgotten melody. The
burst of freshness of a power that draws one back, and anguish, akin
to regrets, over that which is massacred here at your feet each time
anew and gets trampled, you know not what it is. They recapture
that which is extinct and by now is nothing but tenderness, all the
tenderness. Yet in it are preserved all its lost flavour, fully retained,
and its true colours—with a punch that is like a fist-blow to the jaw.
In the great wide world only this time, only for me, only in my case—
won't I, please—some day find you again?

Translated by Raya and Nimrod Jones.

Aharon Appelfeld

COLD SPRING

Born in Czernowitz, Romania in 1932, Appelfeld was deported to a concentration camp at the age of eight. He escaped and spent three years hiding in the Ukraine before joining the Russian army. He arrived in Palestine in 1946. After several years in a variety of schools for refugee children, where he learned Hebrew, he studied at the Hebrew University and thereafter dedicated himself to writing. Appelfeld is fond of stressing that he has never been to school. He is widely recognized as the most effective transmitter in Hebrew fiction of the experience of victims of the Holocaust. His first volume of stories, Ashes *(1962), was the first artistically effective portrayal in Hebrew literature of people whose lives had been affected by the ravages of the Holocaust. His technique is one of allusion and indirection, 'surrounding' the Holocaust, never direct confrontation with it. He therefore writes about communities before and after the Holocaust, the menace lurking in the world on the brink of catastrophe and the aftermath of the tragedy when individuals attempt to rebuild their lives. He has written many novels, notably* Badenheim 1939, The Age of Wonders, *and* The Immortal Bartfuss, *and many collections of short stories.*

Seven days late, we learned that the war was over. We heard that the day after the war ended everyone was very happy. The fact is, sounds reminiscent of the war's beginning did filter into our bunker, but we did not know that these were after-war pangs, so we listened in silence.

When we removed the cover of our hiding place and daylight suddenly descended into the bunker, we did not know what to do. Our faces took on an expresion of naïve amazement, like the face of a stutterer.

Zeitel said, 'Don't rush out into the cold.'

Berel and Hershel curled up, not wanting to move.

The first to leave, rushing out with a powerful burst and thrusting his beard ahead of him, was old Reb Isaac.

'Sonya!' he called, as though she were waiting for him at the doorway.

Outside lay a lucid winter. Great lights glittered in the distance, too strong for the naked eye. The horizon was a firm, solid blue. In the evening we returned and covered the bunker.

'What did you see?' asked Zeitel in the middle of the night, but we were tired and said, 'Nothing.' Then we fell asleep again.

In the morning we were in no hurry to remove the cover again. The army band beat out thunderous rhythms above our heads, the music spiralled happily, and peasants yelled: 'Hurray, the war is over!' In the afternoon a company of Russian soldiers wandered over. 'Do you know the war is over?'

'Yes,' answered Berel, 'only we're tired.'

We did not know where to go now that the war was over, so we sat at the entrance of the bunker, and when we grew thirsty we sucked the white snow that melted nicely between our fingers. Company after company of soldiers passed singing and whooping; their victory yells echoed and passed over us. The snow did not melt. In the evenings sparkling clouds of smoke piled up in the sky. Nights we no longer went out to the fields to search for potatoes, but slept huddled together in a circle. As we lay in hibernation, a heavy shudder ran through our limbs. We posted no watchmen to listen for strange noises, but Zeitel would rouse us at midnight. 'Do you hear?'

Old Reb Isaac could not just sit and wait. The second day, he suddenly fled the bunker, going off into the snowy fields. I remember his hands flapping in the distance like wings.

'Sonya,' he called through the clear air. 'Sonya.' He did not return to the bunker. We were fast asleep and did not notice his absence. Only Zeitel said from time to time, 'Reb Isaac went out without his coat.'

After we had got used to the light, we would go out and watch the Russian soldiers march past singing. We did not go very far, just around the bunker. The idea occurred to none of us that the time had come to take to the road. We had food. The soldiers abandoned piles of bread and sausages and vodka, but we were not hungry. The bunker was full of food but none of us went near it. Zeitel would spread out her hands and say, 'Maybe you'll eat something.' Berel grew fat, so heavy he could barely stand. Hershel, on the other hand, shot up tall, like a plant springing in the shade. Zeitel could not help saying, 'Look at Hershel.' And Berel said, 'You have no appetite. Good. I'll eat all the more.'

Hershel sat apart from us, and fell into a brown study. Nobody went near him; it was clear that he was not one of us any more. He was sailing off somewhere and there was no stopping him, for he could see what we could not.

At times a company of soldiers stopped to eat and rest with us. They were flushed with victory and did not ask any questions. But they let us forage after them, and sometimes were amazed. 'Jews.'

The battlefront moved away, the railroad tracks were repaired, and the snow began to soften—not all at once, but in layers, from the surface down. There were no human voices. You could hear the sound of saws in the forest, and the sound of axes, and the sound of wood being piled up and loaded.

Zeitel said, 'I shiver whenever I hear these sounds. Why haven't I become used to them?'

Max smiled. 'Winter is passing.'

The snow began to thaw, baring the earth. Steel helmets that had been discarded were scattered in the fields. A burned-out jeep lay on its side wearing a helpless expression, one tail-light gleaming red.

Zeitel said, 'It's a good thing we stayed in the bunker and were not so foolish as to follow the refugees.'

We did not bother to repair the leaks in the bunker, as we had done every year toward spring. The water began seeping in, and we had to curl up in the corners of the bunker.

Max and I used to go out and watch the army cars speeding down the road, their wheels throwing up clods of mud behind them.

Zeitel said, 'Children, why are you standing outside?'

One morning we awoke to find the bunker full of water. Now we knew we could not remain. We took our bundles out of the bunker, and Berel grumbled. 'Just when you want to sleep, it fills up with water.'

Max glanced inside and said, 'Our bunker.'

Then we left.

Where were we to go?

Zeitel said, 'Let's go to the village.'

Hershel said, 'Let's go to the road where the cars pass.'

In the distance moved long lines of refugees; their feet seemed to sink in the thawing snow. Huddled together in the bunker we used to talk and talk. Now we five walked in silence.

Zeitel remembered something and said, 'I forgot the wooden spoon in the bunker. Maybe I ought to go back and get it.'

Carts loaded with trees moved very slow, leaving a trail of dripping resin. Cows were taken to pasture.

A peasant woman stood at the door of her house with a little girl, and the woman said, 'Look, Jews! You see, they are going to look for their families.'

'Those are Jews?' wondered the little girl.

After a time we turned off the main road into a narrower one. Facing us was a green hill with a monastery looking down from the peak. Holiday bells were pealing and Hershel said, 'Christian holiday.'

The sun stood in the middle of the sky, it was hot and a mouldy smell rose from our clothes. 'We might go down to the river and wash,' said Max.

'God forbid, God forbid,' said Zeitel. 'Not in this cold weather.'

We sat down to rest in the sun. 'The sun is good,' said Hershel.

And Max remembered the bunker and said, 'Our bunker is full of water.'

We took out the bread and the bottle of vodka. 'I have a bad taste in my mouth,' said Hershel. But smelling the vodka, he said, 'Seeing vodka makes me happy.'

We sat and stared at the red monastery, and saw the sun going down by degrees, and heard the bells hurriedly calling.

At last, Berel stood up and said, 'What are we sitting here for? It's late, it will soon be night.'

Hershel said, 'We should walk along the main road.'

Berel thought it would be better to start off toward the monastery.

Max said, 'It's good to walk.'

Berel grew angry and said, 'If you people don't want to go to the monastery, I'll go alone. I'm not afraid of going alone. As a matter of fact...'

Zeitel interfered and said, 'Sh...sh...Are you quarrelling now? All the years we sat in the bunker we never quarrelled—should we quarrel now?'

We moved slowly in silence. At first we all kept together. Then, gradually, the knot loosened. An angry cloud hung over our heads. Berel lengthened his stride. Hershel dawdled behind. Toward evening we reached the monastery. The walls that had looked low and narrow from a distance now loomed high and forbidding. They were enclosed by rigid iron gates.

'Who is there?' asked the monk.

We told him.

'We have too many refugees already,' said the monk's voice.

'But only for one night,' Zeitel raised her voice.

'Every inch is taken,' he replied.

Berel climbed up the wall, stood on the top, and said, 'I'm a Christian.'

'Look at the Jew pretending he's a Christian,' laughed the monk.

His face smarting, Berel crawled down, and Zeitel said, 'What's all the fuss? We'll sleep here, next to the wall. The winter is over, we can spread straw on the ground.'

When we got up in the morning, the angry cloud of contention had not lifted. We continued to walk. The morning was large and clear and bright. Behind us trailed the monastery prayers.

Zeitel said, 'So hot.' She remembered Reb Isaac. 'I wonder what Reb Isaac is doing now.'

'You're always complaining.' Berel grew angry.

'I don't mean anyone is to blame, God forbid. But why did we let him go? All the years we looked after him—then, on the happy day, we let him go,' said Zeitel.

Berel walked faster. We sensed the anger that was driving him. It forced him to keep going, never to look behind. He ran with his head lowered. By afternoon he was far away.

Max said, 'Maybe we ought to run after him.'

'Even if we ran, we couldn't catch him,' sighed Zeitel.

The footprints Berel left in the earth were deep and we were able to follow them. Max shouted, 'Berel, Berel! We don't have the strength to run after you. Wait, wait.' Toward evening, Berel was swallowed up in the dusk.

'That would not have happened if Reb Isaac were here,' said Zeitel. 'But what are we standing around for?' She hurried us. We knew we would do whatever Zeitel said.

It grew very dark, but Zeitel said, 'We won't rest till we find him.'

At midnight we found Berel, by his groans. He was sitting with his back propped up against a tree.

'Let me alone, let me alone, let me rest,' he said.

Zeitel went over to him and said, 'I'm going to take care of you.' She made him sip some water.

Hershel and Max carried Berel, Zeitel and I trailed behind. We were in good spirits, the way we had been in the bunker. Max hummed Russian marching songs, and even Berel's heavy breathing was part of the celebration. Reconciliation was in the air.

Max said, 'Let go, Hershel. I want to carry him by myself.'

'Look at the hero,' said Zeitel.

We came across a lean dog and Max said, 'Look at the dog,' and ran over to stroke it.

We decided to ask the peasants for a place to lodge.

'You want to sleep at my place?' asked the peasant woman. 'I can tell from your looks you've just come out of a bunker. Now you're trying to locate your relatives, aren't you?'

'We're looking for a place to sleep,' said Berel.

'Ah,' smiled the peasant woman. She seemed to like what Berel had said.

In the ante-room she spread out straw, lit the oven, and said, 'You poor people, lie down and sleep.'

I do not remember that night. But I do remember the tongues of flame that licked my back. The wounds all over my body gaped painfully. A sweet languor dissolved through my limbs. The hayseed crackled in the oven, shooting sparks. I sensed my voice returning. Tomorrow I would be able to speak again. The moment we lifted the cover of the bunker when we learned the war was over, a stream of cold air had numbed my throat, and I had not been able to talk ever since.

The next morning our bodies ached and we could not rise. It was Max who got up at last and said, 'Where's Berel?'

'Woe is me!' screamed Zeitel.

'Where is Berel?' we asked the peasant woman.

'Don't worry, he's in my room.'

'Give us a chance to speak to him,' pleaded Zeitel.

'The nerve of these people! You think he's badly off with me?' asked the peasant woman.

'Berel!' shouted Max, but Berel did not answer.

Zeitel covered her face with a kerchief and said, 'The son of Nachman Katz and the grandson of Rappoport. What have we done to deserve this?'

I had not regained the power of speech. I tried to say something but could not. I felt that if only I could speak I would be able to suggest a solution. A vast loneliness descended on us, the sun's rays seemed to sink, heavy and rough, and Zeitel said, 'If Reb Isaac were with us, such a thing would never have happened. A tragedy.'

Hershel walked behind us. His face was silent. We saw that his eyes were clouded, he was deep in inner meditation. We did not know what visions were being shown him.

We had been walking for an hour or so when Zeitel stopped and said, 'Children, perhaps we ought to go back. He must be sitting alone feeling sorry now. How could we have allowed that filthy peasant woman to steal him from us? What if we meet his father? Could we tell him that we left Berel with a filthy peasant woman? Let us go back, children.'

But even as she spoke, Zeitel knew we could not go back. We felt heavy and weary.

In the distance moved long lines of refugees. Tall peasants stood in the field mowing grass. 'Hey you,' a peasant yelled to us. 'Over there go the refugees looking for their relatives. Don't you have any relatives? Is that why you're in no hurry?'

Hershel was depressed, his face yellow with sadness. Max and I walked at Zeitel's side. Hershel plodded heavily behind, his every step a sigh.

'You remember the night we went into the bunker?' Max broke the silence. 'You didn't want to go in, Zeitel. Now the bunker is full of water. It held up all those years, and on the last day it filled with water. The dampness must have been too much for it '

We took out the last of our bread and sausage and sat down to eat. 'Hershel, if you don't eat, neither will we. A person can't walk if he doesn't eat. You've got to keep up your strength, it's a long trip,' Zeitel reprimanded Hershel.

We came to a cross-road, and Max said, 'I'll walk over and ask where the roads go.'

'Well, I found out,' he said when he returned. 'One road goes to Tulz, the other to Raditz.'

'Raditz,' said Hershel. 'No Raditz for me. They'll never see my face there again.'

'Well, where shall we go?'

We were standing there in a quandary when an old peasant approached us, his cheeks wrinkled in a smile, and began talking to us in our language.

'You're Jews,' he said. 'I like your food. I did a lot of business with Jews. You want to take my advice? It's good advice. Down there, on the slope of that hill, lives a man who is very famous in these parts, there's no one like him when it comes to dealing with spirits. He'll tell you who is still alive and worth searching for, and who has been killed. Why tire yourselves walking the roads? Go over to his hut and he'll tell you. Take my advice.'

'What do you think?' said Max, the blue vein throbbing in his forehead.

Zeitel's face grew very serious. She took off her kerchief.

Hershel raised his head and said, 'I don't believe in magic.'

The straw-roofed hut was low, with a narrow door.

'Do our people believe in magic?' asked Hershel.

'It can't do us any harm,' said Zeitel, taking hold of his sleeve. 'Let's go in, children.'

'Quiet, quiet,' a man greeted us at the door. 'Take your shoes off, take your shoes off. It's forbidden to wear shoes in a holy place.'

Barefoot, we stood outside the room. Zeitel held on to the three of us.

'People have come,' said the doorkeeper. 'They've taken their shoes off. Shall I let them in?'

'In a while,' answered a muffled voice from the large room.

After that we heard, 'It is permitted now.'

The doorkeeper placed himself at the head of our group, and said, 'Follow me.' We walked close together, like links in a taut chain, the way we used to walk on those nights when we left the bunker to hunt for potatoes. We heard the sound of bells, and of wheels, and of a great rushing back and forth. We sensed the darkness growing deeper; in a moment we would be in its dumb heart.

Two candlesticks stood in a corner, the candles flickering.

'Now cover your faces,' said the magician, 'and repeat after me.'

I do not remember what he told us to say, but I remember that we repeated the words loudly and the room was full of trembling and sound.

'Now,' said the old man, 'I have sanctified you and you may see visions from the other worlds.'

One by one they ascended the stage, shrouded in blue, and we recognized them by their rustling and the way they lifted their necks.

Zeitel broke away from us, shouting, 'We are orphaned, children, we are orphaned.' We could not hold her.

'I cannot show you anything with all this noise,' said the magician.

Hershel took off his caftan and said, 'Here's the pay of your magic.'

'This is not magic,' the sorcerer called after him.

We pulled Zeitel outside. Hershel stood bare-armed, the bones of his body sticking out. We did not see Zeitel's face. She covered it with her fists and shouted, 'Children, we are orphans, children, we are orphans.'

Outside, the winter lay cold. Clouds rent the huge silence, the trees were hung with a gleaming red that stained the premature blossoms. When Zeitel caught sight of Hershel's bare body, she started up and said, 'Where's your caftan? Put it on quick, you'll catch your death of cold.'

That night Zeitel awoke and said, 'Did you see, did you see?' She was having a bad dream.

Max took off his coat and said, 'Hershel, let's share this.'

The night deepened, the dogs in the village were awake and howl-ing, Zeitel kept raising her head and covering Hershel. The darkness pressed down on us.

Zeitel said, 'If anybody sees Reb Isaac—my heart tells me he will come—don't let him go to that place, God forbid.'

In the morning we saw a man ploughing in the distance, and a woman walking behind him. Zeitel said, 'I see Berel.'

'No, it's a peasant you see,' said Hershel.

The spring sun passed through the clouds. Max's face shone white. Zeitel became herself again, and said, 'If only we were all together once more, the way we used to be in the bunker, and Reb Isaac and Berel were with us . . . if only . . . I could walk to the end of the world.'

Translated by J. Sloane.

Yaakov Shabtai

THE VISIT

*Born in Tel Aviv, Shabtai (1934–81) began his literary career with short stories col-
lected in* The Spotted Tiger *(Hebrew: Hadod Peretz mamri, 1972) and he is the
author of two plays. His novel* Past Continuous *(1977) immediately signalled a
major and innovative talent. Making no concessions to the reader, it is related in
one ongoing paragraph, a* roman fleuve *moving through the consciousness of each
one of the characters to the others. This technique was refined even more in his second novel,* Past Perfect *(1984), in which Shabtai utilizes a variety of modernist narrative techniques. In these novels, as in his short stories, Shabtai traces the historical
and emotional landscape of modern Tel Aviv with a tragic sense of the past and some
pessimism about the future in Israel. Nevertheless his style is a mixture of humour,
irony, and descriptive brilliance.*

The bookseller held out Maimonides' *A Guide of the Perplexed*. It was
a used copy and he offered it to me for a very low price. But I preferred *Ahitophel's Complete Almanac of Signs and Portents*, which I had
come across by chance after browsing at length among the second-
hand homiletic and exegetical books and prayer-books and other sacred
books lying packed in cardboard boxes and piled up in stacks in the
courtyard of the building. I had never heard of this book, but its title
appealed to me and made me smile. I dipped into it and read a few
sentences here and there, paid and emerged into Allenby Street.

It was a hot summer day. The street was full of blinding light and
the motionless air was damp and stifling. I glanced at the introduction and found the following: 'And if anyone has a question in his
heart or a desire, of his own or another's, or if some evil thing has
entered his mind, and he is troubled by frightening thoughts, and
wishes to set his mind at rest, let him turn to these pages and he will
find in them what he seeks. And if anyone wishes to consult this book,
let him do so only with pious and serious intent, if he indeed desires
to hear a right and true answer to his question.'

I smiled to myself. The truth is that I had intended buying a prayer-book for the High Holy Days, not in order to pray from it, but to read and study it. At this time I was in the throes of a 'return to the fold of Judaism', and it was in this connection that I had begun to dip into the prayer-book and devotional literature, and especially to read various articles dealing with the explication of Judaism and the analysis of its revealed and hidden sides, and with endless attempts to get to the bottom of its essential meaning.

At the end of the Carmel Market crowds of perspiring people milled about in the blazing sunshine, filling the road and surrounding the various stalls. There was a smell of spices and pickled herring in the air. I crossed Allenby Street and walked down King George Street. Suddenly it occurred to me to pay a visit to Haim Leib.

Haim Leib lived with his family in the Nordiyah quarter, and of all my parents' relatives and *landsleit* he was the one I loved most. His hands were thick and heavy and there was something wise and shining and full of life in him and everything he did. He loved eating and drinking, reading newspapers, strolling the streets, aimless chats, political arguments, parties in honour of *briths* and *bar mitzvahs*, weddings and funerals. He lived in frank enjoyment of the world and at peace with God, in whom he believed, but gladly and without stern fanaticism. Often, when he went to the synagogue, or when he set off to deliver a load of washing in the rickety pram to one of his customers, he would dawdle on the way and only come home after half the day had passed. His wife, Mrs Dvora, cooked and cleaned the shack and brought up the children with pleas and screams and terrible aggravation, and she also did her husband's work at the mangle while he dallied on his way. And every now and then she would poke her head out of the window and yell without any hope and with the last of her strength into the empty air of the street:

'Haim Leib!'

I stood in the shade of the sycamore trees opposite 'Fort Ze'ev', the Revisionist Party headquarters, and leafed through the book. I read that 'These are the days on which it is sure and certain and also tried and tested that Moses our Master, May he Rest in Peace, laid down that any man who travels the roads, or who moves goods from place to place, or from house to house, will not profit by it. And if he takes to his bed—he will not rise from it, God forbid. And if he goes to war on them—he will be slain. Even if he is a great warrior . . .' A detailed list followed of all the ill-omened days in every month according to the Hebrew calendar. I glanced at the newspaper and saw that today was not one of them.

I knocked on the door of the shack and waited. A feeling of happiness spread through me, mingled with anticipation and longing. I thought of how surprised Haim Leib would be when he opened the door and of how glad he would be to see me. It was many years since I last visited him at home, and the last time I saw him was two years ago, at Grandmother's funeral. He marched ahead with Mrs Dvora floating behind him like a still feather, a little beige felt hat on her head. When he passed me he smiled his warm smile and said:

'Don't worry. God doesn't forget anybody.'

'My brother, have no fear of those who persecute you without your knowledge, they are full of wiles but fortune smiles on you' caught my eye. I closed the book and knocked again.

The huge sycamore cast a greenish shade. Its trampled fruit lay scattered round about, staining the pavement and the street. It gave off a strong scent, recalling sand lots and virgin fields, vineyards and melon patches and Arabs driving donkeys. Once I used to spend a lot of time in this place. Grandmother used to live in a shack not far from here. I used to stand quietly in a corner of the room, which was full of a good smell of starched laundry, and stare at Haim Leib and the huge wooden mangle moving steadily to and fro. It fascinated me and frightened me with its great rollers and its mysterious power. At any moment I expected a brown devil to jump out of it. Haim Leib fascinated me. He set the rollers in motion and operated the machine and laughed with his eyes and all the wrinkles of his sunburnt face. I knocked a third time and wiped the sweat from my face and neck.

The tar-paper covering the walls of the shack had torn here and there, and the watchmaker from next door had died. His shop had been taken over by a hatter, whom I did not know. In the seedy little display window stood two painted wooden heads. They both wore hats and looked like a pair of dusty English gentlemen. The tinker, Mr Feldman, had moved and his shop was locked up. He had a flat nose like a boxer's and he was never properly shaved. His daughter was called Rucha. Like everyone else, the tinker supported the *Haganah*, whereas Haim Leib supported the right-wing, nationalist *Irgun Tzva'i Leumi* and denounced the *Haganah* and the *Histadrut* Labour Federation. This used to upset me, and I would tell myself that he was only joking.

The door opened and Haim Leib stood on the threshold. His brown eyes were sunk deep in their hard sockets and the skin was stretched taut as dry parchment over the cheekbones of his shrunken face. His black beard had gone grey.

'*Shalom*,' I said happily and smiled at him.

He looked at me with dull, lifeless eyes, like the eyes of an old American Indian.

His body gave off an overpowering smell of old age. His stomach had caved in, and his trousers were gathered in pleats round his waist by means of a belt whose end dangled negligently.

'*Shalom*, Haim Leib.'

He gazed at me blankly and I saw that he was straining to remember me, but to no avail. I waited for a minute and then I told him my name and my mother's and father's names.

'Ah.'

A smile, the shadow of a different smile, appeared on his face for a moment and he took my outstretched hand in his.

His grip was limp and cold. Nothing was left of the old strength and gladness.

'Dvora, a guest,' he announced soundlessly when we stepped inside and mentioned my father's name.

I was on the point of correcting him, but refrained from doing so.

The room, which was once big and high and dim, had grown small and light, and the old furniture now seemed disappointingly ordinary. In the corner stood a white electric mangle.

Mrs Dvora came in from the kitchen. As always when visitors came she was flustered, and she shuffled her slippered feet in agitation. Her wet hands were holding the skin of a chicken's neck, a needle and white thread. When she saw me she shrieked with joy and her long, faded, whey-face lit up. She hurried into the kitchen and came back drying her hands on her apron.

Mrs Dvora was a tall, long-limbed, and slightly stooped woman. For some reason she made me think of a chicken's leg. The blue of her eyes had completely faded and her hair had turned white. She came from a wealthy family, and in her youth she had worn satins and silks and washed her face in lilac milk. Haim Leib had dragged her to *Eretz Israel*, among the Arabs and the heat and the sand, and nothing was left of her former glory but for the little gold earrings in the lobes of her ears.

We went into the other room and sat at the table.

'How are things with the *goyim*?' asked Haim Leib in a brittle voice and smoothed out a wrinkle in the tablecloth, 'Your rabbi is the Marxist Meir Yaari if I'm not mistaken?' And he chuckled dryly.

I told him how things were with me.

'And did you lay *tefillin* this morning?' he said with a weak laugh and pulled *Ahitophel's Almanac* out of my hands.

Mrs Dvora set the table with the bottle of brandy, little clouded red glasses, pieces of pickled herring arranged on a china plate, and home-made onion crackers which she took out of an old 'Quaker Oats' tin, which bore the picture of a man with a sunburnt face wearing a broad-brimmed straw hat.

'Eat your oats,' my mother would urge me, 'It's good for you. Eat. Hundreds of thousands of children like you are dying of hunger right this minute in India.'

We raised our glasses and drank.

'Take a piece of Jewish herring,' said Haim Leib and called me again by my father's name. He himself did not touch the herring, since the doctor had forbidden it.

The conversation proceeded heavily. It dragged along without interest, and all my attempts to arouse him were in vain. I felt disappointed. Even politics didn't interest him. Only once he remarked that everyone would come back to the fold in the end, even Meir Yaari. Behind his shoulders, and behind the net curtains lay King George Street with the sycamore tree and people and cars passing. I remembered that very many years ago I had once seen through this same window an Arab making two bears and a monkey dance in the sand.

'My brother, correct your heart and desist from your double-heartedness and turn away from this question which is wicked, for if not—you will regret it,' read Haim Leib without interest from the *Almanac*.

'Eat, eat,' urged Mrs Dvora, and pushed the onion crackers towards me, 'It's good.'

'And what is your question?' asked Haim Leib mockingly, placing his hand on mine.

I giggled and averted my face slightly. I could not bear the smell of his old age.

'Eat, eat,' repeated Mrs Dvora.

The warmth of my hand was draining into his, but it remained cold nevertheless.

'I saw your grandmother wrapped in a fox-fur,' said Haim Leib suddenly, 'she must have made money in the next world.' And a smile crossed his face.

I withdrew my hand carefully and stood up to take my leave. Out of the corner of my eye I caught a glimpse of the picture of 'The Garden of Eden' hanging in its usual place above the sideboard.

In the middle of the picture stood Adam and Eve, both of them young and beautiful, girdles of fig-leaves around their waists, holding a pink baby in their hands, with a number of animals in the meadow around them: a lion, a tiger, a lamb, a horse, and a squirrel. On either side, on rising steps, one opposite the other, stood a boy-child and a girl-child, a boy and a girl, a youth and a maid, a man and a woman, and lastly, on top of the steps, an old man and an old woman leaning on their sticks, and above them a kind of flying scroll. I knew what was written on it: 'This is the Torah—and this is its reward.'

'Go and visit her,' said Haim Leib from where he sat and sniggered.

'Give regards to your mother and father,' screeched Mrs Dvora in her shrill voice as I opened the kitchen door on my way out.

'All right.'

I went down two steps and trod in the sand. A sudden space stretched out in front of me, still and brightly lit. It was familiar and strange to my eyes at once. The ruins of a few shacks were scattered round-about, uprooted and lost and forlorn as refugees from a war. Here and there stood a gate without a fence, a Persian lilac casting its shade on the floor of a vanished room, a single wall, a tap, a collection of old boards and bricks, a tub, a sheet of tin, a cypress tree. And in the distance, suddenly rising into the summer sky, two blocks of high buildings, white as paper.

I took a few steps and turned my head and saw Mrs Dvora, who was standing at the kitchen window and watching me walk away. I turned back towards the path along which we used to walk to go and visit my grandmother. I could still feel Haim Leib's hand lying on top of my own.

The old path was still visible, although it had been blurred by sand and weeds and smothered beneath the tangled branches of a mulberry tree growing wild. Once I used to climb this tree with Rucha.

I walked round the mulberry tree and came to the place which had once been the front yard of Grandmother's shack. Here, in this yard, the dovecote built by my grandfather had once stood. He was a Zionist. Next to the dovecote he had laid out a few beds of vegetables.

The shack had disappeared, but by some miracle the blocks upon which the walls had rested had survived, so that the essence of its shape remained stamped in the sand.

I went up to the kitchen. This was a dark cubbyhole, stuck onto the façade of the shack, populated by enamel saucepans, brown walls, black iron frying-pans, a salting-board and a kneading board, assorted sieves, china plates, a blue teapot, a bronze pestle and mortar, a mincing machine, two kerosene burners and one deafening primus stove. A large black lock hung on the creaking door, which was made of whitewashed wooden boards.

I stepped into the entrance to the front room. The glass panes in the high door were thick and grainy and they were coloured orange and green and a dense honey-gold. I stood in the place where the table had once stood, covered with a thick cloth decorated with large flowers. On the right stood the brown cupboard and on top of it two copper candlesticks. In this cupboard Grandmother had hidden during the Second World War when the Italians had dropped a bomb on her. On the eastern wall hung Grandfather's portrait, and next to it the portraits of some other man and woman. The golden sand, which had been hidden under the floorboards all those years, was revealed. It was mixed with broken glass and china, dry leaves and stalks and pieces of coal, which the wind had carried here from the yard.

I stepped through the entrance to the second room. It was smaller than the first and stifling. Its air was saturated with the smell of cushions and feather quilts and mattresses, as if it was never aired. Most of its space was taken up by a big bed and an old sideboard. The walls of the room and its ceiling were distempered a harsh white, but nevertheless it was perpetually dark and unbearably stuffy in there. Now everything was dazzlingly light and spacious. Overhead stretched the wide blue sky, and the castor oil plant, which had once rested on the wall of the shack, sent its broad leaves into the room—a fresh purple-green. I looked around me for a moment, and then I stepped through the wall and walked away.

Translated by Dalya Bilu.

Avraham B. Yehoshua

THE LAST COMMANDER

Yehoshua was born in Jerusalem in 1936 and today lives in Haifa after spending four years (1963–7) in Paris. He is at once a novelist, a short-story writer, a playwright, an essayist, and a literary scholar, and is among the most widely recognized authors in Israel and abroad, described by the New York Times as a 'kind of Israeli Faulkner'. His novels indicate a particular gift for capturing the mood of contemporary Israel. His criticism of Israeli culture is demonstrated particularly in his novel The Lover (1977), in which he mirrors Israeli society at its nadir. In his fiction he portrays some of the 'neurotic' deviances that follow the abandonment of Israel for the diaspora. He explores the instincts which threaten the façade of civilized human beings and examines their isolation from each other, the community, and themselves. His subjects have included political allegory (the novella 'Facing the Forests', 1963), psychological analysis (Late Divorce, 1982, Molcho, 1987), and family epic (Mr Mani, 1990), all of which have been translated into English.

The Gnostics, who were the contemporaries of the Jewish Tannaim of the second century, believed that it was necessary to distinguish between a good but hidden God who alone was worthy of being worshipped by the elect, and a Demiurge or creator of the physical universe, whom they identified with the 'just' God of the Old Testament.

Gershom Scholem, 'Redemption Through Sin'

I

After the war there we were in murky offices, pushing pencils and sending form letters to one another on matters which seemed important to us. Had we lost, we would have been in a real mess now. We would have been accounting for murder, for robbery, committed by our dead comrades. Since we had won—we brought liberation, but they had to give us something to do, otherwise nobody would vacate the fast, murderous jeeps, full of machine-guns and rounds of ammunition.

Now our clothes are clean; no grime on our faces. Only adding machines are softly humming at our side, and at night, in the crazy city, we rush from place to place to avoid loneliness. We run from light to light, clinging to our jaded women. Our eyes grow weak.

Each year when summer comes around, the reservists go off for military practice. The commands flutter around the offices like white soft bullets, but they don't touch us—the veterans. At first we felt slighted, but we consoled ourselves: no doubt this world needs us and our sharp pencils. Seven years we fought without stopping. Our nights have become hollow with fear. Now they ask us to rest on our withered laurel wreaths. So we barricaded ourselves behind piles of letters.

But this year when summer came around, strange to say, we too were caught. Our good brothers, the officers in charge of sending out the summonses, remembered us. And the call-up summonses landed on our desks to our amazement. No escape.

One fine day they loaded us dodgers, former military men, onto freight cars, and sent us off to the south, to clamber up the hills.

And now, who knows, we might have picked up the weapons, unfamiliar to our hands by now, and stormed off; carried packs and fought until our strength gave out in new, imagined battles; attacked, retreated, returning again to conquer the wind and ourselves—had it not been for Yagnon—a swarthy, angular character, who was appointed at the last moment and with some trepidation, to substitute for the Commander of the Company who was suddenly called away on some business.

Already at the point of departure near the desert crossroads we could see that the new Commander tarried. While the rest of the companies were very busily engaged in loading equipment to go off to some place of action and trouble, and the commanders were running back and forth, this one went up on a small hill at the side of the road, and there he dozed off all by himself, bared to the sun. I remember our men hanging around idly by the silent machines—grunting and grumbling. The other companies disappeared one by one, and the square quietened down. But that black dot on top of the hill didn't move. No one knew the reason for this delay. Fed up with one another, scorched by the heat, we hadn't yet realized that from now on time was not our own. Darzi and Hilmi, two Division Commanders, approached me, their limbs moving restlessly. In the war they had served as sappers, and they had blown up whole villages together with their inhabitants, and since then they don't move without one another, out of fear.

I could see that the hours were passing, so I climbed up the hill and went over to him. This was the first time that I really saw him. He was lying at my feet—an elongated form with limbs stretched out, sporting a huge broken nose in an ugly face. With bifocals perched on his nose and a long scar deeply imprinted on his forehead. He was sleeping in a state of deep fatigue, but his breathing was barely audible. I knew that he, too, had served in the lower echelon in one of the offices, but he was a bachelor, and in the war he had displayed bold leadership on the southern front. I bent over and touched him. I remember his look—tear-veiled from sleeping in the sun. If death is very close to life, then death had been caught in his eyes. He lifted his head slowly, calmly, like one who had experienced an eternity of death. An old khaki shirt hung limply on his body. No military stripes.

'The other units have already left,' I said, bending over him. 'Isn't it time for us?'

He shot me a look out of another world.

'What?' His lips broke out in a strange drawl.

I repeated what I had said.

A weak smile lit up his mouth.

'You're in a hurry?' he said in a kind of mocking surprise.

Only when the heat subsided and a breeze came up from the desert did he rouse himself, glide weakly down the hill, get up on an old bullet-ridden jeep which had been given to us, a survivor of the war years. The whole column followed in his footsteps.

We travelled for many hours, slowly, with long stops. It seemed as though lead had been poured into the wheels of the cars that were crookedly wending their way at the bidding of the drowsy officer. We pressed deeper and deeper into the heart of the desert, getting ever further away from any shadow of a settlement. Nobody knew where we were going. In the north, we had fought for every house, for every clod of earth; but in this desert only a few small scattered units were roaming about, without direction and without reason. The whole wide expanse was conquered in a swift, seven-day campaign. Anything wider than a narrow parcel of dust cutting through the length of the desert was beyond our ken.

The sun beat down on the cars that wormed their way around in the menacing chalk-white region, sombrely, through sand dunes glistening with fool's gold, oceans of wasteland whose gentleness belied the eye. In the evening we found ourselves ascending a strange mountain, a formidable reddish ridge of Hymettian stone and reddish-black rocks. The wheels of the cars were caught in the steep rise little by little, until finally the spluttering motors gave out and stalled in the middle of their ascent, halfway up the mountain, next to a wide, deep rut with desert brush sticking out of it, their branches twisted as though demented.

We jumped out of the cars, weakened and confused, and a dim, ghostlike twilight encircled us. The drivers unloaded the cases of army rations, unfastened the trailing water tank, and disappeared to the rear down the slope. Like sleepwalkers we began going around among the piles of equipment that were thrown around, among the heaped weapons, coming to a halt and standing at the mouth of the abyss that was but a chain of extinct volcanic craters; their bases either cooled off or still smouldering. Every step opened up long and gaping canyons, small craters that dropped—crookedly—to deep layers of chalk, broken up in a mysterious way. We were still wandering about when the officer, who looked now like a dark brown hawk, stepped down into the rut, spread out a blanket for himself on the ground, curled up, and without a word, fell asleep. We were still bunched together here and there, looking for food, but the utter chaos confused everything. One after another we followed him into the rut, hungry and tired. Soon all had fallen asleep around the new officer, after a day in which nothing had been accomplished.

The camp was asleep and silent until late in the morning. The slow crawling rays of the sun added slumber to slumber. A strange, paralysing heat flowed beneath us all the time, from hidden sources in the mountain itself, as if we had been placed inside a giant furnace. Darzi and Hilmi crept over to me, drowsily and heavily, and snuggled up next to me, among the smouldering rocks. From their mumbling I figured out that they wanted to know whether to awaken the men, since the new officer didn't seem to show any signs of life.

The heat of the sun was now more intense and there was a burning sensation which weakened everybody. From between the slits of our aching eyes, the rocks looked like trembling molluscs, formations of sandstone running amok in a riot of colours. The blue of the sky disappeared and in its place there remained only a stark white heat. No soldier moved a muscle. Here and there somebody would try to move around, but immediately his legs would buckle and he would collapse to the ground. Only the youngest amongst us, the Commander of the fourth unit, an officer of the youth corps, who at the time of the war was still a child and collected bags of bullets, he alone got

up and wandered around, ready for a day's work. He glanced apprehensively at his slumbering Commander, then he settled at the edge
of the abyss, and cleaned his weapons.

The morning hours passed. The bellies of the soldiers of the Division
stretched out around me were glued to the ground. At noon Yagnon
suddenly turned over from one side to the other, opened his eyes and
gazed at the world while lying on his back, took a cigarette from his
shirt pocket, and lit it. The whole camp lay in wait for his every move.
We got up, bent over, and came near him; the youth joined us. We
knelt, all together, at the side of the officer, who tossed his ugly head
in our direction.

'What's to be done today?' the young officer burst out. Yagnon
didn't answer. A queer grimace twisted his mouth. The scar on his
forehead was gleaming like a long, bloody stain.

'Today,' repeated the youth, almost angrily, 'what's to be done
today?'

Yagnon didn't move from his place. His slim, tanned hand was
thrown over his sack, between his mussed-up blankets. Papers rustled.
A smile came over his lips.

'There are plans,' he whispered tiredly. 'They gave me plans,' he
repeated.

The young man tried to seize the practice plans.

'So then what's to be done today? One just can't keep on lying
around like this.'

He was aflame with the heat, and it seemed that he was right.

Yagnon's tiny eyes glided along Hilmi and Darzi's palpitating bellies, lying criss-crossed, at least that is the way I saw them. His lips
mumbled drowsily.

'Today—rest . . . at night perhaps . . . the heat will subside . . . now
—rest.'

Darzi bent his head towards the figure bundled up on the ground.

'Rest,' he repeated with an inward smile.

We looked at each other, all three of us. The young officer wanted
to open his mouth, but we had already disappeared, stooping down
over the rim of the shadow under the scrawny trees, returning to our
sweaty slumber. When the heat subsided, when it started to get dark,
Yagnon again woke up, and sucked on a cigarette. It was clear to all
of us that he was not setting aside the approaching night for anything
but sleep. Again, one after the other, we succumbed to heat-ravaged
slumber, riddled with disturbing fantasies. And in the morning we
were still lying down, only more tired than we were before.

On the third day we had already removed our clothes. Rank disappeared. We wondered suspiciously what schemes the sleeping man was devising. But, after the hours passed without anything happening, we knew that he had decided to lie low on the rocks until the end of the practice period.

We were struck with terror when we realized his clear, simple purpose. We attacked the deceiving shrubs, we uprooted and reduced them to splinters. We made a fire and nibbled without appetite on some dry rations we had at hand. Now there was not even the slightest bit of shade left.

On the fourth day, at noontime, we woke up. A hot wind whispered through the clefts of the rocks. Sun-scorched papers were flying around us, we made weak attempts to catch some of them. Yagnon had let fly away the practice plans. The wireless was cracked, and the sleepy liaison officer had tied it up with blankets, and had placed it under his head. The only possible connection with other units was severed. At twilight the young officer suddenly jumped up, got on the jeep that was left with us, to escape this hell. The roar of the engine shattered the silence. They all opened their eyes, but no one got up from their place. They hoped it would alarm the sleeping officer. The jeep started gliding down the incline; suddenly the dry brakes snapped, and it rolled down to the edge of the abyss and got stuck between two rocks. He was saved by a miracle. He returned shamefacedly to us, his eyes on fire. That night we saw neither the moon nor the stars. Complete darkness covered the mountains.

On the fifth day the sound of a car was heard in the mounttains, horn blowing noisily, and the men inside it shooting in the air, looking for us. Perhaps letters were coming from the cold, far-off city, our memory of which had completely disappeared. Again the young man straightened up, like a roe deer—his blue eyes flustered. The sun scorched his skin, he was all aflame. He cocked his weapon, shot into space, pierced the silence. The dialogue of shots continued for a long time, but the abyss scrambled the echoes. The car went further away. The young man started running among us like a madman, yelling and pleading. Drowsy and indifferent, we observed his thin shadow gliding around us. After the car had disappeared and silence was restored, he was still standing like a hurt child, his fist releasing his weapon, until at last he sank down near Yagnon, who smiled at him tiredly. During the night he disappeared and was not seen again. Perhaps he is still lost among the craters.

We are getting confused as to the number of the days, but already the sixth day has arrived, and as our skin has blackened, so has our human image faded. People who used to pray have stopped praying. The six working days passed in idleness, and on the Sabbath our capacity for sleep doubled. By now we know only the rocks hanging over our heads. We are lying in a group but each one is alone. Our hearing is clearer in the silence, and when we make an attempt to speak, we whisper. Nobody is looking for us, nobody ever gets up here. At times in the winding wadi below there are what appear to be three tiny figures, swathed in black, one in front and two in the rear, in a fixed order. These are our silent, bitter, vanquished enemies, but no one wakens to the danger that it is possible to slaughter all of us with just one dagger—without a single outcry.

Only occasionally, at night, somebody's mind would become lucid, and he would toss around, unable to fall asleep. He jumps up all by himself and sees the mountain very clearly with all its sharply edged outlines. He circles the sleepy camp crying softly to the sleeping men. He too feels like sleeping. When he reaches the ugly face of Yagnon he halts, he seems to think that he hears cries of pain from the neighbouring mountain, into which those black-swathed ones are disappearing. With nothing else to do, he feverishly piles up rocks. Then his passion suddenly subsides, and a dry, ashen look returns to his lips. He sinks down on the spot where he is standing, and returns to forgetfulness. On the next day, in the light, between one fit of sleep and the next he discovers next to him only a pile of rocks.

For seven days we have been captives in this realm in the power of this skinny magician who can't get enough sleep. But there is a kind of bewitching delight in having leaden legs that keep getting entangled, in the waning consciousness.

'God Almighty,' a mumbling cry is heard at times, 'why didn't we come here after the war?'

And at night, again and again, one dreams about the war.

II

Was this Sunday? We were lost in reverie when suddenly we heard a faint rumbling sound over our heads. We lifted our eyes. In the white expanse of brightness a grey dot fluttered over us. We rubbed our eyes, when a roaring, bellowing helicopter in a whirlpool of dust and wind hovered like a bird over the furrow in the earth. Suddenly its flight was arrested in mid-air, a rope ladder unfurled, bags were thrown out, a sturdy figure descended and waved a hand to the pilots who were disappearing in flight like blue angels. Perplexed and tired, we raised our heads from the dirt. He gathered his bags and came towards us with firm strides we could no longer match. Flushed, human, heavy-framed, silver-haired, blue, paternal eyes, and hands that knew how to praise. Insignia gleamed on his shoulders. He held back for a second, surveyed the bunch of shadows that peered at him—black, lean, bare.

We gazed at him. We knew—that was our enemy.

He made a firm decision, stepped over to a soldier who had straightened up in shock, and said curtly:

'I am the Company Commander . . . where is my deputy?'

We led him to Yagnon, who was sleeping, as always. His heavy shadow completely covered the slim figure. We sank down by the side of the slumbering man, we touched him. He opened his small, crafty eyes.

'Yagnon,' we whispered, all bent over and frightened.

The Company Commander measured him with his eyes, undecidedly.

'You are my deputy?'

He nodded his head as he lay on the ground. Our hearts went out to his ugly face.

'What happened? Someone killed?' The sturdy Commander turned his eyes on us.

Our tongues moved without a sound. The words got choked. We are dead, we tried to tell him. But he wasn't looking for an answer. He had already stopped listening. He wiped away his sweat and spoke:

'Why did you come to this furrow? I hovered in the sky for a long time looking for you . . . and it was only with difficulty that I found time to come to you . . . They say that since the end of the war you haven't done a thing.'

No one blinked an eyelash. He surveyed the furrow wonderingly.

'How in the world . . . utter chaos . . . so one lies, like this, naked?'

His voice was sharp like a whip. We kept silent. Yagnon shut his eyes tiredly, his head still lying on the ground. The officer cocked his ear, demanded an answer.

'Today: rest.' Darzi's voice rose at last as if from beyond the grave.

'Rest?' roared the Company Commander, and his roar awakened the remaining sleepers.

'Rest,' uttered Hilmi naively and with frightened eyes, 'Sabbath today?'

A threat rent the officer's mouth. Even I murmured apologetically.

'The days have got mixed up.'

They all nodded their heads with me. Our souls were already

sold to the man who lay on his back, and gazed quietly with dead eyes.

The Commander was taken aback. He was an officer of high rank, and he was not used to insolence. Even during the war they uttered his name respectfully, though he was a civilian. At that time he used to travel around the world, and he was the one who used to bring ammunition to the depleted arsenals. He could have been resting now in his huge office, but he always kept looking for the main action. When he heard that they were conscripting the war heroes, the dodgers, he made himself a Company Commander, and though it had seemed that he would not appear, here he was.

From then on he didn't utter a sound. He bent over his bags and rummaged around in them. Solitary and strong, a white figure. He pitched a small tent outside the furrow and shut himself in it. When evening came he crept out of his tent, and roamed a bit among the piles of equipment that were thrown about until he found a broken lamp. He fixed it and lit it. For the first time we had light. All night the lamp glowed next to him and from behind the canvas of the tent his outline was silhouetted, devising schemes and bent over plans.

On the following day he got us up before dawn, before light. With dictatorial anger he delivered us from the furrow, and soon we were standing before him in sleepy formation, armed and ready. The tardy ones he sent to the mountain peak to light a fire for the rising sun. He dispatched the officers to put on insignia. When the skies lit up with golden rays, and the fire died down, the tardy returned, and then we all climbed after him in a long file, with Yagnon trailing along at the end like a black shadow. It was a difficult climb but we eventually reached the mountain peak, where the blue sky was spread out, a vast expanse. All day we fired into the abyss, until our shoulders were fractured with pain. In the evening we ran after him down the slope, and he did not allow us to eat or drink until we had put up a high flagpole. At night we again climbed up the mountain, under star-studded skies. Until midnight we fired in the darkness, hitting and missing, with the echoes rolling all around us. The remaining half of the night we had alternate guard duty with the commander-who-knew-no-sleep awakening the guards.

We had only slept a few hours, and here it was Tuesday, and he was standing over us—clean, alert, and cross. In the morning twilight, heavy and weak, we fell in to raise the forgotten war flag which he had brought with him, and to hear the order of the day which he composed, a biblical psalm. All that day we dug ditches, camp sites, and pits. Our hands were blistered, as though leprous. There was no rest. From trench to trench he passed, and upbraided the lazy ones. Our eyes searched desperately for Yagnon, but he found himself a deep pit and slept on, and while we were striking the rocks in vain he was in his pit, dozing off. Smoke from his cigarette curled up from time to time. In the evening we dug out holes for lavatories, we covered them with tin, and gathered our scattered excretions into one place. From then on we walked to the edge of the canyon to relieve ourselves. With the setting rays licking the burning rocks, he was the first to go there. The whole company hung around feebly, icy eyes glued to the sturdy figure crouched over there by itself.

At night—a bonfire. He assembled us in circles and talked about the war. About the war that was, about the war that will be. Is there ever a moment without a war? Is there ever rest? He stood before us and read from the book of wars, in a clear, flat voice, as though giving orders. Our heads were nodding and drooping, but he shot pebbles at the dozers and kept them jumping. As midnight approached he demanded all of a sudden that we sing the battle songs that had long since sunk into oblivion. We looked at one another fearfully, as if we were having a nightmare. But he kept right after us. We sang. Hesitating at first, hoarse, but little by little our singing turned into a terrible wail, drunken and wild. Exhausted from a burning hot day of toil, we yelled and bellowed out the old bloody battle songs. He was standing, arms crossed over his heart, a trace of a smile on his lips. After which he turned serious, silenced us by raising a firm hand, and sent us off to our blankets, to our guard duties. There will be a big day tomorrow, he said.

And on Wednesday we charged. The whole art of fighting that we had forgotten came back to us in one day. From hill to hill, from mount to mount, he collected us and showed us where to charge, where to win. Afterward, we would spread out on the rocky hills, running, shooting, and falling until winning as he said. At noon, after we had been running in the wadi, and our eyes were blurred with the heat and dust, there appeared before us, a short distance away, the three figures clad in black. We stopped for a moment, gazing, but the roaring Commander, who was running after us with his helmet falling over his hot face, noticed them, cocked his gun, and fired at them. And immediately they disappeared light and swift into one of the canyons, like a mirage.

Where is Yagnon?

At times it seems to us that we see him treading soundlessly at the

side of the Commander, a dark, shadowy figure. But mostly he would
appear to be going around alone in the mountain chains. The Commander could keep the whole company under control by himself, and
it seemed that he was afraid of his strange adjutant, the tired officer,
who throughout the war was busy with the dead.

In the evening, in a period of slight rest, the Commander busied
himself with a car. He was wonderfully capable and he fixed it right
away. At night its two headlights shone, strange, large lights. The
whole night we charged back and forth within the beams of the light
that it threw over the surrounding hills. Terror gripped us again. The
smell of sulphur that stuck to our clothes brought the war back to
us. The morning chill found us at the foot of the mountain, fainting
with fatigue, but still alert enough to hear with the last ounce of
strength his comments on the methods of a war that he had never
fought. At dawn we returned to the deserted furrow, to the flag, after
a sleepless night. He fixed his blue eyes upon us, smiled to himself,
and said: 'It's Thursday.'

In the morning a new drill was set up. He stood on top of the
mountain, and it was up to us to reach him, without being noticed.
The whole mountain was full of soldiers crawling like insects, trying
to hide from him. It was hopelessly impossible. Whenever we thought
we had got to the top and reached him, his alert eyes would stop us
in time, and turn us back again to the starting-point, to the place
where Yagnon was lying, smiling and blowing clouds of smoke. Before
this we had intended to fall asleep in one of the passes between the
great rocks, but since yesterday we hadn't had a drop of water in our
mouths, and the water was beside him at the top of the mountain.
Crazed with thirst, we were creeping, scratched and dry, until noon.
No one succeeded in reaching him. He won.

In the afternoon, no one paid any attention to the sound of the
car wandering around the mountains, carrying letters. But he heard.
He assembled us at once and commanded us to go and meet it. We
marched a great distance and found it stuck in one of the small wadis.
We freed its wheels from the pits, we cleared the path before it,
we split rocks, and as a reward we received crumpled and yellowed
letters from those who remained in the city. They wrote to us about
their petty worries. We wanted to throw the letters away. He stood
there and demanded of all of us that we send our answers, as in the
war days, so that they would know that we were still living, and
wouldn't mourn. We leaned over and scrawled large letters on top of

the rocks, staring at him with open hostility. We returned to the camp in a trot around the mountain.

On Friday he was feeling good. He said: 'I haven't done anything yet ... I haven't accomplished half of what I want.' All day he spread out and rolled up maps and coloured diagrams which he had brought with him to demonstrate to us what was going to take place, what was still to happen. When he saw that we were dozing off in front of him he dispatched us to pitch tents outside the furrow, in precise squares. There will be a shade over your head, for your damned tiredness.

In the evening he instructed those who prayed to pray. Even the agnostics—it is better for them to pray, to ease their troubled minds. He stood and looked at them until their hurried prayer ended. At night he took out of his pack a box of broken, dried-up biscuits that he had brought with him, and divided them fairly and evenly with us. He was glad, so he said, that he had accomplished a great change in six days; no longer do we crouch dejectedly in the dry furrow. He rubbed his strong hands together, slowly and firmly. And isn't everything all right? We didn't answer. He doesn't really want an answer. And anyway has anybody except him said anything throughout these six days?

A gleaming night is spread over us. A strong dark sky. A deep rumble grows in the distance. The canvas of the tent is flapping in the wind. The mess has disappeared under the precisely folded blankets. We had said: Tonight we shall rest, we shall sleep. But he did not favour that. He wanted to sum up, to give himself credit. Since the war we hadn't done anything. All night he spoke to us about the fighting man.

Sabbath. Stones in our skulls instead of eyes. Hush. Quiet. As in the days when we first came here. Now it seems that we are permitted to sleep, but we can't. We keep opening our leaden eyelids to see what he is doing. How does he relax? Does he rest? The tiny tents are suffocating us. The shade is hot and dirty, not much of a shade. We are dying to close our eyes, we must. We have had a week of terror, and another week of terror is yet to come. The hours were passing, but sleep did not come. Painfully awake, like driven dogs we groped around on the ground to find a place for ourselves.

Yagnon. We remind ourselves of that one individual deep in sleep in the deserted furrow—why has he abandoned us?

And out of the corners of inflamed eyes, against our will, we keep seeing the Company Commander who is making the rounds among the tents, alert and awake, smiling at our drooping faces.

'Why don't you sleep? You say you're tired. At night I hear you crying.'

III

In the evening, at the end of the Sabbath, he assembled the officers and Yagnon in his tent in order to give directions for a taxing march of seven days' duration through the Wilderness of John and its plains, up to a distant well of water at the desert crossroads, where cars will wait for us to take us back home. All night he kept us in his tent and spelled out for us every item of the march with maddening attention to detail. Plans for assaults, charges, entrenchments, retreats, complicated night raids. With his swift red pencil he encircled on the map places where he wanted to stage battles with an imaginary enemy, and the point of his pencil cruelly indicated the many kilometres that we would be carrying the imaginary wounded. He wanted to conduct the march under military conditions, with packs and ammunition, with meagre rations of food and water, without rest. He ordered us to take the tents with us, and to drag along the boxes of ammunition; so that no trace of our existence be left in the furrow.

We bit our lips in anger, looked up at Yagnon who was sucking on a cigarette in the darkness of the tent, but he didn't raise his head. We exchanged hopeless looks. Darzi took heart, extended a weak hand towards the officer, who was bent over the map, his voice wavering.

'Why the tents?' he said sarcastically. 'At any rate there will be no time to fall asleep in them.'

The Company Commander directed his blue gaze at us. Darzi was awed, waiting for the scathing anger of the Commander.

'In vain...' Another word died on his lips. The Company Commander controlled his temper, but rage made his quiet voice quiver. Once more he spoke about the war that was, the war that will be. About the blood, about those who would be killed, about the crying, about the need to learn how to win. Suddenly he turned to the silent spark that was lighting one cigarette with another, as though he knew that in that one's silence lay all the trouble. Yagnon removed the cigarette from his mouth, lifted his eyebrows in mock amazement, and said in his warm, quiet voice:

'Of course these are the plans.'

And he put the live fire back into his mouth. The Commander's eyes softened. He passed his glance over the men who were sitting bent and crushed. He knew that the march would be taxing, but was there really any other choice? Are we the masters? Years ago, in the war, battles took place here, and through the arid Plain of John men went out on offensive marches. He bent his body towards us; his eyes were glistening. Perhaps we would find remains of equipment, or even skeletons of fighters who were killed in the passes. He looked sternly into the gloomy space that was visible from behind the folds of the tent. With unconcealed sorrow. What a pity that he wouldn't be able to lead us on that march.

The last sentence that was swallowed up in the darkness made our hearts leap with sudden joy. We didn't believe what our ears had heard. Only Yagnon didn't bat an eyelid.

'You aren't coming with us?' we asked with unconcealed joy.

'No . . . I only came here for seven days . . . no more.'

We lowered our heads so that he wouldn't notice the relief that engulfed us. Only slow-witted Hilmi slipped in with a delighted voice, 'Who will take you, sir?'

He smiled with sovereign condescension. 'Those who brought me . . . tomorrow morning.'

We shook hands thankfully.

After he finished speaking, we went out of the tent. A desert breeze was blowing. Only a few hours remained before sunrise, and although we were exhausted after a night of planning, we weren't looking for sleep. Hilmi and Darzi lit a small bonfire at the edge of the abyss, and the four of us sat around the fire. The heat enveloped our drowsy limbs. The star-strewn sky was hazy, and the shadows of the mountains long. From time to time we would smuggle a look at Yagnon who was sitting with us. This was the first time that he looked wide awake and his eyes were inwardly twinkling with a strange smile.

The fire attracted the Company Commander. He came over to say goodbye to us in a nice, friendly way, reminding us to carry out his orders. At the edge of the abyss he stepped towards us, somewhat cautious. He came, he seated himself near us, he warmed his strong hands in the fire. The light fell on his handsome face. His eyes lifted up beyond the Plain of John, whose border points to the north, a place where the ridges end. After that he examined us with a steady gaze. No bashfulness in his eyes, no perplexity. He kept looking relentlessly at Yagnon, trying to tear apart the curtains that he was wrapped in. But he kept smoking peacefully away, and his eyes kept lapping up the fire. Suddenly the Commander jerked his head back, partly stating, partly asking:

'You fought here . . . in these mountains.'

Yagnon raised his eyes to him. For the first time they gleamed with interest.

'Yes.'

'They say that some bitter fighting took place here.'

'Yes.'

'Why?'

'We were surrounded.'

'Surrounded?'

'Yes.'

'Where?'

'Here . . . around this very mountain. We hid in this furrow . . . we were hiding.'

'And after that you broke out and beat the enemy.' He wasn't asking. He was stating facts.

'No . . . we fled. We escaped through the Plain of John.'

'The Plain of John,' we whispered.

'Yes,' answered the quiet, somewhat slovenly voice of Yagnon. 'On the road they murdered us all. The retreat lasted seven days.'

'Seven?' We recoiled.

'Seven.'

At dawn the watchmen awakened the camp. The men got up in fear. Already word had leaked out about the long and tiring journey that was arranged. They packed their bags and grumbled, tied up the tents and grumbled, they removed the crates of ammunition from the pits and divided them among themselves, and the grumbling rose to the very heavens, wan in the light of the dawn. They nibbled on their dry rations, formed subordinate groups, and already the packs were on their shoulders, and the polished weapons in their hands. The sun's rays that streamed from the mountain, like broken arrows, lit up the company that stood in formation laden and weighted down with iron helmets, weapons and ammunition, and with the tents rising like squashed towers from the stooped shoulders. Sixty pairs of eyes intent on evil searched for Yagnon. The Commander passed in front of the soldiers, his bag in his hand. The grumblings fell like sheaves.

Seven days he was with us, and each day was branded with a hot iron. He tried to impose order, and what he brought was terror. Now he is trying to clear us out of here to bruise our feet for seven days with the rocks of the arid Wilderness of John. What for? Is there anything we need here? Is there anything we search for here? The ugly vulture, the corpse, spread out here. He didn't demand a thing. We are tired. We have gazed open-eyed into the abyss. The sun has scorched us.

The Commander spoke to the soldiers, described the way, talked about the drills. If we should complete the journey before seven days we could return to our homes earlier. His smile lit up his face. Would we indeed be strong enough to complete the difficult journey in less than seven days? No one stirred. Not a sound. He didn't even want an answer. He finished his short message, and his eyes looked for Yagnon; he crept out from the rear of the company, saddled with a helmet, and a cane in his hand. In that same instant a faint buzzing noise was heard. They all lifted their eyes to the sky. A grey dot was moving on high.

The Commander said to Yagnon, and his voice cut the air:

'Take your men and get on your way!'

Yagnon raised his dark eyes to him, but did not stir. All were glued to the manoeuvring plane in the sky, looking for us. Our feet stuck to the ground. If we should go down the slope we wouldn't ever come back here.

The Company Commander bristled with a stern look.

'What are you waiting for?' he roared at the bunch of platoon officers, who were standing at the side and were looking intently at him, petrified. They shifted unwillingly from foot to foot. The men lifted the crates of ammunition, ready to march. But the pupils of their eyes didn't budge from the plane that was getting bigger, flying like something from outer space. Suddenly Yagnon picked up his feet, marked time slowly, and came and stood in front of the Commander, bending over with a sort of slight bow. The scar on his forehead looked like a dark, wide-open hole.

The Commander gaped in astonishment.

'Mister,' his lips stammered out the civilian term, and his eyes narrowed, 'they want to see how they're going to take you out of here . . . so that we will remember . . . please, mister . . .'

The noise of the plane turned into a frightening blast. A whirlpool of winds went wild all around us, a smarting and very fine dust covered us. The helicopter, agitated and stormy, started to come to a stop very slowly on to the ground. Now to our joy we couldn't understand a word of the shoutings of the Company Commander. We only saw his moving lips. A door opened in the helicopter, and a rope ladder unfurled. The pilots, wearing sun visors and earphones, smiled at us who were standing laden with arms and packs.

Yagnon poked among the rocks with his cane. Everybody was

waiting in hushed silence. Only now did the Company Commander understand what we were planning, burdened and silent as we were. Like a madman he ran between the lines, but the awesome vehicle drowned out his voice. Tears stood in his eyes, his hands trembled all of a sudden. The pilots accelerated the noise impatiently, laughing. Strange and removed—from a blue, swift world.

He waved his fists at them, alone under the sky and on the earth, his back bowed, for the first time we saw him at a loss, helpless. He climbed the rope ladder, then stopped suddenly and turned his chiselled head to us. His lips twisted in a sort of shudder. He murmured a few quiet, mute last words. Curses. We bowed our heads. His body was swallowed up inside the helicopter which at once ascended from its place. The noise was dying down, the clouds of dust settled on the ground. The plane melted into the sky, and calm returned to the everlasting mountains.

Without a word, each man turned full circle. We unloaded the packs, we threw down the arms. We threw away the crates of ammunition. Quietly, on tiptoe, like someone walking with the fear of God, light-footed and intoxicated with the light. Spellbound we made our way to the kitchen tent and threw it to the ground, someone kicked the lamp until it fell apart. The toilets that we had put up were smashed in a twinkling, the tins were flying in the air. Two tackled the deserted flagpole and broke it in two. Everything returned to its former state, and before much time had elapsed, we were again sprawled out inside the furrow, exposed to the morning light, to the growing heat of the sun rays. Yagnon had already shut his eyes.

The horror of white heat is burning on us. The sun does not leave us alone. We are tired and we are growing wearier by the hour. We have returned to the tender mercies of Yagnon's bony hands. Many days are still left for us to sleep here.

Day after day passes. A sleepy, paralysed camp. Only from time to time does one of us lift his eyes to the gleaming expanse of white, which is called sky, in case a grey dot is fluttering, trying to come down to us and bring him back again.

Translated by Pauline Shrier.

Yitzhak Ben-Ner

CINEMA

*Ben-Ner was born in the village of Kfar Yehoshua in 1937. His central topic is the
Israeli situation, including the sense of change within Israel. He frequently uses distant countries as contrasts to his troubled homeland. His massive novel, Protocol
(1983), traces the history of communism in Israel and his later novel of 1989, entitled
Ta'atu'on (roughly, 'hocus-pocus' or legerdemain), is a powerful evocation of Israel
at the time of the Intifada. Ben-Ner is one of the most original voices in Israel today,
with a style and content that transcends Israeli realism. In his latest novels he has
utilized a series of monologues to advance the narrative. In these monologues he pre-
sents varieties of language to accord with his characters, the most evocative language
style being the crude, brash street-language of Israel. Ben-Ner has written thirteen
books, novels, stories, and children's stories.*

Every Tuesday they used to show a movie in our village. One Tuesday
they showed a real shocker. Mother and Father had gone to visit my
aunt and uncle, and my sister and I ran home in the darkness along
the muddy paths, gripping each other's hand so tightly that our fingernails dug into the flesh. We locked the door and shut the blinds so
the Nazis wouldn't come inside, and we couldn't fall asleep for hours.
To divert me, my sister read chapters from George Sand's *Little Fadette*.
I looked out into the darkness and waited for the beak-faced German
officer, with his glistening boots and leather strap that stretched from
shoulder to waist.

I sat up in bed and listened to my sister reading from the book,
herself frightened to death but full of sisterly responsibility, I thought
about that officer and the deserter who had eluded him. My ears were
alert to the winter sounds outside, my eyes heavy from fear and
fatigue. I could see pictures from *The Reel*, the magazine that used
to bring the war to us in glossy British photos. And right there, in
the tractor garage in our village—meeting to discuss world affairs—
were Stalin, Roosevelt, and Churchill. Stalin wore blue overalls like
the tractor-drivers, and he had a bicycle. He took me for a ride when

the meeting was over. As I clung to his waist from behind, the winter wind froze my cheeks, and mud from the road sprayed all over my pants. Then my sister woke me up so I should keep an eye open to the dangers lurking around us.

The Nazis reached our house before dawn. They were movie Nazis: cruel, cunning, terrifyingly polite, speaking to each other in English with a German accent. They stamped around the rooms in their boots, and we hid under the bed. The beaky, clamp-lipped *Reichsgeneral* slapped his gloves on his tight breeches. Failing to discover the fugitive, they left before the farmhand arrived for the morning milking. Soaked in sweat, we climbed back into our beds, regretting that we had gone to a movie that was not for children.

The fugitive's name was Dane Clark. He was short and slender with penetrating eyes. At the end of the movie he hid in a cave, in complete despair, bristling like a cornered mouse. I was only eight then, but knew that he was in complete despair. The German officer waited smiling, pistol in hand, for the end of the sixty seconds he had allowed the fugitive. The loudspeaker in the village packing house struck out the seconds, one by one, like a gigantic heart, and Dane Clark stretched a rubber band between his fingers. Out flew the golden arrow of death, a token of love from a girl, into the heart of his captor, just as the lead bullet entered his own heart.

This moment was so stupefying that the man who ran the Hebrew subtitle-projector forgot what he was doing. At the bottom of the screen the rounded handwriting still flickered: 'I shall giff you vahn minute, Sergeant. Vahn minute!'—while the words THE END appeared above the numbers 1, 2, 3, 4, 5, 6, 7. Then there was light in the hall, and the people, wrapped in coats, got up to make their fearful journey home. The Australian soldiers in their heavy trenchcoats and rough shoes returned to their camp on the edge of the village, and my sister and I fled for our lives.

Since then I have lost Dane Clark. If that was his name—perhaps I'm mixing his face up with someone else. On rainy days I sometimes sit in the print shop, hidden from my three hostile workers, and follow my memories through the stacks of yellowing magazines and old movie photos. I look for him but cannot find him. Pretty girls in swimsuits with short skirts, actors in felt-brimmed hats and wide trousers, splendid women wrapped in halos of light, oversized Fords and Packards after the fashion of the day. I lift them from the papers my uncle has sorted into bundles for future use, and the laughter of the three workers—two old men and one young—filters down to me from the old printing press.

They used to show a movie in our village every Tuesday. In wintertime, in the empty packing house; in the summer, on the school playground. The men would come to set up their equipment at noon and we would stand in a circle watching them work, school satchels in hand.

They were father and son. During the week they went to the different villages putting on movies, and on Saturday nights they showed them in the town. On their free evenings, the rumour went, the two of them sat in their womanless house and watched movies alone, the projector humming in the dark.

They knew their work. Their skilled hands unloaded the equipment from the pickup and assembled the heavy black projector piece by piece; they took out the film and ran it through, reel by reel; they ran wires up to the kerosene generator, screwed in lightbulbs; they set up the loudspeakers; they fenced in the area with wire and hung ten bedsheets on the schoolhouse wall to form a single screen. If we helped them, we were rewarded with celluloid strips cut from the film during the run.

In the evening the yard was completely filled with wooden benches and bales of hay. Big Ephraim (the son's name was Ephraim; we didn't know the father's name, so we called him Big Ephraim) stood by the cash-box. His son was busy with the big black machine and the small Hebrew subtitle-projector. In a little while two strips of light joined the snouts of the projectors to the linen screen, and a world of fantasy was ours. Margaret O'Brien wept, and little Butch Jenkins contorted his freckled face. Alan Ladd stood on deck with his mutinous sailors, and Hurd Hatfield examined his painted profile. Summer fireflies hovered spark-like in the darkness; children sank into sleep in their parents' laps; and a certain Epstein, a British Mandate functionary, would laugh before everyone else: he laughed at what was being said and not was written in the subtitles. Sometimes Big Ephraim would accidentally show the final reel before the penultimate: the Partisans would free their bold comrade Zoya from the gallows, but a half hour later the Nazis would be leading her up the gallows steps. Everyone was forgiving, since the cinema, by its very nature, demands some concessions. And so it was every Tuesday.

Some time later my friend Uri received a movie reel from Young Ephraim—thirty metres of black-and-white celluloid, with Joel McCrea on his horse and a band of wild Indians—in exchange for half a bag of Astrakhan apples. After school we spent hours looking at this acquisition, frame by frame—the redskins' war cries—along with the gunshots and the pounding of horses' hooves—rose from the tiny frames. Cinema, by God, cinema.

Not long after this Big Ephraim and Ephraim stopped coming to the village. There was a rumour that on one of their trips they picked up a girl and did things with her, the father and son together. When it was discovered, we heard, young men from the girl's village jumped them, beat them to a pulp, and destroyed their machines and their films, as if the blame lay with the cinema.

Somehow or other, our villagers acquired a projector with their own funds. Movies were shown as usual every Tuesday, but there was no joy in it.

During summer vacations I used to visit my uncle in Tel Aviv. In his small print shop near the central bus station, I would walk with him between the typesetting machine and the printing press, which was later turned over to me. I did not know my aunt or my cousin, since they had left the country before I was a year old. I was just a young boy, but my uncle would often tell me, in wonderment, how my aunt, his wife, had tearfully requested the separation. There is a picture of her in his apartment on Halperin Street, the apartment in which I live now. A pretty woman, her unsmiling face gazes past me.

'Your aunt's a cunt,' said Francesco, the oldest of the three workers, as he smeared black printer's ink on the press cylinder.

'Don't talk so loud,' said Pinchas, the younger of the two, and laughed. 'The boss'll hear you.'

'Let him!' said Francesco. 'So why'd he let her run off with that English pilot? What is it—whoring British better than us Jews?'

The workers showed their hatred for my uncle in front of me, but I don't know why.

At home I told my uncle what the worker had said. He just grinned, and foggy memories were in his eyes. He never said much; he spoke like the heroes in American movies through Hebrew subtitles.

'I think,' said my uncle, 'that Francesco was in love with her a bit. You should have seen him when she visited the plant.' That's what my uncle called his miserable print shop, 'The plant', a single composing room and a single press. 'She wasn't what he said she was,' my uncle continued. 'What could I have done? She really loved him . . .'

'And the boy?' Francesco asked me, his jaws tight with anger, his eye on the clamping forks that were seizing the sheets of paper one by one. 'When did you hear of them letting a Jewish boy go to the *goyim* in England—a Jewish boy?'

'The child,' said my uncle that evening, as we were getting ready to go to the movies, 'the child was hers. Not mine. What could I have done?' He finished washing the dishes and wiped his hands on his wife's apron, careful not to let drops of water fall to the floor. 'I know she'll come back with the child. I'm waiting.' His smile was so understanding. 'I mean, this Kinsley was married and everything looked different when she went to him in England with the child. Sheffield, I think. It was a tremendous crisis for her.'

My uncle took off his apron and sat down at the table. 'The whole thing is that she loved him with all her heart. You see, he offered to get an apartment for her and for the boy and support them. But she's not that kind of woman. I mean, you know, she's so proud. So, she left him. She started working as a waitress in some restaurant. She'll come back. I know she will. I mean, the moment she lets go of her stubborn pride. The child never gives her any rest. He pestered Arthur Kinsley the whole time. He loved me so. As if I were his father.' My uncle grew silent a moment and then continued, as if cautioning me: 'But don't mention a thing about this. It's our secret.' His wife had left eleven years before—and she hadn't written a word. I was twelve then, and already a witness to his most confidential secrets.

My uncle loved the cinema more than anything else. At 2:00 p.m. Francesco used to take his seat at the desk, and my uncle and I would go to the daily matinée. Afterwards, still immersed in visions, we would return on bus number 4 or 5 to the central bus station to lock up the shop. Back in the apartment on Halperin Street, we would fix ourselves a meal, bathe, and look at my uncle's movie magazines. At the appointed time we would leave for the early evening feature, see the marvels, and then return bedazzled and go to sleep.

I can remember my uncle gazing at the screen beneath the flickering light, his eyes and mouth open wide like a child's, his face grave like a monk's. He would watch the films in silence, in his private world. Tall, erect, and frozen. My uncle didn't like me to ask questions during the film, so I didn't. Even after the movie was over, he didn't talk about it much. He didn't talk much about the cinema at all. Even though he shared other secrets with me, the cinema was the best-kept secret of all. When I tried to get him to talk about it, his pale, ascetic face would blush, his words were confused, and he would answer curtly, unwillingly.

For many years, the small press printed a movie magazine. My sister received the thin volumes in their yellow and green covers. My uncle would let me peer into this magazine and others he had collected out of his love for the cinema.

The movie magazine was owned by a family which was quite poor. Even though they couldn't always pay their bills on time, my uncle never pressed them. He even took it upon himself, free of charge, to go over the page proofs. For hours on end, in frozen solemnity, he pored over the large sheets of paper. Some time later, a young woman came to the shop and took over this task, since my uncle had left too many errors uncorrected. My uncle bore no grudge against this girl; by her second year there was already a bond of friendship between them. The young woman was quiet and prone to blushing; she was paid very little even though she had a great amount of work. My uncle treated her with respect, since she dealt with the cinema and was a woman.

'He', my uncle told her proudly as he slapped me on the back, 'will go into writing. His essays are the best in the class.' He grew silent, and the girl smiled and looked down at her ink-stained fingers. 'Maybe he'll even write for the magazine,' my uncle said. 'He loves the cinema.'

'That's not such a great honour,' laughed the girl, and my uncle was startled. 'If he loves the cinema, let him work with the cinema itself.'

'But what's wrong with writing, I mean, in a magazine like yours?' asked my uncle.

'It's silly!' said the girl. 'Cinema, cameras, films, projectors. See? that's a more respectable thing to go into.' With a tinge of loathing she pushed the actors' photographs aside. 'This is really silly!' Francesco and Peretz stood to one side and ogled her breasts, whispering crudities to each other.

The next day my uncle paid cash for a small movie camera and a roll of 9.5 millimetre film. The perforations were beneath the picture-frames. On Saturday we went out to take some movies at the beach, near the target-shooting stands and game booths. The camera spring was wound as tight as it would go. We chose some subjects and aimed the camera, finger on lever.

'Well, press the button, shoot,' the boys urged. My uncle and I got a lot of attention. 'They're from the movies,' said the boys.

We came home tired, with sand in our hair, and movie film still unexposed. The next day, when I told this to the girl at the print shop, she laughed.

'Well, so what? I mean, this was the first time. We're experimenting,' my uncle said. 'The next time we'll really shoot something.' But his voice lacked certainty. The girl laughed again, winked at me, blushed, and went back to work on her papers, leaning her full chest against the table. From the other side of the typesetting machine, Pinchas said to Peretz: 'My God, I'd like to slip it to her.' Peretz gave an evil laugh and pushed his friend with his shoulder.

The camera is still in my uncle's desk drawer, in a small box. The film in its belly never saw the light of day. When money is tight, I tell myself I must sell it; then the need passes, and the camera my uncle gave me for my *bar mitzvah* is still with me.

Not long ago I was at the same beach. The shooting galleries and billiard halls have disappeared, but where Gordon Street runs toward the sea some people in jeans and sweatshirts were aiming a heavy black camera and silver reflectors at a very pretty young woman in an orange swimsuit. I stood there and watched them film her as she walked up and down the steps. A young man kept coming up to her saying, 'It's useless. Mark doesn't agree.' The girl lifted her hands to her mouth, as if holding back a scream and said: 'What shall we do?'

Again and again the two of them appeared and reappeared, rehearsing their parts before the camera. The crowd of observers dwindled, but I stayed until the girl, gesturing apprehensively in my direction, whispered in the ear of one of the men. I turned and walked away. Silly fool, I can't even remember the colour of her hair.

There was a certain girl on Halperin Street in the building facing my uncle's apartment house. One evening, as my uncle did the dishes before we went out to the movies, I stood on the dark balcony and watched her as she undressed by the open window. I was fourteen then, and her body—she was about twenty-five—was white and full, and her nakedness blinded my eyes. She saw me looking at her and stationed herself before me, naked and angry. When I lowered my eyes, I heard her laugh. I looked up, and she was waving at me in friendship. While I stood there amazed, a man entered the yellow-lit room, looked this way and that, lost his temper, slapped her hard and shoved her away from the window. I heard her crying, as the man lowered the blinds with a crash, sealing in the voices and lights.

Those were the days right after the War of Independence, and there were still bomb-dugouts in people's yards. One day, while my uncle was at the shop and I was going out for a walk in the city I saw the girl wearing a light summer housecoat of faded flowers, standing at the opening of the bomb shelter in her yard. She was holding an empty garbage pail and laughing at me.

'Come here!' she commanded.

I went up to the gate. Up close her body was not so shimmering white, and there were pimples on her face. She wasn't as pretty as in the evening from across the street.

'How old are you?' she asked.

I told her.

'You from here?' she asked.

'No,' I said.

'You wanna go with me down the pit?' she asked and put down the pail.

'What for?' I asked.

'Have some fun together,' said the girl. Her robe was open at the neck, and her bosom heaved at me, and the street was deserted.

She took my hand, and I followed her down the stairs.

'We'll go down deep, deep,' she whispered, as if choking.

In the darkness of the dirt stairs she stopped and clung to me, grasping me with her warmth. 'Hug me tight and it'll come,' she said quickly in a low, cracking voice, gasping as if she had just been pulled out of a lake. There were two tiny holes in her ear lobes, and her sweat-soaked robe stuck to my body. I escaped her embrace and ran upstairs, pursued by her pleading voice until I reached the next street.

In the evening, when my uncle and I returned from the matinée (for the first time my mind wasn't on the movie we had seen that day), she was waiting in front of her yard. When she saw me she began hurling stones at me and cursing loudly. My uncle was startled and pulled me into the house. We locked ourselves in, and I could see how white his face was; he didn't ask me what had happened. From the balcony I saw people gathering to watch the screaming woman until that man came out of the building and dragged her inside.

When I entered the kitchen, my uncle was chopping cucumbers for a salad, trying to overcome the shaking in his hands. Again he spoke like a movie hero.

'She's a pitiful girl,' my uncle said. 'I mean, the whole world mistreats her.' Then he told me that her fiancé had fallen in battle when she was seventeen, so she had married an older man who treated her badly. To this day I don't know where my uncle got that story. He had never met his neighbours. The woman at the grocery store told me about the girl the next morning as she packed my goods: 'She's crazy. We've told her father a thousand times to have her put away. She hasn't gone to school since she was seven, and her father thinks that he can beat her craziness out of her. People don't understand that lunacy is like an illness.'

I didn't see the girl again for many years. They said her father locked her in her room after what had happened. From my uncle's balcony I looked over toward her room in search of her distant, brassy loveliness, but I couldn't find her. About a year ago, I saw her leaving the house, childishly holding on to her scowling father's hand; she's not a child, yet she's not a woman either. She wore creased over-sized khaki slacks and high-heeled shoes. A worker's hat was pulled over her ears. Her face was wrinkled like a newborn infant's, but her flesh was full and flabby like an old woman's. Years ago her father put her in an institution, and twice a year, on holidays, he brings her home to eat at his table.

One afternoon, during the same summer vacation, the girl from the print shop invited herself to join us on our way to the matinee. My uncle's face paled in excitement. The girl got up from her desk and put on a blue corduroy coat, since the end-of-summer evenings were chilly.

After the show she came with us to my uncle's apartment, as if it were the expected thing to do. While my uncle hurried to fix a spiced cheese salad and some omelettes, the girl and I looked at the magazines.

After dinner, when she didn't hasten to leave, we sat down to talk, but our conversation was awkward and full of silences. I was four-teen then and already understood things. I got up and went to my room. A moment later my uncle came to me, embarrassed, and whis-pered to me to come back and sit with them. Together we rode the bus with the girl back to her apartment and then walked back to my uncle's. We walked half the way in silence, but my uncle found it oppressive. He stopped on the corner of Zamenhof Street and King George and asked me if I had seen the movie *Casablanca*.

'No,' I replied.

'With Humphrey Bogart,' said my uncle, urging me to remember.

At home, while turning down my bed, he asked me what I thought of the girl.

'She's nice, I guess,' I said awkwardly.

My uncle said nothing and tucked in my sheet. Then he stood up and gazed at the window: 'I hope she'll keep coming. It was a pleasant evening, I mean.'

That night we sat with Humphrey Bogart on a sand dune in short pants and sandals. Bogart played with the gravel pebbles and told my uncle that the United States had made a mistake in entering the First World War. His Hebrew was quite good. My uncle told him that Peter Lorre and Erich von Stroheim were better than any other Hollywood actors at portraying Nazi officers, with a fiendishness that was really convincing. I dozed on the sand. Across from us, the contraband arms ship *Altalena* was sunk in the water up to her stern.

The girl kept coming with us to the cinema in the days that followed —and as before, we made a silent trio. My continued presence surprised her and after a while she stopped coming. That day, at three in the afternoon, when my uncle asked her if she wanted to see *The Wages of Fear* with us, she looked at him with a wry grin, as if to say, 'What's the point?' We went alone, and my uncle was somewhat dejected. After that the girl never came to our apartment.

On my last day in the city, before returning home to the village, my uncle and I stopped by the print shop after the matinee to lock up as usual. The stairwell in the old building was dim as we walked up to the second floor, and so, too late, we saw the girl. She jumped up from the step she was sitting on, and after her, languidly, a man stood up. Her clothes and hair were dishevelled. My uncle stopped, astonished.

'Let the people pass, baby,' said the man and pulled her by the arm over to the wall. My uncle passed by them and went upstairs in silence and I followed, and neither of them said anything to us.

My uncle fumbled with the locks to the ramshackle door for a long time, deliberately, and I watched his delicate hands, overcome by trembling, and his fingers which seemed to have been drained of blood. When we went down to the lighted street the girl was no longer there, nor was the man who had been with her. We passed through bustling crowds of people at the bus station, and my uncle, sunk in thought, said: 'It's a dangerous thing, that nitroglycerine. I mean, one toss—and the whole business . . .'

I kept silent.

'What do you say?', my uncle looked at me, interested.

I remained stubbornly quiet, my eyes on my sandals.

'You saw the movie,' he said.

I said nothing.

'The old guy was terrific, eh?'

I didn't answer.

'I think I'll see that movie again,' continued my uncle. 'Too bad you're leaving tomorrow.' He looked at me warmly, like a good uncle. 'Maybe you'll stay, I mean, another day or so?'

'She's a fucking whore,' I said, enraged. 'She's a cunt. If she comes in tomorrow, I'll kick her out the window. I swear I will.'

People walking by looked at me dumbfounded. 'What's the matter with you?' he asked stunned. 'Such language . . .' He had never preached to me before. We boarded bus number 4 and didn't exchange a word till we got off at Arlozoroff and Ben-Yehuda streets. I stood, my thoughts moving back and forth between the neighbour girl in the bomb shelter and my good uncle.

In the empty street my uncle chastised me gently. He knew why I was angry—but I didn't understand a thing, he said. The girl, he said, was incurably sick. Yes, that's right. Francesco told him. She had only a few weeks to live. The flickering street lamps cast their mysterious white light upon his face.

Entering his apartment, he stopped in the doorway. 'Besides, you know, your aunt is coming, with the child. I mean—who knows? Tomorrow, the next day, a letter might come, or maybe in a month or two . . . You can't foresee these things, but it's a good idea to be smart.'

The next morning my uncle wasn't at home when I got up. Breakfast was waiting for me on the table, as usual. I packed my bag and crossed the central bus station to tell my uncle goodbye. The girl sat at her desk as usual, her head bent sideways as she worked, and her soft brown hair falling upon her shoulders. As I walked by her she looked up at me and smiled. My uncle was busy with Peretz and Pinchas at the typesetting machine which had broken down. It broke down once a day. The lead in the cylinder had hardened, and my uncle, who didn't know the first thing about machines, was at a loss.

I went up to Francesco, who was sullenly feeding paper into the press, and asked him about the girl.

'What do you mean, sick?' the worker asked and glowered at me threateningly. 'I said that? What are you—nuts or something? How the hell do I know *what* she is?'

I immediately regretted having spoken. Francesco despised my uncle. And now, as if he had been waiting for the opportunity, his rage boiled over. He grabbed me by the arm and dragged me past the printing press to my uncle, whose delicate white fingers were stained black.

'Mr Bach!' Francesco spoke in a loud voice, his cheekbones, twitching angrily. 'Mr Bach, say, why are you mixing me up in all your crap?' My uncle straightened up and looked at him without speaking. 'What's this, this kid comes up and says I said something? What do I care if that girl is sick or not. You leave me out of it. What are you doing, screwing with his head just because you're impotent.'

The girl looked up from her work, startled, and the other two workers laughed loudly. My uncle was pale, and the skin on his face stretched tight over his jaw. He said nothing.

Francesco spat on the wood floor. 'What kind of shit is this? We sit around for days with nothing to do—we never get any new orders— just some wedding cards and that crappy movie magazine—and now he gives us this shit. What the fuck's going on here.'

My uncle's eyes had a quiet look, as if he were daydreaming about something else, but the girl got up from her desk to fight his battle: 'You ought to be ashamed!' she shouted at Francesco. 'What's wrong? Your wages don't come on time? What are you yelling for?' And to my uncle she said: 'If I were you, I'd fire him. You'll find someone else, for sure. He's always causing you trouble with that dirty mouth of his.'

The worker let go of me and his body tensed: 'Looky here, you slut. I'm polite to girls, but don't you stick your ass into my business, you hear, Madam?' With measured, studied movements he dried his hands on a sheet of expensive chromo paper. 'What do you think I am, bitch, a kid?' he asked and looked over at his two friends, his moustache curling in a mean smile. 'What, there's no *Histadrut*?—no printers' union?' He balled up the dirty paper and tossed it out the window, then picked up his shirt and put it on carefully as he looked over at us and said: 'Now I'm mad, Mr Bach. You'll have a strike on your hands thanks to your personal problems, Mr Bach. You can tell that to Comrade Friedman from the *Histadrut*! They'll all take my side!'

The girl collected her papers and looked as if she were about to cry. All three workers rose and marched out to the stairwell. My uncle smiled in relief, as if he had been holding his breath until now, and muttered to himself: 'They've printed the whole form already, I think. We have eight pages, right?' The girl said nothing and my uncle continued: 'Maybe we can take in a movie at the Tamar Cinema—I mean, before you go home?' He looked at me, amused. I agreed. My uncle, with uncustomary boldness, asked the girl if she'd join us. She shook her head. Her name was Aliya.

I turned my eyes to the window. Through the panes, like the square frames of a celluloid clipping, I saw the three workers cross the street toward the nearby restaurant.

The next year I didn't come to the city on my vacation. Two years later, in the summer, I found my uncle nearly old, and ill. When he spoke to me he would clutch his chest suddenly, as if to stop some pain from breaking forth. Sometimes his left leg was swollen for several days, causing him great pain.

The cinema magazine stopped coming out; the girl Aliya no longer sat at the old desk. But the workers were the same, and Peretz now ran the typesetting machine. The customers now were passers-by who came in to order greeting cards and invitations to parties and weddings, but my uncle treated them as if they were old, established clients. He took time to explain about the paper and lettering and methods of folding. He still went to the movies, although sitting in the wooden seats was agony for him—but without the movies his suffering would have been much greater.

One day my uncle was tending with great respect to a young man with a beard and checked slacks, who had stopped in to visit the little print shop. He was a producer who needed some prints for a short film. My uncle treated him with solemn awe, and though he didn't say it, I knew what he was thinking: Just imagine—this man is in the movie business.

While the young man waited for his order, he and my uncle discussed films. My uncle mentioned a movie everybody was talking about then, Limelight. The young man sneered and waved his hand, cutting short my uncle's enthusiasm: 'Just a moment. Just a moment,' he said. 'What's in it besides the self-pity of its creator? Has it got any profound meaning? What startingly new message do you find in it?'

My uncle looked at him in amazement. Then he asked, without a trace of mockery in his voice: 'And what profound meaning is there in anything else? I mean, for instance, in shoemaking?'

The young man was quick to answer: 'Just a minute. You view the shoemaker and the artist in the same light?'

'Yes. I mean, one creates something, and so does the other,' my uncle explained.

'Are you serious?' asked the man.

My uncle nodded.

'I don't get it,' said the producer. Then he paused and thought a moment. 'If that's your opinion, it seems you don't think much of the cinema, do you?'

My uncle laughed, and I said: 'He sees, on the average, eight movies a week.' 'Wait a minute,' said the young man. 'That doesn't show he loves the cinema. I see just one film a week. You see? . . . To *really* love the cinema, is . . . ,' he struggled to define it, '. . . is a lifelong dedication, nothing more and nothing less. It's a sacrifice. You understand? It's a severing of all relation to reality outside the cinema.'

He spoke with enthusiasm and I couldn't stand him. He, whose entire stake in the matter was four films a month and a thirty-second film he had made himself, was trying to teach my uncle about love of cinema. He kept asking: *You see? You understand?* But my uncle accepted his word as law and didn't argue. I left the room and went down to the restaurant when Pinchas brought in the print the producer had ordered, advertisements for some soap.

When I returned to the shop, the young man was no longer there, but my uncle was caught up in excitement: 'Extraordinary,' he exclaimed. 'Extraordinary. I mean, this is your first break. You must sit down and write.'

In answer to my question, he told me how he had drummed up enough courage to tell the producer that I was a keen writer. The man showed a benevolent interest and finally said I might bring him some samples. Something. Maybe something could result from this, he said.

My uncle looked at me solemnly. Then, his face bathed in light from the square window, he intoned in his most cinematic voice: 'This is your chance, my boy. Don't miss it.'

In the days that followed my uncle became nearly tyrannical. He wouldn't let me come to the shop any more. Every morning, when he rose to go to work, he would wake me up and make me go sit at the writing-table. His visions turned my vacation into a nightmare.

When he left, I tried to put some words down on paper, but a few opening sentences were all I could manage. I soon got up to look at old magazines or walk along the streets. When he returned, my uncle wanted to know what I had done. I lied to him, and his face took on an expression of solemn joy that I had rarely seen. So it was for a week or two—and I didn't know how things would end.

In the final week of my vacation my aunt and her son showed up at my uncle's home, sixteen years after they had left it. It was morning, and I was at the table, listening to the press review broadcast on radio: '*Hatsofeh*, the religious workers' daily, warns President Eisenhower that his present approach to the problem is liable to create a bridgehead for . . .'

Then the doorbell rang and in the doorway stood a small, elegantly dressed woman with blonde, coiffured hair, and a young man of about twenty-two in a dark suit. I didn't recognize them as my long-lost relatives—not even when the woman asked, in stilted Hebrew, if I was Mr Bach's son. It came to me all of a sudden, like a lightning flash.

'No. I'm his nephew,' I answered. They came in and looked about the room curiously. 'I remember you as a little baby, like that,' said the woman. She sat down in the armchair in the living-room, as if she had never left. Her son took off his coat and lit a cigarette.

'You know who I am?' the woman asked. I nodded my head. She exchanged a few rapid and incomprehensible sentences with the young man. They both laughed and looked at me.

I put on a shirt and said I'd go call my uncle. They carried on with their conversation and I went down to the grocery store to phone the restaurant across from my uncle's print shop. Five minutes passed before I heard his soft, hesitant voice through the receiver.

'It's me, uncle,' I said.

'Oh, have, you finished?' he sounded pleasantly surprised.

'No,' I said, 'it's something else. Listen!' I considered what to say and how to say it, but I'm bad at formulating things, so the words didn't come out the way I intended. 'Your ex-wife and her son have arrived from abroad. They're sitting in the house waiting for you.'

This dry bit of information didn't seem to sink in on the other end of the line. I repeated it, word for word. There was silence, and I heard only static rustling through the receiver. Had my uncle stopped breathing?

After a long silence he said, in a strange voice: 'That's nonsense. I mean, it can't be them.'

'It's them,' I said. 'I talked with them.'

My uncle was silent.

'Well, are you coming?' I asked.

'What on earth did they come for?' asked my uncle in a cracked voice.

'You've been expecting them,' I said. The grocery lady kept sneaking glances in an effort to snatch bits of conversation.

'You told me yourself.'

My uncle was silent.

'Are you coming?' I pressed him.

'Listen. It's been years.' My uncle's voice sounded light years away. 'I mean, I'm not young any more.' He grew silent a moment, then asked softly: 'How does she look?'

I didn't know what he wanted to hear: 'Like a woman—what do I know? Tell me, are you coming?'

'And the child?' my uncle's voice inquired. The sounds of the restaurant filtered through—was that Francesco's laughter I heard?

'What child? He's twenty-three, or more.'

'Right,' said my uncle, and again there was a pause.

'Okay, really. When are you coming over?' I asked.

He hesitated. Finally, in a weak voice, he told me he'd leave for home right away. I returned to his apartment and found the two visitors wandering about glancing at the few things that distinguished it from any other apartment. As I ground some coffee, the sound of their laughter carried: they were making a mockery of memories.

Before the water boiled, I folded the bedsheets and made the beds. Then we sat down for coffee, and I was a stranger in their midst. The little woman and her son talked in English with each other and laughed a lot. They didn't ask me a thing. I knew, though I understood only a little of what they were saying, that they were talking about my uncle.

An hour passed, and then two. The woman took her shoes off and lay down on the living room sofa, and the son loosened his tie. They didn't seem to be in a hurry. I went back to the grocery and rang the restaurant. They made me hold a few minutes, and then came back and said that my uncle had left the print shop a little while ago.

I returned home and told the visitors in my best English: 'My uncle shall arrive soon.'

The woman said okay, and her son wandered over to the stacks of papers on the table, picked up one of the pages, and went back to her to ask about the strange letters and words. Again they both laughed. I walked out on the balcony to wait for my uncle and saw the father of the girl across the street returning home, an evening paper under his arm and two cartons of yoghurt in his hand, his face scowling as always. A garish billboard touting a new movie caught my eye, and I knew I wouldn't write a single line for the cinema again, even if this broke my uncle's heart.

Sixteen years have passed since then. No, more than that. Sometimes I sit in my uncle's print shop, which is mine now, and which barely provides a living for me and a pension for my uncle, who for many years has been in a nursing-home. I sit at the desk, and when the three workers leave for lunch, I take a smooth sheet of paper and try to write something. It's not important what. But my pen refuses to budge; my skills remain barren, and then the three grumbling workers return and I retreat.

That day back then—when I turned from the balcony, it was already afternoon. My aunt was reclining in her pink, fringed slip on the sofa, and her son had taken off his shirt and fallen asleep in the chair; and my uncle had still not returned.

At three in the afternoon my aunt got up and went to the refrigerator in the kitchen, opened it, looked inside and took out some tomatoes and chicken. Her son got up and sliced some bread. Then the two of them sat down at the table.

'Want to eat something?' the woman asked in the little Hebrew she remembered, without turning her head to me.

'No,' I said. I went out to the balcony again, but the poignant figure of my uncle, limping down the street on his bad leg, did not appear.

I returned to the kitchen. The two of them were laughing together at the table.

'I must ask you to go,' I said in Hebrew.

They didn't turn to look at me. I repeated what I had said.

'What'd he say?' asked the son in English.

'I said for you to get up, please, and leave the house now,' I said it in English.

'What's this?' asked my aunt, unsmiling. 'Where is Mr Bach?'

'I don't know,' I said. 'Get up and get out!'

'What's happening?' the son demanded of his mother.

They exchanged some fast, nervous words in English. The young man shrugged his shoulders, finished his dinner, wiped his hands on a towel and got his shirt. My aunt cleared the dishes and put them in the sink. Then she put her dress on as I stood over them like a guard.

Just then the doorbell rang. My uncle! No. In the doorway stood a tall, slender man with his hair combed back, wearing horn-rimmed glasses and dressed like a tourist. He asked me something politely, but before I could figure out what he was saying, the little blonde woman rushed over to the door and dropped her arms around him, saying, 'Arthur dear'.

'Hello there,' said the man in English in the same voice my teacher used when reading from *English for Beginners*. He kissed my aunt on the cheek: 'Well, did you find him?'

My cousin buttoned his shirt: 'No, Dad. But we've had a jolly time all the same.'

Two hours after my relatives left, my uncle still had not returned, so I went out to look for him. I locked up the shop and began a search of the city's movie houses. I had to purchase tickets three times before I finally found him at the Tamar cinema, sitting amidst the sparse audience of the first show and totally immersed in a movie entitled *The Happy Time*. On the screen Charles Boyer hugged his son, Bobby Driscoll, and gave him a lecture about growing up, as I entered and sat down beside my uncle.

'Have they gone?' asked my uncle, without taking his eyes off the screen, as if he had been expecting me.

I nodded my head. Despite the darkness I could sense his body slacken in relief, as if he had been holding his breath till now.

'I couldn't,' my uncle said. 'I mean, this damned leg. It hurts like hell. I had to come in here to ease the pain.'

We watched the rest of the movie in silence, and hurried over to the Ophir cinema to catch the second show.

Translated by Robert Whitehill.

Shulamith Hareven

MY STRAW CHAIRS

Shulamith Hareven, who lives in Jerusalem, was born in Poland in 1931 and reached Palestine in 1940. She served as a medical orderly during the siege of Jerusalem in 1948. She is now a columnist for the daily Yedi'ot Aharonot. She has published fifteen books, including poetry, anthologies of short stories, novels, novellas, essays, children's books, and thrillers. Her work is marked by a wide variety of subject-matter. Whether her central characters are biblical prophets in the desert or cosmopolitan women living in modern-day Jerusalem, their predicament is the same, invariably involving loneliness and alienation, their relationships strained and peculiar.

Just then many shallow and frivolous people had begun to dabble in literature, which pained me considerably. Perhaps that was what got me into the predicament I'm in. Why should I care about literature, you ask, I who am a lonely woman about to retire from my job as a bookkeeper for the Sick Fund? After all, I deal with numbers, not authors. But I do like to go to lectures, of which Jerusalem has no end. All this because I love literature—and not sentimentally either, the way amateurs do, because I'm a harsh critic and not your emotional type. I'm not one of your high-school girls who discovers boys and poetry all in one week.

What I wanted to say was that lately all sorts of poseurs have been permitted not only to publish but even to lecture in public. Often I sit through some talk and I suffer, actually suffer, so that I go home feeling personally insulted. I'm sure I must have been feeling that way the day I brought my straw chairs to be fixed, because otherwise what happened would not have. And what happened was this.

Since the wicker chairs in my kitchen had dried out from many days of desert heat, and the straw was beginning to snap, I brought them for repairs to a man in a dark little den of a workshop on one of those narrow Jerusalem alleys where electric drills and saws whine all day.

How people can even work in such places without shutting their ears is beyond me. The cart-driver who brought my chairs put them down in the middle of the vaulted alley, took his fare, and left. It grieved me to see them standing like unwanted guests: in my kitchen they were handsome to look at; here in the street they resembled penniless beggars. The repairman took them disparagingly and tossed them into a corner with some other destitute furniture, between a rocking chair whose belly had burst and a large chest filled with rags. In two or three weeks, he said. Better yet, come back in a month. It was so dark in his shop that I could barely make out his face. I didn't know why it took so long to do such relatively simple work, but he told me with obvious displeasure that he didn't attend to such things himself—meaning, of course, to cheap chairs like my own. He gave them to a group of old people, who worked on them slowly, more as a hobby than a job. When I enquired why I couldn't save time by bringing the chairs directly to the old people myself, he replied that their address was confidential. Suddenly he flew into a rage. Lifting one of my chairs with a menacing hand, he said:

'Listen, lady, I don't need them, you can take them back if you want. They're nothing but trouble for me—trouble with the old people, trouble with the customers, trouble with the income tax. A person tries to do a favour and this is what he gets.'

I stared at the floor and said nothing, since there was no one else around who would take my chairs at all. He turned a cross and burly shoulder to me, and said:

'All right, then. Give your name to the woman over there, and pay her something in advance.'

Only now did I notice the squat woman sitting in a corner of the shop behind an ancient, paper-piled counter that might have been a century old. Real junk it was, though good enough perhaps for the accounts of a workshop like this. The woman behind it was staring at me, staring, I could see, with bold, disconcerting eyes. For the life of me I couldn't understand why there was so much hostility in this place. She told me how much to pay and I asked if I could pay her by cheque.

'What's your address?' she snapped.

Why, I'll never know, perhaps because of her curt tone, perhaps because I was still thinking of last evening's lecture, which had annoyed me greatly, having been given by a fraud, I replied:

'Authors House.'

'Ah,' said the woman. 'So you're an author.'

To this day I don't know why I nodded that I was. I could blush for shame when I think of it. But facts are facts, and, know why or not, that's what I did. There are lies that a person will tell in a dark, noisy shop that she never would tell in broad daylight where people can see. To make matters worse, I don't even like the word *author*, which seems less a title that authors take for themselves than one appropriated by critics, professors, fraudulent lecturers, and all the others who spend their time on the noisy periphery of the small, still voice. At most, it seems to me, a person is an author only at the moment that he actually writes and ceases to be one as soon as he stops. You can call him a pedestrian then, or an eater, or a sewer-on-of-buttons-on-his-coat, but certainly not an author. I swear I don't know what got into me then.

The woman rose slightly from her seat and pointed a hand at me, extending her fat little arm to its full length:

'So what are you writing about me for? Who gave you permission to take people's lives and write them up?'

Her shouting frightened me. Years ago, before I was a bookkeeper for the Sick Fund, I worked as a receptionist in the clinic. Because there were always bullying patients shouting at me, and I couldn't stand their anger, I became very ill and had to be transferred to the accounting department. These days you can never be sure that you know all there is to know about yourself. Everybody in the street knows more than you do. Psychologists, statisticians, journalists. If someone stands up and accuses you, there's no saying you aren't guilty. And even if you aren't, your subconscious is.

'But I don't even know you,' I tried saying. This just made her shout even louder.

'That has nothing to do with it. You authors know everything. Bad people tell you things, people with big mouths, and you listen and write it all down and get rich. You live off our miseries. I hope you all burn.'

I asked her what story and whose life she had in mind. She began to laugh.

'Just look at her playing the innocent. Butter wouldn't melt in her mouth.'

'But I don't know what you're talking about.'

'Of course you do,' she declared, leering at me meanly.

She sat down again, very stout, her eyes glittering triumphantly in the darkness like black patent-leather buttons. All this while the repairman stood looking off into another corner with his back to us, though he was clearly not unaware of what was happening. Two people can sit at opposite ends of a room and still talk to each other with their bodies, even with hidden love. Yet the language spoken here was the language of war. Of ancient, backbiting hostility.

I left. Strong sunlight streamed through an opening in the vaulted archway outside the shop. Where it fell on the sidewalk stood a young man in a grey undershirt who was smoothing a large board on a hand-lathe. Chips of wood shot off in all directions, gleaming like gold sparks as they flew into the dark alley. Sparks that did not hurt, for the young man failed to flinch when several fell upon his shoulder.

'Excuse me,' I said to him. 'There's something I'd like to ask you.'

He stopped and frowned at me for interrupting his work. I was no longer so sure that I wanted to ask the question, but since I had already intruded, I said:

'Tell me, isn't there something strange about that woman at the counter in there?'

The minute I asked I felt sorry. What did I know about it, perhaps the young man was the woman's son, and here I was opening my mouth. But he answered me tranquilly enough:

'There's nothing strange about her.'

He paused and repeated:

'There's nothing strange about *that* woman.'

He returned to his lathe.

I regretted having bothered him, a young working man like him, where would the world be if not for a man who works with his hands? This wasn't my lucky alley, and so I hurried to leave it, skipping over piles of wooden chips lying between light and shade, over wrenches and heavy doorlatches. I turned into another roofed alley in which lay torn sacks of wormy vegetables from the nearby marketplace and finally re-emerged into sunlit streets and the sights I knew well.

Without its chairs my kitchen was strangely empty, yet it was still mine. I knew every inch of it. I noticed that where one of the chairs had stood some paint had peeled and left a crack on the exposed wall. Well, I'm a scrubber. I like things to be orderly and neat. I took a small paintbrush and a can of putty such as I always keep handy and retouched the wall, smoothed it out, and painted it over. The kitchen was spick and span. I didn't feel up to a lecture, who knows what a person will encounter once he leaves his own house, the surprises there are in this world—sometimes I have the strength for them and sometimes I don't, so toward evening I went out for a walk, as I do on lectureless days. In the street I met Theo Stein, who was out walking too. We stood by Government Place, where the ravens flock.

Jerusalem is full of ravens. Theo Stein used to say that they were reincarnations of the soldiers of the Tenth Roman Legion that captured Jerusalem after the long siege. They looted and stole so much, he said, that they lost their soldierly bearing. The proof of it was that no one ever saw a dead raven. Dead sparrows, yes, run-over pigeons, yes, dead thrushes fallen from their nests, yes, but never a dead raven. He talked Latin to them and claimed they understood him perfectly, although they acted clever and tried to conceal it. Nevertheless, they gathered wherever he walked, their raucous voices dry and mocking, like self-important beggars or perhaps like an old group of emigrants that will never return, whether in the woods of Augusta Victoria, by the road leading off into the desert, or by Government Place. Large, grey-black, hoppity birds whose every hop was a little hill in the air, connoisseurs of the city's conspicuous stones. Last, decrepit Romans.

In recent years Theo Stein has taken his evening walk by himself, without his wife. I like Theo Stein, like to see him walking in the distance in his short pants with the broad stride of an elderly athlete, a small rucksack slung over one shoulder as though it were a map case, his glasses and knees reddening in the great swath of sunset light. Until several years ago he walked with his wife, a woman with a wonderfully beautiful face and hair clipped short like a boy's. One never got used to the contrast between her boyish head and her bloated body, which defied all attempts at demarcation as though it were a blob of liquid held in by her dress. It was all the fault of the tranquillizers that she took day and night on orders from the doctors and that were practically her only food. Since a cure was impossible, the next best thing was to sedate her—although if you ask me, all these sedatives simply mean that the doctors have failed. When Theo Stein walked with Lotte, he didn't stride like an athlete or carry a rucksack; he walked slowly, supporting her weight, as though fearful of spilling her. Toward evening, when the heat fades and the air is blessedly refreshing, Jerusalem is full of old couples out for a walk. Sometimes I don't know what I've done to deserve to live in Jerusalem. The city gives so much of itself, so much, cool breezes and lovely sunsets and lately even municipal gardeners who work hard and plant lovely things for us. Once I saw the Steins walking when a truck suddenly cut in front of them on Saadia Ga'on Street. It was not a particularly unusual occurrence in this age of reckless driving—who isn't startled at least a few times a day by such a truck roaring by? Yet Lotte Stein's panic was out of all proportion, there was something not sane about it. 'Theo, Theo,' she started to cry in a high-pitched howl, until he seized her shoulders like a vice and shouted, 'Quiet, I want quiet right now!' They continued on their way, he scolding her roundly while she cried.

Since her illness Lotte has stopped saying hello to me. In recent years, however, she hasn't gone out at all, so that I only run into Theo, who always stops to chat a bit with me. Even if we are both out walking, we never walk side by side. We just stand in one place for a while, which is no accident, because generally people who walk together are couples, but Theo Stein and I are not a couple, we are just two people who happened to have met in the street. There is a tactfulness between Theo Stein and me. We stop to chat but do not walk together.

Lotte Stein has been repeatedly hospitalized, released, and rehospitalized, and Theo has had time for walking only when she is put away. When she is home he has to take care of her, to cook and resew her dresses, which are always bursting at the seams because of her drugged awkwardness and swollen limbs, so that he gets out at most for a quarter of an hour in the evening to stretch his legs a bit. When he leaves he carefully locks the door and makes sure to disconnect the telephone and the doorbell with a small screwdriver that he always keeps in his pocket, so that his wife is protected from all contact with strangers. A strange voice, a strange face can frighten her to tears, so that not even all the drugs in the house can calm her. Sometimes he has had to return her to the hospital in the middle of a vacation. Such things have happened more than once.

They say that Lotte Stein already needed treatment as a high-school student. She was nineteen when she arrived from Europe and still hadn't finished high school—in fact, there was nothing she could start and finish properly—and it was pointless for her to sit with sixteen- and seventeen-year-olds who were abler and nimbler than she. Perhaps she shouldn't have married either. Yet Theo Stein was determined; she was unhappy in school; and her family seized at the straw. Instead of improving, however, she only deteriorated. Two or three years after her illness had been officially diagnosed, and declared to be incurable, there was an incident with a plumber who had been working in several apartments of the building. He was a laconic, curly-headed young man who wore old army fatigues to work and had no idea that Lotte had fallen in love with him—indeed, that she was bent on a courtly, European-style romance with bouquets of flowers and tender love letters. Who is to say that she didn't deserve one? In those days she wasn't yet bloated from the drugs, there was just a wild cunning in her eyes. But the plumber noticed nothing and may never have looked in her eyes; if her immediate and total surrender from the moment he entered her kitchen surprised him, he let it go at that. He finished changing the fittings in all eight apartments of the building and—being a skilled worker whose services were much in demand—went off to other jobs.

From then on Lotte Stein took a turn for the worse. She still more or less functioned as a housewife—sometimes more and sometimes less, so that Theo Stein never knew if he would find a meal waiting for him when he came home from work—but even on days when she functioned she set the table for three, for, as she explained to Theo, the plumber was apt to return any moment and she wanted the house to be ready for him, since they were lovers and were going to elope. Afterward, when she stopped functioning entirely, Theo obediently went on setting the table for three, because he didn't want to upset her. Until one day he felt that he had had enough and told Lotte's doctor that he wasn't setting three places anymore even if all the psychiatrists in the world should counsel him otherwise. He had taken as much as he could.

I don't know what the doctor said to Lotte. Perhaps he told her that the plumber had gone off to America, perhaps he was drafted by the army. Unfortunately there are times when one has to resort to deception, though both the world and the deceiver are diminished in the process. At any rate, from now on Lotte agreed to a table set for two, just for her and Theo, only occasionally reminding him, as though some signal had flashed in her brain: 'Yes, yes, but next week we'll need three place settings again, won't we, Theo?' And Theo would grit this teeth and say, 'Perhaps, we'll have to see.'

This too was a temporary phase. Eventually Lotte Stein took to sleeping most of the time. When she didn't sleep, she ate sweets. The door had to be locked at all times.

For a while Theo refused to accept the situation and fought back. His gestures in those days were those of a man who is chasing off flies, or water from a relentless sprinkler that pursues him wherever he goes. I know a fair amount about what went on in their house at this time, because Theo Stein came to visit me now and then. Sometimes, agitated, he would tell me about things that happened in plain words, but more often it would be indirectly. It wasn't easy for him. He would sit there on tenterhooks. Once he even bent the prongs of a cake fork out of shape, one by one, without noticing it, so that I had to bring it in to a shop near the market to be fixed. And once he said:

'This generation thinks that it invented sex. Its mothers and grand-mothers did more and talked less. I'll tell you what a woman used to do when her lover left her. She went to her wash basin and scrubbed and beat all day, all day long on the washboard until her hands were raw. By evening the wash was done, there was a meal on the table, and nobody could guess that anything was wrong, not her husband and certainly not her children. Today everyone has a washing machine or a laundry, there's nothing to beat, so they all run to psychiatrists.'

I served him good coffee. You won't find any of your instant coffee or tea-bags in my house. Tea is tea with me and coffee is coffee. He sipped it avidly and said:

'Blessed be the coffee-makers of this world.'

He thanked me and left.

So you see, years ago Theo Stein used to visit, and if he stopped coming, this was only because of an embarrassment between us. The fact of the matter is that a woman I worked with at the Sick Fund had already suggested to me that Theo Stein would be a good 'solution' for me, which hurt my feelings a great deal. What did I need a solution for if I didn't have a problem? And then, in that period of his life when Theo was still resisting his fate, thrashing about like a swimmer in a whirlpool who creates more whirlpools with every stroke, he came to me one Saturday afternoon and half-heartedly propositioned me, pessimistic in advance about the outcome. I declined in no uncertain terms. He himself, so it seemed, hadn't expected anything else. Since then we have retained our twilight-time friendship, but only in the street, no longer in my house. As I've said, there is a tactfulness between Theo Stein and me.

It took me a few days to get over this incident. His proposal offended me. It was like the time the thieves broke into the Sick Fund office at night, though everyone knows that I keep only accounts at my desk, and certainly no money or anything else worth taking. Still, they searched everywhere and made a mess of the room. The sight of it in the morning made me physically ill, because I'm such an orderly woman, and here was everything upside down. It was the same with Theo Stein. I hope I'll be forgiven for saying so, but I, who am a woman of nearly fifty on the verge of retirement, have always looked for a certain beauty in people, and there is nothing beautiful about Theo Stein. Nothing at all. Perhaps I should explain what sort of beauty I mean. The beauty I look for in a man should be like the beauty of this country in which I live—this country that I love with an undivided love, it is all that I have. What I miss in people is a kind of starkness; there is so much superfluity about them. Theo Stein is too articulate, too cultured, if I may say so, too foreign in his speech. And the way he gesticulates. And all his apologies and self-explanations. What difference does any of it make? There are people who make you want to take a broom and sweep half of their words out the door. I won't say that Theo Stein is the worst of them, but you certainly can't call him stark. True there is something forceful about him, but it is not the kind of forcefulness that I like. I don't know why people wonder so at my stubbornness. I'm stubborn about a lot of things. The idea of that woman at the Sick Fund, looking for solutions for me.

All this happened years ago, and I'm only mentioning it now because there is a connection between Theo Stein and my chairs. Just last week we stood chatting by the Israel Museum, praising the gardeners for doing such splendid work for us. The trouble with all this splendour, though, is the foolishness it has led to. A custom has sprung up in Jerusalem that whenever a young lady gets married, she comes to be photographed among the flowers in her fancy bridal clothes, her young man hopping after her. The photographer stands or lies among the flowers and snaps the happy couple from every angle, more her than him: the Hall of the Scroll is a halo for her head, the Valley of the Cross a vanquished backdrop at his feet, then both of them, all flowers, buttons, and bows. They make the whole place ridiculous and depart amid a popping of flashbulbs as if they were movie stars.

Theo Stein and I were in the middle of talking when we saw an unusual sight: a bride dressed all in white, coarse-faced, a cigarette stuck in her mouth, was driving a car very fast by herself with her veil thrown back over her head and an expression of undisguised rage

on her face. We had no idea where she was coming from, or where
she was going to, or why she looked so annoyed, or why there was
no one to drive her to her destination on such a day. If Theo Stein
and I were the laughing type, we might have laughed. But we didn't.

'Just so, just so.' said Theo Stein, 'there are all kinds of conquerors.'

The ravens sat on a rock that bore the sign 'Kiryat David Ben-Gurion'
as though it were a coffee-house of theirs, and mocked in Latin. Theo
Stein stood by my side and sniffed a branch of rosemary that he had
picked in the Valley of the Cross. It had a good, dry, sharp smell. Suddenly he asked if he might come to drink coffee at my house some
day, because coffee like mine he had drunk nowhere else but my
kitchen. The thought of Theo Stein and me in my kitchen discon-
certed me, and, in any case, my kitchen had no chairs. Six weeks had
passed since I'd brought them to be fixed and I still hadn't gone to
retrieve them, so unpleasant were my memories of the place and the
squat woman who had caused me to lie. I had no chairs. I was used
to not having chairs, the things that are annoying are the things that
one has, not the things that one doesn't. And without the chairs to
sit on, my kitchen seemed larger and cleaner. What really did I need
them for? I could always grab a slice of bread and drink a cup of coffee standing up.

I told Theo Stein lamely that my kitchen was empty at the moment.
Once I had my chairs back, I'd be glad to have him over, why not?
He noticed my hesitation and must have thought that I didn't want
him because of the last time he had come. He exchanged a few more
words and went his way, smelling the rosemary.

This episode prompted me to go the next day for my chairs. How
long, after all, can one put off doing what has to be done? Moreover,
I decided that as soon as I had the chairs I would call Theo Stein on
the telephone at work to invite him. On the whole I'm not one to
use the office phone for private calls, who is there for me to call anyway, but a single exception to the rule couldn't hurt.

I returned to the vaulted alley and walked the full length of it looking for the little workshop. There was no lack of shops: I passed a
jeweller's shop, a shoemaker's shop, and the shop of a man who sold
plastic toys and a few kitchen utensils, but I couldn't find the shop I
was looking for. The noise was its usual deafening self. Drills whined,
saws rasped, yet my shop was nowhere to be found. I walked up and
down the narrow street several times without understanding how I

could be wrong, because I knew the street well, from childhood in fact, and couldn't possibly be lost. I shut my eyes halfway and tried walking blindly in the hope that my legs would be better guides, but this didn't help either. The shop was not there.

I opened my eyes again. A young man stood sawing something by a table in the sun. The chips flew all around him, but he was not the same young man I had talked to, nor was the shop across from him the dark, sunken den I remembered. It was a regular store, painted a fresh, bright colour inside, with some light-coloured rustic furniture standing in the doorway. I understand now why the shop had eluded me. It was because the vaulting covering the alley had been torn down at this point, so that sunlight was everywhere. When the light changes, places change with it and become unrecognizable. I was standing in light when all the time I had been looking for darkness.

I asked the young man sawing wood what had happened to the repair shop that had been here. He didn't know.

'Have you been working here long?' I asked.

'I just started. Maybe the manager knows.'

He wiped his hands on his pants and went inside with me to ask the manager. I hadn't meant, God forbid, to interrupt his work, but he must have wanted to take a break himself, or else was curious. The manager of the store was a young man too, with a plump and nimble appearance and a politeness that seemed to come less from the heart than from the calculation that it paid to be polite. Two or three gold rings adorned his fingers. He had no idea what had happened to the shop's previous owners. He too was new here. He was an agent for Mr Urfalli, whom I had no doubt heard of if I was an old Jerusalemite, the same Urfalli family that owned shops and whole streets all over the city. Mr Urfalli was a hard taskmaster, but well worth sticking to. How did the saying go? If you rubbed up against big money, some of it was sure to rub off on you. As a matter of fact, he remembered now having heard something when moving in here, some business about the police—there had been blows, someone had a stroke, he wasn't really sure. As Madam knows, when you associate a man with trouble, you no longer remember if he was the victim or the culprit. The less said about it, the better. Why rehash ancient history? Yes, perhaps there were some old shabby items left behind when the shop changed hands. No doubt they were thrown out long ago, Mr Urfalli wouldn't have kept them. Chairs? Old ones? Of straw? But what did I want with straw chairs? I wasn't an old woman, after all, that I needed to be attached to old things. Whoever was young at heart deserved to have something new—and he could tell by looking at me that I was nothing if not young at heart. If I would just step this way to look at his stock, I would forget all about my straw chairs. Perhaps I would like something made of beech? Or of teak? Spanish-style was all the rage now.

Since he was courteous and not ill-natured, I asked him if he knew where I could find the group of old people who had done wicker work for the shop. Perhaps the chairs had been given to them before whatever it was that had happened with the police. He didn't know, but being eager to please he telephoned a friend in another store, which belonged to Mr Urfalli too, and soon had the address for me: a workshop by the old-age home in Kiryat Yovel. A Jerusalemite like myself should have no problem finding it. The old-age home was in an old house on a hill where once had been the Arab village of Bet-Mazmil. There were new housing projects there now, but the old house still stood. It had the kind of doors with high thresholds that don't suit old people at all, an old person had trouble lifting his leg that high, he might even break it, worse luck, and broken bones were no joke in old people. On the other hand, it was said that the thresholds had been put there on purpose to keep the old people from running away. Everyone knew that old people sometimes lost their memories and couldn't even recall their own names. Then the whole police department had to be called out to look for them, which was a huge waste of public funds. Good luck, Madam, he said, I've got to hand it to you, and I'm sure we'll see you again here, even if it's just to visit and see the new stock.

I took the bus to Kiryat Yovel. I found the old-age home, hidden almong tall new buildings whose balconies on every floor were draped with wash hung out to dry. It was probably just as well, because if it weren't for the wash I might have thought I was looking at an army barracks, God forbid. It's good that people have at least their own private wash. When I reached the old-age home, I discovered that it wasn't an ordinary day there; a party was going on in the workshop. A woman with black hair, which came to a point on her forehead, and a flat, white face like a barn owl's intercepted me at the door. Not that I couldn't enter, I certainly could, I could even drink a glass of cocktail juice, really I was welcome—but it would be impossible to ask about my chairs until the party was over. When would the party be over? There was no way of knowing: once the old people began to celebrate, it was hard to get them back to their beds. 'Far be it from me to begrudge them a little pleasure in life,' said the owl woman. 'They suffered plenty before coming here, and they haven't much time left. Let them enjoy themselves while they can.'

I stepped inside. The back wall was covered with an Israeli flag. Flowerpots filled with sparse, sleepy plants decorated the other walls, rubber-plants and philodendrons and Wandering Jew. The old men and women looked well. They stood or sat or hopped gingerly in one place with bright smiles. A few wore colourful cardboard dunce caps strapped to their bald heads, which upset me, because I don't like old people to play the clown. No one ever saw my father or grandfather in an undignified moment, and no one will ever see me in one either. Yet there was nothing base about it, just a kind of childishness, as though they wished to announce with the same beaming countenances that they no longer counted for anything in life, that they had long since renounced all tastes, beliefs, opinions, and disagreements, and were left only with the sunbeams dancing on their cheeks, with party cake and party juice, yum yum. How could I possibly ask what had happened to my vanished straw chairs? One old man came up to me and urged me to eat a piece of cake, my child, my child. I ate a bit to please him and walked out, feeling very out of sorts. I had forgotten about the high thresholds and would have tripped on one of them as I left had the barn-owl woman not gripped me by the elbow. Her hand was very cold. I was frightened.

I didn't know what to do. It was nearly evening and the sun was low in the sky. It occurred to me that I didn't even know what was happening at Authors' House that night. Ever since that foolish lie I told I'd been going there less and less, as though the shame of it were written on my face. It seemed to me that the truth was very near and that only my own blindness kept me from seeing it. Perhaps I should try to sleep, I told myself, perhaps I'll dream the answers that can't be found in waking life. My kitchen looked terribly empty without its chairs. There could be no question of inviting Theo Stein— God in heaven, not even to have any chairs! For a moment I thought of returning to the plump, foxy man in the alley, Mr Urfalli's henchman, and ordering some beechy-teaky from him. Even though it wasn't really me and never could be. Give in, give in, everything seemed to be telling me, don't be such a stubborn old maid, the world likes compromisers. One way or another I saw that the crack in the kitchen wall that I had refinished so carefully was back again. The problem was apparently not just the paint, but a structural fault in the wall itself, which was a much more complicated matter. Bigger solutions are called for, I said out loud to myself, without having the vaguest idea of what they might be. My straw chairs, which I had already given up on, floated before me in space in a slow, weightless dance.

Translated by Hillel Halkin.

Yehoshua Kenaz

THE THREE-LEGGED CHICKEN

Kenaz was born in Petah Tikva in 1937. He studied at the Hebrew University and later at the Sorbonne, and published his first short story in 1960. He has subsequently published four novels, a play, and a book of short stories. His early stories, collected in Musical Moment, *have become classics of the genre. Rites of passage to adulthood and the destruction of innocence are the principal topics in the four stories in this collection of which 'The Three-Legged Chicken' is one. His novel of 1991,* The Way to the Cats, *on the difficult topic of the elderly living in a geriatric home, earned Kenaz many superlative reviews, and* Heart Murmur, *which is set in an Israeli army camp, is regarded as his finest social novel.*

One day at the end of summer they laid the old man they called grandfather on the floor in the big room, lit candles at his head and closed the double doors on him and on the people standing around him. The last rays of sun filtered through the coloured panes of glass at the tops of the windows and the veranda door to say their last farewells, staining the walls, the floor, and the body with violet, green, and orange lights and making the flames of the candles look very thin and pale in comparison.

When his mother emerged from the big room she stood opposite the boy and bent over him, bringing her face level with his so that she could say what she had to say to him in a very soft voice. She smiled for a moment, a strange smile that he had never seen on her face before, and he did not know if it was anxiety or malice glittering in her eyes when she said to him: our grandfather is dead, our grandfather is dead—but it was obvious to him that she knew she was hurting him for nothing, and that this was what she wanted, and in this matter there would be no concessions.

He asked when his father was coming, because he knew that at a time like this his father was bound to come and restore order and security, but there was no reply. The old man they called grandfather, who used to come every evening when the boy got into bed, to urge and beg him again and again to say 'Hear Oh Israel', if only for his sake, did not come to his room that night, just as he had not come on any of the previous evenings of his brief and final illness. And knowing this, he wanted to say 'Hear Oh Israel' to make him happy, to repeat the words after him as he wished him to do and to give him love in return for the love he had given him.

All night long it seemed as if people were walking about on tiptoe in the rooms and passages of the house in the dark, seeking, secretly labouring at all kinds of tasks whose meaning there was no way of knowing. For hours the boy racked his memory for the words of the prayer which had suddenly vanished, as if the old man had taken them with him on his journey. For hours he could not fall asleep, and no one came to the doorway to peep into his room and see how he was. All night long he waited for his father to arrive home from work and to hear his voice and know that he had someone to take care of him. Until late at night the quiet bustle continued, and when the searching and silent prowling between the rooms ended there were only the brief, businesslike whispers of people parting from each other for a while until they met again to set out on a journey together.

And when silence fell the boy heard the voice of the woodworm again, friend of the sleepless, burrowing in the depths of the old wardrobes, labouring and pausing in her labours and beginning her nibbling again, momentarily taking fright and listening to the sound of his breathing in order to ascertain that it was rhythmic and he was indeed asleep: and if not—she would stop and make an effort not to disturb him and wait until he fell asleep; but no sooner had she conquered her drive for a moment than it would reassert itself and overwhelm her with its strength. And the boy would outwit her and restrain his breath. And the worm would wonder if he had really fallen asleep and she could go ahead without anything to stop her, and she would send out tentative signals, groping in the dark. Very hesitantly she would venture an experimental nibble, nibbling and stopping, afraid of exaggerating, trying to discover how much she could dare at once without bringing wrath and catastrophe down on her head. She was so full of a sense of the significance of the deed she was destined to do, and so full of the prudence demanded by the importance of the task and the need to perform it stealthily, obsequiously, and ingenuously. And nevertheless, as soon as she plucked up courage, or simply succumbed to her drive and went back to work, she would be overcome by an urgent, panic-stricken need to cram as much as she could into one short moment, in order to make up for the time lost in the pause of the past and counteract the paralysis that would take hold of her a moment later, when her senses were alerted to the danger again. With blind enthusiasm she would plunge into her labours, the other possibility receding as she did so, and until the fear came back again she would accomplish whatever she could. And when she stopped, it was obvious that she was in the grip of terror and great remorse, and that she was playing a cunning game of deceit and make-believe: clinging tightly to her place, shrinking into herself as far as she could, and pretending to be bodiless and spaceless, a concentrated point of alertness to spy out the silence. And whenever she stopped work for longer than usual, breaking the accustomed rhythm, the boy would cover his face silently with the sheet and roll his whole body into it, very slowly, so that not the slightest sound would reach her, and he would lie motionless, barely breathing and imagining that he, too, was all closed in and wrapped up in himself, and since his eyes were closed his bed turned into one of the deepest, most hidden veins of the wood, shrouded in eternal darkness, warm and protective, and thus he and she would listen to each other in the silence, and she would always be the first to give in to the illusion of safety, send out a tentative, experimental signal, a tiny sound to test the reaction: and since nothing happened to arouse her suspicions that a trap was being set for her in the silence, and since her appetite had been whetted and her passion had blinded her to all sense of caution and danger, she would fall to work again. And sometimes she would go on for longer than usual in her enthusiasm and oblivion, and the boy would wonder how far this eagerness of hers would deafen her to the danger signals from outside. After a long moment during which she did not stop he would cough loudly and she would fall silent immediately, and her silence would go on and on, as if it were taking her a long time to recover from her terror.

At that moment the boy remembered the big room and the old man they called grandfather, who had been left there by himself. He opened his eyes and suddenly the sounds of the night broke into his room from outside: the sound of the crickets rising from the furthest reaches of the house, and the yard, and the chorus of frogs gathered by the cow shed and in the garden, and the howling of the jackals in the citrus groves—all these silenced the soundless game between his breathing and the whispering of the woodworm, and with them the ample light of the moon came flooding into the room. And since he was accustomed to this pattern of sounds and its regular sequence, he did not even raise his head from the pillow to see what was happening around him. The shadow of the oil lamp standing at the end of the passage stretched like a long dark triangle from the threshold of his room to a corner of the house which was invisible from where he was lying. And he wanted to get up and see what was in the big room at this hour of night, but his body refused to respond to his will, as if it had been turned to stone.

From all the corners of the room the dark and loathsome thing advanced on him. He opened his mouth to scream, but his lips and voice were paralysed, and only the muscles of his throat strained to call for help or break the evil spell of the moment, but in vain. He felt that he was not dreaming, but this was how he always felt when the thing came at him out of the dark, and only in the morning, when he recalled it to his memory, he would wonder if he had been dreaming or if he had really been awake when he saw it. And only the vestiges of the scream that he had wanted to utter but couldn't, remained like a painful sensation in his throat.

In the morning he would get up and look for the trickle of powder that had fallen from the wardrobe, the worm's nightly work and a concrete proof that those moments were real, and he would crumble the powder between his fingers until it disintegrated and was absorbed into his skin, and much as he wanted to derive some secret knowledge from it and its touch, all his efforts were in vain.

The quilt and mattress renovator sat on an empty crate next to one of the citrus groves, took a hard-boiled egg, about a quarter of a loaf of black bread, and a few olives and tomatoes out of the little haversack slung over his shoulder and got ready to eat his breakfast. The instrument he used to tease the cotton wool, which resembled a big harp with one string, stood leaning against the fence and at its foot a bundle of tools tied up in a coarse cloth of a blue-grey colour. There was not a soul to be seen and the only sound was the murmur of the water in the irrigation canals coming from the citrus groves. It was already quite late in the morning. The quilt and mattress renovator took the egg and aimed it at the middle of his forehead. Although there was no audience to witness his tricks he could not suppress the buffoonery which in the course of plying his trade had become second nature to him. He held the egg opposite his forehead, squinted at it with both eyes, moved it away again, with his eyes squinting at it all the time as if in alarmed anticipation of the blow which was about to descend at any minute, and which indeed materialized immediately as the man smashed the egg on his forehead and burst out laughing. He held the egg with its shattered shell in his left hand and began removing the bits of white shell very slowly and meticulously. When he had finished he inspected it carefully to see if there were any bits left. His face was serious now, but his eyes hinted to the empty sun-washed spaces in front of him that there was one more joke in store for them: again he squinted at his nose and all at once he dropped the whole peeled egg into his wide open mouth, where it vanished without a trace. He looked about him as if to test the reaction of his non-existent audience and then slapped his cheeks with both hands, as if to hit the egg from one side of his mouth to the other, like a tennis ball. After this his shoulders heaved convulsively, as if he had swallowed the whole egg. Then he spat it out into the palm of his hand, took a few olives from the handkerchief spread out in front of him, stuck his teeth into the quarter loaf of black bread and started chewing with his mouth open, while at the same time humming a cheerful tune and swaying his head from side to side in time to the tune.

Two men appeared at the end of the road, one of them carrying a suitcase and the other a kind of square box covered with a sack, and began advancing towards the quilt and mattress renovator. When they reached the place where he was sitting they stopped and exchanged a few words with him. Then they consulted with each other, put the suitcase and the sack-covered box down on the ground, sat down next to the man, and began to roll themselves cigarettes. They rolled one for him too. The three of them smoked peacefully in almost total silence.

The two men lay back on the ground, rested their heads on their hands and closed their eyes. The quilt and mattress renovator kept darting glances at the sack-covered box and an ugly smile appeared on his face, as if he had remembered an obscene joke. Then he looked at the two sleeping men and his face suddenly fell. He stared at the fields and citrus groves and his eyes scanned the dirt road beside which he was sitting, which twisted and turned and receded into the distance until it disappeared around a corner next to the horizon. He remembered to cast a glance from time to time at his one-stringed harp and his bundle of tools, but he would immediately turn his head away and start staring into space again, and there was a great sadness in his eyes. He too would have liked to lie back like them and take a nap, but since he had promised them to look after their things until they had recovered their strength he did not stir from his place, nor did he dare to hum his songs for fear of disturbing their sleep.

When the two men rose after a little while he asked them to take him with them, and they laughed at him. They pointed at his tools and he promised that he would sell them and give the proceeds to them, or even abandon them where they lay and follow them with no more ado. He took their hands and begged them, saying that he would do anything for them if only they would let him join them. They laughed. They straightened their clothes. One of them picked up the suitcase and the other the box covered with the sack, and the quilt and mattress renovator called out to them. They set out. He leapt up and ran after them.

They did not turn their heads and he walked along behind them. Until the man with the suitcase picked up a stone and threatened to throw it at him, but still he was not deterred. And seeing that the man was still following them and that he was already far away from the citrus grove and the fence where he had left his tools lying, they stopped and turned to face him. The man with the suitcase picked up a stone again and this time he threw it with all his strength at the quilt and mattress renovator and hit his leg. He jumped into the air as if he had been bitten by a snake and stood rooted to the spot again. They continued on their way without turning their heads again, and he yelled curses and entreaties and abuse after them, until they disappeared from view and he returned unwillingly to the place where he had left his tools. He sat down on the crate and began humming his songs and staring into space again.

In the morning they sent a cart to the ice factory to fetch ice and the boy did not know what they wanted the ice for. His uncle, his mother's brother, stood in the back yard facing the cowshed, and he looked at him for a long time without saying a word. The sound of the Arab playing his fiddle drifted out of the dark doorway together with the smell of the cows and their fodder. No one had told the Arab to stop playing his fiddle. His uncle called the boy to him softly, gave him a few coins and told him to go to the little market to buy the newspapers. They wanted to see how the funeral notices had been printed. And the boy really wanted to stay and wait for his father to come and see when the cart came and what they would do with the ice and if they would leave any of it unguarded. But the people who up to that day had belonged to him were now busy with their own affairs. And also the old man they called grandfather who, during the boy's illness, had prowled restlessly around his bed, sighing bitterly and bringing him glasses of lukewarm water sweetened with sugar to sweeten the pill of his sickness a little, and saying indulgent things to him in a broken voice with his peculiar accent, and stroking his forehead with a heavy, hesitant hand—he too had joined the conspiracy and lay motionless on the floor in the big room with candles burning at his head, waiting for the blocks of ice they had sent the cart to bring for him for a purpose the boy could not fathom.

His father was working then in one of the army camps near Haifa and came only for Saturdays. On Friday evenings the boy would go and stand in the street long before the time his mother told him to, waiting to see the figure of his father appearing in the distance and coming towards him from the top of the road, to examine his face and his body and touch his clothes that had come from far away and get to know him anew all over again and wait for him to throw him into the air and hug him. His father had not yet come but he knew that he would come, even though it wasn't Friday evening.

He put the money in his trouser pocket and went to put on his sandals.

That morning they brought Bruria home for the summer vacation from school, which was far away from the village. Her mother and father got up early in the morning so that they would have time to bring her back and take her home before too many people saw her. When the bus arrived Bruria refused to get off until her parents promised to buy her new shoes. She was wearing laced-up boots and her parents tried to persuade her that these boots were healthier for her feet and prevented them from getting tired. But Bruria stamped her feet and said that she would not budge from her place in the bus until they promised to buy her the most modern high-heeled shoes, and in Tel Aviv, nowhere but Tel Aviv would do. All the way from the bus station to their house next to the little market they kept her quiet with arguments and promises: Whoever buys new shoes just like that on an ordinary day in the middle of the year? On Passover eve we'll buy you new shoes. And anyway the ones you've got on are still new, they look as if they've just come out of the shop.—When's Passover eve? asked Bruria. It'll be here soon. In a little while.—After these holidays? asked Bruria.—Yes, said her father.—After the winter? —Yes, said her father. Bruria reflected for a moment and her father said: But only if you're good and do what you're told and listen to your mother and don't talk to people.

Passover eve, said Bruria, Passover eve, Passover eve. After the summer and after the winter. In a little while. Soon. And in Tel Aviv, in the most modern shop? And thus she gave in to them and went home with them, dreaming about her new shoes. But as soon as they got there she forgot all about their promises and sat down on the sofa and scowled angrily at her big boots.—What's got into your head about your shoes? Did somebody at school say something about them? asked her mother. But Bruria did not reply, only stamped her feet in hatred and humiliation and then fell furiously on her boots, quickly undoing the laces and taking them off and hurling them into a corner of the room. Afterwards she took her socks off too and sat barefoot. Her father said to her: If you don't behave yourself we'll take you back to school and we won't buy you new shoes on Passover eve or ever in all your life.

When the boy went into the street there was still no sign of the cart returning from the ice factory. He saw Molcho sitting next to the notice-board and whispering something to himself, as if he were hatching some evil. Molcho was hostile to the boy because of some forgotten quarrel, or perhaps there had never been a quarrel at all and the boy had simply walked past his house on the street of the Sephardis and Molcho had tried to hit him. And when he saw him coming Molcho stood up and started shaking the dust from his trousers. He gave the boy a hard look and his lips were parted in a challenging smile. The boy started walking without looking at him. But he imagined he could hear his bare feet padding behind him like some wild cat, and he knew that the moment he heard them quicken he would run away as fast as he could. But as long as he kept on padding softly behind him he wouldn't anger him by sudden flight. He concentrated all his senses on listening and on the effort to check the flight begging to break out in his feet and keep them on the alert so as not to miss the moment when it would become necessary to bound forward and run. For a moment it seemed to him that he no longer heard the bare feet padding behind him but he was afraid to turn his head and look. Until he gathered up his courage and looked and saw Molcho standing a few steps behind him and beckoning him to approach. But the boy did not budge. Come on, I won't hit you, said Molcho. The boy approached. Your grandfather's dead, said Molcho.— It's not true, said the boy: Who said so?—I'll hit you if you lie, said Molcho. And the boy said nothing. They've brought Bruria home for the holidays, said Molcho. I saw her. He looked for a moment at the windows of the house, and since there was nothing to see he turned his back on the boy and walked away. The boy let him go, and when he was about to turn into the little market to buy the newspapers he heard her voice calling him from the window: Little boy, little boy, come here for a minute.

He went into the yard and stood facing the window. He saw her face, the face of a pretty child, pale, dark-eyed, and her hair which was already full of grey streaks. Don't be frightened little boy, you can come into the house, my mother and father have gone out and I'm alone, said Bruria. But he stayed where he was and went on looking at her face. In the window frame she looked like a figure in a portrait, from the waist up. She leant with her elbows on the sill, one hand dangling and tapping the wall and the other patting her hair into place. On Passover eve they're going to buy me new shoes, in Tel Aviv, the most modern shoes there are, with high heels. She fell silent for a moment and closed her eyes. There was a triumphant smile on her pale, pretty face: And at night I'll dance with all the boys! And I'll be the belle of the ball! And I'll dance with the boys all night long!

Opposite the big tap next to the cowshed, in the back yard of my house, a long time before, before all the times I have ever known, I experienced something like an awakening from a dream into a new dream. I always spent a lot of time sitting opposite the big tap and playing with it, because the handle of the tap had been removed to stop it from dripping, and also perhaps to prevent me from opening it and playing with the water as I loved to do. But I kept plugging away and never gave up trying to open it with stones and bits of wire, nails, and even my teeth.

Until I resigned myself at last and passed my fingers over the thick, cold pipe, seeking something to take hold of, some secret catch which would make everything work like magic. The cowshed with the two steps at its door and the dim light inside it always looked blurred, and the Arab sat inside it playing his fiddle.

And as I sat stroking the stem of the tap a great and mysterious spirit passed over me, over me and the world around me: the wall of the cowshed and the two steps took on before my eyes their final, definitive form, and the strains of the Arab's fiddle emerging from the doorway sounded as if they were coming from the bowels of the earth. And the earth steaming with a pleasant warmth and the dusty sky and the wooden fence and the trough and the little back shed next to the urinal and the smell of the cows and the sourness of the sacks of fodder and the flock of birds suddenly startled into flight from the roof of the cowshed, shooting like an arrow of little black dashes to the tops of the trees and from them to the limits of the horizon: the more fixed and formed and self-sufficient they became the further they receded from me, shrouded in strangeness and perhaps even hostility. And at the same time—from unknown depths inside me—there rose a voice, the voice said: I, I, I, I. And although the voice came from inside me, it wasn't my voice. And the voice was quiet, solemn, redeeming and very dangerous, and it stiffened my hand on the chilly metal of the big tap, which had become rounder and more slippery, trying to shake my fingers off and put an end to all my games. And the voice filled me with dread and a joy whose cause I could not tell, but I felt that it was greater than I was. Out of the twilight silence the voice spoke to me and I looked around me, tried to rise to my feet and could not, like at night in my bed when the dark, loathsome thing came at me from all the corners of the room. The vividness of the shapes awakening to a life of their own before my eyes and the painful and liberating current flowing through me, strong and silent, coming from an unknown source and spreading through all my limbs, brought the scent of the greatest of all possible adventures before me. And the voice rising from the depths of my being pushed onto my lips the words which slipped out as silently as if it were not I saying them but a stranger sitting inside me and calling without stopping, in great astonishment: I, I, I, I.

A heavy load descended on my shoulders and squatted there, like an uninvited guest with the right to stay forever.

My hand fell from the snub-nosed tap and the Arab went on playing his fiddle inside the cowshed. The sound of the Arab's fiddle with its thin notes dragging out endlessly like the voice of some strange beast, heartbreaking in its sobbing, moaning its longings for other places, told me that from now on every step I took and everything I did and everything I touched would be a secret known only to me and never to be revealed to anyone else in the world. For my hands had touched the last wall of all—behind which there was nothing.

A hidden hand dragged Bruria away from the window and her cries rose from inside the house: Handsome boys and girls in party dresses are dancing together all night long, and I'm going to dance with them too!

And then the boy heard the sound of blows and Bruria screaming. Her old father came out onto the porch and approached the boy: What are you doing here, he asked, with your grandfather dead?!

She called me, said the boy.

Go home, said her father.

And he stood on the porch waiting for the boy to go. The sound of Bruria's shrieks rose from the house and her mother drew the blind and shut the window where Bruria had been standing before, as if she were in a picture.

When he went into the street the boy saw the little market in front of him and a crowd of people outside Yardeni's cafe. He approached the people and they told him that the three-legged chicken was on display inside the cafe. Two men, they said, had obtained the chicken on loan from its owners, who had brought it from abroad, and there was nothing like it anywhere in the world. The two of them were passing through the village on their way and they had agreed to stop for a few hours to put the monster on display. The next day they would leave for a tour of the surrounding villages and then they would take their show overseas. The sound of laughter rose from Yardeni's little cafe, which was packed with people. Strange, obscene cries were heard from the interior. The entrance fee, explained the people standing outside, was divided equally between the owner of the chicken, the two men travelling around with it, and Yardeni, who had made his cafe available for the show. The faces of the people emerging from the cafe after the five minutes paid for by the entrance fee were exhausted with laughter and astonishment. The boy drew nearer the doorway, pushing his way through the crowd of curiosity-seekers and people waiting in line to pay the entrance fee. Suddenly he felt a hand on his shoulder and Molcho's face was very close to his, steaming with heat and smelling of sweat.

You want me to look after you? I'll look after you for ever, just like my brother.

And Molcho did not cease clutching his shoulder.

A chicken, with three legs, said Molcho. It talks and dances and pulls faces.

The boy put his hands in his pockets and felt the coins and knew that he would not buy the newspapers which he had been sent to fetch and that he would never again see the face of the old man lying on the floor of the big room, and the cart they had sent to the ice factory, and a great anxiety swept through him and drew his heart towards unknown things. He stretched out his hand to Molcho's shoulder and clasped it in great fear.

And you can come and swing on the swing in our yard whenever you like, with my brother.

He gave him the coins he had taken out of his pocket.

I'll look after you for ever, said Molcho, even more than my brother.

The monster stood inside its little cage made of flimsy wooden slats, which had been placed on top of a high box. There was a handful of corn grains in the corner of the cage but she did not touch them. She kept rolling her eyes around and swivelling her head from side to side so as not to miss anything that was going on around her. And she would hop on her two healthy legs and jump backwards, as if she was trying to escape from the danger surrounding her on all sides, and her extra leg, her sick leg, stuck out behind her, defiant and provocative. Yardeni stood next to the cage guarding it against the blows of the people who were trying to tease the chicken and elicit grotesque and surprising reactions from her. And a certain cart-driver, a very heavy man who always wore a sweaty cap on his head, kept circling his mouth with his hands like a trumpet and imitating a cock's crow in order to awaken her longings for a male and every movement she made would then be interpreted as a response to this simulated mating call, seductive and very obscene, giving rise to loud guffaws of laughter. The two men who had brought the chicken sat at a table next to the door and took the entrance fees. And every now and then Yardeni glanced in their direction to make sure that they weren't putting any of the money into their pockets before giving him his share.

The drunkard sat at his usual table in the corner, untouched by all the commotion. He was in a quiet and very thoughtful mood. And only when a very loud burst of laughter rose from the crowd around the cage, in reaction to one of the spectator's comments or one of the monster's movements, the drunk would raise his eyes, shake his head dismissively, and whisper: Vanity of vanities, vanity of vanities.

There was a bad smell in the crowded cafe, and the boy did not connect it with the congestion and the sweat but with the presence of the chicken, and especially her third leg, infected with some disease from foreign parts. Molcho stood next to him opposite the cage and stared at the spectacle, fascinated and perhaps a little anxious too. The boy knew that his father would not have come to stand among these people and stare at a chicken with three legs, and he missed him very much. And although no one had ever condemned such spectacles to him, he knew that they were wrong. The anxiety that had been in him before he entered the cafe and had drawn him to the spectacle and the company of these people and the friendship of Molcho now brought ominous pictures before his eyes. Every now and then the corners of Molcho's lips twitched in a smile, as if he were seeing things in a dream. And the boy pretended to be very amused and tried to look closely at the chicken, who was hopping from side to side of her little cage, as if she were fighting some hidden enemy, and he was ashamed of his ignorance of the secret which would have enabled him too to enjoy and admire the spectacle. He waited impatiently for the time he had paid for to be up so that he could leave. During those moments he felt such a sense of desolation that he thought it would never leave him.

The sound of a quarrel broke out at the entrance to the cafe, where the quilt and mattress renovator could be seen trying to force his way in past the two men sitting by the money-box, who were pushing him back and hitting him. Yardeni looked anxiously at the door, wondering whether to leave his post by the cage and to go investigate the reasons for the fight and restore order, or to let it alone and guard the chicken.

The quilt and mattress renovator shouted something from the doorway to the people inside the cafe, and the people asked one another: What's he shouting there, what does he want?—With carpenter's glue, he says, they stuck the leg on with carpenter's glue.

The alarmed Yardeni was driven to take a few steps forward again, in order to have a few words with the two men, but before he could reach the doorway he had to return to his post by the cage to guard it and restore order in the cafe, where the outcry was growing louder by the minute; and there was no knowing if the outcry was due to excitement and high spirits or to indignation at the fraud, or whether the people's frenzy was simply seeking a pretext for erupting after it had been inflamed by the sight of the freakish, contemptible chicken: in any case, the heavy cart-driver with the sweaty cap brushed Yardeni out of his way, lifted the cage into the air with both his hands, hit the flimsy wooden slats with his fist and shattered it with a couple of blows. He removed the chicken, brushed aside her tail, and inspected her third leg. All the people crowded round and the chicken flapped her wings and squawked in pain as the cartdriver attempted to tear the third leg out of her flesh. Again and again he tried to part the leg from the flesh of her body, pulling harder and harder as Yardeni entreated him: Have pity on dumb animals!

And suddenly they all saw the leg lying on the palm of the cart-driver's hand and drops of blood falling from the chicken's white feathers. The people in the cafe burst into angry cries and laughter and they all rushed to the doorway to see the two men in all their guilt. But their places next to the table were empty, and the money-box was gone too.

The cart-driver dropped the chicken and threw the third leg in disgust at Yardeni, who recoiled in horror. Although drops of blood were still falling from underneath its tail, the chicken ran frantically about the cafe looking for the door, but she could not find it for the people filled the room and hid the light from her.

And when she bumped into the legs of the people who recoiled from her in disgust, because they had not forgotten her third leg, she flapped her wings and tried to fly away, as if she were a bird. Only the drunk, who was in a very quiet and thoughtful mood all this time, smiled at the panic-stricken chicken, held up an admonitory finger, and repeated: Vanity of vanities, vanity of vanities.

They stuck it on with glue, with glue, said Yardeni and clapped his hands despairingly, remembering the two men who had escaped with the money and left him with the chicken and the uproar in his cafe. The crowd began to leave the cafe. When they were outside Molcho said to the boy: You want to come and swing now or some other time?—Some other time, said the boy.—What a chicken, sighed Molcho, remembering with emotion the impact of the experience.—They stuck it on with glue, with glue. It's a shame my brother didn't see it. And once again he stretched out his hand to clasp the boy's shoulder, as a gesture of friendship. But the boy evaded him. Molcho went on his way without another word, and the boy knew that next time he encountered him Molcho would try to hit him again, as he always did, but he no longer cared.

When the boy reached home he stood outside the gate for a minute looking at the windows. Then he climbed the steps and the front door was locked. No one answered his knocking. He walked around the house and everything was shut up tight. He went into the back yard and saw the Arab sitting on the steps of the cowshed, without his fiddle, his head on his hands and his eyes staring vacantly.

In the afternoon Bruria's parents left the house and walked with her to the bus station. Bruria was quiet all the way, but when she saw the bus she shrank back and promised that she would be good. But her parents paid no attention to her promises. She wept silently and her mother too wiped a tear from her eye. But her father said: Let this be a lesson to you for next time, let this be a lesson to you.

I don't want the shoes anymore, said Bruria, I'm sorry. They got on the bus and Bruria covered her face with her hands and cried without stopping. Her mother, who sat beside her, embraced her and put her head on her shoulder, and her father, who sat in front of them, pretended not to know them.

The boy circled the house again, to see if anyone had come back in the meantime, but the doors and windows were all shut, and there was no one to be seen. He returned to the back yard and sat down opposite the big tap. He held the stem and wondered if the same thing that had happened before would happen again, but everything stayed the same and the afternoon hours stretched out endlessly.

In one of the deserted fields behind the citrus groves, outside the village, the quilt and mattress renovator lay on the ground with his eyes open, staring at the sky. A column of ants crawled over his arm and climbed up to his neck and down to the ground again, as if he too was part of the earth, a hump on its back.

It was a dreary summer afternoon and everything was empty and too quiet. The Arab rose lazily to his feet and went into the cowshed and started raking the manure into the gutters and from the gutters outside. The raking sounded like a scratching in the heart of the darkness. A slow drag of the rake, then a short silence, then a drag of the rake, then silence again. And the boy looked around him and waited for the thing to happen again, and he was seized with rage at the indifferent touch of the big tap, and affronted at being left alone. He said softly: I, I, I, I—and the magic did not work.

And suddenly his body was lifted sky-high in a familiar, well-beloved movement, and immediately he felt his father's face with its prickly stubble against his cheek. And the boy could find nothing to say to his father for shame filled him with a kind of fog. But he was afraid that his eyes would fill with tears and betray him if he did not open his mouth and say something, and so he whispered into his ear: Our grandfather is dead, our grandfather is dead. And his father hugged him and said nothing in reply, but carried him to the house and put him down next to the door and took him by the hand. Together they entered the house and his father led him into the big room and there was a secret smile on his face. They went into the big room and the boy looked around him and saw that nothing had changed and the room was the same as always. As if no one had ever lain there on the floor, and there had never been candles or anything. The colours of the window-panes as always cast purple, green, and orange stains on the walls and tiles. The boy did not understand what was before his eyes or the contradictions rising in his memory. He looked questioningly at his father, and then again at the room, and afterwards he smiled at his father as if to ask: Did it really happen? And his father smiled back at him as if to say: Indeed it did.

Translated by Dalya Bilu.

Amos Oz

STRANGE FIRE

Oz, one of the best-known Israeli novelists and political spokesman, was born in Jerusalem in 1939. At the age of fifteen he went to live on a kibbutz, where he remained for many years. He studied philosophy and literature at the Hebrew University in Jerusalem and was then visiting writer at Oxford, author in residence at the Hebrew University, and writer in residence at Colorado College. He has been named Officer of Arts and Letters in France. His work has been widely translated and he has been awarded many international honours, including the 1992 Frankfurt Peace Prize. He has written numerous novels, collections of short stories, essays, and articles. He is a respected political commentator and a founding member of the Peace Now movement in Israel. His fiction is rooted in the history of Israel, presenting in graphic style its people, its political tribulations, and its biblical landscape. In the 1990s his novels displayed greater introspection and concern with the protagonists' interior lives.

Night spread his wings over the peoples of the world. Nature spun her yarn and breathed with every turn of the wheel. Creation has ears, but in her the sense of hearing and that which she hears are one thing, not two. The beasts of the forest stir and search for prey and the beasts of the farm stand at the manger. Man returns home from his labour. But as soon as man leaves his work, love and sin are digging his grave. God swore to create a world and to fill the world. And flesh shall draw near to flesh . . .

Micha Yosef Berdyczewski *Hiding in the Thunder*

1

At first the two old men walked without exchanging words.

On leaving the brightly lit and overheated clubroom they helped each other on with their overcoats. Yosef Yarden maintained a dogged silence, while Dr Kleinberger let out a long series of throaty coughs and finally sneezed. The speaker's words had left them both in a state of depression: All this leads nowhere. Nothing ever comes out of these discussions. Nothing practical.

An air of weariness and futility hung over the sparsely attended meetings of the moderate Centre Party, of which the two friends had both been members for many years. Nothing will ever come of these meetings. Precipitate action is dragging the whole of the nation into an orgy of arrogant affluence. The voice of reason, the voice of moderation, the voice of common sense is not heard and cannot be heard in the midst of this jubilation. What are they to do, the few men of sense, no longer young, the advocates of moderate and sober statesmanship, who have seen before in their lifetime the fruits of political euphoria in all its various forms? A handful of men of education and good sense cannot hope to put a stop to the intoxication of the masses and their jubilant, light-headed leaders, all of them skipping with yells of triumph toward the abyss.

After some thirty paces, at the point where the side street opened into one of the majestic and tranquil boulevards of the suburb of Rehavia, Yosef Yarden stopped, thus causing Dr Kleinberger to stop as well without knowing why. Yosef Yarden fumbled for a cigarette and, after some difficulty, found one. Dr Kleinberger hastened to offer his friend a light. Still they had not exchanged a single word. With delicate fingers they shielded the little flame from the wind. Autumn winds in Jerusalem blow strongly, ferociously. Yosef thanked his companion with a nod of his head and inhaled smoke. But three paces further on, the cigarette went out, for it had not been properly lit. Angrily he threw it down on the sidewalk and crushed it with the heel of his shoe. Then he thought better of it, picked up the crumpled cigarette, and tossed it into a trash can that the municipality of Jerusalem had placed on the iron pole of a bus stop.

'Degeneracy,' he said.

'Well, really, I ask you,' replied Dr Kleinberger, 'is that not a simplistic, almost vulgar definition for a reality that is by definition complex?'

'Degeneracy and arrogance, too,' insisted Yosef Yarden.

'You know as well as anyone, my dear Yosef, that a simplistic definition is a form of surrender.'

'I'm sick of this,' said Yosef Yarden, adjusting his scarf and the collar of his coat against the freezing daggers of the wind. 'I'm sick of all this. From now on I shall not mince words. Disease is disease, and degeneracy is degeneracy.'

Dr Kleinberger passed his tongue over lips that were always cracked in winter; his eyes closed like the embrasures of a tank as he commented:

'Degeneracy is a complex phenomenon, Yosef. Without degeneracy there is no meaning to the word "purity". There is a cycle at work here, some kind of eternal wheel, and this was well understood by our Sages when they spoke of the evil side of human nature, and also, on the other hand, by the Fathers of the Christian Church: apparently degeneracy and purity are absolute opposites, whereas in fact one draws the other out, one makes the other possible and makes it flourish, and this is what we must hope for and trust in in this decadent age.'

An arrogant wind, sharp and chilly, blew in the streets of Rehavia. The street lamps gave out an intermittent yellowish light. Some of them had been smashed by vandals and hung blind on top of their posts. Birds of the night had nested in these ruined lamps.

The founders of the Rehavia quarter planted trees and laid out gardens and avenues, for it was their intention to create amid the sun-bleached rocks of Jerusalem a pleasant and shady suburb where the piano might be heard all day and the violin or the cello at nightfall. The whole neighbourhood basks beneath a cluster of treetops. All day the little houses stand sleepily on the bed of a lake of shadow. But at night dim creatures roost in the foliage and flap their wings in the darkness, uttering despairing cries. They are not so easy to hit as the street lamps; the stones miss their mark and are lost in the gloom, and the treetops whisper in secret derision.

And surely even these opposites and not simple but complex; in fact, one draws the other out and one cannot exist without the other, et cetera, et cetera. Dr Elhanan Kleinberger, a bachelor, is an Egyptologist with a modest reputation, particularly in the European state from which he escaped by the skin of his teeth some thirty years ago. Both his life and his views bear the mark of a brilliant stoicism. Yosef Yarden, an expert in the deciphering of ancient Hebrew manuscripts, is a widower who is shortly to marry off his eldest son, Yair, to a girl named Dinah Dannenberg, the daughter of an old friend. As for the birds of the night, they roost in the heart of the suburb, but the first fingers of light drive them away every morning to their hiding places in the rocks and woods outside the city.

The two elderly men continued their stroll without finding anything further to add to the harsh words they had heard and spoken before.

They passed by the Prime Minister's office on the corner of Ibn Gabirol
Street and Keren Kayemet Street, passed the buildings of the secondary
school, and paused at the corner of Ussishkin Street. This crossroads
is open to the west and exposed to the blasts of cold wind blowing
in from the stony fields. Here Yosef Yarden took out another cigarette,
and again Dr Kleinberger gave him a light and shielded it with both
his hands like a sailor: this time it would not go out.

'Well, next month we shall all be dancing at the wedding,' said the
doctor playfully.

'I'm on my way now to see Lily Dannenberg. We have to sit
down and draw up a list of guests,' said Yosef Yarden. 'It will be a
short list. His mother, may she rest in peace, always wanted our
son to be married quietly, without a great show, and so it will be.
Just a modest family ceremony. You will be there, of course, but, then,
to us you are like a member of the family. There's no question about
that.'

Dr Kleinberger took off his glasses, breathed on them, wiped them
with a handkerchief, and slowly replaced them.

'Yes. Of course. But the Dannenberg woman will not agree to that.
Better not deceive yourself. She's certain to want her daughter's wedding to be a spectacular event, and the whole of Jerusalem will be
invited to bow down and wonder. You will have to give in and do as
she wishes.'

'It isn't that easy to make me change my mind,' replied Yosef Yarden.
'Especially in a case where the wishes of my late wife are involved.
Mrs Dannenberg is a sensitive lady, and she is certainly aware of per-
sonal considerations.'

As Yosef Yarden said that it would not be easy to make him change
his mind, he began inadvertently to squeeze the cigarette between his
fingers. Bent and crushed, the cigarette still did not go out but continued to flicker. Dr Kleinberger concluded:

'You're mistaken, my friend. The Dannenberg woman will not do
without the big spectacle. Certainly she's a sensitive lady, as you so
admirably express it, but she's also an obstinate lady. There is no contradiction between these two qualities. And you had better prepare
yourself for a very tough argument. A vulgar argument.'

A mutual acquaintance, or perhaps one whose silhouette reminded
the two friends of a mutual acquaintance, passed by the street corner. Both put their hands to their hats, and the stranger did the same
but pressed on without stopping, hurrying, head bowed, against the

wind. And he vanished in the darkness. Then a hooligan roared past on a motorcycle, shattering the peace of Rehavia.

'It's outrageous!' fumed Yosef Yarden. 'That dirty gangster deliberately opened up his throttle, just to disturb the peace of ten thousand citizens. And why? Simply because he's not quite sure that he's real, that he exists, and this buffoonery gives him an inflated sense of importance: everybody can hear him. The professors. The President and the Prime Minister. The artists. The girls. This madness must be stopped before it's too late. Stopped forcibly.'

Dr Kleinberger was in no hurry to reply. He pondered these words, turning them this way and that during a long moment of silence. Finally he commented:

'First, it's already too late.'

'I don't hold with such resignation. And second?'

'Second—yes, there is a second point, and please pardon my frankness —second, you're exaggerating. As always.'

'I'm not exaggerating,' said Yosef Yarden, teeth clenched in suppressed hatred. 'I'm not exaggerating. I'm just calling the child by his name. That's all. I've got the cigarettes and you've got the matches, so we're tied to each other. A light, please. Thank you. A child should always be called by his name.'

'But really, Yosef, my very dear friend, but really,' drawled Dr Kleinberger with forced didactic patience, 'you know as well as I do that usually every child has more than one name. Now it's time to part. You must go to your son's future mother-in-law, and don't you be late or she'll scold you. She's a sensitive lady, no doubt about that, but she's hard as well. Call me tomorrow evening. We can finish that chess game that we left off in the middle. Good night. Take the matches with you. Yes. Don't mention it.'

As the two elderly men began to go their separate ways, the children's shouts rose from the Valley of the Cross. Evidently the boys of the Youth Movement had gathered there to play games of hide-and-seek in the dark. Old olive trees make good hiding-places. Sounds and scents rise from the valley and penetrate to the heart of the affluent suburb. From the olive trees some hidden current passes to the barren trees, which were planted by the landscape gardeners of Rehavia. The night birds are responsible for this current. The weight of responsibility infuses them with a sense of deadly seriousness, and they save their shrieking for a moment of danger or a moment of truth. In contrast, the olive trees are doomed to grow in perpetual silence.

2

Mrs Lily Dannenberg's house lies in one of the quiet side streets between the suburb of Rehavia and her younger and taller sister, the suburb of Kiryat Shemuel. The hooligan who shattered the peace of the entire city with his motorcycle did not disturb the peace of Mrs Dannenberg, because she had no peace. She paced around the house, arranging and adjusting, then changing her mind and putting everything back in its original place. As if she really intended to sit at home and quietly wait for her guest. At nine-thirty Yosef means to come over to discuss with her the list of wedding invitations. This whole business can bear postponement; there is no need for haste. The visit, the wedding, and the list of guests, too. What's the hurry? In any case, he will arrive at nine-thirty precisely—you can count on him not to be a second late—but the door will be closed, the house empty and in darkness. Life is full of surprises. It's nice to imagine the look on his face—surprised, offended, shocked as well. And nice to guess what will be written on the note that he will certainly leave on my door. There are some people, and Yosef is one of them, who when they are surprised, offended, and shocked become almost likeable. It's a sort of spiritual alchemy. He's a decent man, and he always anticipates what is good and fears what is not.

These thoughts were whispered in German. Lily Dannenberg switched on the reading lamp, her face cold and calm. She sat in an armchair and filed her fingernails. At two minutes to nine her manicure was complete. Without leaving her chair she switched on the radio. The day's reading from the Bible had already finished, and the news broadcost had not yet begun. Some sentimental, nauseatingly trite piece of music was repeated four or five times without variation. Lily turned the tuning knob and passed hurriedly over the guttural voices of the Near East, skipped over Athens without stopping, and reached Radio Vienna in time for the evening news summary in German. Then there was a broadcast of Beethoven's *Eroica*. She turned the radio off and went to the kitchen to make coffee.

What do I care if he's offended or shocked? Why should I care what happens to that man and his son? There are some emotions that the Hebrew language isn't sufficiently developed to express. If I say that to Yosef or his friend Kleinberger, the pair of them will attack me, and there'll be a terrific argument about the merits of the Hebrew language, with all kinds of unpleasant digressions. Even the word 'digression' does not exist in Hebrew. I must drink this coffee without a single grain of sugar. Bitter, of course it's bitter, but it keeps me awake. Am I allowed one biscuit? No, I'm not allowed to eat biscuits, and there's no room for compromise. And it's already a quarter past nine. Let's go, before he appears. The stove. The light. The key. Let's go.

Lily Dannenberg is a forty-two-year-old divorcee. She could easily claim to be seven or eight years younger, but that would be contrary to her moral principles, so she does not disguise her true age. Her body is tall and thin, her hair naturally blond, not a rich tint but deep and dense. Her nose is straight and strong. On her lips there is a permanent and fascinating unease, and her eyes are bright blue. A single, modest ring seems to accentuate the lonely and pensive quality of her long fingers.

Dinah won't be back from Tel Aviv before twelve. I've left her a little coffee in the pot for tomorrow morning. There's salad in the fridge and fresh bread in the basket. If the girl decides to have a bath at midnight, the water will still be hot. So everything is in order. And if everything's in order, why am I uneasy, as if I've left something burning or open? But nothing is burning and nothing's open and already I'm two streets away heading west, so that man Yosef isn't likely to meet me by chance on his way to the house. That would spoil everything. Most young Levantines are very attractive at first glance. But only a few of them stand up to a second look. A great spirit is always struggling and tormented, and this distorts the body from within and corrodes the face like a rainstorm eating limestone. That is why people of spiritual greatness have something written on their faces, sometimes in letters that resemble scars, and usually they find it hard to keep their bodies upright. By contrast, the handsome Levantines do not know the taste of suffering, and that is why their faces are symmetrical, their bodies strong and well proportioned. Twenty-two minutes after nine. An owl just said something complicated and raucous. That bird is called *Eule* in German, and in Hebrew, I think, *yanshuf*. Anyway, what difference does it make? In exactly seven minutes, Yosef will ring the doorbell of my house. His punctuality is beyond doubt. At that precise moment I shall ring the doorbell of his house on Alfasi Street. Shut up, *Eule*, I've heard everything you have to say more than once. And Yair will open the door to me.

3

A person who comes from a broken home is likely to destroy the stability of other people's homes. There is nothing fortuitous about this, although there is no way of formulating a rule. Yosef Yarden is a widower. Lily Dannenberg is a divorcee whose ex-husband died of a broken heart, or jaundice, less than three months after the divorce. Even Dr Kleinberger, Egyptologist and stoic, a marginal figure, is an ageing bachelor. Needless to say, he has no children. That leaves Yair Yarden and Dinah Dannenberg. Dinah has gone to Tel Aviv to pass the good news along to her relatives and to make a few purchases and arrangements, and she will not be back before midnight. As for Yair, he is sitting with his brother, a grammar-school student, in the pleasant living-room of the Yarden household on Alfasi Street. He has decided to spend the evening grappling with a backlog of university work: three exercises, a tedious project, a whole mountain of bibliographical chores. Studying political economy may be important and profitable, but it can also be wearisome and depressing. If he had been able to choose, he might have chosen to study the Far East, China, Japan, mysterious Tibet, or perhaps Latin America. Rio. The Incas. Or black Africa. But what could a young man do with studies such as these? Build himself an igloo, marry a geisha? The trouble is that political economy is full of functions and calculations, words and figures that seem to disintegrate when you stare at them. Dinah is in Tel Aviv. When she comes back, perhaps she'll forget that unnecessary quarrel that we had yesterday. Those things I said to her face. On the other hand, she started it. Dad has gone to see her mother, and he won't be back before eleven. If only there was some way of persuading Uri to stop sitting there picking his nose. How disgusting. There's a mystery programme on the radio at a quarter past nine called *Treasure Hunt*, broadcast live. That's the solution for an uncomfortable evening like this. We'll listen to the programme and then finish the third exercise. That should be enough.

The brothers switched on the radio.

The antics of the night birds do not abate until a quarter past nine. Even before the twilight is over, the owls and the other birds of darkness begin to move from the suburbs to the heart of the city. With their glassy dead eyes they stare at the birds of light, who rejoice with carefree song at the onset of the day's last radiance. To the ears of the night birds, this sounds like utter madness, a festival of fools. On the edge of the suburb of Rehavia, where the farthest houses clutch at the rocks of the western slope, the rising birds meet the descending birds. In the light that is neither day nor night the two camps move past each other in opposite directions. No compromise ever lasts long in Jerusalem, and so the evening twilight flickers and fades rapidly, too. Darkness comes. The sun has fled, and the rear-guard forces are already in retreat.

At nine-thirty, Lily had meant to ring the doorbell of the Yardens' house. But at the corner of Radak Street she saw a cat standing on a stone wall. His tail was swishing, and he was whining with lust. Lily decided to waste a few moments observing the feverish cat. Meanwhile the brothers were listening to the start of the mystery programme. The first clue was given to the studio panel and the listeners by a jovial fellow; the beginning of the thread was contained in a song by Bialik:

> Not by day and not by night
> Quietly I set out and walk;
> Not on the hill or in the vale,
> Where stands an old acacia tree . . .

And at once Yair and Uri were on fire with detective zeal. An old acacia tree, that's the vital point. Not on the hill or in the vale, that's where it starts getting complicated. Yair had a bright idea: Maybe we should look the poem up in the big book of Bialik's poetry and find the context, then we'll know which way to turn. He pounced on the bookcase, rummaged around, found the book, and within three minutes had located the very poem. However, the lines that followed did not solve the puzzle, but only tantalized the hunters still further:

> The acacia solves mysteries
> And tells what lies ahead . . .

Yes. I see. But if the acacia itself is the mystery, how can it be expected to solve mysteries and even tell the future? How does it go on? The next stanza is irrelevant. The whole poem's irrelevant. Bialik's no use. We must try a different approach. Let's think, now. I've got it: the Hebrew word *shita* isn't only the name of a tree. It also means 'method'. *Shita* is a system. These inquiries would do credit to that buffoon Kleinberger. Well, then, let's think some more. Shut up, Uri, I'm trying to think. Well, my dear Watson, tell me what you make of the first words. I mean 'Not by day and not by night.' Don't you understand anything? Of course you don't. Think for a while. Incidentally, I don't understand it yet, either. But give me a moment, and you'll see.

The doorbell rang.

An unexpected guest stood in the doorway. Her face was set, her lips nervous. She was a weird and beautiful woman.

An alley cat is a fickle creature; he will abandon anything for the caress of a human hand. Even at the height of rutting fever he will not turn away from the caress of a human hand. When Lily touched him, he began to shudder. With her left hand she stroked his back firmly, while the fingers of her right hand gently tickled the fur of his neck. Her combination of tenderness and strength filled the animal with pleasure. The cat turned over on his back and offered his stomach to the gentle fingers, purring loudly and contentedly. Lily tickled him as she spoke.

'You're happy. Now you're happy. Don't deny it, you're happy,' she said in German. The cat narrowed his eyes until two slits were all that was left, and continued purring.

'Relax,' she said, 'you don't need to do anything. Just enjoy yourself.'

The fur was soft and warm. Thin vibrations passed through it and ceased. Lily rubbed her ring against the cat's ear.

'And what's more, you're stupid as well.'

Suddenly the cat shuddered and stirred uneasily. Perhaps he guessed or half-sensed what was coming. A yellow slit opened in his face, the wink of an eye, a fleeting glimmer. Then her fist rose, made a wide sweep in the air, and struck a violent blow at the belly of the cat. The creature took fright and leapt away into the darkness, collided with the trunk of a pine tree, and dug in his claws. From the murky height he hissed at her like a snake. All his fur stood on end. Lily turned and walked to the Yardens' house.

'Good evening, Yair. It seems you're free. And on your own.'

'Uri is here and we . . . but isn't Dad on his way to see you?'

'Uri here, too. I'd forgotten about Uri. Good evening, Uri. How you've grown! I'm sure all the girls must be chasing you. No, you needn't invite me inside. I just came to get something straight with you, Yair. I didn't mean to intrude.'

'But Mrs . . . but Lily, how can you say that. You're always welcome. Come in. I was so sure that just now you'd be at your house drinking coffee with Dad, and suddenly . . .'

'Suddenly your dad will find the door locked and the windows dark, and he won't understand what's become of me. He's disappointed and worried—which makes him look almost agreeable. Pity I'm not there among the trees in the garden, secretly watching him, enjoying the expression on his face. It doesn't matter. I'll explain everything. Come on, Yair, let's go out, let's go for a little walk outside, there's something I need to straighten out with you. Yes. This very evening. Be patient.'

'What . . . Has something happened? Didn't Dinah go to Tel Aviv, or . . .'

'She went like a good little girl, and she'll come back like a good little girl. But not until later. Come on, Yair. You won't need your coat. It isn't cold outside. It's pleasant outside. You'll have to excuse us, Uri. How you've grown! Good night.'

In the yard, near the pepper tree, she spoke to Yair again: 'Don't look so puzzled. Nothing serious has happened.'

But Yair already knew that he had made a mistake. He should have brought his coat, in spite of what Lily had said. The evening was cold. And later it would be very cold. He could still excuse himself, go back, and fetch his coat. Lily herself was wearing a coat that was stylish, almost daring. But to go back to the house for a coat seemed to him somehow dishonourable, perhaps even cowardly. He put the thought aside and said:

'Yes. It's really pleasant out here.'

Since she was in no hurry to reply, Yair had time to wonder if there really were acacia trees in Jerusalem, and if so, where, and if not, perhaps *shita* should be taken as a clue to the verb *leshatot*—'to jest'. Who knows, maybe the treasure's hidden in one of the wadis to the west or the south of Rehavia. Pity about the programme. Now I'll never know the solution.

4

After a brief moment of astonishment and confusion and a few indecisive speculations, Yosef Yarden made up his mind to go to Dr Kleinberger's house. If he found him at home he would go in, apologize for the lateness of the hour and the unexpected visit, and tell his friend about this strange incident. Who would have thought it? And just imagine the look she would have given me if I had been a few minutes late. And there I was, standing and waiting, ten o'clock already, two and a half minutes past. If something had happened to her, she would have phoned me. There's no way of understanding or explaining this.

'And for the time being you have avoided a vulgar and possibly painful argument,' said Elhanan Kleinberger, smiling. 'She wouldn't have given in to you over the guest list. She'll send invitations all over the city, all over the university. To the President of the State and the Mayor of Jerusalem. And really, Yosef, why should you expect her to give up what she wants in deference to what you want? Why shouldn't she invite the Pope and his wife to the wedding of her only daughter? What's the matter, Yosef?'

His guest began to explain, patiently:

'Times are not easy. In general, I mean. And remember, all these years we have been preaching, both in speech and in writing, the need to "walk humbly". Yair's mother wanted an intimate wedding, a small circle of relatives, and that is a kind of imperative, at least from the ethical point of view. And . . . then there's the cost. I mean, who wants to go into debt for the sake of a society wedding?'

Dr Kleinberger felt that he had lost the thread. He made coffee, set out milk and sugar. And at this point he also took the opportunity to add something to his previous remarks concerning the interplay of opposite extremes. The conversation soon diversified. They discussed Egyptology, they discussed Hebrew literature, they conducted a scathing inquiry into the workings of the municipality of Jerusalem. Elhanan Kleinberger has a great flair for linking together Egyptology, his professional field, and Hebrew literature, which is his heart's love, as he puts it, and of which he is a passionate lover, as he also puts it. In general, Yosef is used to having his views overruled by those of his friend, although he tends on most occasions to reject the particular wording adopted by Elhanan Kleinberger. So their arguments end with the last word going to Yosef Yarden and not to his old friend.

Were it not for the cold, the two friends would have gone out together to stand on the balcony and gaze at the starlight on the hills, as was their habit in summer. The Valley of the Cross lies opposite. There old olive trees grow in bitter tranquillity.

In passionate, almost violent hunger, the olive trees send out their tendrils into the blackness of the heavy earth. There the roots pierce the rocky subsoil, cleaving the hidden stones and sucking up the dark moisture. They are like sharpened claws. But above them the green and silver treetops are caressed by the wind: theirs is the peace and the glory.

And you cannot kill the olive. Olive trees burned in fire sprout and flourish again. A vulgar growth, quite shameless, Elhanan Kleinberger would say. Even olives struck by lightning are reborn and in time clothe themselves with new foliage. And they grow on the hills of Jerusalem, and on the modest heights on the fringes of the Coastal

Plain, and they hide away in the cloisters of monasteries enclosed within walls of stone. There the olives thicken their knotted trunks generation after generation and lasciviously entwine their stout branches. They have a savage vitality like that of birds of prey.

To the north of Rehavia lie sprawling suburbs, poor neighbourhoods with charming streets. In one of these winding alleyways stands an old olive tree. One hundred and seven years ago an iron gate was erected here and the lintel was supported by the tree. Over the years the tree leaned against the iron, and the iron bit deep into the trunk like a roasting spit.

Patiently the olive began to enfold the iron wedge. In the course of time it closed around it and set tight. The iron was crushed in the tree's embrace. The tree's wounds healed over, and the vigorous foliage of its upper branches was in no way impaired.

5

Yair Yarden is a young man of handsome appearance. He is not tall, but his shoulders are powerful and his torso is trim, well proportioned, and athletic. His chin is firm and angular, with a deep dimple. Girls secretly long to touch this dimple with their fingertips, and some of them even blush or turn pale when they feel the impulse. They say, 'And what's more, he thinks he knows a thing or two. He's about as brainy as a tailor's dummy.'

His arms are strong and covered in black hair. It would be wrong to say that Yair Yarden is clumsy, but there is a certain heaviness, a kind of slow solidity, perceptible in all his movements. Lily Dannenberg would have called this 'massivity' and returned to her theme of the inadequacy of the Hebrew language, with its dearth of nuances. Of course, Elhanan Kleinberger is capable of refuting such barbed comments and of suggesting in the twinkling of an eye a suitable Hebrew adjective, or even two. And at the same time he will come up with a Hebrew expression to fit the word 'nuance'.

It may be that this fascinating 'massivity' with which Yair Yarden is endowed will change within a few years into the patriarchal corpulence for which his father is noted. A sharp eye may detect the first signs. But at present—Lily has no intention of disguising the truth—at present, Yair is a handsome, captivating youth. The moustache gives a special force to his appearance. It is blond, droopy, sometimes flecked with shreds of tobacco. Yair is studying economics and business management at the university; his whole future lies before him. Romantic follies, kibbutzim, and life in border settlements hold no attraction for him. His political views are temperate; he has learned them from his father. To be precise, Yosef Yarden sees in the political situation a wasteland of degeneracy and arrogance, whereas Yair sees a wide-open prospect before him.

'Will you offer me a cigarette, please,' said Lily.

'Of course. Here you are. Please take one, Lily.'

'Oh, thank you. I left mine at home, I was in such a hurry.'

'A light, Lily?'

'Thank you. Dinah Yarden—a name almost as musical as Dinah Dannenberg. Perhaps a little simpler. When you have a child you can call him Dan. Dan Yarden: like something out of a ballad about camels and bells. How much time are you going to give me, how long will it be, before you make me a grandmother? A year? A bit less? You needn't answer. It was a rhetorical question. Yair, how do you say "rhetorical question" in Hebrew?'

'I don't know,' said Yair.

'I wasn't asking you. It was a rhetorical question.'

Yair began scratching the lobe of his ear uneasily. What's the matter with her? What's she up to? There's something about her that I don't like at all. She isn't being sincere. It's very hard to tell.

'Now you're searching for something to say and not finding it. It doesn't matter. Your manners are perfect, and for heaven's sake, you're not in front of a board of examiners.'

'I wasn't thinking of you as a board of examiners, Lily. Not at all. I mean, I . . .'

'You're a very spontaneous boy. And quick and witty replies don't matter to me. What interests me is, rather, your . . . how shall I put it, your *esprit*.' And she smiled in the dark.

Chance led them to the upper part of the suburb. They reached the centre of Rehavia and turned north. A passerby, thin and bespectacled, definitely a student of extreme views and crossed in love, passed in front of them with a transistor radio in his hand. Yair paused for a moment and turned his head, straining to catch a fragment of the fascinating programme that Lily had interrupted. Not on the hill or in the vale, where stands an old acacia tree. Thanks to her he had gone out of the house without a coat, and now he was cold. He did not feel comfortable, either. And he had missed the climax of the programme. Time to get to the point, and get it over with.

'Right,' said Yair. 'OK, Lily. Are you going to tell me what the problem is?'

'Problem?' She seemed surprised. 'There's no problem. You and I are going for a stroll on a pleasant evening because Dinah has gone away and your father isn't at home. We are talking, exchanging views, getting to know each other. There are so many things to talk about. So many things that I don't know about you, and there may even be things that you would like to know about me.'

'You said before'—Yair scratched his ear—'you said there was something that you—'

'Yes. It's just a formality and really quite unimportant. But I would like you to sort it out as soon as possible. Let's say tomorrow or the day after, at the latest by the beginning of next week.'

She put out her cigarette and refused the offer of another.

Many years ago a famous architect sketched the plan of Rehavia. He wanted to give it the character of a quiet garden suburb. Narrow shady lanes like Alharizi Street, a well-tended boulevard called Ben-Maimon Avenue, squares like Magnes Square, full of the pensive murmur of cypresses even at the height of summer. An enclave of security, a sort of rest home for fugitives who have suffered in their lives. The names of great medieval Jewish scholars were given to the streets, to enrich them with a sense of antiquity and an air of wisdom and learning.

But over the years, New Jerusalem has spread and encircled Rehavia with a noose of ugly developments. The narrow streets have become choked with motor traffic. And when the western highway was opened and the heights of Sheikh-Badar and Naveh Shaanan became the heart of the city and the state, Rehavia ceased to be a garden suburb. Demented buildings sprouted on every rock. Small villas were demolished and tenements built in their place. The original intentions were swept away by the exuberance of the new age and the advance of technology.

The nights give back to Rehavia something of its plundered dreams. The trees that have survived draw a new dignity from the night and sometimes even act like a forest. Weary, slow-moving residents leave their homes to stroll at dusk. From the Valley of the Cross a different air arises, and with it a scent of bitter cypresses and night birds. It is as if the olive groves rise up and come into the lanes and the courtyards of houses. By electric light, book-laden shelves appear through the windows. And there are women who play the piano. Perhaps their hearts are heavy with longing or desire.

'That man on the other side of the street, the one feeling the sidewalk with his stick,' said Lily, 'that's Professor Shatski. He's getting old now. I don't suppose you knew Professor Shatski was still alive. I

dare say you thought he was something out of the last century. Perhaps
you'd have been right. He was an elegant and venomous man who
believed in mercy, and in his writings he demanded mercilessly that
all men show mercy to all men. Even the victim should show mercy
to his killer. Now he's blind.'

'I've never heard of him,' said Yair. 'He isn't exactly in my field, as
they say.'

'And now, if I may just ask for one more cigarette, let's talk about
your field, as they say.'

'By all means. Take one. I'm curious to know about the formality
that you started talking about before.'

She narrowed her eyes. Tried hard to concentrate. Remembered
moments of pain that she had lived through long before this clumsy
cavalier was born. She felt a momentary nausea and almost changed
her mind. But after a while she said:

'It has to do with an examination. I want you to have a medical
examination as soon as possible, certainly before we announce the
wedding officially.'

'I don't understand,' said Yair, and his hand stopped halfway to his
ear. 'I don't understand. I'm a hundred per cent fit. Why do I need
an examination?'

'Just a screening examination. Your mother died of a hereditary disease. Incidentally, if she had been examined in time, she might have
lived a few years longer.'

'I had a physical two years ago, when I started at the university. They said I was as healthy as an ox. I know very little about my
mother. I was young then.'

'Now, Yair, don't go making a big fuss over a little examination,
OK? There's a good boy. Just for my peace of mind, as they say. If
you knew any German, I'd make you a present of all the economics
books that Erich Dannenberg left me. He's someone else that I'm
sure you don't remember. A new leaf, as they say. I shall have to think
of some other present for you.'

Yair said nothing.

As they walked up Ibn Ezra Street, they were confronted by an elegantly dressed old woman.

'There is a personal link that joins all creation. God is angry and
man does not see it. One meaning to all deeds, fine deeds and ugly
deeds. They that walk in the darkness shall see a great light. Not
tomorrow—yesterday. The throat is warm and the knife is sharp. To
all of creation there is one meaning.'

Yair moved away from the madwoman and quickened his pace. Lily paused for a moment without speaking, then caught up with him. A poisonous, twisted sort of expression spread over her face like a disease. And then passed. In Jerusalem they called the elegant woman 'One Meaning.' She had a startlingly deep voice and a German accent. From a distance the madwoman of Rehavia blessed the two who were walking by:

'The blessing of the sky above, and the blessing of the water beneath, from Düsseldorf to Jerusalem, one meaning to all deeds, to those that build and those that destroy. Peace and success and full redemption to you and to all refugees and sufferers. Peace, peace, to near and far.'

'Peace,' replied Lily in a whisper. From there until they reached the Rothschild School, not a word was said. Yair was humming or murmuring to himself, 'Not by day and not by night . . .' and then he stopped.

Lily said, 'Let's not quarrel over this examination, even though it may sound to you like a whim. Your mother died only because of negligence, and as a result your father was left alone again and you became an orphan.'

Yair said, 'All right, all right, why make an issue of it?' Then, with a slow realization, he began to see the significance of something she had said. He put his tongue to the edge of his moustache, caught a fragment of tobacco, and said:

'Again? Did you say that my father was left alone again?'

Now Lily's voice had a cold and authoritative sound to it, like that of a clerk at an information counter:

'Yes. Your father's second wife died of cancer when you where six. Your father's first wife did not die of cancer; she left him. She was divorced. Soon you will be a married man yourself, and it's time your father stopped hiding elementary facts from you as if you were still a child.'

'I don't understand,' said Yair, hurt. 'I don't understand—you say my father was married before?'

In his puzzlement he raised his voice beyond what was appropriate to the time and place. Lily was anxious to restore things to their proper level.

'Your father was married for four months,' she said, 'to the woman who later married Erich Dannenberg.'

'That's impossible,' said Yair.

He stopped. He took out a cigarette and put it between his lips but forgot to light it. Then for a moment he forgot his companion and forgot to offer her a cigarette. He stared into the darkness, deep in thought. At last he managed to say:

'So what? What has that got to do with us?'

'Be a dear,' Lily said, smiling, 'and give me another cigarette. I left mine at home. You're right. I myself find it hard to believe that there ever was, or could have been, such a marriage. I myself can hardly believe what I've just told you. But you should know, and you must learn what there is to be learned from that episode. Now, please light the cigarettes, mine and yours. Or give me the matches and I'll light them. Don't let it upset you. It happened in the past. A long time ago. And it lasted less than four absurd months. It was just an episode. Come on, let's walk a little farther. Jerusalem is wonderful at this time of night. Come on.'

Yair began to follow her northward, lost in thought. And she was filled with a savage joy. A car honked and she ignored it. A night bird spoke to her and she did not answer. She watched her shoes and his on the sidewalk. And she took the lighter from his distracted fingers and lit both the cigarettes.

'And I was never told anything about it,' said Yair.

'Well, you've been told now. That's enough. Relax. Don't get yourself all worked up,' said Lily warmly, as if to console him.

'But it's . . . it's so strange. And not very nice, somehow.'

She touched the back of his neck. Caressed the roots of his hair. Her hand felt warm and comforting to the boy. They walked on, out of Rehavia and into the neighbouring quarter. The winding streets became sharp-angled alleyways. And there in front of them was the olive tree, embracing and crushing the iron gatepost.

6

Elhanan Kleinberger and Yosef Yarden were engrossed in their game of chess. A lamp styled in the shape of an old Bavarian street lamp shed a dim light on the table. On the bindings of the scholarly books danced gold letters which gave back a light still dimmer than the one they took from the lamp. All around stood Dr Kleinberger's bookshelves, set out along the length and height of the walls of the room, from floor to ceiling. One special shelf was devoted to the Egyptologist's stamp albums. Another was reserved for Hebrew literature, Elhanan Kleinberger's secret love. In the few spaces among the rows of books there were African miniatures, vases, primitive statuettes of a crudely erotic style. But these statuettes also served as vases, holding coloured paper flowers that never wilted.

'No, Yosef, you can't do that,' said Dr Kleinberger. 'In any case, you have no choice now but to exchange your knight for my rook.'

'Just a moment, Elhanan, give me a chance to think. I still have a small advantage in this game.'

'A temporary advantage, my friend, a temporary advantage,' replied Dr Kleinberger playfully. 'But think, by all means. The more you think, the better you will appreciate just how temporary your advantage is. Temporary and irrelevant.' He leaned back comfortably in his armchair.

Yosef Yarden thought hard: Now I must concentrate. What he says about the weakness of my position is just tactics in a war of nerves. I must concentrate. The next move will decide the game.

'The next move will decide the game,' said Dr Kleinberger. 'Should we call a ten-minute break and have a cup of tea?'

'A Machiavellian suggestion, Elhanan, and I don't hesitate to call the child by his name. A diabolical suggestion designed to upset my concentration, and you have succeeded in doing that already. Anyway, the answer is: no, thank you.'

'Did we not say before that every child has more than one name, Yosef? We were talking about that only two or three hours ago. It seems that you have already forgotten our conversation. Pity.'

'I have already forgotten what I was intending to do to you. To your rook, I mean. You've succeeded in distracting me, Elhanan. Please, let me concentrate. Look, so. Yes. I am here and you are there. What do you say to that, my dear doctor?'

'For the time being I don't say anything. All that I will say is: let's break off for a moment and listen to the news. But after the news I shall say "check", Yosef, and then I shall say "checkmate"'.

It was nearly midnight when the two men parted. Yosef bore his defeat with dignity. He consoled himself with the glass of brandy that his host offered him, and said:

'At the end of the week we shall meet at my house. On my territory you will be the loser. You have my word on it.'

'And this,' said Dr Kleinberger, laughing, 'this is the man who wrote that eloquent article "Against the Politics of Revenge" in *The Social Democrat*. Sleep well, Yosef.'

Outside were the night and the wind. An ill-mannered owl urged Yosef to hurry up. I forgot to phone her to ask what happened. Better wait until tomorrow. She will phone and apologize and I won't accept her excuses. At least, not right away.

7

The acacia solves mysteries / And tells what lies ahead, / I shall ask
the acacia tree / Oh, who is my bride to be?

The insistent tune takes no account of circumstances and will not
leave Yair alone. Already he has whistled it, hummed it, and sung it,
and still the song gives him no peace.

Lily has questioned Yair about his professors, about his studies,
about the girl students who were sure to be mad with grief at the
thought of his forthcoming marriage.

Yair was thinking: That's enough. Let's go home. What she's told
me isn't necessarily true. And even if it is true, So what? What does
she want? What's the matter with her? Time to put a stop to all this
and go home. Besides, I'm cold.

'Perhaps,' he said cautiously, 'perhaps we should start heading back
home. It's late, and there's a dampness in the air. It's cold as well. I
don't want it to be my fault if you catch a chill.'

He gripped her arm, just above the elbow, and began gently drawing her toward a street corner lit by a lamp.

'Do you know, my dear child,' she said, 'the amount of patience
that is required of a man and a woman to prevent their marriage from
turning into a tragedy after a few months?'

'But I think . . . Let's talk about that on the way home. Or some
other time altogether.'

'For the first few months there is sex and sex is all that matters.
Sex in the morning, at midday, and at night, before and after meals,
instead of meals. But after a few months you suddenly begin to have
a lot of time to sit and think—and you think all kinds of thoughts.
Infuriating habits come to the surface, on both sides. And this is when
subtlety is required.'

'It'll be all right. Don't worry. Dinah and I . . .'

'Who said anything about you and Dinah? I'm talking in general
terms. Now I can also tell you something from my personal experience. Put your arm around my shoulders. I'm cold. Yes. Don't be so
shy. Be a nice boy. Like this. I'm going to tell you something about
Dinah and something about you, too.'

'But I already know.'

'No, my child, you don't know everything. I think you should know,
for example, that Dinah is in love with your outward appearance and
not with you. She doesn't think about you. She's still a child. And so
are you. I don't suppose you have ever once been depressed. Don't

answer me now. No, I'm not saying that you're a crude boy. Far from it. I just mean you're strong. You're straightforward and strong, as our young people should be. Here, give me your hand. Yes. Don't ask so many questions. I asked for your hand. Yes. Like this. Now, squeeze my hand, please. Because I'm asking you, isn't that reason enough? Squeeze. Not gently. Hard. Harder. Harder still. Don't be afraid. You're afraid of me. There, that's good. You're very strong. Have you noticed that your hand is cold and mine is warm? Soon you'll understand why. Buy stop whining and trying to persuade me to go home all the time, or I'll begin to think I came out for a walk with a spoiled toddler who just wants to go home and sleep. Look, child, look at the moon peeping out from behind the clouds. Do you see? Yes. Just relax completely for a few moments. Don't say anything. Hush.'

The dim wailing of jackals is heard from far away. Words flee from him. Something other than words now strives to assert itself but finds no outlet. A sharp and mischievous wind rises from the desolation on the fringes of the town and comes to play in the stone-flagged side streets. Windows are shut. Shutters closed. Drains with iron gratings. A long procession of trash cans frozen on the sidewalk. Cats prowl on the mounds of Jerusalem stone. Lily Dannenberg is sure that the things that she has said to Yair Yarden are 'educational'. She tries hard to keep to the rhythm of events, lest everything be wasted. But the blood is pounding in her temples, and some inner agitation urges her to go racing on without drawing breath. Here among the houses there is no acacia solving riddles. The two walkers emerge from the side streets and pass through the market of Mahaneh Yehuda toward Jaffa Road. Here Lily leads the young man to a cheap café that caters to the all-night taxi drivers.

Beneath the electric light the moths are singeing their wings in token of their love for the yellow bulb. Mrs Danenberg orders black coffee without sugar or saccharine. Yair asks for a cheese sandwich. He hesitates and asks for a small glass of brandy as well. She lays her hand on his broad brown hand and carefully counts his fingers. In a state of mild dizziness he responds with a smile. She takes his hand in hers and raises the fingers to her lips.

8

In this taxi-drivers' café in the Mahaneh Yehuda district there was a certain driver, a giant named Abbu. All day he sleeps. At midnight, like a bear, he wakes up and goes out to prowl Jaffa Road, his kingdom. All the taxi drivers willingly defer to him, for he is strong and goodhearted, but a hard man, too. Now he was sitting at one of the tables with three or four of the younger members of the flock, showing them how to load the dice in the game of backgammon. When Yair and Lily came into the café, Abbu said to his young cronies:

'Here come the Queen of Sheba and King Solomon.'

And when Yair said nothing and Lily smiled, he added:

'Never mind. Health is what matters. Hey, lady, are you letting the kid drink brandy?'

His fellow drivers turned to look. The café proprietor, a tubercular and melancholic man, also turned to watch the approaching scene.

'And as for you, little boy, I'm damned if I understand what you're playing at. What is this, is it Grandma's Day today? Giving your grandma a treat? What are you doing going around at night with a vintage model like that?'

Yair leapt to his feet, his ears reddening, willing and ready to fight for his honour. But Lily motioned him back to his seat, and when she spoke her voice was warm and happy.

'There are some models that a man of experience and taste would sell his soul for—and not just his soul, but any number of these new-fangled toys of today, all tin and glass.'

'Touché!' said Abbu, laughing. 'So why not come over to my place and get a good hand on your wheel, an experienced hand with clever fingers, how about it? Why go around with that slip of a boy?'

Yair sprang up, his moustache bristling. But once again she got in first and snuffed out the quarrel before it began. A new light danced in her eyes.

'What's the matter with you, Yair? This gentleman doesn't mean to insult me but to make me happy. He and I think exactly the same thoughts. So don't lose your temper, but sit down and learn how to make me happy. Now I am happy.' And in her happiness the divorcee pulled Yair toward her and kissed the dimple in the middle is his chin. Abbu said slowly, as if about to faint at the sweetness of the sight:

'Lord God of Hosts, where, oh, where have you been all this time, lady, and where have I been?'

Lily said:

'Today is Grandson's Day. But maybe tomorrow or the day after, Grandma will need a taxi, and maybe Grandpa will be around, or he will discover where the Queen of Sheba is enthroned and bring her tribute of monkeys and parrots. Come on, Yair, let's go. Good night, sir. It's been a great pleasure meeting you.'

As the couple passed the drivers' table on their way to the door, Abbu murmured in a tone of reverent awe:

'Go home, young man, go home and sleep. By God, you're not fit
to touch the tip of her little finger.'

Lily smiled.

And outside Yair said angrily:

'They're a gang of thugs. And savages.'

9

The tips of her little fingers were pressed in the flesh of his arm.

'Now I'm cold, too,' she said, 'and I want you to hold me. If you
know by now how you should hold me.'

Yair embraced her around the shoulders in anger and shame, emotions that breathed violence into his movements.

Lily said, 'Yes. Like that.'

'But . . . I think, anyway, it's time we turned around and headed
back. It's late,' he said, unconsciously gripping the lobe of his ear
between thumb and forefinger. What does she want from me? What's
the matter with her?

'It's too late now to go home,' she whispered, 'and the house is
empty. What is there at home? There's nothing at home. Armchairs.
Disgusting armchairs. Erich Dannenberg's chairs. Dr Kleinberger's.
Your father's. All the miserable people. There is nothing for us there
at home. Here outside you can meet anything and feel anything. Owls
are bewitching the moon. You're not going to leave me now, outside
in the night with those wild thugs of drivers and all the owls. You
must stay and protect me. No, I'm not raving, I'm perfectly rational
and I'm almost frozen to death; don't leave me and don't say a word,
Hebrew is such a rhetorical language, nothing but Bible and commentaries. Don't say another word to me in Hebrew, don't say anything at all. Just hold me. To you. Close. Like this. Please, not politely,
please, not gently, hold me as if I'm trying to get away from you, biting and scratching, and you're not letting me go. Hush. And that
wretched *Eule* can shut up as well, because I shall hear and see nothing more because you have covered my head and my ears and gagged
my mouth and tied my hands behind my back because you are much
stronger because I am a woman and you are a man.'

10

As she spoke, they walked through the Makor Baruch quarter toward
the Schneller Barracks, approaching the last of the dirt paths and the
zoo in North Jerusalem, which lies on the frontier between the city
and enemy territory.

The treasure hunt had come to nothing. Nobody had interpreted correctly the clue of the old acacia tree, and the treasure was not found. Uri was asleep curled up in the armchair when Yosef Yarden returned from his visit to Dr Kleinberger. The house was in chaos. In the middle of the table lay an open volume of Bialik's poetry. All the lights were on. Yair was not at home. Yosef Yarden roused his younger son and sent him off to bed with a scolding. Yair must have gone to the station to meet his fiancée. Tomorrow I will let Lily apologize for not being home tonight. She will have to apologize profusely before I agree to accept her excuses and forgive her. The most disagreeable thing was the quarrel with Kleinberger. Naturally I had the last word in the argument, but I have to admit that I was beaten, just as I was in the chess game. I must be honest. I don't believe that our wretched party will ever succeed in shaking off its apathy and depression. Weakness of heart and weakness of will have eroded all the good intentions. All is lost. Now it's time to sleep, so that tomorrow I won't be sleepwalking like the majority of people. But if I get to sleep now, Yair will come home and make a lot of noise. Then I won't be able to sleep until morning, which means another dreadful night. Who's that shouting out there? Nobody's shouting. A bird, perhaps.

Dr Elhanan Kleinberger had also put out the light in his room. He stood at one end of the room, with his face to the wall and his back to the door. The radio was playing late-night music. The scholar's lips moved silently. He was trying, in a whisper, to find the right word for a lyric poem. Unbeknownst to anyone, he was composing poetry. In German. He, the passionate lover of Hebrew literature and the defender of the language's honour, whispered his poetry in German. Perhaps it was for this reason that he concealed what he was doing from even his closest friend. He himself felt that he was committing a sin and was guilty of hypocrisy as well.

With his lips he strove to put ideas into words. A wandering light flickered among the dark shelves. For a moment this light danced on the lenses of his spectacles, creating a flash as of madness or of utter despair. Outside, a bird screeched with malicious joy. Slowly, and very painfully, things became clearer. But still there were things for which no words existed. His frail shoulders began to shake in choking desire. The right words would not come; they only slipped by and eluded him like transparent veils, like fragrances, like longings that the fingers cannot grasp. He felt that there was no hope for him.

Then he switched on the lamp again. Suddenly he felt a vicious hatred for the African ornaments and the erotic vases. And for words.

He stretched out his hand and casually selected a scientific volume from one of the bookshelves. The title shone in gold letters on the leather binding: *Demons and Ghosts in Ancient Chaldee Ritual.* All words are whores, forever betraying you and slipping away into the darkness while your soul yearns for them.

11

The last wood. In its centre stands the Jerusalem Biblical Zoo, and its northern flank marks the frontier between Jerusalem and the enemy villages across the cease-fire line. Lily had been married to Yosef Yarden for less than four months, and he was a delightful youth, full of dreams and ideals. All this happened many years ago, and still there is no peace. It is the way of flesh to hold its grudges, and it is the way of the moon to hover with calm and cold insolence in the night sky.

Within the zoo is a nervous silence.

All the predators are asleep, but their slumber is not deep. They are never totally free from smells and voices borne on the breeze. The night never ceases to penetrate their sleep, sometimes drawing from their lungs a low growl. Their hide bristles in the frozen wind. A tense vibration, a ripple of fear or of nightmare, comes and goes. A moist, suspicious nose probes the night air and takes in the unfamiliar scents. Everywhere there is dew. The rustling cypresses breathe a sigh of quiet sorrow. The pine needles whisper as they search in the darkness, thirsty for the black dew.

From the wolves' cage comes a sound. A pair of wolves in heat, lusting for each other in the darkness. The bitch bites her mate but his fury is only redoubled. In the height of their fever they hear the cries of the birds and the vicious growl of the wildcat.

A blue-tinted vapour rises from the valleys. Strange lights twinkle across the border. The moon sheds her light upon all and shrinks, enchanted, in the whiteness of the rocks: cancers of shining venom in beams of sickly, primeval light.

Moon-struck jackals roam the valleys. From the murky groves they call to their brothers in the cages. These are the lands of nightmare, and perhaps beyond them lie those gardens that no eye has seen, and only the heart reaches out to them as if wailing: Homeward.

Out of the depths of your terror lift up your eyes. See the tops of the pine trees. A halo of pale-grey light enfolds the treetops like a gift of grace. Only the rocks are as dry as death. Give them a sign.

Translated by Philip Simpson.

David Grossman

CHERRIES IN THE ICEBOX

Born in Jerusalem in 1954, Grossman studied philosophy and drama at the Hebrew University and later worked as an editor and broadcaster on Israeli radio. His first novel, The Smile of the Lamb, *was published in 1983 and later translated into English. In it he reflects the tendency in Israel of the 1970s and 1980s to produce politically committed literature. In addition to two further novels, one being* See Under: Love *(1986), a play, a number of short stories, and children's stories, Grossman has compiled two books of interviews with Palestinians and Israeli Arabs. Both have provoked much controversy.*

Tonight, after we made love, Tamar cried. What is there to add? The wounded pillow, ravaged in her mouth; the foul sap oozing from her wounds; perhaps the bristling tension of my muscles, or the hiss escaping from the cracks in my body as they are hastily sealed against the particles of pain that float in the room. Or this: My lying there beside her, splayed on my back and snoring lightly, rhythmically, exuding the manliness expected of me as I lie there, stupid with pleasure and exhaustion, a naked man devoid of all desire beside a seeming-woman, beside her nine-faces which are now reabsorbed into her resting features, the face that was drawn into his own cries, when he clenched his teeth tight so that he would cry out the correct name of the nine, of the ninety, so that, afterwards he would sink, masking his face with contentment.

Tamer cried soundlessly. I felt the sting of sweat behind my knees and neck. I snored insistently. When we were making love, everything was as usual. Before, too. We brought the twins from Tamar's mother's, then the bedtime ritual—the gurglings over the sink, the car pool arrangements for tomorrow—and then—the tears.

I shift slightly in place. Sigh at the echo of a dreamy unease. There a woman is crying. She'll calm down in a minute. These deep sobs, they rend her body. Furrows are ploughed slowly, rustling over the marzipan surface of our bed. Tamar is crying.

Seven years of marriage. That afternoon I picked up the girls from kindergarten and brought them to Tamar's mother's. The young waitress smiled when I said we were celebrating a private holiday, and so would order the finest wine. Tamar screwed up her face grudgingly, but I gave her a lengthy stare, making her smile. We're not watching our pockets today. It's not just the money, Tamar said, and don't drink today.

The girl brought us two violet cyclamens. Her fingers were long and brittle. From the management, she said, and all the best to you. While we ate, she never ceased darting loving, moist glances at us. She's writing our story, I said, and drank from the pungent wine. Tamar followed the movements of my hands. I ask for the best wine, I said, and she brings me *havdalah* wine. Don't make a scene, Tamar said. I poured another glass.

Tamar sliced her quiche with precision. One for Daddy and one for Granny and an itty-bitty one for Annie. Tamar's hair is a bit sparse and short, her forehead white and smooth. What are you looking at me like that for? Here: The dance of the time-honoured glances has already begun tracing a delicate pattern on the cheeks' parchment. What do you mean—'like that'? The lines of separation beginning to show. Even in her. Like *that*, like you've never seen me before. This, too, should be remarked: A faint, tired wing of destruction on the childlike chin; the earth, gently tempting, draws the corners of the mouth to it. Hey, Tami: You're cute.

It was in this vegetarian restaurant that we sat seven years ago, the afternoon of the wedding. Tamar was then twenty-three, and I twenty-six. But I love you much more today, I say to the red silhouette of my face on the wine glass. We were such children, says Tamar. I drink my winey, wavy image. Such children, she repeats.

We ate. That morning someone had hinted that next month my employment at the university might be terminated, because of the cutbacks. I didn't mention it to Tamar. Rumours like that had come and gone. I didn't want to see her nostrils flare as if in anticipation of great danger, see the determined responsibility well up in her eyes. The soup came.

What did we talk about then? I promised you I would be unfaithful within a year; I said I wouldn't pretend, not even on that day, and that I detested the idea that anyone would think so little of me as to trust me. Really, lovely things to hear the morning of your wedding day, Tamar said, leaning her chin on her hand and glaring at me. And I'm ready, I said, gulping some soup so that steam would fog up my glasses, to renew that promise today. But I know you, she said, and I believe in you even more, now. She smiled. I smiled.

Spoons touched plates. Back then I held to the absolute honesty of evil. Things need to be said, even painful ones. Especially painful ones. Terrible, Tamar said, grinning, you were a terrible child, and I don't know how I fell in love with you. It was my money, I said. Somewhere in the basin of my brain pain began to pound. And my mother's letter of recommendation. How impudent you were—a haughty, worldly, spoiled brat. Uh-uh, I raised a finger, that confidence is what captured you. No, she said sweetly: It was the fear behind it.

Seven years. The body is now smoothed. The rings of age only add beauty, ease our movements one inside the other. Saturday at your parents'; Maya drank the syrup by herself; go to bed, Tamar, I'll write a little longer. Suddenly, it's easy.

But I'm lying, she giggles; I didn't sense your fear; you were a thousand years older than me, and smart and talented and bold. Now: the loving joy kindled in her eyes; her guileless, luminous knowing that together we overpowered it, overpowered me; my diving inside; my slack, circular trawling to the cadence of pain. You used to taunt me, she giggles, because I thought Osnat was the best and most perfect of friends, because for years I let her torment me in the pretence of love. You used to blanch to hear me talk about my parents—about us, too—with a tongue like an ice-pick—that's what you called it. And you revelled in feeling like a cursed man, the definitive exile and outcast. And you, and you.

The girl brought tea of fragrant herbs. We're getting married tonight, I told her with a smile. Tamar's lips pursed under the girl's slim arm. I moved slightly, catching them inside the curve of the teapot handle. I knew it, said the waitress, it's written all over your faces. Her watery eyes welled up a bit. I sipped some wine.

And those compulsive little lies of yours, Tamar said briskly, brusquely, the incessant writing of life, the cunning for its own sake. And, I said languidly, your aversion to my writing; your childish hostility toward me on the days when I have a story. Why are we bickering today, Tamar asked, her eyes suddenly extinguished. I extended a hand and drank straight from the bottle. Festive days depress me, Tamar said. I'm actually happy today, I said. A fleeting searing in my temples now joined each dull thud of pain. Someone had welded the exposed edges of the nerves together, by accident. I rhymed to myself, quickly: Last hired, first fired. Why not fire the one you just hired? Also (this is pretty good—): 'The prof. is in the pudding.' By then Tamar had noticed that I was blinking nervously but didn't say a word. She touched a finger to my finger. You're having a hard time now that you're not writing, she said.

Now she cries into the pillow. A continuous, honeyed drop of sorrow drips from her, evaporating in its own warmth until it is a thin whistle, a thought, cooling and freezing like a sharp, glinting shard of glass above my carefully closed eyes. We love each other, I repeat. No outside force could spoil the movement of this relationship, because we have a kind of incessant love, I continue, etching the words on the soft inner shell of my eyelid. Now and then it creates hardship and doubt, but only so they can be resolved wisely, with a controlled flare of pain and desire; it has, I whisper to my frightened self, a complete understanding, a deep grasp of the whole process.

Afterwards we went for a walk in Yemin Moshe, down streets paved with stone. We walked hand in hand and at every third step swung an imaginary child who kicked smooth legs. But there were no children that day. I sat down on a stone bench. The orange beak of a blackbird flashed on the grass. You've changed a great deal, I said; of the two of us, you've changed more. Thanks to you, she said and sat down, placing her purse between us, her thin hair lifting as if fluttering in the wind, her eyes greyer than they were blue. The clouds caused that. Thanks to you, she said again, and in spite of you, because at first I lost myself beside you. Everything about you was clear and absolute, even your fears; only when the first years of shock had passed did I begin to fight. And you're still fighting, though sometimes it's unnecessary. After all, I'm an enlightened dictator. No; with you, she jokes, with cunning, one has to fight constantly. I've learned to do it without getting too tired. With a weary hand I dragged myself for anger and bitterness, but dredged up nothing.

You were so—she says with wise sorrow—so aggressive, so demanding. I had to fight for a me-I-didn't-know. And now, I said, the results I've achieved sometimes frighten me. I know, she said, but this is the only way, adding, surprised: I really have learned. You've changed more, I said.

After that we got up, leaned into one another, and embraced. The skies greyed. Let's go to the four o'clock showing and kiss in the dark, Tamar said into my coat. Let's go to the train station and go away, I said in a pensive Russian accent. I hope my mother's coping with the girls. Today we have no girls.

On the way to the café we passed a playground. It was empty, and its shrubs and benches were furled. The slide shone like the outstretched tongue of a child, breathing and curving with steely torpor. We sat on the rope swings, side by side. The wind whispered at our backs. The swings shifted a bit, and their damp ropes squeaked. Closing my eyes, I flooded my brain with the thick reek of a seaport. Legs kicked at the layer of gravel; muscles stretched from the gut to the tips of the toes and beyond; suddenly, the air freshened.

I remained faithful to her in an old-fashioned way. Even when the expanse of the world was for me a humid, close hothouse; even when the scented trails of glances and veiled meanings were wound around my face. I stitched my desire to her. But the heat of the body melts the iron threads, and the slivers that don't totally evaporate float in the veins, and wound. Women's-eyes' wounds. Perfume's wounds. The wounds of a lover who protects himself from the wounds of women.

And this, too: the potent agility of the imagination's sexual conscience; the longing for a sense of revulsion, which might hint at a chance of salvation; the body that rebels against you. That growls desire at you. At what is left of you. Only the bitter exile in Tamar's placid loins. Only your love of her, her love of you, a childish pain-reliever that you doubtfully swallow.

Stretching, bending the knees, leaning, Tamar passes me with blissful languor, her head arched back, her eyes closed, and I—already I sense the sinewy consistency of my muscles; already this flight sends balls of fire through me that burst in my guts and my groin and under my arms. I've been kidnapped, I'm flying, I'm the eye of the storm, I am devoured. I drag after me the slackened and the rotted. Again I weld to my body the splintered slivers. Even though I can hear Tamar's legs thud against the gravel, hear her clumsy braking; even though I can picture her wondering, still-smiling gaze. I let wildness wail in the arc of my throat, make leaden the iron weighting my body, until I become a giant pendulum slicing the air with my movements, slicing space and time in the semicircle of the swing's arc, again and again slamming against impotence to which the ropes give way at the peak of flight as they hurl me backwards with determined softness.

Nevertheless, Tamar said at the café, we're much more alike now. Because you've managed to contaminate me a little with your dismal outlook, and I've taught you to love; you're not all sharp angles, and I'm not all soft circles.

We insisted on sitting in the café garden. Rain cubs tussled in the bellies of the clouds (I should write that down). An older waitress, short and short-tempered, was forced to clean the bird droppings off the blue plastic table. Beyond the fence the street cleared the mucus from its throat. Tamar blew onto her palms. I asked for two hot chocolates and a snifter of brandy. That tooth hurts, I said to her. Her lips curled in anger. I didn't have the strength to explain what the pain meant: for the last few minutes I had realized, astounded, that the message my nerves had been sending me was one of—hunger. A live, reptilian hunger. As I said, someone inside me bungled the welding. Tamar averted her gaze. Tamar smiled uncomfortably.

She learned fast; she was very innocent when I first met her. That's how she was sucked into the wind tunnel where I roared. She choked on the dust of my fragmented words. That's how she was sucked into the fear that shrieks suddenly, into the froth of frightened violence. In a seemingly lost whisper, she is an opaque, corked bottle which sinks deeper into the maelstrom in my pupils.

And yet. From within her momentary helplessness springs the matador's charm: the slight sway of Tamar's slim back, and the danger—projecting onto soft hammocks of astonishment, the sweetness of gentle mockery—is caught. A thin scarf is tossed weakly at the smoke gathering at the nostrils. You're like that, I'm like this. You see, we can be together like this, too. An evasive leap, a smile: I will not leave you, my little boy. A thick tendon pulses on a bulging neck. You make love to me as if you were at war. From on high a voice is heard, a bitter, lowing call: The bull loves the matador.

The waitress brought hot chocolate and a glass one-third full of brandy. A leather pouch was strapped to her belly by a greasy belt. We're getting married today, Tamar said suddenly, stealing a childishly crafty glance at me. Yeah, that's how it goes, said the waitress, looking at us with fleeting surprise before turning to leave.

We drank. If they fire me I'll go back to writing advertising slogans and technical instructions. They'll be pleased to have me back at the offices of Peled-Arnon. Remedy precedes rot. The cigarette smokes you. These are both mine, and I waste my time teaching literature at the university. Even the tourist office pays well for propaganda leaflets. Follow the gun and come to Israel.*

Anyone seeing us from a distance, Tamar said, would think we're strangers. And from up close? I scowled into the glass. Her gaze flickered. You just have to—her lips whitened—say everything, don't you, test the effect of every possible combination of words. Words are

---

* In English transliteration in the original.

my business, I said half-heartedly. No; it's a kind of joy in destruction. I remember the things you used to tell me when I was pregnant, the evil prophecies about the inevitable hatred between parents and children. I hurt myself that way, too. After all, you know there are things I must say. Angry to be telling her this yet again, I got carried away and added: Besides, you already know that it's the most banal things that hurt me, that I can never accept them—like what you said before.

What, that you have to say everything?

No; that we're alike.

Sometimes I gnaw myself in sorrow over her. Over her being sentenced to me. The path of life for which she was intended is so clear. Of course she would have to have known me, but only as a slight burning sensation. As a lighthouse of danger. Maybe as a friend of hers and her husband's. An amusing curio you must be careful of, careful of the white-hot barbed wire cutting it in half. Someone to tell friends about, to try half-heartedly to fix up with single girlfriends, sighing fondly: He's a challenge; you'll see.

It's these clouds, Tamar said, and the empty garden and the waitress with the dyed hair, that are making us melancholy just now, tempting us to forget that, really, on a day-to-day basis, we're pretty happy together; that we have two wonderful, healthy girls; that I'm successful in my work and you enjoy teaching and writing. That we have friends and lives that are so full and strong we can afford to talk openly like this about our relationship. No, I think we're forgetting too many things just now. It's just that you enjoy being the child you were at twenty.

I crushed the wet sugar in the bottom of the glass with the spoon. That child still has hold of my throat; he demands attention for his pain. I spurn him because that's what I've been trained to do. But I keep him hidden away, sneak food to him. When the war's over, I'll let him be discovered.

The grains squeaked under the pressure of the metal spoon. When we met we were impossibly different from one another. Love buffeted us against each other. So we fought together to change our dreams. From this came the unknowable wonder of the blossoming of our two girls: the code of our bodies, deciphered.

Except that all this—what is all this?—it's a fraud, a detour Tamar's learned to make. Burns she sustained passing through me before she returned to herself. From here forward: her even steps; the thin, transparent slices of herself she parcels out to the world; her calm eyes. It was only in my envy of her that I understood: There was a message hidden in that corked bottle. A concealed, relentless directive: Me. Me. Me.

But now, all of a sudden, her bitter tears—the secret of Tamar in a tear—what are we two, what is left?

Really, we're happy together, I say, taking her hand in mine and kissing her on the mouth, and really, there's no need to say everything; how silly of us to expect that today of all days, on a day like this, we'd be dripping with love and optimism made to order. There, she said; you really do quite please me; perhaps I'll renew that contract with your parents after all, and lease you for another seven years. I laughed. The pain in my head suddenly abated. I laughed again. Tamar looked at me, uncomprehending, ready to smile. I laughed aloud. Perhaps I've discovered the cure, I said. She didn't understand. Come, I winked at her, let's go home. There are cherries in the icebox.

It should be noted that the house was very empty. Tiny articles of clothing were strewn in every corner. Also, blocks, coloured-on pages, pencils, and dolls. We took off our coats. My eyes throbbed. I stood in front of the open refrigerator, furiously gobbling food. Tamar hummed to herself in one of the rooms. Suddenly I heard her voice beside me. What aggressive eating, she said, then vanished. I slammed the refrigerator door shut. Now what. I picked through the record albums. Peter and the Wolf and Let's Learn to Count with the Count, and 50 Holiday Songs for Children. The bottom of the pile yielded prehistoric layers: Leonard Cohen and Theodorakis and Carole King. But somewhere a distant needle skipped out of its mechanical slumber and began revolving in my head in rhythmic circles, translating the grooves into sounds and sights in my memory. A rented room with the lavatory outside. A dedication in a book of poems. Hands meeting in the dark. I gave up. A pickle was still clenched in my mouth when I placed an album on the turntable; I tried to balance the pickle between my teeth, my head angled back and my arms spread out to the sides. One, two, left, right, arms on friends' shoulders. Shlomit is building a bright green *sukkah*, that's why she's busy today. That's why I'm now a smiling, trained show-dolphin, a seal poking through a hole in the ice, the harpoon already stuck in its brain and tasting of sour pickle. And it's not just any bright green *sukkah*, left and right, caught up in the rhythm of the music, in the flashing of the sabres of pain, Shlomit is building a *sukkah* of peace, a bower of peace; my neck arches toward the ceiling and I gulp the sourish shaft, suddenly silence, Tamar is beside the turntable, her eyes wide. The pickle glides across the room like some comic bird.

Later, after we'd brought the startled twins back home and Tamar had tried to put them to bed, I went into their room. The three of them lay side by side, and for a moment seemed to be a mirage. They were so alike, entwined. I smiled at them and went out. I rubbed my eyes roughly. That usually worked for a while, but not this time. I think I was also a bit drunk, because inside the pangs of biting hunger were slow, insistent stirrings of nausea. I stood in the hall and tried to laugh soundlessly. I contracted my stomach muscles; I pawed through my thoughts for funny things. The dance of the sour pickle, for one, or the look on Tamar's face when she was standing there. Breathing like that in the silence, my face radiant, I exhaled all the ironic poison that had collected since that morning at the university. That didn't work, either. Suddenly I knew I was ripe for a great defeat. Tamar came out of the girls' room and closed the door after her. She saw me and let out a frightened giggle. She said I looked like one of those dingy dogs that hang around gas stations. I liked the image. I pressed her to me. As if I felt better.

Afterwards even though we were a bit dejected and careful of one another, we made love with the old passion, and Tamar's body was again my only possible home. She was tense, and when we finished she said that this time she had made love against me. Within minutes she fell asleep. *Tonight after we made love Tamar cried*—but that's only an imaginary lasso of words I was caught in, that wrung startling seeds of pain from my whole body. The humming in my head became a straight, shimmering line. I knew I had to move, had to keep from being a motionless target. But I continued to lie there and wait.

Translated by Marsha Weinstein.

Yitzhak (Auerbach) Orpaz

TALITHA KUMI

Born in the USSR in 1923, Orpaz emigrated to Palestine in 1938. He worked for some time on a kibbutz and studied philosophy and literature. He has published short stories, novellas, and novels as well as a book of essays. One of his most famous works is Tomozhenna Street, a series of loosely connected stories relating to childhood and the family. The stories describe a diaspora Jewish lifestyle that has largely disappeared. His latest collection of stories, Loves and Follies, from which 'Talitha Kumi' is taken, was published in 1992.

In September everyone's looking for an apartment. Especially in Jerusalem. Especially students. This is the busy season for Yochanan Dvir, apartment renovator and owner of a few of them himself. Two small apartments which he renovated in Nahlaoth he rented immediately for 400 dollars each. He was on the point of renting the third, a one-room apartment in Abulafia Street, for 300 dollars, but before he signed the contract Haimke Levine called him from Tel Aviv and said: 'Listen. Maybe you've got something for my daughter. She's been accepted at "Betzalel" and she needs a one-room apartment.'

Yochanan said 'Yes.' Without hesitation.

Haimke Levine had helped Yochanan when he was in big trouble. He had fallen in love. Suddenly he understood the meaning of the words 'for love is fierce as death'. And the girl—a high-school student. He stopped working and ran around like a lunatic. One day he began taking an interest in the Shalom Tower, walking around and counting the floors. Haimke went with him, ate with him, refused to leave him alone. And all the time he told him horror stories about this one and that one and how they all, thank God, survived in the end. And were getting along nicely too. Once he even jumped into the Gordon pool for him. He shouted 'I'm sick if it!' and jumped in at the deep end. He didn't know how to swim. Yochanan naturally jumped in after him and pulled him out. Afterwards it turned out that Haimke was once the junior swimming champion or something. He simply never left him alone. This was four years before. Yochanan got over it, and in the end he even got married (and divorced again). They didn't see much of each other. But Yochanan kept a warm spot in his heart for Haimke. And when he called and asked a favour for his daughter, he immediately saw before his eyes Haimke's floury face, his soft laugh, and the exposed gums at the front of his mouth. He wouldn't hear of an implant or a prothesis. He claimed that he couldn't afford it, that the alimony he paid for his two daughters ate up everything he earned teaching mathematics at a crammer's. As far as this was concerned Yochanan didn't believe him. In Yochanan's opinion, Haimke knew that the exposed gums were part of his elderly charm. In any case, Yochanan was delighted to have the opportunity to repay him. He had never seen Haimke's daughters.

'Her name's Dana,' said Haimke Levine. 'You'll recognize her immediately. Innocent-looking with big eyes.'

They arranged for Yochanan to meet Dana the next day at seven o'clock in the evening next to Talitha Kumi,* to show her the apartment and give her the key.

'How much?' asked Haimke.

'Don't insult me. We'll talk about money later.'

His watch was fast. Sometimes ten minutes and sometimes twenty. This didn't bother him. He liked feeling that he was running ahead of time. He took his shoulder bag, but instead of wearing his regular jeans, which he used for work too, he put on a striped shirt and wide cotton trousers. He checked his beard after shaving too, smelled his armpits after showering, and combed his short, strong hair, and suddenly it occurred to him, and he wasn't even surprised, that he was getting ready for a blind date.

But he didn't change the contents of his shoulder-bag. The usual pliers and screwdriver, he never left the house without them. Any repair or renovation, big or small, you began with them.

And there was also a thick notebook with a hard black cover in the shoulder bag, on whose first page, under the word 'Diary', the opening date was written in green ink, and after that nothing. And there

* *Talitha Kumi*: 'Arise, little maid', words spoken by Jesus (Mark 5: 41) on resuscitating a young girl. When the school by this name—a school for Arab Christian girls established by German missionaries in the last century—was demolished to make way for a shopping complex in downtown Jerusalem, some of the features of the historic building, including an arch with a clock, were preserved and reconstructed as a little edifice on the plaza in front of the Mashbir Letzarhan department store.

was also a thin book published by the open university in a soft cobalt-blue cover, the colour of his Subaru car, on the subject of quantum theory. The fate of the universe had been worrying him lately.

Equipped with all the above, he made for Talitha Kumi. The clock on the façade of Talitha Kumi said six-thirty. He compared it with his wrist-watch, which said six-forty. He trusted the Talitha Kumi clock, which left him enough time to duplicate a key for Haimke Levine's daughter, who appeared in his imagination as a pale, fragile girl who spoke in a whisper and whose big soft eyes shyly caressed his face.

At about the time Yochanan put the finishing touches to his mental portrait of the girl he was going to meet next to Talitha Kumi, the man finished duplicating the key. Yochanan was pleased by this synchronization, it seemed to him like a vestige of some longed-for, harmonious world which had once existed but was now lost. It also held out a promise for a successful meeting. He looked for a key-ring and found a gilt medallion with a picture of Madonna. He supposed that she would want Madonna. He himself detested Madonna. The duplication of the key cost him four shekels. The key-holder eight. This seemed exorbitant to him, and he almost bought one in the shape of a Dutch clog for four shekels, but at the last moment, for the sake of Haimke Levine, he decided to buy the medallion with Madonna nevertheless.

A wonderful feeling of generosity flooded him. He didn't exactly know what to do with it. He dropped a whole shekel into the violin case of a street musician, and called up one of his two tenants, a new immigrant from Russia, and asked him what he could do to help him. The new immigrant said: 'Everything. Everything. *Nye harasho.*' Yochanan promised to come and see what he could do. Maybe that very evening. He knew, of course, that the taps had to be fixed, but his experience as a landlord told him that if he didn't do it, the tenant would. The tenant, however, who misunderstood the landlord's good intentions, said something in Russian which sounded to Yochanan like a curse.

Yochanan thought that this was unfair. But he made up his mind not to let it spoil the rendezvous. He returned to the Talitha Kumi plaza. On his arm he carried a black anorak. As a native Tel Avivian he mistrusted the Jerusalem weather: suddenly in the middle of summer, especially here, you would be hit by a freezing wind. Even without a wind, it was September now, and September evenings in Jerusalem meant sweaters and anoraks.

Talitha Kumi is the place where everybody meets everybody,

especially at this hour. The light took on a a kind of blueish hue—
he was always astounded by this colour of light in Jerusalem, in the
last ten minutes before darkness gathered. Perhaps they would be in
time to meet inside the blue. Now he saw her as a Japanese silk doll.
Deathly pallor worked well on his hormones. He was glad that he
had been given the opportunity to discover this side of himself. Not
only would he give her the gilded key-ring studded with glittering
stones, he would show her the apartment and ask her what it lacked,
and after she told him shyly what it lacked, he would say to her, casually: 'At the landlord's expense.'

He liked these thoughts. He wanted to cry. His ex-wife's words still
rang in his ears ('You only think of yourself'), and in view of all this
abundance he was about to shower on his friend's daughter, he was overwhelmed by a swelling surge of self-love. After a long time of dulling
his mind with house renovations and apartment rentals, together with
abstract concern for the fate of the universe—he suddenly felt good,
and he was almost happy.

The watch on his wrist said ten past seven. Another ten minutes
at least, he said to himself. Maybe fifteen. He looked forward to a
delightful hour, and in the mean time, in a kind of eagerness hith-
erto almost unknown to him to do something for others, he went up
to a particularly vociferous group clamouring near the edge of the
plaza, and suggested that they state their case quietly. One of them,
holding a placard with the clenched fist of the *Kach* movement, bent
down and roared into his face: 'Are you for or against?'

Yochanan thought that the man was joking, but he was afraid to
laugh. At a distance of a few steps from there a young man in a teeshirt and short trousers was standing and muttering: 'No more war,
no more bloodshed.'* Yochanan wanted to tell them that now, when
the world was about to collapse anyway, there was no point in worrying about trifles. Most of all he wanted to shout: '*I'm happly! I'm
happy!*'

But the lout with the placard, puzzled by the mumbling of the
weirdo—who at this moment opened his arms as if to embrace the
world—lowered his heavy head with a roar:

'Are you for or against?'

The question was definitely unfair. Yochanan saw the dagger flash
under the flapping shirt of the armed giant with the cobalt face who
was threatening the world.

---

* In English in the original.

He thought of inviting him to discuss the problem over a cup of coffee in the Cafe Atara, but in view of the urgency of the matter, he immediately declared:

'I'm for or against.'

The clenched fist of his interrogator remained suspended in the air, enabling Yochanan to withdraw in a more or less orderly manner.

As he retreated, walking backwards, Yochanan admitted to himself that the Cobalt Man's question had a certain justice, if not in its style then in its content. He had never completely made up his mind whether he was for or against anything. It seemed to him a little besides the point. For example, if he happened to bump into a high-school student with a murmuring voice and caressing eyes, he wouldn't ask himself if he was for or against, he would simply die for her.

Dana, for instance.

At this moment he realized that he was imagining the kind-hearted Haimke's daughter as a kind of double of the high-school student for whose sake he had almost thrown himself off the Shalom Tower. This moved him, and he couldn't come up with any good reason to fight against this wild flight of his imagination. Somewhere deep in his heart he was always ready to forget his apartments and the alimony which had turned him unwillingly into a landlord with apartments to rent, and the never-ending worry about the imminent destruction of the world, which appeared to him in the form of a cobalt-coloured booklet shooting out of his bag and exploding into a million scraps of coloured paper—a real celebration!—and to begin the adventure of his death from the beginning.

A few useful details about the life history of Yochanan Dvir:

Motherless from the age of six, a bookworm to the age of sixteen, fatherless from the age of sixteen, apprenticed to a renovations contractor from the age of sixteen, non-registered student in the departments of Jewish Mysticism and Business Administration at Tel Aviv University, a six-month course in Japanese flower arrangement, two years as a pilgrim at a temple in Nepal, whence he returns bearded, smiling, and silent, to work from the age of twenty-four at odd jobs, and between one job and the next to lie on his back and smile at the ceiling. Sometimes he announces, alone or among casual acquaintances over a glass of beer, in reponse to urgent events: 'It's impossible to know anything.' In this manner ten years go by. At the age of thirty-four he is pushed into marriage by two of his acquaintances, themselves married, who are unable to bear his provocative bachelorhood.

From the age of thirty-nine divorced with a child. At this age, one day after his divorce, he bought a thick notebook with a hard cover and wrote under the word 'DIARY', printed in large letters: *'Begun on the 15th of September 198– Yochanan Dvir.'* The date was important, since it was his birthday. But Yochanan did not believe in horoscopes and the signs of the zodiac, and accordingly he did not see the date as having any significance beyond the date itself. Ever since then he had carried the notebook around with him wherever he went, in a special compartment in his shoulder-bag. Apart from the opening date he didn't write a single word in the notebook. After his divorce, his wanderings, the death of his parents, and his first love, he was sure that he would have something to write in the diary. But when he sat down to write in it, everything seemed to him trivial, meaningless, and incomprehensible, and the notebook remained empty. Nevertheless he never stopped believing that one day he would find something to write in his diary. When he fell in love with the beautiful high-school student, who spoke to him—her private tutor in mathematics—in a soft voice and with a caressing look, he decided that this was the thing he had been waiting for, and everything assumed a tremendous significance. Her name was Dana. In his dreams she would smoke his pipe (he had never smoked a pipe) which had a gigantic stem. He immediately understood that the sights of Nepal were intruding here and signalling to him: This is your bride. This is your betrothed. He almost began to write in the diary, but then the girl made it clear to him that she had a boyfriend, and that if he continued to harrass her she would call the police, and he began to contemplate suicide. Yochanan was sure that there had been a misunderstanding here, that she was meant for him, and that it was only because of some fault or hitch in a dark corner among the stars—of which he could know nothing because of the immanent uncertainty stemming from quantum theory—that it had not come off, and the little high-school student had exchanged him in her blind naïvety for some stupid athletic boy who still had pimples on his face.

According to the same logic, Yochanan argued in his own favour, as he lay on his back for days at a time looking at the ceiling, it was possible that some other, opposite fault, a kind of anti-fault, in some other corner of the universe, would cancel them both out, and the girl would return to him as naturally as the sun returns to its course in the morning, and his life would be saved.

Equipped with these thoughts and a full measure of self-pity, he stood for hours in front of the Shalom Tower and counted the floors from top to bottom, without any intention of committing suicide, but full of gratitude to Haimke Levine who took his tears and threats seriously. From the age of thirty-nine he worked as a renovations contractor, both because of the need to pay alimony for his son, whom he hardly ever saw, and because of the opportunities offered him by the Jerusalem building market, which began to boom with the mass immigration from Russia; but mainly because of an inner consciousness that Jerusalem was a place in which everything was still possible. He soon found himself with apartments to rent. He had an accounts book, also in a hard cover, in which he wrote down his income and expenditure at the end of the day, but he did not take this notebook with him in his shoulder-bag. He thought: If what he had heard a scientist saying on the radio was true, that it was enough for a butterfly in Kamchatka to flutter its wings in order to create a cyclone in the constellation of Sirius, then mixing up the two notebooks could be really dangerous.

Yochanan shook his arms as if they were crawling with vermin, but for safety's sake he also sent a conciliatory wave in the direction of the lout, who had not yet recovered from his stupefaction.

The twilight blue dissolved into the cold neon lights of the evening, and Yochanan asked himself if he had done everything possible to be worthy of the frissons of delight awaiting him at the appointed hour. In the mean time he scratched his back between his shoulder-blades, where a kind of scabies had taken up permanent residence during one of his journeys. A cold wind descended on the plaza and went away again, and the crowds of people, of all races and ages, who momentarily raised their heads as if to see where the cold wind was coming from, immediately returned to their searches or their wares, jewellery and balloons, knitwear, missionary leaflets and prayer-books for the High Holidays; the violinist to his violin, the messiahs to their demented mutterings, and the quarrellers to their quarrels, and a rabble of faces and garments moved to and fro like sleepwalkers around the stone arch bearing the name of a young girl who had come back to life—and they all looked as if they were searching for their blind date.

Yochanan put on his black anorak, which up to now he had been carrying over his arm, examined the way it lay over his white shirt with the brown stripes, and leaving the sleeves unbuttoned for an effect of careless grace, he looked at the Talitha Kumi clock and was shocked.

The clock still said half past six.

The anticipated frissons of delight gave way to confusion. On principle he was against confusion. And so he resolutely exchanged the
confusion for paternal concern. What had happened to the girl? His
dear friend Haimke had entrusted her to his care, and now where
was the girl? Irrelevantly he remembered that he hadn't had any supper. He bought a hotdog for three shekels, demanded mustard, crammed
half of it into his mouth with one bite, and immediately spat it out
into the municipal litter bin, into which he also disgustedly threw what
was left in his hand. There. In spite of his hunger, he had given up the
hotdog. This seemed to him a worthy sacrifice. His watch said seven
forty. How was he to tell if his watch was fast or slow? Suddenly he
no longer trusted his watch. He wanted to swear, but he couldn't
find the right word, and so he ripped it furiously off his wrist, but he
couldn't bring himself to throw it away and he put it in his pocket
instead. He asked someone who looked serious: 'What's the time?'
'I'm not from here,' said the man. Another man asked Yochanan if
the number 4 bus went to Kiryat Yovel. Yochanan, who believed in
the supreme importance of maintaining your presence of mind under
stress, explained patiently that he could go to Kiryat Yovel with 18,
20, or 27, and that the nearest bus stop was in Jaffa Street. But the
man interrupted him with a dismissive gesture and said: 'All I asked
was if number 4 went to Kiryat Yovel.'

Suddenly he had the distinct feeling that all the people here, waiting on the steps of the monument and milling around it, had been
waiting and milling around since yesterday, since the day before yesterday, and maybe forever. And they had all missed their appointments
because of this bloody Talitha Kumi clock, which had probably stopped
two thousand years ago at least. In the grip of this defeatist thought,
he turned to a pale young girl, who was sitting and writing from left
to right on a letter pad, and asked her, after apologizing in two languages, what the time was. She said: 'Eight o'clock.' In Hebrew.

Her voice was soft, something delicate and painful tightened her
lips. For a moment he hoped that she was Dana. In the terrible pressure he felt in his guts, he was ready to compromise, and so he asked
her if she was by any chance Dana Levine. She whistled a few words
between her almost-closed lips, among which he identified one English
word he know: 'Asshole.'

A mumbling, bearded messiah-freak who was standing with his back
to the big display windows of the Mashbir Letzarhan went on mechanically repeating, in a nasal American accent: 'The last train, gentlemen. It's not too late.' Only now, perhaps under the influence of the

words of the mad, self-anointed messiah, Yochanan grasped his new position: that he was late. By a simple calculation, while he was duplicating the key, phoning his tenant and messing around with the morons from *Kach*, Dana had been looking for him. He was at least half an hour late. Dana had waited for him for half an hour and left. He dismissed out of hand the possibility that she had not recognized him —in such cases your eyes met with the force of an electric shock. By a simple calculation, the cold wind had descended on the plaza at exactly half past seven, and that was supposed to be the minute at which it would happen. I'm thinking like a madman, thought Yochanan. He immediately formed a two-pronged plan. One: call Haimke—Dana had undoubtely phoned him to tell him what had happened. And if the first move failed, then the second came into operation: he would go to the apartment in Abulafia Street, within spitting distance, and there—he could see the picture in front of his eyes—she walks past the entrance, lingers for a moment, and her big eyes caress the iron door, and she rings the bell, and listens, and when nobody answers she leans against the doorpost and waits.

He inserted ten tokens, anticipating a long conversation with his Tel Aviv friend. There was no reply. He proceeded immediately to the second move. But half-way there, as he crossed Mesilat-Yesharim Street, he remembered that he hadn't retrieved the telephone tokens. He decided not to make an issue out of it and to continue on his way. But in the narrow alley, Avi, a skinny youth with a stealthy step, known in the quarter as something between a thief and a junkie, barred his way. Avi's mother was sitting on the steps of the Hagoral synagogue, holding a chicken in her lap and stroking it. She always sat on the same step with a chicken in her lap. In the quarter they said that she saw everything, but she had one eye stuck together permanently shut. Her son, Avi, stood barring the way with his legs wide apart, and took a deep drag from his cigarette. The alley was narrow, barely one and a half metres wide, and it was impossible to pass without pushing up against him.

'I've got somebody for you.'

His voice was menacing.

'Thank you. I've already got someone,' said Yochanan.

'A girl, right?'

'How do you know.'

His heart was full of foreboding.

'There was some female here,' said Avi. 'Don't worry. I'll give you a girl you can rely on, just right for you. Two hundred, maybe two hundred and fifty—what the hell's the matter with you!'

Yochanan charged forward, almost knocking him over. He ran, but immediately slowed down. He rang the bell and knocked on the door of his house, as if Dana were inside. But Dana wasn't even outside.

He went up to his apartment. For a moment he wondered why Dana wasn't there. Then he wondered at his wonder. In the mean time he promised himself that even if she wasn't there, she would come back, of that there could be no doubt. After all, she belonged here.

The thought that Dana belonged here and that she would therefore simply return here, was so pleasing to him that he awarded himself a laugh in front of the mirror, rubbed his teeth with his finger and smelled it, and in order to give full expression to the feeling of relief he stretched his arms out to the empty room and yawned a deep yawn. And then he was seized by a terrible panic.

Maybe something had happened to her!

Yochanan Dvir found himself at this hour, inside his house, in a state of total uncertainty as to where to go and what to do, but with the clear knowledge that he had to do something, come what may. This being the case, he took his accounts book and began to write down his expenditures for the day: Duplication of key 3 shekels, keyring for Dana Levine 8 shekels, hotdog, telephone calls—

A police car, or maybe an ambulance, drove past with a wail, right under his window. The situation seemed urgent, even threatening, but on no account could he clarify to himself where things had gone wrong. The Talitha Kumi clock appeared before him, confident and eternal, its hands on six-thirty. He tried to phone Haimke and found the line dead. It must have been that junkie Avi who had cut the line. The neighbourhood boss. Skinny as a dried fig, and lording it over everybody like a rooster. He had to phone the police, but the phone was dead.

Yochanan resolutely dismissed the idea that everyone had conspired against him. The effort he invested in this refusal made him sweat, especially in his armpits. He smelled his armpits. The smell wasn't so bad, but nevertheless he sprayed himself with a deodorant. He liked deodorants that smelled of tobacco. He liked his body. He still saw himself going to keep his appointment with Dana. He drew encouragement from his short, hard haircut, and decided to act with presence of mind.

And immediately, as if he had gone beserk, he began to run. In his catastrophe-haunted heart he immediately connected the nervous wailing of the police cars and ambulances arriving from the direction of the Talitha Kumi plaza with the inevitable death of Dana, hope of his life. As he ran he tried to connect his permanent anxiety about the collapse of the universe with the death of Dana, but they wouldn't connect. The little pimp with his eternal cigarette barred his way, this time facing the opposite direction. Yochanan decided that with the wailing of the sirens in the background and Dana hovering between life and death it wouldn't be so terrible if he knocked the little bastard out of his way. He did it. 'I don't believe it,' he said to himself in surprise. 'I don't believe that I did it.' Judging by the squawking of the chicken, Yochanan guessed that the little pimp had rolled onto his mother.

But Yochanan's heart was already elsewhere. His Dana lay dying on the Mashbir plaza, at the feet of the Talitha Kumi archway, covered with a blanket, and they were already pulling a stretcher out of one of the ambulances. He heard shouts: 'Kill them. They work for Jews and come at you with knives.' He crossed knots of people, shouts, wailing sirens. He sensed huge powers in himself. Policemen grabbed him and he eluded them, and fell on the body. He tore the blanket off the body and lay down on it full length and shouted '*Kumi*, get up, Dana my soul, get up, Dana my heart—'

That was as far as he got. The policemen grabbed hold of him and dragged him behind the arch of Talitha Kumi and seated him on the concrete step.

Someone brought water.

Yochanan rejected the water. The sweat was pouring off him. A policeman wiped the blood off his face.

'Take it easy,' said the policeman. 'Is this yours?'

Yochanan nodded and the policeman hung the shoulder bag on his shoulder.

'Are you related to her?'

'She's my brother's daughter.'

'What's your brother's name?'

'Haim Levine.'

His answers were lucid. He didn't look anywhere. He knew that all in all he was the hero of a tragedy and the victim of a great love, and decided to act accordingly.

'What's your name?'

'Yochanan Dvir.'

'How do you know that she's your brother's daughter?'

'That's an idiotic question' said Yochanan.

The policeman put the side of this hand in position for a dry chop. But another policeman intervened:

'Leave him alone. Can't you see? The guy's in shock.'

'What's her name?'

'Dana. Dana Levine.'

The second policeman, the one who had spoken before, rummaged in a small jeans knapsack and pulled out a document that looked like a passport. He paged through the passport and showed Yochanan the photo.

'Do you know this woman?'

'No.' Said Yochanan.

'Her name's Sandra Lee, Arkansas, USA. Is that your brother's daughter?' asked the policeman.

'No. But . . .' said Yochanan, 'its not too late.'

He stretched out his finger and pointed it at the level of their eyes. The second policeman exchanged a glance with the interrogating policeman.

'You can go,' said the interrogating policeman.

Yochanan felt slighted at not having been taken in for more serious questioning. What could you expect from policemen who saw the world through the nickel of their police badges? There had been a big mistake here, of that there was no doubt. A colossal mistake in his opinion, but completely comprehensible. If they had given him a chance he would have opened their eyes to see that there was some-thing more, something else, more than anything visible to human eyes, and that it was an everyday matter. Yochanan's mind, which had in a certain sense been clouded, but in another sense been granted clarity, immediately connected everything with the great imminent collapse, when the bodies racing toward nothingness, toward the gath-ering darkness, would open up to each other like lovers at the hour of their last farewell. What's the wonder that my Dana, Dana my soul, came back to life.

Pityingly he now looked at the two ignorant policeman, who didn't understand what they saw. One thing was absolutely clear: as long as he waited for his Dana, as long as he waited for his Dana, his Dana was alive.

These are good thoughts, said Yochanan to himself. He went up to the battery of public telephones to call Haimke, but remembered that he had no tokens left, and turned round to go home. His whole body hurt, but the sacrifice was worth it. Even if he never saw Dana as long as he lived, he had done his bit. At the same time, however, he wasn't sure if the cosmic forces which had assisted him to bring

Dana back to life would be enough to protect him from the swift knife of the little pimp, who was presumably lying in wait for him in the alley. Accordingly he made a detour round the quarter via Agrippas Street and approached his house from the rear, stealthily, and immediately phoned Haimke.

He was sure that Haimke knew everything. The hand which had previously cut the line had now repaired it. Haimke was on the line.

'Listen, Yochanan. It's a good thing you phoned. Danka's found something else. A friend of hers has rented a two-room apartment and she's going to share it with her. Not far from you, by the way, in Bezalel Street.'

'But. . . .' said Yochanan in bewilderment. 'She. You know. That's to say . . .'

'Yes. Of course. She came to tell you. You sound . . . is anything wrong?'

'No.'

'Then bye for now. Drop in some time.'

Yochanan leant on the table. He was very tired. And now he also felt a pressure at the base of his head, where it joined his neck. This he imagined was where the plug connecting all the positive cosmic forces was situated. He felt exhausted. He wasn't sure that he would be able to play his role in maintaining the system. He needed concrete proof. Accordingly he phoned his Russian tenant and the moment he heard the word 'taps' he went for him and told him not to expect any refunds or repairs from him: 'Listen here'—he yelled at him—'you fix those taps yourself. I'm telling you. Everyone has to do his bit, and that's that.'

What he said sounded to him barbaric. But completely justified. It was high time they learnt Hebrew.

He went into the bathroom and tested the hot water. There was hot water. He left the tap open. He liked seeing the steam rising from the hot water. As he pulled off his anorak and kicked off his sandals, he reviewed his day with detached interest, like a person examining someone else's clothes. He vaguely remembered the clock set into the stone arch of Talitha Kumi. The clock said half past six. Why half past six for God's sake?

'Here's something to open the diary with,' he said to himself.

In the mean time he got into the bath.

'It can wait till tomorrow,' he said to himself.

Translated by Dalya Bilu.

Orly Castel-Bloom

HIGH TIDE

Orly Castel-Bloom was born in 1960 in Tel Aviv, where she still lives. She studied film at Tel Aviv University. She is the recipient of many major literary prizes. Her second novel, Dolly City, *is set in a mythical city which sometimes recalls Tel Aviv, and describes both its squalor and its vitality. Her book of short stories,* Hostile Surroundings, *from which 'High Tide' is taken, was published in 1989. The banal situations with which her stories are concerned are inspired by everyday life but they are written in a style that borders on surrealism, described as both hyper-fantasy and hyper-realism. Castel-Bloom is one of the generation of Israeli postmodernist writers.*

Something was wrong with my and Alex's way of life. The pace was frantic, there wasn't a drop of air. He left home at seven and came back at ten, eleven at night. I left quarter of an hour after him and came home at about the same time. We had different-coloured diaries, in which we wrote down where we would be and when. Our diaries were filled up a month and a half in advance. I don't know how he managed with meals, I always ate fast food: sandwiches that I ate while waiting for the green light.

We had a number of advantages. Like two fast and very comfortable cars each with air-conditioning, and a double bed with a special orthopaedic mattress to soothe the cramps in our back and leg muscles. We always had hot water in the bath, there were always cold soft drinks in the fridge, and our bar was always full. I had someone in three times a week to clean and take care of the housekeeping for me. For an extra pittance she also ironed and did the shopping, and that really made my life easier.

We worked weekends too. Each of us has a study furnished according to own personal taste. We would sit there, summing up the week and making plans. Alex is an importer. He imports whatever he feels like, he has a sixth sense that tells him what will sell. Naturally he travels a lot, but his trips are short. I'm in clothing. I own a quality chain that everybody's heard of. I have twelve shops in the centre, five in the north, and another three in Beersheba and its suburbs. I go from shop to shop, travel abroad for the shows, and buy more clothes for the chain. Sometimes I meet women who want me to design a dress for them like this and like that. I always say to them: You're the customer, but I'm what I am. You want to tell me what's running through your head, I'm prepared to listen, but I'm not some little dressmaker. I don't take orders from anybody, and the money makes no difference to me. I have something to say in the matter too, and a lot.

Once I did much more designing. Today I only design bridal gowns, and if they make it worth my while, I might agree to run up something for the mother of the bride or the mother of the groom as well.

My prices are probably the highest in the country, and only those who can afford it walk into Sisi's shops. A lot of women stand outside looking at the window displays and dreaming of the day when they'll be able to buy one of our creations for themselves. Dream on, girls, dream on.

Above each of my shops is a sign with the name of the owner: Ronit, Simone, Shirlee, Ofra, and so on, and underneath in different letters, in my opinion letters of a different class entirely, Sisi One, Sisi Two, Sisi Three, and so on. They actually belong to me, all these shops, I only rent them to Ronit or Ofra or Pazit or whoever, and they pay me a fortune for the name Sisi, and also give me a share of the profits.

So what was I saying before?—when I start talking about my shops there's no stopping me—yes, the tempo of our lives was frantic. Alex had already begun feeling aches and pains in all kinds of places, and my back was giving me problems. We decided to take a few days' vacation. Alex said: 'Haifa.' I said: 'Haifa? What kind of a holiday is that? I'll drive down the streets and bump into one or another of my shops, suddenly I'll see something not right, I'll go in and start reorganizing the place? I haven't got the strength for it.' He said: 'Eilat.' I said: 'Eilat's the same story.' He said: 'So let's leave the country.' I said: 'What for, so I can walk round the streets and do shopping? Does that sound to you like a proper holiday for me? Europe and the United States are the same story for me as Givatayim or Jerusalem or any place you care to mention.' Alex said: 'Okay, Sisi, okay. So what do you suggest? Kenya? Or how about the Far East—you need a new dressing gown.'

At that moment he cracked me up with laughter. After I recovered,

I must have laughed for about five minutes flat, that Alex is a real joker sometimes. I said: 'Let me arrange a place where there's nobody and nothing to disturb us.'

A friend of my cousin's has a house on a cliff in Normandy, not far from Le Havre. There are steps carved in the cliff going down to the sea. I was there once, twenty years ago. I remember thousands of seagulls and dark ocean waves breaking on the cliff. I was there with my cousin and her friend. This was before I married Alex, when I was still going out with Benny, whom I married afterwards and divorced three years later. There was a lot of publicity at the time in the gossip columns. They said he cheated on me, and I kept repeating that we didn't get on, and that was all there was to it.

I don't remember having a whole lot of fun on that visit to Normandy, except for before we arrived back in Paris, when my cousin suddenly let out an exclamation of alarm and cried: 'The fish! I forgot the fish in the fridge! Boy, will that fish stink in another day or two. Will it stink!' After that we laughed for a kilometre or two.

I phoned her. She's my age, still with the same boyfriend, and I asked her about the country house in Normandy. She said she had no problem with letting us stay there, we didn't even have to come through Paris to pick up the keys, we could go straight there, and she described the hiding-place under the big flower-pot standing at the entrance to the house.

What was left but to pack, say goodbye, issue instructions to the girls, and fly.

We hired a car at the airport and a few hours later Alex was already moving the flower-pot. We turned it over, we crumbled clods of earth to powder, we dug up the flower-beds, our hands and clothes were full of the brown dirt. It was a real drag.

'It's a scandal,' I said. 'So much for relying on your family.'

'Yes,' agreed Alex.

We returned to the village and phoned my cousin.

'Under the flower-pot, under the flower-pot,' she kept repeating.

'But there's nothing there,' I said.

'How can that be? Jean-Pierre, Jean-Pierre!' she called to her boyfriend. 'Where are the keys to the house? Under the flower-pot, right?'

'Under the flower-pot. Yes yes. Exactly so,' I heard him in the distance.

'Under the flower-pot, Sisi.'

'Well, it's not there. Okay? I'm telling you it's not there.' I tried to control myself. If it had been Simone Nurit Pazit or Ofra I would have told her a long time ago to go find herself another Sisi.

'I don't know what to tell you. It was under the flower-pot. Nobody's been there for ages. It's been under the flower-pot ever since we bought that house. I think we even bought the flower-pot specially so we could put the key under it. Right, Jean-Pierre?'

'Right, right, exactly so.'

'Okay. What do we do now?'

'Break down the door and get a new lock. It'll cost next to nothing. I'll pay you back. Just don't forget to put the new key under the flowerpot.'

'Never mind the money,' I said to her and put the phone down. 'Now go find a break-in expert and a locksmith in this hole.'

Okay, we found them. When we finally got into the house it was late in the evening. We brought the luggage in, and I took the car back to the village to buy a few groceries. An hour later I was back with baskets of crabs and other seafood, cheeses and a freshly baked baguette. I went inside and made for the kitchen to put the groceries away. When I opened the fridge I saw a fat shiny fish lying on a wooden plate.

'Alex,' I called in alarm.

'What's up? I'm in bed taking a little rest.'

'What the hell is this fish? Where did this fish come from?'

'What fish?'

'The big fish in the fridge.'

'Aha, there are a few more in the freezer. I caught them. There's a rod here with a long line. I was bored and I threw it into the sea. Suddenly I felt that I'd caught something. There must be a lot of fish in the ocean here if you can catch fish from this height, no? I thought we could grill them. Did you bring lemons?'

'I did.'

'Excellent.'

I arranged the groceries in the fridge, and on one of the bottom shelves I encountered the skeleton of the fish that my cousin had forgotten years ago. I picked it up and it disintegrated almost immediately. Disgusting. I laid the table. I looked for candles in the cupboards and lit them. We sat down to eat and I cut the fish in half, one half for each of us.

'Mmmm—delicious,' said Alex. 'What an exceptional fish. And the shellfish? Have you tasted them? Why aren't you eating? You know what I feel like? Crayfish. Tomorrow we'll go and get some. What a meal you made. Fantastic!'

'There's a salad too.'

'Perfect. With a lot of lemon?'

'Yes.'

We ate in silence. We opened clams and sucked them out, seafood shells piled up on our plates.

Suddenly the house rocked slightly. The lamp rocked. The table rocked. The fishbones fell.

'What is it? What is it?' asked Alex and stood up. 'An earthquake.'

'What,' I trembled and held onto the swaying table.

'An earthquake, let's get out of here.'

He seized my hand and ran for the door. The élite fashion designer Sisi and her husband Alex die in an earthquake in Normandy. Tens of thousands of others perish too. Two hundred thousand left homeless. These were the headlines I saw in the seconds that passed before we reached the path where the car was parked. I looked towards the village.

'Look, everything seems stable there.'

'Yes,' he said. 'It must have been a minor earthquake. Still, I don't think we should stay in the house.'

'Hey, Alex, look,' I pointed to the white foam that looked very close to the house.

'Aha, it's just the tide.'

'Aha.'

'It affects the foundations of the house. Rots them. Would you like to go to a hotel?'

'Yes.'

We went back into the house to pack. From time to time a wave rocked the house.

'What am I going to do with all these shellfish?' I asked.

'Throw them into the sea.'

I opened the window and threw out the shellfish, the salad and the baguette. Down below everything was black with only a bit of white foam on the water here and there. I heard the fish leaping and snatching crumbs from the meal and disappearing again beneath the surface of the deep water.

Translated by Dalya Bilu.

Yeshayahu Koren

TOGETHER WITH THEM

Yeshayahu Koren was born in Kfar Saba in 1940, near Tel Aviv. He studied philosophy and Hebrew literature at the Hebrew University in Jerusalem and today lives in Jerusalem. He has published a number of collections of short stories. His stories are generally rooted in often brutal Israeli reality and written with a sparseness of style which avoids emotional description. He has written one novel. The collection Those Who Stand at Night, *from which 'Together With Them' is taken, was published in 1992.*

The first day after the war we were given the job of searching a road which the army hadn't passed through during the course of the battles. The road went from west to east, crossed the Seir road, and ended in the vicinity of the Dead Sea. We passed the maps from hand to hand. From the density of the contour lines on the map it was clear that it would be out of the question to descend from the cliffs to the sea.

At five in the morning the Arab village of Za'atara, the village from which we set out, was mute and deserted. The rays of the sun were not yet sharp. They didn't penetrate the cold dust kicked up by the wheels of our four jeeps. Dovik, the platoon commander, rode in the first jeep. Hochman, the sergeant, was in the last jeep. And so was I.

We drove slowly. The steel helmets were lying on the floor of the jeep. A bloody field dressing was stuck to the camouflage net. Next to the village, at the sides of the road, green thorns were growing. The mists covering the mountains had already evaporated, but the rocks were still damp with dew, sometimes dazzling. We passed an overturned APC. Afterwards a burned-out truck barred the road. The jeeps driving ahead of us found a way to go around it, but Hochman told the driver to stop. He got off the jeep, cautiously opened the blackened door and poked about in the driver's cabin.

'What are you doing there?' called Dovik, the only one of us wearing a steel helmet.

Dust came down on Hochman's face, hiding the grey hair covering his head. Only after Dovik shouted at him again, Hochman said quietly: 'Just souvenirs. For the kids.' As if he was talking to himself.

The road wound among the hills, but I saw the white sand covering it, the footprints of the retreating Jordanian soldiers, and the prints of the bare feet of the escaping peasants. There was no wind to efface the footprints. Only the wheels left marks on them. A colourful striped mat was caught, torn, on the thorns next to the road. The smell of a corpse rose from one of the shelled tanks.

The ridge rose steeply and the road curved north. On the slopes of the ridge there were a few caves, and opposite us, in the dust which was full of golden sunlight, a donkey limped. It was emaciated, long ribs stuck out of its grey skin. Its forelegs were tied together with a piece of rope. Its suppurating eyes were fixed on the ground. Its back was one big, bloody sore. Because of its bound legs it took tiny, slow steps.

'Stop,' called Dovik.

Behind the donkey there might be people too. We put on our steel helmets and our jeep climbed onto a looming hill to the left of the road, to cover the rest of the force.

The other soldiers got out of the jeeps and, fanning out, they climbed the hill to search the caves. Hochman paused next to the donkey. He pulled the dagger out of his webbing and cut the rope binding its forelegs. Then he took one of the sandbags protecting the sides of the jeep, emptied it, and laid it on the animal's painful back.

'Stop messing around there,' called Dovik.

Hochman quickly poured the water from his canteen onto the donkey's head, and then he joined us. There were flies crawling over his helmet.

There were two caves on the side of the hill, and another one, with a narrower opening, on its summit. Dovik divided the men into three teams. One team to a cave. The cave at the top of the hill was quite far, and the soldiers who had to search it walked quickly. The space in front of the cave was paved with white rocks which created a steep escarpment. The escarpment held the soldiers up and they began climbing it slowly, helping each other.

They were already very close to the cave, when two grenades rolled out of it towards them: the first one—a fragmentation grenade, which exploded without hurting anyone and the second—a smoke-grenade, which masked the escarpment and the rock-paved area giving off it.

The smoke swallowed up the soldiers who were still hanging onto the escarpment. Two men came out of the cave and got away. One of them was wearing khaki army trousers and a grey civilian shirt. The other one was wearing a *galabiyeh*. Their heads were cropped, exposed to the sun.

Dovik went down to the road. He spread out maps, called Hochman, and pointed to a deep wadi crossing the road at a distance of about half a kilometre from the caves.

'Drive there,' he said, 'and block the wadi. They'll have to pass there.'

Before we came down from the hill I saw the donkey limping slowly along the road. There was a bloodstain on his back. The sack which Hochman had spread over his back didn't cover the whole wound.

The force was divided in two. Two jeeps under Hochman's command went to block the wadi. The others, under Dovik's command, stayed on the hills and went on searching them.

When we reached the wadi Hochman left one jeep on the road. We went down into the creek.

'Do you really think they'll pass here?' I asked.

'Either they will or they won't.'

'If they've got any sense they'll go into the mountains and disappear there.'

'Why are you so worried about them?' said Hochman.

There was a feeling that nothing would happen, as usual. We took off our helmets. Only Hochman went on looking through his binoculars at the bare creeks running irregularly down the hillsides.

'The flies are eating him up,' I said.

'Who?'

'The donkey. That sack you threw over his back's useless. His wound's completely exposed.'

'Check the radio,' said Hochman.

The radio was making a noise.

'I asked for a Piper to search,' said Dovik.

The binoculars slipped out of Hochman's hands. 'We don't need one now,' he said. There was a lot of sand left on his webbing, from the emptied sandbag. Little beads of sweat, like bubbles of saliva, broke out on his forehead.

On the slope opposite us the two men descended slowly. Under the *galabiyeh* of the one walking in front something sharp protruded.

The driver started the jeep. Hochman shouted at him and told him to stop, but it was too late. The two men froze for a moment where they stood. Then they turned round abruptly and ran into the creek.

The echoes of the shots went on reverberating between the walls of the wadi. The machine gun attached to the engine of the jeep shook. The two men fell. Then it was quiet again. Like before.

'Stop it,' said Hochman.

We went up to them. The man in the khaki trousers was dead. The one in the *galabiyeh* was wounded in the stomach. His face was bathed in sweat. Next to his feet, underneath the *galabiyeh*, a carbine stuck out.

It was hot in the wadi and the sun beat down on our heads with all its strength. The strap of the binoculars cut into Hochman's neck. His canteen was empty, the black cork swung against it. 'What's the time?' he asked.

'Half past eight,' I said.

'I thought it was already noon,' he said. Hot vapour rose from the barrel of the machine gun.

A few minutes later Dovik arrived. He gave orders to bandage the wounded man, and after contacting the regiment he sent us to the main road, where an ambulance was supposed to be waiting for us.

Dovik and the rest of the jeeps went on, according to the plan, to the Dead Sea. We drove with the wounded man to the main road.

Between the wrecked vehicles and the footprints filling the dirt road we felt lonely. Dust covered Hochman's goggles. He took them off, blinked, and drove on without them.

Before the village, next to the colourful torn mat spread on the thorns, we saw the donkey again. Its forelegs were close together and its steps were small and teetering, as if Hochman hadn't cut the rope binding them to each other. There was still no sign of life in the village. Only the wounded man lying on the jeep groaned. Hochman remembered now that he hadn't covered the entire surface of the wound on the donkey's back. He stopped the jeep, threw the sack off the donkey's back, pulled the multi-coloured striped mat off the thorns and covered the wound.

'I don't think you should cover that sore,' said the driver. 'It's better to leave it open.'

'The flies will eat him alive,' said Hochman.

'That's not important.'

The donkey's eyes were fixed on the ground all the time. Indifferent to what was happening.

I looked back. Between the sharp crags I suddenly saw the Dead Sea. 'Pity I didn't bring my camera,' I said, but Hochman wasn't listening. A strong wind blew up opposite us, rolling dry bushes down the hills. It swept the road, raising dust to the sky.

'What a wind,' said Hochman. His eyes were red. His neck was streaked with stripes of dried sweat under the binocular strap.

We reached the main road, transferred the wounded man to the ambulance, turned round and began to drive back. The wind didn't stop blowing. Flat, grey rocks appeared on the ground. The road was already swept smooth. Only small, dry bushes still trembled on it. Hochman rubbed his goggles hard, cleaned off the dust and put them on again. After that he took over from the driver, stepped on the gas and drove like a lunatic. He knew that in a little while, from the crags, his friends would see the Dead Sea, and he wanted to be together with them.

Translated by Dalya Bilu.

Yehudit Katzir

SCHLAFSTUNDE

Born in Haifa in 1963, Yehudit Katzir studied general literature and cinema at Tel Aviv University. She is currently a teacher of creative writing at Tel Aviv University and she has also worked in the research department of Israel Television. She began publishing short stories in the Israeli press in the 1980s and both her individual stories and her collection, Closing the Sea, *from which 'Schlafstunde' is taken, have been awarded literary prizes and translated into Dutch, English, and Italian. A central theme of her writing is disappointment in love and the failure of trust. Katzir has recently published her first novel,* Matisse Has the Sun in His Belly.

Once, when summer vacation stretched over the whole summer and tasted of sand and smelled of grapes and a redhead sun daubed freckles on your face and, after *Sukkot*, the wind whistled into a gang of clouds and we galloped home through the ravine in a thunderstorm and the rain stabbed your tongue with mint and pine and the neigh-bourhood dogs set up a racket, barking like uncles coughing at the inter-mission in a winter concert, and suddenly spring attacked with cats shrieking and the lemon trees blossoming and again came a *hamsin* and the air stood still in the bus but we got up only for Mrs Bella Blum from the Post Office, a dangerous child-snatcher who comes to us in bed at night with the wild grey hair of a dangerous child-snatcher and narrow glasses on the tip of the sharp-as-a-red-pencil nose of a dangerous child-snatcher and who smiles with the cunning flattery of a dangerous child-snatcher and pokes dry-ice fingers into our faces, and only if we'd give her all the triangular stamps could we somehow be saved or if we prayed to God, who disguised himself as a clown in the Hungarian circus and rocked, balancing himself on the tightrope under the blue canvas of the tent, in high-heeled shoes and wide red-and-white checked trousers and then disguised himself as an elephant, turned his wrinkled behind to us and went off to eat supper.

Once, when the world was all golden through the sparkling Carrera vase in the living room on the credenza, which maybe vanished with all the other furniture as soon as we left the room and we peeked through the keyhole to see if it was still there but maybe it saw us peeking and rushed back and a horrible gang of thieves was hiding out in the garage under the supermarket and only Emil and you could solve the mystery because obviously you were going to be an important detective they'd write books about and I'd be your assistant and we experimented with invisible ink made of onion skins and we heated the note in the candle so the writing would emerge and then we trained ourselves to swallow it so it wouldn't fall into enemy hands and we did other training exercises, in self-defence and in not revealing secrets even if they torture you and tie you to a bed and put burning matches under your toenails, and we mixed up poison from dirt and leaves and crushed shells and we kept it in yoghurt jars and we drew a skull and crossbones on them and hid them with all our other treasures.

When the summer vacation stretched over the whole summer and the world was all gold and everything was possible and everything was about to happen, and Uncle Alfred was still alive and came for afternoon tea and Grandfather and Grandmother went to rest between two and four and left us endless time, we snuck up the creaky wooden steps behind the house to our little room in the attic which was headquarters and we stood at the window where you could view the whole sea beyond the cemetery and you touched my face with your fingertips and said you loved me.

Now we're gathered here, like sad family members at a departure in an airport, around the departures board at the entrance, where somebody's written in white chalk, two zero zero, Aaron Green, funeral, and I look at the woman sitting on the stone bench next to you, a round straw hat shading her eyes and ripening her mouth to a grape and the sun polishes two knives of light along her tanned shins and then I go up to the two of you, take off my sunglasses and say quietly, Hallo, and you stand up hastily, Meet each other, this is my wife. My cousin. I discern the sparkle of the ring and the white teeth among the shadows and touch her soft hand with long long fingers and say again, Hallo. And the undertakers, busy at work like angels in their white shirtsleeves, bearded faces, sweaty, carrying on a stretcher the shrivelled body under the dark dusty cloth, the head almost touching the fat black behind of the gravedigger, the legs dangling in front of the open fly of the second one, and a frosty wind blowing inside me, as then, and I seek the memory in your eyes but you lower them to her, take hold of her arm and help her up and my spy's eyes freeze on her rounded belly in the flowered dress and see inside her all your children you buried behind the house, in the grove, in the summer vacation between seventh and eighth grade, when on the first morning, as every year, Grandfather came to pick me up from home in his old black car, with Misha, the office chauffeur, who dressed himself up in my honour in a white visor cap and a huge smile with a gold tooth. Misha put my red suitcase in the boot and opened the back door for me with a bow and a wink and we went to pick you up from the railway station near the port. On the way, I stuck my head between him and Grandfather and asked him to tell me again how he played for the King of Yugoslavia and Misha sighed and said, That was a long time ago, but I remember it as if it was yesterday. I was a child then, maybe nine, maybe ten, and I played the trumpet better than anybody in the whole school and one day they brought me a blue suit with gold buttons and a tie and stockings up to my knees and a cap with a visor and said, Get dressed, and they put me next to a flag and said, Play, and I played so beautifully and strongly and King Pavel came in and the flag rose to the top of the pole and the trumpet sparkled like that in the sun and so did the gold buttons, who would have believed a little Jewish boy like that playing trumpet for the King and he came to me and stroked my head and asked, What's your name, and I told him, Misha, and Mama was standing there and crying so they had to hold her up and Papa said to her, Now I'm happy we have him, because at first he didn't want me at all, they went to Austria just for a vacation and when they came back Mama said, I'm pregnant, and Papa told her, Five is enough, get an abortion, but Mama was very stubborn, like Albert Einstein's mother, his father didn't want him either, and then he was terrible in school and the teachers called the father and the father said to him, Albert, you're seventeen years old now, not a child, what will become of you, but when he was twenty-six he met Lenin and Churchill and showed them the theory of relativity and there were a lot of discussions, and he became famous all over the world, so when I hear about abortions I say, Who knows what can come out of that child, why kill a human being. Misha sighed again and lit a cigarette. In the distance you could already see the big clock over the railway station. At five to nine we arrived. Grandfather and I went down to the platform and Misha waited in the car. Two porters in grey caps were leaning on their rusty carts, looked at one another from time to time with

half-closed eyes and smoked stinky cigarettes from yellow packs with
a picture of black horses. I was so excited I had to pee and I hopped
around from one foot to the other. At nine o'clock on the dot we
heard a long happy whistle of the locomotive pulling five rumbling
carriages. The porters woke up, stomped on their cigarettes with huge
shoes and started running back and forth along the platform shouting, Suitcases, suitcases. Terrified, I looked for your face among the
hundreds of faces, crushed and scared, against the glass of the windows. Then the doors opened with a hiss and you came down, the
very first one, wearing the short jeans all the kids had and a green
shirt with emblems on the pockets that only a few had and a checked
detective hat they had brought you from England and no other kid
had, and you stood there like that next to your father's black suitcase,
and looked around with eyes scrunched up like two green slits under
your dishevelled fair curls, and once again I felt the pain between my
throat and my stomach that clutched my breath every time I saw you
and even when I thought about you, and I shouted, Here Uli, here
Uli, and I ran to you, and then you saw me and smiled and we
embraced, and Grandfather came too, and tapped you on the shoulder and said, How you've grown Saul, and he didn't take your suitcase because you were already thirteen and a half and stronger than
he, and you put it in the boot, next to my red one. And Misha took
us to Grandfather's office on Herzl Street, whose walls were covered
with big shiny pictures with lots of blue, pictures of beautiful places
in Israel, the Kinneret and the Dead Sea and Rosh Hanikra and Elat,
where there were rest homes, and the government paid him to send
Holocaust survivors there, and I always imagined how they arrived
there by train, wearing funny coats and hats with sad yellow faces
underneath them as in the pictures they showed us in school on the
day commemorating the Holocaust-and-Heroism, and they line up
there in a long row with all their suitcases tied with rope, and everybody enters in a line and takes off his coat and hat and gets bright-
coloured clothes and an orange pointy cap, and they sit in *chaises-longues*
in the sun and swim in the sea and eat a lot and convalesce and after
a week grow fat and tanned and smiling like the people in the advertisements and then they're sent home because new survivors came on
the train and are already waiting in line. Until once, on Saturday, we
went with Grandfather and Grandmother and Misha to visit one of
those rest homes, called Rosh Hanikra Recreation Village, and there
was no line of survivors at the entrance, and there was no way to
know who was a Holocaust survivor and who was just a normal

person because they all had fat, droopy pot-bellies and nobody looked especially sad, they were all swimming in the pool and gobbling sandwiches and guzzling juice and talking loudly and playing bingo. So we made up a system to check who was a real survivor, but I didn't have the courage, I just watched from a distance as you passed among the *chaises-longues* on the lawn next to the pool and whispered into everybody's ear, Hitler, and I saw that most of the people didn't do anything, just opened their eyes wide in a strange kind of look, as if they were waking up from some dream and hadn't had time yet to remember where they were and they closed their eyes right away and went on sleeping and only one man, big and fat with a lot of black hair on his chest and on his back like a huge gorilla, got up and chased you all over the lawn huffing and puffing, his eyes red and huge, and finally he caught you and slapped you and shook your shoulders hard and barked, *Paskutstve holerye, paskutstve holerye*, and you came back to me with red ears, and you didn't cry and you said it didn't really hurt, but from then on, every time they mentioned Hitler, in school or on television, I would think of the gorilla from the rest home instead of the real Hitler with the little moustache and dangling forelock.

In the afternoon we went down, as always on the first day of vacation, to eat in the Balfour Cellar, and the tall thin waiter, who looked like a professor, Grandfather told us that many years ago he really had been a professor in Berlin, wearing glasses in a silver frame and a beard the same colour and a black bow-tie, gave a little bow because he knew us, and especially Grandfather, who was a regular customer, and pulled out the chairs for us to sit down, and quickly put menus in front of us and said, What will you have, Herr Green, even though Grandfather always ordered the same thing, roast with puree of potatoes and sauerkraut, and a bunch of purple grapes for dessert, and the regular customers around the tables knew us and smiled and waved at us with white napkins, and as I ate I watched the two plywood cooks hung on the wall in their high chef-hats and long aprons and black moustaches curving upward like two more smiles on their mouths, and they looked back at me leaning on half a wooden barrel sticking out of the wall and full, I was sure, of very very good sauerkraut. And once you told me that the restaurant had a secret cellar right underneath us and that was why it was called the Balfour Cellar, and in the cellar there were lots more barrels like those and all of them were full of sauerkraut that could last a long time in case of another Holocaust, and then the limping newspaper-seller came in wearing a dirty grey undershirt soaked with sweat and yelled, Paper get your paper, until the whole restaurant was filled with his sour breath, and Grandfather beckoned to him, and he came to our table and gave him the paper with a black hand, and Grandfather paid him even though right next door to the restaurant there was a clean kiosk that had papers and lemonade and ice-cream-on-a-stick. Then we went back home on the steep road that went by the gold dome and you could see the whole bay from there, and on the way we fooled around on the back seat and played pinch-me-punch-me and boxed and yelled and called each other names, and Grandfather suddenly turned around and said quietly and earnestly, Don't fight, children, human beings have to love and pity one another, for in the end we all die. And we didn't understand what he meant but we stopped, and Misha winked at us in the mirror, and told about Louis Armstrong, who was the greatest trumpet-player and had the deepest lungs, and when Betty Grable, who had the prettiest legs in Hollywood, got cancer he came with his whole orchestra to play for her on the hospital lawn under her window. Then we got to the house, and Grandmother opened the door, her tight hairdo rolled in a braid around her scalp, and pecked each of us on the cheek and said, Now *Schlafstunde*, which always sounded to me like the name of a cake like Schwartzwalder Kirsch-torte or Sachertorte or Apfelstrudel, which she would bake because they reminded her of her home overseas, and the steamy fragrant café when outside it was cold and snowing, but Dr Schmidt didn't allow her to eat them because she had high blood sugar which is very dan-gerous for the heart. So she only served it to us and Uncle Alfred and Grandfather, who always said politely, No thank you, and refused to taste a single bite even though he was very healthy. But sometimes, when he went to walk Uncle Alfred to the gate, Grandmother would cut herself a small slice and eat it with quick bites, bent over her plate, and Grandfather would come back, stand in the door and observe her back with a tender look, and wait until she was finished, and only then would he come into the living room and sit down with the news-paper, pretending he hadn't seen. They went to their room, and we went out to the grove behind the house and stretched a strong rope between two pine trees and tried to balance on it like that clown we once saw when we were little and Grandfather took us to the Hungarian circus in Paris Square, where there were pure-bred horses and pan-thers with yellow eyes and trained elephants and a beautiful acrobat with long blond hair and the face of an angel who danced on the tightrope with a golden parasol in her hand, and we decided we'd run away and join that circus after we were trained, but now we only managed to creep along on the rope, and you explained to me that it's important to know in case you have to cross over water. Then we climbed up to our espionage headquarters under the roof, which sometimes was Anne Frank's hiding-place, where we'd huddle together trembling under the table and munch on potato peelings and call each other Anne and Peter and hear the voices of German soldiers outside and drop onto the green velvet sofa which Grandmother brought with her when she came to Israel in the ship, and when one of the two wooden headrests collapsed they bought a new sofa for the living room and brought this one here, because it's a shame to throw out a good piece of furniture, and suddenly you said in a pensive voice, Interesting what you feel after you die, and I said, After you die you don't feel anything, and we tried to close our eyes tight and block our ears and hold our breath to feel dead, but it didn't work because even with our eyes closed we could see colours and you said, Maybe by the time we get old they'll invent some medicine against death, and I said, Maybe you'll be a scientist and invent it yourself and you'll be famous like Albert Einstein. Then we played writing words with our finger on each other's back and whispering them. First we wrote the names of flowers, narcissus and anemone and cyclamen, and names of animals, panther and hippopotamus, and names of people we knew, but after a while you said that was boring, and it was hard to guess because of our shirts, so I took off my shirt and lay down on the sofa, my face in the smell of dust and perfume and cigarette smoke that lingered in the upholstery from days gone by, and I felt how your nice finger slowly wrote words we never dared to say, first a-s-s and then t-i-t and finally w-h-o-r-e, and while I whispered the words in a soft voice between the cushions of the sofa I felt my face burning and my nipples which had just started to sprout hardening against the velvet.

In the afternoon Grandfather and Grandmother came out of the bedroom with pink cheeks, twenty years younger, and at five o'clock on the dot Uncle Alfred came and we never understood exactly how he was related to us, maybe he was one of Grandmother's distant cousins, and her mouth grew thin as a thread whenever his name was mentioned and Grandfather would roar with rage, Bastard, and we didn't know why they didn't like him, whether it was because he was poor or because he once tried to be an opera singer in Paris or some other reason we couldn't guess, and why they entertained him so nicely in spite of it, and Grandmother served him tea and cake, which he would drink and eat and smack his thick red lips and tell again, his eyes melting with regret, about how he was a student in the Paris Conservatoire and lived in a teeny-tiny attic without a shower and without a toilet in Place de la République, and ate half a baguette with butter a day, but at seven in the evening he would put on his only good suit and a bow-tie and sprinkle eau-de-Cologne on his cheeks and go to the opera, where he would stand under a decorated lighted vault and steal the occasional notes that slipped out through the lattices and caressed the statues of the muses and the cornices of the angels, and in the intermission he would mingle with the audience and go inside, because then they didn't check tickets, and find himself an empty seat in one of the balconies, and so with sobbing heart and as damp as a clutched handkerchief he saw the last acts of the most famous operas in the world. And here he would usually stand up, sway like a jack-in-the-box, clasp the back of the armchair with his plump fingers, and burst into an aria from Rigoletto or La Traviata or The Marriage of Figaro, and his voice was frail and fragrant and sweet like the tea he had just drunk, and only at the end did it squeak and break like glass, and Grandmother's thin hands smacked one another in dry applause and Grandfather lowered his eyes to the squares of the carpet and muttered, Bravo, bravo, and we didn't know why Uncle Alfred was thrown out of the Conservatoire one day and didn't become a great singer in the Paris opera, and Grandmother wouldn't tell us, she only clenched her mouth even tighter, as if a huge frog would leap out if she opened it. And Uncle Alfred would sit down and sigh and wipe his reddish nose like a strawberry with a wrinkled handkerchief he pulled out of the left pocket of his jacket, and he would hold out his arms to invite us to ride on both sides of the chair, and hug our waists and tell about the cafés of Montparnasse and Montmartre, which was a meeting-place for writers and artists and students, and from his mouth strange names flowed with a wonderful sound I'd never heard before anywhere, like Sartre and Simone de Beauvoir and Cocteau and Satie and Picasso, and then he'd caress your hair and say, You'll be an artist too some day, and stroke your back and say, Or a writer, and press his little white hand on your leg with the short jeans and say, Or a musician, and go on strumming with his fingers on your smooth bare thigh as if he were playing a piano, and he didn't say anything to me. He couldn't know that some day, on a steamy, shuddering mid-summer afternoon, we'd be standing in the old cemetery at Carmel Beach, our shamed backs to his tombstone, on which were the words, in gold letters as he requested, of the Chinese poet from Mahler's Lied von der Erde:

When sorrow draws near,
The gardens of the soul lie wasted,
Joy and song wither and die,
Dark is life and so is death.
Now it is time, companions!
Drain your golden goblets to the dregs.

Our backs to his tombstone and our faces to Grandfather wrapped
in a sheet, he hurrying to slip into an eternal *Schlafstunde* next to
Grandmother, who died in the winter many years before, but they
didn't take us to the funeral because they didn't want us to catch cold
and miss school, and our faces to the cantor, whose closed eyes were
turned to the sky as he trilled his *El male rakhamim shokhen bamromim*,
and to your father who had turned completely grey, muttering *Yitgadal
v'yitkadash sh'me raba*, and to my mother hiding her face in her hands,
ripping her shirt, and to the old people responding Amen, their familiar faces mocking me under their wrinkled masks, waving at me sometimes and smiling around the tables in the Balfour Cellar which isn't
there any more, and sometimes dozing off in the *chaises-longues* of the
rest home which was closed years ago, and here's Misha, who almost
didn't get old but without the visor hat and the smile with the gold
tooth, and he's wearing a black *kippa* and noisily wiping his nose, and
my gaze is drawn to the shrivelled sharp face of a stooped little old
woman which is stamped on my memory as if it had accompanied
me throughout my childhood, though I can't remember where, and
I turn to you and seek in your eyes which don't look straight at me,
in your worn-out face, in the white threads in your hair, desire in me
a sharp wild pain like the whistle of the train now galloping along
the shore on its way to the new station at Bat-Galim, but only tatters of memories are pulled from me, connecting to one another
with their tails like the coloured handkerchiefs from the box of the
magician in the Hungarian circus, and about a week after vacation
started you didn't want to join the circus or practise balancing on the
tightrope between the pines and you didn't want to play Anne Frank
or Emil and the Detectives, you didn't want to play anything with
me, you just sat under the big pine tree all day long and read little
books with crinkled bindings and you looked worried and sad and
full of secret thoughts under your checked cap. At first I tried not to
disturb you even though I was insulted, but by the third day I had
had enough. I waited until afternoon and when Grandfather and
Grandmother went for their *Schlafstunde*, I crept up behind you, grabbed
the book named *The Confession of the Commander's Lover* with a

picture on the cover of a soldier in a brown uniform with black boots up to his knees aiming a huge pistol at a blonde sprawling in the snow between his legs and wearing only panties and a bra. I hid the book, and said I wouldn't give it back until you told me what was going on. You looked at me strangely through your long light lashes and said, Swear on the black grave of Hitler that you won't tell anyone in the world ever. I swear, I whispered solemnly, and to myself I imagined a deep black hole where the big hairy Hitler of the rest home was standing. Then you told me that recently, ever since you started reading those books, it swelled up in your pants and became so hard you had to rub it with your hand until a kind of white liquid sprayed out of it and that was the most wonderful feeling you ever had in your life, like the explosion of a shooting star, but afterward you were worried because in school they explained to you that women get pregnant from it, and when you wash your hands it goes into the pipes of the sewer along with the water and flows into the sea and a lot of women swim in the sea and it could get into them under their bathing suits, and not all of it would go into the sink either because among millions of little seeds some twenty or thirty were bound to be left on your hand, and sometimes you had to go on the bus afterward or to basketball or scouts, and it could get on the money you paid the driver, and from the driver's hands to the tickets he gives the girls and women of all ages, and then they go back home and go to the bathroom and tear toilet paper and wipe themselves and it gets inside them and they don't even know, and now thousands of women are walking around the streets with babies from you in their swollen bellies, and not only here in Israel, because the sperm can be washed away in the water and even go as far as Europe. An ashamed spark of pride glimmered in your eyes for a moment and died out. I sat silently awhile and thought, chewing on dry pine needles. That was a really serious problem. Meantime you were tossing pine cones, trying to hit the treetrunk opposite, thunk, thunk, thunk. Suddenly I had an idea. I stood up and ran to the kitchen, opened the drawer next to the sink which had all kinds of things you need in a house, matches and bandaids and rubber bands, and took out a few plastic sandwich bags Grandmother used to pack food for the road when we went on a visit Saturday to one of the rest homes, and I ran back and gave it to you and said, Here, do it in this and bury it in the ground. From that day on, the worry and the pride disappeared from your face and we were friends again and played all the old games, and only sometimes did you suddenly stop and give me long pensive looks, and at night I'd creep into the kitchen and count the bags to know how many were missing, and I'd go out barefoot to the fragrant dark grove with gloomy treetops and the sound of rustling and chirping and howling and mysterious hissing, and I'd find the places where dry pine needles were piled up and the earth was loose, and I'd dig with feverish curious hands and panic and bring up the plastic bags from their graves and look at the wonderful liquid in the moonlight for a long time. One day you added the crinkled little books to our treasure and said, I don't need this garbage anymore, I can invent better stories myself, and I said, You'll surely be a writer some day, and I remembered that Uncle Alfred had said it before me. So we tore the pages out of the books and sat down to cut out the words, especially the coarsest ones, and pasted them into scary anonymous threatening letters to the gang of criminals under the supermarket and to Mrs Bella Blum of the Post Office, and we gorged ourselves on the chocolate we had stolen earlier from Grandmother's kitchen, where she kept it for baking her cakes, and it tasted a little like almond paste, and suddenly you touched my face with your fingertips, as if to wipe off a chocolate moustache, and you went behind me and wrote slowly on my back, word after word, I love you, and hugged me tight. You lay on the sofa, and I lay down on top of you, my face in the soft shadow between your shoulder and your neck, a smell of paste and starch from your green shirt, and your damp fingers stroked the back of my neck for a long time, trembled, hovered over my hair. Stuck together without moving, almost without breathing, only our hearts galloping like horses in a mad race, and I slowly stroked your face, as if I were sculpting it anew, your fair curls and your smooth brow and your eyelids and underneath them is a whole world and your little nose that a finger could slide down like a ski to your lips, where a hot draught breathes on my frozen finger, and you pull up my shirt, your cool hand on my back down and up, then up and down to that nice place where if we were cats our tails would grow out of, and I put my mouth on your mouth, taste the stolen chocolate, our tongues meet, circle, and push each other like two panicky wrestlers, and I tug the shirt up off your smooth chest and my shirt up off my breasts, to press my nipples hard from the cold against the warm soft skin of your panting belly, and I feel a sweetness between my legs as if honey had spilled and a little of it drops on my panties, and that makes me open them and move back and forth on your thigh, and you hug me tight and suck my lips like lemon drops and you put my hand on the hard bulge in your shorts and your face becomes serious and fragile so in it I can see what no one before me has ever seen, and I breathe fast-fast like a little animal without memories, my melted belly stuck to yours the sweetness in my panties more and more until it hurts until I can't and suddenly those spasms inside me the first time so strong and sharp and long and then shorter and faster like flutterings but I don't shout so they won't wake up and I want it never to end but finally it does end and I fall on you breathless as if I had run the sixty-yard-dash, and I see that you too are half fainted, struggling to swallow air, your face burning, and I get off you and lie beside you and discover a big spot on your pants and, excited, I inhale the sharp smell rising from the two of us, a smell not like any other.

Then you looked at me with flashing green eyes and you smiled and kissed me on my cheek, and you wildly pushed aside the hair stuck to your brow and sat up and took off your shirt in one movement and said, Take off yours too. And I took off mine, and you laid your head on my stomach, and we rested like that awhile, my hand stirring your damp hair, and fingers of sun pierced the chinks in the shutter and spread golden fans on the walls. Then I stroked your back and said your skin was soft as velvet, and you said mine was soft as water, and you kissed my stomach and drew strange forms on it with your lips, and you said, When you lie on your back your breasts are as flat as mine, and you licked my nipples, and your tongue was a little rough like a cat's, and you licked and licked until they got hard as cherry pits, and again I felt sweet and smooth between my legs and I wanted it to go on as before, but Grandmother's voice rose from downstairs, sharp and probing, like the periscope of a submarine, Children, where are you, five o'clock tea and cake. We put on our shirts fast and came down and you went to change your pants, while I looked in the gilded mirror in the vestibule. My eyes sparkled like cups of sky, and the whole world, the furniture in the living room and Grandfather and Grandmother and Uncle Albert looked far away and unreal but sharp and clear, as on a stage.

That night I couldn't sleep because I missed you too much, you were sleeping quietly in the room at the end of the hall and maybe your body was dreaming of me. I wanted so much to come to you in the dark and hug you and hear you breathing, but Grandmother was always strict about you sleeping in your father's old room and me in my mother's room, next to their room, so I controlled myself and thought about tomorrow, about the ceremony we planned down to the smallest detail after dinner, when Uncle Alfred had gone and

Grandfather and Grandmother sat down in the living room to watch the Friday night news on television, and we whispered back and forth in the kitchen, and we could hear Menachem Begin the new Prime Minister giving a speech about Auschwitz and the Six Million, and then he announced he was willing to meet in Jerusalem with President Sadat, and Grandfather said, At last that idiot came out with something good, and Grandmother called us, You should see this, important news, but we knew that tomorrow's ceremony was much more important, and especially what would come afterward, and there was no way I could stop the film that kept repeating over and over on the dark screen, the film we starred in. And suddenly, from their room, I heard Grandmother scream in a whisper, Aaron, Aaron, and Grandfather woke up and said gently, Yes, Minna, and Grandmother said she couldn't fall asleep, and she told him quietly, but I could hear every word, that in the morning, as she was walking around in the supermarket with the cart to buy food for the Sabbath, she suddenly felt that her mother was standing next to her, in a black fur coat, the one she wore years ago when they said goodbye at the railway station, and her face was as pale and terrified as it was then, and she told her something, but Grandmother didn't pay attention because she said to herself, It's summer now, why is Mother wearing a fur coat, and before she could understand, her mother wasn't there anymore. I've been calm ever since, Grandmother went on in a harsh whisper, I'm sure it's something very bad. From her face I know something awful is going to happen. Grandfather didn't say anything, he just sang her something very quiet, a tune of yearning without words, and repeated it over and over until it filled me completely, until I fell asleep.

The next day was the Sabbath. Grandfather and Grandmother woke us early to go with them to visit the rest home in Tiberias, and were surprised when we muttered from under the covers that we were tired and wanted to stay home, but they gave in. I remembered what I had heard at night from their room, and I thought to myself, How can ghosts wander around in our supermarket, and why didn't Grandfather comfort her and tell her it was all her imagination and nothing bad would happen, and suddenly I thought, Maybe that whole conversation didn't happen and I only dreamed it, and I decided not to tell anybody, not even you. Grandmother made hard-boiled egg sandwiches for our lunch, and prepared food to take on the road, and my heart began to pound when I heard the drawer next to the sink open and Grandmother whisper to herself, Funny, I remember there was a whole package here. Finally she wrapped it in wax-paper because Misha was already honking for them outside, and pecked each of us on the cheek and said, We'll be back by seven thirty tonight, behave yourselves, and they left. As soon as the hum of the motor disappeared around the corner, we leapt out of bed and met in the hall, and we started to do everything exactly according to the plan we concocted last night down to the last detail. First each of us took a long and thorough bath, shampooing our hair and cleaning our ears. Then we wrapped ourselves in our sheets, which we tied at the shoulder like Greek togas, and I put on perfume from all the bottles I found on Grandmother's dressing table, and I smeared my lips and cheeks with a lot of red, and my eyes with blue. Then we cut off the tops of the pink flowers Grandmother had bought for the Sabbath, in the golden vase on the credenza, and we plaited two wreaths for our heads. Then we went into the kitchen but didn't eat breakfast because we couldn't swallow a thing, but from Grandmother's hiding-place for candles, next to the hiding-place for chocolate, we stole six *Yahrzeit* candles, she always kept it full of them because there was always a *Yahrzeit* for somebody in her family who had remained over there, and from the sewing box covered with flowered cloth we took a pair of scissors, and from Grandfather's linen drawer we took a white handkerchief, and from the pantry a glass of wine, and from the library a small Bible your father got as a *bar mitzvah* present from his school, and barefoot we went up to our room in the attic with all those things. Then we closed the shutter on the day and on the cemetery and we made it absolutely dark, and we lit the *Yahrzeit* candles and put them about the room, which was filled with the shadows of scary demons dancing on the ceiling and the walls, and we left one candle on the table, and we put the Bible next to it, and you asked, You ready, and I whispered, Yes, and my heart was pounding, and we stood facing each other, and we put one hand on the Bible and we raised the other with thumb and pinkie together as in the scouts' oath, and I looked straight into your eyes where the flames of the candles were burning and repeated after you slowly, solemnly:

> I swear by God and by the black grave of Hitler,
> I swear by God and by the black grave of Hitler,
> I will never marry another woman,
> I will never marry another man,
> And I will love only you forever,
> And I will love only you forever.

Then we hugged each other and almost couldn't breathe because we knew that that oath was as strong as death and to make it even stronger we cut the words out of the Bible and pasted them on a sheet of paper in the light of the candle. The two Gods we found right away in the creation, and woman in the story of Adam and Eve, and grave in the part about the cave of Machpelah. Then we found man and swear and I and of and you and another and love and the and black and will and never. The rest of the words, Hitler and marry and for ever, we couldn't find, so we pasted them together from separate letters. When it was all ready, you wrapped the glass in the handkerchief, put it on the floor and stamped on it hard with your bare foot. The glass broke and a big spot of blood spread over the cloth. You dipped your finger in it and signed your name under the oath. Now you, you said. I took a deep breath, picked up a piece of glass, and scratched my big toe hard, from the bottom, so nobody would see the cut, squeezed a drop of blood onto my finger and signed a shaky signature next to your name. Then we wrote the date, the regular date and the Hebrew date, and the exact address, Presidents' Boulevard, Mount Carmel, Haifa, Israel, Middle East, Continent of Asia, Earth, Solar Syatem, Galaxy, Cosmos. Now we'll tear the oath in two and each of us will keep the half with the other's signature, I said what we had planned to do, and you were silent for a moment and suddenly you said, No, let's wrap it up and bury it under the big pine tree, some place where we can always find it. I thought to myself that we were forbidden to change the plan, but I didn't say anything. We folded the paper in the aluminium foil of yesterday's chocolate and put it in an empty matchbox, which we wrapped with more paper and in a plastic bag you had left over from the ones you stole from the drawer, and we went downstairs. We dug a deep pit with our hands next to the trunk and hid our package, more important to us than anything in the world, but when we covered it with earth and tamped it down with our feet and piled pine needles on it, I became very sad all of a sudden, and I didn't know why.

When we got back to the room, the *Yahrzeit* candles were still burning and the demons kept jumping wildly on the walls. I knew what was about to happen but I wasn't scared. I thought about Anne Frank and how the Germans caught her before she really had a chance to love her Peter, when she was exactly my age, and I said to myself, I will have a chance. We took off the wreaths and the Greek togas and we spread one sheet on the sofa underneath us, and we lay down, and covered ourselves with the other one, and I caressed your whole body which was warm and breathing fast, and I walked my tongue among hills of light and soft shadows and paths of soap and sweat under the sheet, and suddenly you were over me on all fours and looking at me with sparkling yellow eyes and a savage smile, and I wanted that to happen, and I whispered, Come, and you asked, Does it hurt, and I said, No, and I could hear your heart drumming on my breasts rhythmically I-love-you-I-love-you, and I was filled with tremendous pride.

Then heavy steps grated on the stairs and I whispered, The Germans, and I started trembling, and we held each other tight and clung to the wall, and the door opened, and in the opening in a halo of light stood Uncle Alfred. They apparently forgot to tell him they were going away and that he shouldn't come today for tea. He looked at our sweaty bodies and the handkerchief spotted with blood and the pink flowers scattered over the floor and the *Yahrzeit* candles, and he rubbed his strawberry nose in embarrassment, and his eyes were fixed on some point on your stomach, maybe your belly button, as he stammered, What's this children, it's forbidden, at your age, you shouldn't, if Grandmother finds out. We covered ourselves with the sheet and looked at him cautiously and silently like cats. He lowered his eyes to the shiny tips of his shoes and went on, Of course I'll have to tell her, who would have thought, children, cousins, and God forbid there'll be a baby with six fingers on each hand, or two heads, or a little tail like a pig, this is very dangerous, who would have thought. And he wagged his head from the right shoe-tip to the left shoe-tip, as if he were setting up a shiny-shoe contest. Then he looked at you again, and said with no stammering now that he was willing not to tell anybody on condition that you agreed to meet him here, tomorrow afternoon, so he could talk to you and explain what a serious thing it was we had done. Why only him, I burst out to defend you, and Uncle Alfred said he regarded you as responsible and that with your sense and talent he hadn't expected anything like this from you. I agree, you said quietly, and he left. As soon as the door closed behind him we jumped off the couch, stood at the window again, with one hand on the Bible and the other in the air, with thumb and pinkie together, and I repeated after you the oath we composed on the spot:

> And even if we have a baby
> With six fingers on each hand
> Or two heads
> Or a little tail like a pig

We will love it as if it was a completely normal baby
With five fingers and one head
And no tail at all.

Then we dressed and cleaned up everything fast before Grandfather and Grandmother got back home. Except the dark red spot, blossoming on the green velvet, that we left as a souvenir. Before I fell asleep, I could hear Grandmother whispering into the golden vase on the sideboard, Funny, I remember buying flowers for the Sabbath, and Grandfather comforting her gently, Well, my memory's not what it used to be either, how could I forget to tell Alfred not to come today for tea.

In the middle of the night I felt horribly nauseous, ran to the bathroom and stuck my finger down my throat and suddenly I felt I was throwing up sand, enormous amounts of wet sand, it filled my mouth and gritted between my teeth, and I spat and threw up, threw up and spat, and then something else was vomited up from me with the sand, and I looked into the toilet. A tiny black dog floating stiffly on his side, his legs spread out, his gums exposed in a creepy smile, watching me with a gaping dead eye. In horror I slammed down the lid. Outside it was beginning to turn light.

I wandered around among the trees with my hands in my pockets, kicking pine cones. You'd been up there for more than half an hour, closed in the room. What did he have to tell you that took so much time. I couldn't control myself anymore. I went up very quietly, opened the door a little, and peered in. The two of you were sitting on the sofa. With big opera gestures Uncle Alfred was explaining something to you that I couldn't hear and from time to time he put his cotton hand on your leg. Then he wrapped his arm around your shoulders and put his face which was always flushed, almost purple, close to your face which was ashen. Suddenly he looked up and saw me. A shadow passed over his eyes. I fled downstairs. I lay under the big pine tree, right over the oath we buried yesterday, and I looked at the green sparkling needles that stabbed the clouds which today were in the shape of a huge white hand. I waited. Time passed, more time, a lot of time passed, and you didn't come down. I remembered the dream I had last night, and I shivered with cold. At last the door opened and Uncle Alfred came out breathing deeply as he went unsteadily down the steps. He buttoned his jacket and rang the front door bell. Grandmother opened the door, said, Hello Alfred, and he went into the house. Then you came running out, you lay down beside me, hid your head against my belly, and muffled your howls of anguish. Your whole body shook. I held you. What happened, what did he tell you, I whispered. We have to kill him, you cried. Your hot tears were absorbed by my shirt. I had never seen you cry like that. But what happened, what did he do, I asked again. We have to kill him we have to kill him, you wailed, your feet kicking the ground. But what did he do, hit you, tell me what he did, I pleaded. You lifted your burning wet face where the tears and the snot were running but you didn't care, and you said quietly, Today I'm going to kill him. I looked into your red eyes, with two black pits in them, and I knew that today Uncle Alfred would die.

Within minutes we had a fatal solution of poison made of shells ground up with two ants, a mashed piece of pine cone, and yellow dog-do. We mixed it all up with pine tar so the ingredients would stick together. My job was to ask Grandmother if I could make the tea today, and to pour the poison into Uncle Alfred's cup. I chose the big black cup for him so I wouldn't confuse it with another and also because I thought the poison would work better in a black cup. I added five spoons of sugar and stirred it well, trying to hear what they were saying in the living room to make sure he wasn't telling on us in spite of everything. They were talking very quietly and only separate words reached me, Dr Schmidt, chest X-ray, diagnosis, and Dr Schmidt again. They were talking about diseases. I calmed down. On the tea cart I also put the special two-layer Schwartzwaldertorte that Grandmother baked and I didn't understand what it was in hon-our of, maybe it was his birthday today. As soon as I entered with the tray, they shut up. Uncle Alfred said, Thank you, and a sad smile clouded his face. You came in too, your eyes dry now, and we huddled together in the chair, waiting with awful tension to see him drink and die on the spot. First he greedily polished off three pieces of cake. Then he sipped noisily, smacked his lips, faced us, and declared, Now I will sing you the first Lied from Mahler's Lied von der Erde. He cleared his throat twice, clasped his hands on his stomach, and started singing in German which we couldn't understand. His voice burst out of his chest as a solemn trumpet blast, rose to a great height both bold and trembling like a tightrope walker, and suddenly it fell and plunged into a dark abyss, where it struggled with fate, pleaded, prayed, shouted like a hollow echo, whimpered, abased itself, the face that of a drowning man, tears flowed from his eyes and from Grandmother's eyes too, she understood the words, and even Grandfather blew his nose a few times, and we looked at each other and knew the poison we mixed was also a magic potion, and we held our breath to see him sink into the carpet in the middle of the song, but Uncle Alfred finished it with a long endless shout and his arms waved to the sides and hit the credenza, and the gold vase teetered a moment in surprise and then slid off and smashed on the floor into sparkling slivers. Uncle Alfred sat down, panting heavily, and whispered, Sorry, and Grandmother said, It's nothing, and she came and kissed him on the cheek and Grandfather didn't look at the squares of the carpet and didn't murmur, Bravo, but shook his hand and looked into his eyes and said, Wonderful, wonderful, and Uncle Alfred took another sip of the poisoned tea, and stood up to go, and said to us, Goodbye, and caressed you with his gaze, but we didn't answer, we only looked at him with hatred, and they accompanied him to the door, and wished him good luck, and Grandfather patted him on the shoulder and said, Be strong, Alfred, and Uncle Alfred said hesitantly, Yes, and the door closed behind him and Grandfather and Grandmother looked at each other a moment, and Grandmother nodded her head and brought a broom and dustpan and swept up the slivers.

At night I woke up to the sound of coughing and an awful screeching laughter and I heard Grandmother telling Grandfather in the kitchen, Now I know what she said, now I know what she wanted to tell me then. And the awful laugh was heard again, as if it weren't Grandmother laughing but some demon inside her. I got up to peer from behind the door, and I saw her sitting at the table, her long hair dishevelled and in her nightgown and her mouth stained with cherry juice and chocolate, a knife clutched in her fist over the ruins of Alfred's two-layer cake, and Grandfather in pyjamas grabbing her wrist and pleading, Enough, enough now, you've already eaten too much, and Grandmother struggled to free her hand and the screeching voice of the demon burst out of her, Just one more little piece, just one more little piece, and Grandfather held her and cried, Don't leave me alone, Minna, please don't leave me alone, I can't make it alone. I ran away from there to your room. Your breathing was heavy, uneven. I got in under your blanket and hugged you and put my head next to yours. The pillow was soaked.

The next day we went with Misha and Grandfather and Grandmother who sat in front, her braid now pinned together, and Misha let them off at Rambam Hospital and took us to the beach at Bat-Galim, and we took off our clothes and had our bathing suits on underneath, and Misha looked like a lifeguard with his visor cap and broad chest, all he needed was a whistle. He sat down in a *chaise-longue* at the edge of the water, and you ran into the sea with a spray splashing

colourfully and you plunged into the waves, and I ran in behind you
and also plunged because I wanted to feel what you were feeling, and
my eyes burned and I swallowed salt water, and when I came back to
the shore, you were already standing there and shaking your curls, and
we sat down on the sand next to Misha, leaning against his sturdy
legs, and we watched the sea and were silent because none of us had
anything to say. Then I asked Misha to tell us again how he played
for the King of Yugoslavia because I knew how much he liked to tell
it, and I thought maybe that would save the situation. He was silent
a moment, and suddenly he said quietly, It wasn't I who played for
the King, it was another boy, he was also called Misha, and he played
better than I did, so they chose him to wear the uniform with gold
buttons, and the trumpet sparkled in the sun, and the flag went up
to the top of the flagpole, it was so beautiful I'll never forget it, and
King Pavel came and patted his head and his mother cried so they
had to hold her up, and I stood there in the line with all the children
and I cried too. He wiped his nose, and then he went on, as if to himself, But that Misha isn't here anymore, Hitler took him, all of them,
all of them, my parents too, my brothers and sisters, I'm the only one
alive, the sixth child, the one they didn't want, because Papa and
Mama got married very young, they were cousins, but the family
decided to marry them off at thirteen, that's how it was done in those
days, and every year they had a baby, every year a baby, until Papa
said, enough. But then they went for a vacation in Austria and when
they came back Mama was pregnant again. Misha fell silent and lit a
cigarette, and then he said out of the blue, Your grandfather is a fine
man, there aren't many people like him. We quietly watched a young
man who finally managed to walk on his hands and a man who threw
a stick in the water and his big dog charged in barking and swam and
brought the stick out in his mouth and the man patted his head. I
took an ice-cream stick and drew a house and a tree and the sun on
the wet sand, and the waves came and erased my picture. And the
sea slowly turned yellow and we got chilly so we dressed and went
to get Grandfather and Grandmother, who were waiting for us at the
entrance to the hospital with grey faces and looking suddenly very
old.

A few days later Grandmother told us that Uncle Alfred had died
in the hospital. She wiped her tears and said, He had a disease in
his lungs and the operation didn't succeed. But we knew the real
reason, and we didn't dare look at each other as we walked with
Grandmother, who was weeping for Alfred and for herself, and with

Grandfather, who was weeping for Grandmother, and with our parents and the other three people we didn't know, behind the undertakers busy like angels in white shirtsleeves and sweaty faces, carrying
the shrivelled body on a stretcher under a dark dustcloth, the head
almost touching the fat black behind of the first gravedigger, the legs
dangling in front of the open fly of the second one, and I thought, It
could be anyone under the cloth, maybe it's not him, but when we
got to the open grave the cantor said his name and a desperate crying burst out of me because I knew you couldn't move time backward. And you stood silently on the other side of the black grave, and
I knew that Uncle Alfred would always be between us, and after the
funeral your father would take you home, long before the end of
summer vacation because Grandmother already didn't feel well, and
in a few months, in the winter, she would die too, and Grandfather
would close the office on Herzl Street and move to an old people's
home, and he would go on talking to her all those years as if she
were still beside him, and we would never again be together in our
little room under the roof, and only sometimes, before sleep came,
you would crouch over me on all fours and look at me with yellow
pupils and I would whisper to you, Come, and I would feel your heart
drumming on my breasts, until the last flutter. I wipe my tears and
go with all the old people to put a little stone on the grave, and now
everyone is turning to go, but I stay another moment at Uncle Alfred's
yellowed marble, I know you're standing here next to me. Up close
you can see that I too have lines at the corner of my mouth and many
grey hairs, and the two of us read by heart the lines from the first
Lied of Das Lied von der Erde, whose words we didn't understand
then, and I put a little stone under the words and you put a little
stone and then you put your hand on my shoulder and say, Let's go.
My mother and your father are walking in front of us, whispering
about the city's plan to destroy the old house and dig up the grove
to build an expensive apartment building on the site, and I see the
ground, which can't still be holding all we buried there, it will split
open and the highrise will crack and collapse. Misha comes behind
us and sighs and says, If you could only go backward in life, even one
minute, and I know exactly what minute he wants to go back to. And
at the gate stands the stooped-over old woman whose shrivelled face
is so familiar, and she grabs my sleeve with a trembling hand and
screeches, Maybe you don't remember me but I remember your grandfather very well, he was a regular customer of mine, in the old Post
Office. You're Mrs Bella Blum from the Post Office, I whisper and my

heart turns pale, and for a split second I see eyeglasses on the end of a sharp nose, grey hair, icy fingers reaching out for the necks of children and triangular stamps, and I remember the anonymous threatening letters, and I glance over at you, but you're looking at your shoes covered with dust and you say, I have to go, we have a meeting at the factory, and once again I touch her soft hand under the purplish straw hat. Suddenly a strong wind comes from the sea and snatches the hat off her head and rolls it down the path, and she runs after it among the tombstones in her fluttering flowery dress, with her rounded belly, with the strips of her chestnut hair, flinging out her full arms to catch it, but the hat mocks her, it flies into the sky like a purple butterfly, and just as it's about to light on the sharp top of the cypress, it changes its mind, flips over twice and lands on the tombstone of Abba Hushi the famous mayor of Haifa, and you and Misha and all the other men volunteer to get it for her and you jump around among the graves, but the hat is already far away from there, crushed and ashamed between Hanoch ben Moshe Gavrieli born in the city of Lodz and Zilla Frumkin model wife and mother, who lie crowded next to each other, and all of you are flushed and sweating, but the hat pulls away again with a splendid somersault and soars, and you chase it, look up and wave your hands, like survivors on a desert island to an airplane, then the hat loses its balance and spins around itself like a dancer with a jumble of purple ribbons and lands with a bang outside the gate and lies on its side and laughs with its round mouth, and she runs to it, heavy and gasping and bends over and picks it up and waves it high in the air and brimming with joy she turns to you with sparkling eyes, I got it, I got it.

Translated by Barbara Harshav.

Yehudit Hendel

A STORY WITH NO ADDRESS

Yehudit Hendel was born in 1926 into a rabbinical family in Warsaw. She emigrated to Palestine as a child in 1938 and was raised in Haifa. Her first novel, The Street of Steps, *was dramatized and staged by the Habimah National Theatre. She has written four novels and collections of short stories. Her stories often constitute a set of variations on the theme of the brevity of life. Taken together they create a detailed study of psychological and physical confrontation with death. The collection* Small Change, *from which 'A Story With No Address' is taken, was published in 1988.*

On Friday, when I went to the store on the corner to buy a news-paper, a tall woman in a white dress was standing there smoking. Next to her was a little dog and I saw her lean over to the dog and then there was a hoarse shriek: You crazy, putting out cigarettes on the floor? That's how you smoke?

The woman straightened up slowly and adjusted the white collar of her dress.

I'm sorry, she said.

Sorry, the shriek again; sorry? You put out cigarettes on the floor? A pasty saliva foam bubbled on the girl's lips and she stuck out her tongue and licked it off.

I'm sorry, said the woman.

The coarse voice kept on.

Some nerve you got to say you're sorry, it shrieked, burn my foot and say you're sorry, stand in a store with a great big dog and burn my foot and say you're sorry, that's how you smoke, lady?

The woman, very pale, didn't budge.

I'm sorry, she said.

The girl stamped. She went on in a hoarse voice, arms flailing, eyes blazing back and forth, as if she had two heads, the one in front and the one in back.

You're crazy, you say you're sorry, you burn my foot and say you're sorry, you don't see you burned my foot, you don't see I'm barefoot? The dog stood up on his hind legs and clambered up the woman. I'm sorry, I'm really sorry, she said. She was growing paler. I didn't see you were barefoot.

The girl kept stamping both feet. They were bare and particularly big, the toes splayed like asymmetrical stems growing out of the floor. A narrow pasty strip fizzed on her face.

You didn't see? she screamed. Puts out cigarettes on my foot and says she didn't see. Where'd you grow up, lady?

Quiet, said the newspaper man.

What do you mean, quiet? screamed the girl. She licked her chin which was also covered with the damp white pasty foam. What quiet? she screamed.

The dog shrank back from the woman's legs. All of a sudden he whined.

Can I have a chair? said the woman.

Burns up my foot and wants a chair, shouted the girl. These women have some nerve—

The dog was whining faster, drier.

Can I have a chair? whispered the woman. Her face took on the shade of a paper bag. Do you have a telephone? she whispered.

The newspaper man didn't hear.

Do you perhaps have a telephone, she whispered.

The dog jumped on her, clasped her in the heat of his despair with his mouth and paws. He twisted around, riveted himself into a circle, backed off and stood up on his hind legs, his thin ankles rigid.

The woman sighed a soft sigh of pain. She tottered back a bit and forward a bit, her head resting on her shoulder. Then she dropped onto the chair, with a thump, as if she were falling onto the floor.

I think you should call an ambulance, someone said.

Ambulance? screamed the girl. Burns my foot and needs an ambulance. They get away with murder, she shouted.

The dog stood erect on his hind legs. A strange noise was coming from his belly.

By the time the ambulance came, the woman was barely breathing. The doctors refused to take the dog in the ambulance. He twisted around again, riveted himself into a circle, hanging on the back door that was still wide open. Then I saw him running among the cars like a wild animal, whining all the while.

In the evening I went to Ikhilov Hospital. That night it wasn't the hospital on call for emergencies so the yard was almost empty. The dog lay outside, scratching himself. When he saw me he turned his head and stared at me. His eyes were red as two red cherries.

In the hospital admissions office, no one knew anything. I said that a woman with a dog was brought in at noon.

No dog, said the clerk.

I said he was still outside, the dog.

What dog? said the clerk.

The doctor sitting at the desk twitched his shoulders.

Oh, the one from the newspaper store, he said. He looked very tired. He said there was no address. They looked in her purse. No address. He asked if I would like to identify the body.

I said I didn't know the woman.

Too bad, he said, somebody has to identify the body.

I asked when she had died.

Oh, he said, she was dead on arrival. He looked at me for a moment, steadily, blankly. There wasn't any dog. He looked at me again with that same blank, glassy-eyed stare. You can get her clothes in the morgue, he said.

I said she was wearing a white dress.

Could be, he said, I didn't see a white dress.

Yes, she was buying newspapers, I said, she was wearing a white dress.

Maybe, said the doctor, there weren't any newspapers. He raised his head and looked at me again. He said he hadn't seen any white dress. A vague smile hovered over his face.

He asked if it made a difference that she was wearing a white dress. Anyway, somebody has to identify the body, he said.

The clerk said there was a dog.

Now the doctor stared at the clerk. He said he didn't know if they'd take a dog's identification.

In fact, why not? said the clerk.

Yes, said the doctor, But anyway, the dog won't be able to take care of the funeral arrangements.

The dog leapt up wildly as if he had been shot. He jumped on the doctor.

Oh, no, said the doctor.

The dog didn't let go. Afterward he walked silently behind the doctor and I didn't see him go into the morgue. I only saw him come out. He walked slowly, rubbing his back on the wall. Instead of saliva, drops of blood came from his throat. Then he fixed himself to the

chair in the corridor, his back twisted, as if he were glued to the chair.
He scratched both eyes with one of his legs and uttered a strange
sound, like someone sawing through a board.

I returned home along King David Boulevard. By now it was dusk.
The boulevard was empty. The trees were tall, thin, pale, noisy and
quiet. Next to me walked a guy with a Walkman clamped to his
ears. Behind me, mute and patient, walked the dog. His small body
was big and he walked along dead, his jaw stiff as a hoof. The guy
with the Walkman came very close to me. He was wearing a bright
red teeshirt which glowed like a traffic light on the boulevard. He
took the earphones off for a moment. He said: A million men built
the Great Wall of China. I didn't catch what he said. He smiled and
turned around to me. A million men built the Great Wall of China,
he repeated and again took off the earphones. He asked if I wanted
to hear. I said there was a dog walking behind me. He looked at me
very closely and said there wasn't any dog here. I said I clearly saw
him walking. The guy with the Walkman smiled again. A million men
built the Great Wall of China, he said, and that's the only thing they
see from outer space, you understand? He put his earphones back on
and turned the knob which emitted a wild music. You understand?
he repeated. The music came from him as if it were coming out of
his body, like a long chromatic wail. He made a half-turn to me.
Whales love the saxophone, he said, I don't know what dogs love. He
lowered his voice and smiled a bit too broadly. Maybe the saxophone,
too, he said. In the dusk, the pupils of his eyes looked very bright. I
love the saxophone too, he said, don't you? There wasn't anybody
on the boulevard except me, the guy with the Walkman and the dog
who went on walking dead, his jaw stiff, walking like stray dogs who
walk around on the roads for years. The guy with the Walkman took
another step. He walked slowly, absorbed in his wild music, long and
shut tight like a suitcase.

It was a solemn night. The boulevard was still empty and the streets
were empty too. The guy with the walkman took another step and
then was swallowed up in the boulevard, his red teeshirt glowing. He
lifted his head from time to time. He looked as if he were bobbing
up and down in the sea.

I thought it was time to go home. But the dog kept walking behind
me dead and I said to myself, because he was dead he would walk
behind me forever. His face was sad and thin and the leaves wrote a
tattooed inscription on his back. Once again I saw him leap onto the

woman in the white dress, caress her in the heat of his despair with his mouth and his paws. Suddenly, I recalled that the Egyptians would touch the eyes and mouth of the dead to restore their senses and that's just what the dog had done. Wrapped in sawdust and rags, the dead gradually dried out there. When it dried, the mummy was adorned with a mask and the coffin was borne on a wooden litter shaped like a boat to eternity. Then they embalmed the soul of the dead and made a sarcophagus for the soul.

When I entered the house the television was on. They were announcing a plague of locusts in South Africa and a release of prisoners in the Philippines. The announcer said it was a yellowish-white locust and millions of the pests were spreading over forests and fields, destroying every strip of green and they showed jeeps riding and spraying poison and black workers celebrating because, for them, the locust was a delicacy. Then they showed the funeral of a youth blown up by a mine in Lebanon. The mother was waving her hands and shouting. The rabbi was nodding his head. Saying Holy Holy. It was hot and he was sweating a lot. The mother was tearing at her arms. The rabbi kept nodding his head. Saying Holy Holy. The mother was kneeling on the earth. They showed the dignitaries who attended the funeral. They were wearing big sunglasses and were sweating under their sunglasses and wiping away their sweat. The rabbi began the *El Male Rakhamim*. The mother was eating the earth.

I turned off the television and made some coffee. I thought about the woman in the white dress. Then I thought about the dog and I wondered if anyone had come to identify the body. All of a sudden I remembered Paul Celan and that his body had floated on the Seine. The Paris gendarmes no doubt cursed when they found his body floating on the Seine. I didn't know if he had had papers on him and if they had had to identify the body, I didn't know what bridge, I didn't know if it was day or night, summer or winter and it seemed to me that he had floated in a black suit. I called my friend in Haifa. She said: What? What suit? Oh, no, he didn't think about that. He closed himself up in a room and didn't come out. It was in a school. He taught in a school. He couldn't. Couldn't what, I asked. Live, she said. I asked if it was summer or winter. She didn't remember. And the bridge? I asked. She was silent. No, she didn't know if there had been a bridge. No, she didn't know where it was. Again she was silent. The Seine is so slow, she said. Now I remembered when we were in Venice we went to the island where Saint Francis had talked to the birds. They were selling jars of coloured Venetian glass there. The glass was beautiful but the jars were ugly and I asked: Where are the birds? And Zvi said: You see, they sell eyes of crystal and you can buy yellow eyes here you can buy red eyes you can buy horse's eyes, cats have green pupils, he said, and here they're selling a green pupil, it's the iron-oxidation that makes it green that makes them see at night, that's because the glass is strong under pressure that's why it's so fragile, lets the light through so much, ninety per cent of the light so many years so many generations, come, he said, there must be the birds. My friend in Haifa asked why I had broken off the conversation. I said I hadn't broken off the conversation.

The next day I went back to the hospital. There wasn't any dog there and I returned along the boulevard. There wasn't any dog there either, neither living nor dead nor walking along the boulevard. I remembered my mother once told me there is no need to be afraid of the dead. That was back in Nesher, when we lived near the cemetery, when I was a little girl. How old was I then? How old am I now? How old was she? How old is she now? There's nothing to fear from the gravestones, she said, they're made of stone. You think there's no life in stone? I said to my mother. The wind changes the shape of the stone, I said to my mother. Oh no, said my mother, only time.

She used to comb her hair in front of a small mirror on a white lacquered board. I was a girl when they brought her personal belongings. What happened to them, to those personal belongings of hers? She didn't die, said my father's father. She just went away. My father didn't answer. And my father's father left. Then he came back. His coat was wet and his face was wet too and he didn't go to my father, he just wiped his face with his coat and said: First day last day they blow the *shofar* and shout and pray, and my father didn't answer.

It was early in the morning when she went away. She was forty years old when she went away. I didn't know then how young she was. They use the cypress to make musical instruments, she told me once. That was when the cypress near our shack died. Maybe it will be a musical instrument, she told me once. Dry wood is strong, she said.

I was alone with her that early morning. The balcony was filled with light. The garden was filled with light. She sighed one weak sigh. I went out to the balcony and stood there. Even today I remember the light.

How old was she then? How old is she now? What did I know then? What do I know now? You think you learn that, she told me once. Look at the windows when they're closed, she said. Those black holes absorbing distress, oh no, this she didn't say.

I went home quickly. I quickly made myself some coffee and quickly turned on the radio. Someone on the radio was saying that in Portugal they decorated the city with tens of thousands of paper flowers, the whole city was paper flowers, all the houses and all the people and even the electric poles. I changed the station. Someone was talking about spots on the sun. The sunwind is emitted from the areas of sunspots, he said, and the convergence of a few sunspots absorbs enormous amounts of radiation. His voice was soft and I stayed tuned to the station. He spoke slowly and I listened to his soft, musical voice. How the sun emits a sunwind like a sprinkler and something about the space surrounding the sun and how the sunwind there is strong and great. Why do sunspots appear in various areas, he asked, why is it a cycle of eleven years. The activity of the sun isn't guaranteed either. Will changes take place in the sun, in the sunwind, he asked. I pressed my ear to the radio. He said there was a period of seventy years without sunspots. Without sunspots? I said into the radio. The corona of the sun disappeared, he said from the radio. I turned off the radio.

The next day I went back to the hospital. The doctor wasn't there this time either. The clerk said she didn't know anything. Every day there are dead people here, she said.

I asked if they had buried the dog too.

She said you have to ask about dead dogs at city hall.

I returned along the boulevard. The boulevard was empty now too and I sat down on a bench. It was hot. The trees were tall and sharpened like tips of white thorns and a narrow white path was hanging over the trees.

Translated by Barbara Harshav.

Yitzhak Oren

THE MONUMENT OF THE RESURRECTION

Oren was born in Siberia in 1918 and lived in China until his family emigrated to Palestine in 1936. His style is among the most unusual in Hebrew literature, whimsical, paradoxical, and fantastic. His stories dislocate reality and present heroes impassively enduring bizarre situations. He has written three novels and numerous collections of short stories, the first of which, Somewhere, was published in 1950.

I

Everything was perfectly organized and beautifully planned—a doubly worthy achievement considering that the whole matter had to be kept secret. No one, other than those who were directly involved in the operation, knew anything at all about it. And really, to this day I remain amazed that I was privileged to be one of those select members of the species who knew in advance about the great thing, I mean that event without precedent in human history that was going to take place eighteen hours from the time I was told about it.

I am not an expert in the complexities of the various sciences that have the audacity to predict the future. Therefore, I do not know whether it was the astronomers or the astrologers, the physicists or the statisticians, the psychologists or the sociologists who predicted that the Messiah would come on the date, the hour, the minute, and the second that they determined. All I know, and even that knowledge is no more than conjecture, is that someone forecast and calculated and predicted, raised a supposition, proved it to the point of scientific certainty, and transmitted the information to his superiors. His superiors investigated and probed, organized and planned, and kept it all a secret until the time came.

Of course, I myself had no part in either the predicting or the planning—and there is nothing surprising about that. On the contrary, the astonishing thing is that even though I am as I am, I was, as I have said, one of the few who knew the great secret some eighteen hours before its public revelation.

When I say that 'I am as I am' I do not mean, heaven forbid, to disparage my personality. I am a person like any other. I do not fall short of the majority of my kind. To tell the truth, though, I am not superior to the majority of my kind, and certainly I fall short of the minority, that minority which has been blessed with qualities that make their lives a continuous march of triumph and who succeed in their every endeavour. But, as I said, I was not blessed with those traits and I cannot take pride in triumphs. But although I cannot claim triumphs, neither can I point to defeats. For before a person can suffer a defeat he must fight, and I have never fought in my life; neither with valour nor with force nor with spirit.

There is hardly any point in my telling you about the pageant of my life, if only because my life does not deserve to be called a pageant. Suffice it for me to describe myself as I am, and knowledge of my present condition will enable anyone who may be interested to infer my past. And the only reason I take even that trouble is to explain why I found it so astonishing that I was suddenly privy to the secret counsel of the leading personalities of our generation concerning the leading personality of all time.

In any event, I am about thirty, married, and the father of two children: a boy and a girl. My son is six and my daughter is two. My wife is an unqualified mercy-nurse and works in a hospital. We all live in a two-room flat in one of the suburbs. The apartment is my private property, but it still has a mortgage on it that I pay off in monthly instalments from my salary and from my wife's salary.

I myself work in one of the factories of the military industries. I will be absolutely frank: I do not have the foggiest notion what the factory makes. First of all, because the final product is a military secret, and second, because I was never interested in knowing what the final product is.

For eight hours a day I sit by myself in a small chamber that has no windows and whose only door is closed, other than when I open it occasionally. And I only open it four times a day: in the morning, when I enter the chamber; at the lunch break, when I go to the cafeteria to wash down my lunch of sandwiches that I bring from home with a cup of tea; at the end of the lunch break, when I return from the cafeteria to the chamber; and toward evening, when I leave it until the following day. The ventilation that operates in my chamber is artificial, entering through small perforations in the ceiling, and the light comes from fluorescent bulbs. I sit in a kind of large armchair, and across from me on the wall is an instrument that makes you think of a large thermometer, by which I mean an outsize tube, made of glass (or perhaps some other transparent material), that fills up with mercury (or perhaps some other liquid that resembles mercury). The filling process takes place from bottom to top, in other words the pillar structure begins small and rises continually, constantly increasing— at times rapidly, at times more slowly—until it fills the tube completely. When the tube is totally filled, I empty it. How? With my right hand I hold the end of a rope that goes into a hole in the wall. Take note, ladies and gentlemen: not a lever or a button, not a handle or a knob, but a rope. The simplest kind of flax rope. Whenever my eyes see that the tube is full, I pull on the rope and it empties.

I do not know the processes that are involved in my task, just as I do not know why it should be that in order to empty a tube I have to pull on a rope in our era, when every mechanism in the Creator's world is regulated automatically and every facility oversees itself mechanically. I have lived in my flat for five years now, and I do not know any neighbours in the entire building (with the exception of the flat above mine). I would say that this lack of curiosity is one of my characteristic traits. Because of that trait, I do not listen to the news and I do not read the papers, because of it I know so few things and I do not know so many things, because of it I have no formal education beyond elementary school. I stress: formal education, for until that day on which I married a woman and produced children and became indentured to work in the chamber of a factory of the military industries, I used to read a lot—with no method or order, whatever came to hand: detective stories and Spinoza, Scripture legends and Marcel Proust, Plato and popular science—they were all part of my spiritual menu. The thing is, though, that my reading is not like the reading of ordinary people, because for the most part I do not take in things as they are actually written but as I fantasize and mend and improve them in my imagination. As a result, I do not remember even one iota of what Prince Bolkonsky (I refer to Tolstoy's *War and Peace*) whispered to his passionate love, Natasha, but engraved on the tablets of my heart are the words I would say to Natasha if I should encounter her one day, and those are sentiments that no one can erase or uproot. I think that the number of detective novels I have read must run into the hundreds, but anyone who asks me how Sherlock Holmes or Poirot or Perry Mason discovered the perpetrators of the murders will be none the wiser for having asked. Still,

I have my own method of exposing all those criminals, and if I had even a fraction of the talent of Conan Doyle or Agatha Christie or Erle Stanley Gardner, I would rewrite their stories and expose the criminals more quickly and more efficiently. Even when it comes to establishing exemplary states, I have a better idea than Plato's, even though the idea popped into my head just when I was reading Plato's *The Republic*. I am ready to reveal my conception publicly, and the only reason I do not is that I am positive that no one would want to listen to me. Even more: from books like *How I Split the Atom*, *Electronics for Youth*, *Stars for Everyone*, and *One, Two, Three... Infinity*, and other compositions of the same kind, I tried to learn something about the motion of the celestial bodies and the particles of the atom. I read them but I did not go back to them a second time, and if I did go back a second time I did not go back a third time, so that the main points have escaped my memory. But I do not have the slightest regret about that, either. On the contrary, stored in my mind there is a system of laws according to which all the matter in the world— from the electron to the Milky Way—might move in space in a manner completely different from the way it now moves. But I prefer to keep that system of laws locked up within the recesses of my mind, knowing, as I do, that even if I voice my ideas, my voice will be as a voice calling in the desert, for in our day, when people can enact laws that apply only to themselves, anyone who tries to dictate laws to all of creation will be thought a trickster.

So I sit in my chamber and enjoy my work. And the reason I enjoy my work is that my mind is free to reflect and to fantasize about the past of all living things, the present of the cosmos, and the future of the human species. My eyes are glued to the tube and my hands pull the rope whenever the liquid reaches the highest level of that tube.

For six years now I have been looking at the liquid, pulling the rope, spending a third of every day in pleasant contemplation, and while doing so destroying old worlds and building new and better ones.

II

On that day someone knocked on the door of my chamber. The time was nine forty-five.

My eyes were glued to the tube, my hand held the end of the rope, but even so I remember very exactly that the time was nine forty-five—which means that I must have had time to grab a quick look at my watch before asking in a loud voice:

'Who is there?'

'Yona Schwartz,' came the reply from the other side of the door. In fact, it was the voice of Yona Schwartz.

Yona Schwartz was the only worker in the factory who came into my chamber once a month during the past two years to give me my monthly wages. Why only during the past two years? For until two years ago, the wages in the factory were paid in cash, whereas two years ago they began to be paid with cheques. As long as the wages had been paid in cash, I would trudge over to the pay-booth after work, stand in line and wait until I reached the window. After they introduced the cheques, Yona Schwartz would bring them to all the workers—myself included. No longer did I have to stand in line, and as soon as I got home on the first of the month I would countersign the cheque and hand it to my wife.

When I heard Yona Schwartz's voice, I pressed the pedal at my feet. At once the door opened and Yona Schwartz entered. The pedal had been installed by the security authorities so that the door would not be opened from the outside unless I found it necessary. Only those who had been issued a special key—the key that was frequently in my possession—could open the door without needing the push of my pedal.

I was amazed that Yona Schwartz was paying me a surprise visit in the middle of the month, and astonished sevenfold when he opened his mouth and said to me:

'You are wanted by Management. It is urgent. I will fill in for you.'

'Me, to Management?'

Never had I been summoned to Management. I had no idea what its members looked like. Six years earlier, when I had been hired, I was brought in to see a smiling fellow. He had sad blue eyes and his locks were curly and greying at the edges. To this day, I did not know whether he was a member of Management or not. Since then I had not been troubled from my chamber by my superiors even once.

'Yes, to Management,' Yona Schwartz said, and it seemed to me that the ends of the coarse hairs of his ashen beard bristled a bit. (Yona Schwartz would shave once a week, on the Sabbath eve, and today was Tuesday.)

After the hairs of his beard reverted to their normal state—or after I imagined that they had returned to their normal state—Yona made a gesture from which I gathered that he was about to take my place on the seat that I have described as being a kind of armchair.

I got up, and as my grip on the rope loosened and my eyes followed the rise of the liquid in the tube, I prepared myself to give him a brief lecture on the essence of my job. However, Yona Schwartz gave me a look with his yellow eyes (I am assured, for some reason, that in principle Yona Schwartz's eyes were brown, but since he was from the Third *Aliyah* and had endured everything its members had endured, such as paving roads and digging ditches, fishing in Lake Kineret and doing guard duty in Galilee, defending posts in Jerusalem and hiking in the Negev, the colour of his eyes had faded and yellowed because of the sun), and a smattering of contempt emanated from the depths of his glance. While I was still trying to grasp the import of that look, he sat himself in my seat, stared at the tube, and with his hand held the end of my rope.

The upshot was that there was no room for me in the chamber. I left it and walked across a broad courtyard to Management.

Having crossed the courtyard, I entered a high-rise building. I stood next to the lift and rang the bell. A dial that was luminous with a yellowish light pointed up—a sign that the lift was going up.

I sat and waited until it would reach whatever floor it might be going to and would then descend in response to my ring. In the meantime, a few more people arrived and they also waited for the lift. But they were all impatient. So they waited standing up. Whereas I was forbearing and waited sitting.

While I was sitting and waiting, I discovered that the special key to my chamber was still present in my pocket.

At that time I did not yet know that I would never return to my chamber. On the contrary, I thought that I would return there in a few minutes. And it was a good thing that I thought as I did, otherwise the key would have tugged at my conscience until finally I would have run back to give it to Yona Schwartz and forced Management to wait a long time for me—and that might have boomeranged on my future.

III

It turned out to be absolutely certain that the smiler with the sad blue eyes and the curly hair greying at the edges—I mean, the person who hired me, at the time—was in Management. This was proved by the fact that it was he who sat at the head of table in the room on the door of which was a sign reading 'Management' and which I entered without first knocking. I thought that having been invited to Management, I was exempt from knocking on the door.

However, when I opened the door and went in, my confidence failed me and I did not know whether I had done the right thing or not. True, it was not at my initiative that I had come; I had been summoned from on high, but nevertheless it might have been my duty to knock a few times. That inner doubt brought about my weak-kneed feeling as I made my way from the doorway toward the table. But when I saw the curly-haired smiler, with his sad blue eyes and the face I recognized from six years ago, my heart was filled with courage and my anxiety disappeared as though it had never been.

So the sad-eyed smiler sat at the head. On his two sides sat two people whom I had never before had the opportunity to see. One of them was skinny and ruddy-faced, his hair slashed and grizzled so his skull looked like a field of nettles after harvesting, and he himself was a bundle of raw nerves; sometimes he would tap with his fingers on the table and sometimes he would twist his face in successive, rhythmic contortions, either by pouting with his lower lip or by winking his left eye and contracting the whole area of his face in the proximity of that eye.

This jittery guy sat to the left of Curly-Hair, while to his right sat Jittery's complete opposite: he looked part sculpture and part bald flesh and blood, his eyes the shade of rusted metal, his face frozen like a glacier—unmoving, ungesticulating, not batting an eyelash. After Lot's wife turned into a pillar of salt, she must have had a face like that guy.

Smiler gave me his melancholy look and indicated the chair opposite him. His lips assumed an even more intense smile.

'Have a seat, Mr Kornstein,' he said placidly.

'My name is not Kornstein,' I replied, still standing.

'Not Kornstein?' snapped the jittery one.

The glacier did not stir.

'No. My name *was* Kornstein. Now my name is Karni.'

'When did you change your name?' asked Curly, and even though he spoke placidly, the echo of a hidden worry could be detected in his voice.

'Five years ago. The truth is that it didn't bother me to be called Kornstein, but my wife insisted on it.'

'What did your wife insist on?'

'On changing the name.'

Jittery riffled through the file that was on the table in front of him. Glacier raised his brows. Curly emitted some strange humming noises.

I was perfectly calm. Now I realized that I was still standing on my feet, even though I had some time ago been offered a seat—or maybe even ordered to take a seat. I sat down, and not only that, but I made myself comfortable as I sat. I did not care any longer whether any behaviour was proper or improper.

Jittery pushed the file over to Curly and showed him a particular document. Curly nodded and whispered something to Glacier. The frown left Glacier's face and together with the frown went the last trace of any expression at all.

'Lot's wife as a man, after the upheaval in Sodom and Gomorrah,' I reflected in my mind.

It turned out that I had not been content with inward reflections and had spoken my thoughts aloud, for it is out of the question that Smiler had read my thoughts. He said:

'Not Lot's wife but the Monument of the Resurrection and not the upheaval in Sodom and Gomorrah but a fateful upheaval in the history of the human species and all of creation, and not after the upheaval but before it.'

While I was still trying to clarify to myself the meaning of this verbal stew, Glacier's lips moved and from between his clenched teeth a short, categorical statement filtered through:

'Tomorrow before dawn, at oh four hundred hours, the Messiah will come.'

As I have already mentioned, I am to this day astonished at the privilege that befell me to be one of the few to whom it was thought necessary to divulge the news of the most important event that was about to take place in the history of mankind, and perhaps even in the history of the cosmos. However, I was not in the least amazed when Glacier made his pronouncement. If he had said that the alarm clock next to my bed would go off the next day at oh four hundred I would have been far more amazed, because that clock usually rings at oh five hundred hours and not at oh four hundred.

'This is a deep secret, a deep secret, a deep secret. Do you hear?' Jittery emoted, his left eye winking and shrinking the whole area of his face around it within a radius of a few centimetres.

Curly the smiler lowered his eyes, waiting for Jittery to finish his stirrings. Then his face lit up as he turned to me and said placidly, as was his wont:

'I supposed, Mr Karni, that you have heard that the coming of the Messiah is accompanied by the resurrection of the dead. Naturally, the addition of such a large number of people to the planet (we estimate the number of candidates for resurrection at several billion, based on the report of our intelligence service, which considers that the rebirth order will apply to all persons irrespective of creed, race, nationality or views—everyone who was ever born will come to life, the just and the wicked alike), the addition of such a large population is liable to produce innumerable problems, particularly in the realms of food and housing. Therefore, all the requisite arrangements have been made to fly those who come to life—immediately after they rise from their graves—to the moon, to the planets, and perhaps to other celestial bodies as well. The facilities that are needed and their crews are on standby. As for the secrecy, it is essential in order to prevent panic among the inhabitants of the planet. We are doing everything we can to carry out the operation according to a tight schedule, without shocks to the inhabitants of the planet, and as far as possible even without their knowledge. At the same time, we are determined to commemorate the event by building a monument, the Monument of the Resurrection. The mission of setting it up—or, more accurately, of raising it—has been assigned to you.'

Curly inhaled. Jittery raised the palm of one hand and readied his fingers for tapping on the table, but his hand remained suspended in the air. Glacier stretched out his arm and pointed at me with his finger as though he were firing a pistol.

My lips went dry. I wanted to lick them with my tongue, but I didn't dare. I swallowed the saliva that welled up in my mouth and felt a sharp pain in my throat.

'The mission is simple, it is simplicity itself,' Curly the Smiler continued. 'Tomorrow at two fifteen a.m., you get up, leave your house, and walk along the road that leads to Ramallah. Some believe it is Beit-El, the place where Jacob's Ladder was situated at the time and its top reached into heaven. Exactly! You will go on foot. When you reach the barrier at the border, turn left and keep going until you see the end of a rope sticking out of the ground. Lower yourself onto the ground near that place and wait until the time is oh four hundred. At oh four hundred you will hear a sound—something between a trumpet and a siren. Know that this is not an air-raid siren but the blast of the Messiah's *shofar*. As soon as you hear the *shofar*, pull on the rope. Exactly! Do not wait until the end of the blast, pull it when the first sounds are heard. That is all. Now go home and lie down. Rest is a very important element in the operation, and should be seen as the first stage in the execution of your mission. Remember: not a word to any other person!'

'I am not going back to my chamber?'

'No. You must rest.'

'And the key?'

'What key?'

'The key to my chamber. A special key.' I pulled the key out of my pocket.

All three of them burst into laughter. Curly curled even when he laughed. Glacier produced metallic sounds from his throat. Jittery's shoulders shook.

I went out and walked to the bus, carrying the key in my clenched fist.

IV

While I was standing in the bus that took me home, worry gnawed at my heart and gloomy thoughts stabbed at my mind. It was not myself I was worried about and not myself that I thought about. Inwardly, I was certain that I would fulfil the mission faithfully and execute efficiently the task I had been assigned, even though there was no objective reason for that self-confidence. It was in fact the Messiah I was worried about. I had read somewhere that Napoleon had been defeated in the Battle of Leipzig because he had a cold. What will happen, for example—I thought to myself—if just as the Messiah draws his face close to the *shofar*, just then he will be smitten with an unbearable stomach ache.

These and similar fears bothered me the whole way. Yet, after arriving at the threshold of my house I stopped fearing for the Messiah and under the circumstances I began to fear for myself.

When I stood by the entrance to my flat the time was ten fifty-five. As I had been ordered to rest, I planned my day. Immediately upon arriving home, I will take off my clothes and lie down on my bed, cover myself with a blanket, and fall asleep. I will sleep deeply until my son comes home from school and my wife from work. My wife works until one o'clock and on her way home she picks up my daughter from the nursery school. At one thirty the entire family, except for myself, is at home, and at two o'clock they have their midday meal; since I too will be home today, we will all eat together. After lunch I will wash the dishes. As a result, my wife's rest will be perfect and she will be able to go back to work (from five until seven-thirty) fresher than on any other day. While my wife is at work, I will amuse myself with my daughter and help my son prepare his lessons ('Hello, father,' 'Hello mother,' 'Happy New Year'—in gigantic letters).

Because my wife will be less tired than usual in the evening, we will go out together to the cinema and we will ask the neighbour who lives in the flat on the top floor—right above us—if she can come down and watch the children. She also has children of her own, and she sometimes asks us to do her the same service—'You watch mine and I'll watch yours', so to speak.

True, I was ordered by Management to rest, but the cinema is just like a rest.

I worked out that plan at ten fifty-six. The first hitch came at ten fifty-seven. There are many thoughts in a man's heart, but the counsel of the Lord alone will stand firm.

I approached the door to my flat, the key to my chamber in my clenched fist. Absentmindedly, I inserted it into the keyhole, or, more exactly, I tried to insert it, for the structure of that key was unique and under no circumstances could it be inserted into the keyhole of my flat. Nevertheless, I kept thrusting it and pushing it very stubbornly until I grew weary. Only after I had become weary did I notice my mistake and it became apparent that all my efforts were for naught. I extracted the right key from my pocket and opened the door. As I was standing in the doorway I heard my neighbour's voice from above, the one with the flat above ours, the same one who was meant to watch our children that night. I lifted my eyes and saw her coming hastily down from the stairs with my little daughter in her arms. As she descended and approached me her voice became louder and by the time she stood in front of me her voice had become a wail. The neighbour wailed, but my little daughter did not emit a sound. She opened her eyes wide, pursed her lips, and held out her arms to me.

I did not yet know what it all meant, but I was already annoyed. And when I found out what it did mean, I was even more annoyed. It turned out that the owner of the nursery school had brought my daughter home this morning because of the fact that the toddler was burning up with a fever. There was absolutely no doubt that the girl had taken ill, perhaps even with a contagious disease. The nursery school teacher's fear was that the other toddlers would catch the disease and she had been quick to bring my daughter home. She had found our flat locked tight. She had gone up to the second floor and given the little girl to the neighbour. Since the neighbour was the mother of three children, she feared for their wellbeing and refused to accept my child, and only after an argument did she do what the nursery school teacher asked. Now she poured her wrath on me, even though the vilifications she levelled at me were spoken in the feminine and according to all the signs they applied not to me but to my wife, such as: 'A witch, not a mother, sending a sick little girl to the nursery school, bitch, she should be raising children? I wouldn't trust that one with baby animals', and other such railings and denunciations that did not attest to very warm feelings, although until then I had thought that pleasant neighbourly relations prevailed between my spouse and her neighbours in general and the neighbour above us in particular.

I took my daughter from her, laid her down in the cradle, and gave her tea to sip from a spoon. The little one spat out the tea and burst into tears. I rocked the cradle, at first gently and then furiously, until the baby fell asleep. Having fallen asleep, she began to breathe heavily and to emit snores and snorts. I rushed to the grocery store and phoned the hospital where my wife worked. After absorbing various bizarre noises—some of them men's voices and some of them women's voices—I was finally put through to the head nurse in my wife's ward. The head nurse informed me that this morning someone had told them on my wife's behalf that she was ill and would not be coming to work. I put down the receiver and picked it up again. I dialed such-and-such a number of times and called the *Kupat Holim*. I was asked by whomever what degree of fever my daughter had. To this I had no ready response. The voice advised me to give her Asialgin and to phone the next day in order to set up an appointment. I tried to protest, but the call was cut off.

I went back home. My son was standing by the door. His pants were torn and his shirt was filthy. My hand went out automatically and slapped him on the face. It was the first slap I had ever doled out to my son in his whole life. He opened his mouth in astonishment and stood frozen to his spot. I felt a pang of pain in my heart, but as my thoughts were not free for my suffering, I disregarded the pang and entered the house. My daughter was asleep. The snores and snorts had stopped. I sat next to the cradle and touched her forehead. I let my palm rest on her forehead but I was none the wiser, because I had never known how to determine a person's degree of a fever by touch. I bent over her and put my ear next to her chest. The chest rose and fell alternately and her breathing was regular and calm. My mind was at rest. My mind being at rest, I remembered my son. I walked over to the door and found it open. I thought that in my haste I had forgotten to close it. I stood in the doorway and cast my eyes about for my son. I surveyed the entire surroundings but I did not find him.

I returned to my daughter's cradle, brought a chair to it, and sat down. I tried to think about the Messiah who was due to arrive at oh four hundred hours and I glanced at my watch. The time was one forty-seven—the time that my wife usually comes back from work. Yet even though today, as I had learned, she had not been at work, she returned at exactly the same time. When she saw me sitting next to my daughter's bed, she froze on the spot and looked at me in puzzlement. Her eyelids were red as though from crying.

I related to her all my activities, other than the affair of the Messiah, keeping from her the news of his expected arrival at oh four hundred hours. I also kept from her the fact that I knew that she had not been at work today.

She asked:

'What in the world are you doing here at this time of the day?'

To my shame, I found that I had no response to that question, even though one would think that I should have been ready for it. The words came and emerged from my mouth by themselves, saying:

'I was fired.'

Why it was just these two words that came out, is a wonder.

Whenever I am excited or shocked by bad news that comes upon me suddenly, I am gripped by the desire to lie down on my bed and dive into fantasies. Whereas my wife, whenever she is excited or shocked by bad news that comes upon her suddenly, is gripped by tremendous hyperactivity. When she heard about the imaginary firing, she rushed over to the baby, brushed her lips on her forehead, and fixed her blanket. Then she rushed to the kitchen and set a few pots and a kettle on the stove. While they were on the stove, she took vegetables from the refrigerator and peeled them with a special instrument, part-knife and part-saw. With lightning swiftness she put the peeled vegetables into one of the pots and dashed out. She did all this without saying a word.

The baby woke up and burst into tears. Again I tried to calm her: I patted her, gave her sweet tea to drink, and rocked the cradle, but this time I was unsuccessful. I do not know how much time I spent in these vain attempts. It seems to me that they lasted many hours, but according to the exact calculation they lasted only about half an hour. After half an hour had gone by, my wife appeared and with her my son and Dr Tamir.

My son moved off to a far corner and observed me sullenly. Dr Tamir approached the cradle and remained by it. My wife changed my son's clothes and joined Dr Tamir.

Dr Tamir is like his name. Besides being lanky, he is light-haired like a Northern European.

Both of them—my wife and Dr Tamir—were busy with my daughter and I drew near to my son and tried to make it up to him in all kinds of ways. At first he did not respond and all my little pranks were of no use. Finally I related to him a story about a mouse that swallowed an elephant and stayed as small as it had been. That tale caught his fancy and was the occasion for a full reconciliation. I had no choice but to repeat it a second time.

In the meantime Dr Tamir had finished examining my daughter and was writing a prescription. My wife handed me the prescription and asked me to go to the pharmacy. I went to the pharmacy and my son accompanied me. On the way I regaled him for a third time with the story of the mouse that swallowed an elephant.

When I returned from the pharmacy, my wife was sitting deep in the armchair—it is the only armchair in our apartment and came to us from my wife's parents—and behind the armchair stood Dr Tamir. He cast his eyes far past my body, as though I were not made of matter but was a void in an empty space, while my wife gave me a long look that began as a greenish flash of hatred and ended with an expression of guilt mixed with fawning like that of a dog that had misbehaved. That sharp transition from a greenish flash to the expression of a dog that had misbehaved was familiar to me and did not bode well.

Dr Tamir said: 'A spoonful three times a day', and left.

Again I tried to think about the Messiah and the Monument of the Resurrection. Apparently I was unable to direct my heart properly to the Day of God that was approaching like a thief in the night, but at least I was able to divert my mind from everything that was going on around me. This is proved by the fact that I remember absolutely nothing of what transpired from the moment Dr Tamir left our house until the moment that I awoke in my bed to the sound of the sobbing of my wife, who was lying by my side. A full moon flooded the room in a greenish-yellow light. By the light of the moon I glanced at my watch. It was oh twelve hundred hours. My wife's shoulders shook. Her face was buried in the pillow.

I was not blessed with a good memory and I never succeeded in learning a single verse by heart, but at the sight of my wife's trembling shoulders, at the sight of the nape of her neck falling and rising (I did not see her face as it was buried in the pillow), at the sight of her hair that scattered with every motion of her nape, there suddenly played within me (indeed, truly played, for not only the words but the melody sounded inside me) a whole stanza from the poem by Bialik:

> And tell him also: In my bed
> At night I swim in my tears,
> And beneath my pale flesh
> Every night my pillow burns.

I said to her:

'You are in love with Dr Tamir.'

Her shoulders shook even more violently and she made no reply. 'And does he love you too?' I asked.

She raised her head, shot me a look of triumph from her tear-filled eyes, and said:

'Yes.'

At that moment I determined to murder them both; and my decision was a just one, for I knew that at oh four hundred hours they would both be resurrected and flown to one of the planets. I might have done the deed had the images of my son and my daughter not suddenly arisen before my eyes. How shall I sew my son's torn pants when every thread between my fingers misses the eye of the needle? How shall I get a physician for my daughter (be it even Dr Tamir) when the *Kupat Holim* cuts off my calls?

I said to my wife:

'I will go. Curly has ordered me to leave at two fifty a.m.; I will leave the house at two fifty a.m.'

Fortunately, my wife heard only the last sentence. Indeed, God favours fools, for if she had heard the first part of what I said, you can be sure she would have pressed me to say who Curly was and bombarded me with questions, and who knows whether in the end I would not have failed and told her a bit of what I knew about the redemption, the resurrection, and the monument. As she had heard only the last sentence, she raised half her body and pounded with her fists on the pillow:

'Not at two fifty, not at two fifty; now, you will go now. Now, this minute,' she screamed, gripped by hysteria.

It is a miracle that the children did not wake up at the sound of her screaming.

I got up, got dressed, and went out.

Not far from my house a public park had been planted. The saplings were still small and the park was more of a wish for the future, but the benches they had installed were real benches.

I sat on one of them and waited for two fifty.

V

At two fifty I left the park and walked on the road leading to Ramallah. Some believe it is Beit-El, where Jacob's Ladder was once placed, its top reaching to the sky. I walked. Upon reaching the barrier at the border I turned left and kept walking until I saw the end of a rope sticking out of the ground.

By the light of the stars I saw it in the blackness of the night, for the moon had gone down and the dawn had not yet come up.

I lay on the ground next to the place and waited for oh four hundred hours.

The stars dimmed and the universe grew blue. Dark shadows shimmered on the horizon of the peaks of the Judaean Hills. Some of them looked like pairings of trees driven by the wind and some looked like a platoon of soldiers doing guard duty and shaking from the cold pre-dawn dew.

At oh four hundred hours I heard a sound—it sounded like something between a trumpet blast and a siren. I knew it was not an air-raid alarm but rather the sound of the Messiah's *shofar*. As soon as I heard the blast I pulled the rope. I did not wait until the end of the blast. I pulled upon hearing the first sounds.

And as I pulled I felt myself sinking into the earth. I am sinking and in front of me a statue is rising. The more I pulled the deeper I sank and the statue kept rising before my eyes.

I must have pulled for a long time, in any event until the time when the sun came out and lit up the earth. As I was immersed in my work, the sacred work, I did not see the Morning Star or the purple of the dawn. I saw the sun in the full power of its blazing.

And when the sun lit up the world with the full power of its blazing, I was already sunk in the ground up to my neck, with only my right hand, of which the palm held the rope, sticking out of the earth.

The statue was almost completely upright—if it still inclined a bit backwards, it was no more than an incline of five or six degrees. Another few minutes and the Monument of the Resurrection will stand before me at a straight angle relative to the ground.

When the god of the Hindus revealed to Arjuna his divine form, it was like a thousand suns shining in the sky at once. He spoke from

infinite mouths, saw through myriads of eyes, was clad in paradais-
ical attire, and anointed with oil of myrrh, with its heavenly fragrance.
The son of Pandu was privileged to see the whole of creation, with
its array of lights and shades, enfolded in the body of the god of gods.
I saw neither hide nor hair of it.

The Monument of the Resurrection, which grew increasingly erect
as I watched, was nothing more than the image of a girl whose brown
hair was clipped like a boy's, the slit of her blue eyes slightly mon-
goloid, her teeth protruding a bit, her nose delicate and narrow, and
her face radiant with a smile in which innocence and insight, love and
security were fused in supreme perfection; her neck was ever so slightly
inclined forward, her shoulders . . .

No. I did not manage to see her shoulders, because the moment
she was vertically erect in front of me, straight and firm, the earth
covered my eyelids and I could no longer see anything.

In one of his journeys, Ilya Murometz, or perhaps another hero
of the ancient Russian epic, comes across a purse on the road. Ilya
Murometz got off his horse and tried to lift the purse. The purse did
not budge, but Ilya Murometz sank into the earth.

As God is my witness, it was not for a purse that I sank into the
ground, it was because of the Monument of the Resurrection that I
was covered by earth. And although the earth covered my eyelids, my
ears were not sealed from hearing, and the sound of the Messiah's
shofar reached them.

My arm was still thrust out of the ground, but my palm was paralysed and my fingers turned to stone. I ceased pulling on the rope.

When I ceased pulling on the rope the sound of the Messiah's
shofar faded and in its place arose a great din. I well knew that the
resurrected were being flown to the celestial bodies.

And me? Now that I am buried in the earth, am I not one of them?
Should I not be treated as they are?

It is a matter of doubt that requires clarification. What requires
no clarification is the certainty that my wife and my children and Dr
Tamir remained on the earth.

Were it not for the layer of earth that has sealed my mouth and
hindered my breathing, I would burst out laughing.

Translated by Ralph Mandel.

Savyon Liebrecht

MORNING IN THE PARK WITH NANNIES

Savyon Liebrecht was born in Germany in 1948 and reached Israel as a small child.
She now lives in Tel Aviv. She has published a number of collections of short stor-
ies. Liebrecht's stories concern memory and family conflict; troubled Israeli lives are
interpreted in terms of family ancestry and traumas passed down through the gen-
erations. Many of her stories concern the nature of survival, particularly after the
Holocaust. It's All Greek to Me, He Said to Her, the collection from which
'Morning in the Park with Nannies' is taken, was published in 1992.

When you showed up at the playground in the public park, I recognized you right away. It had been decades since I last saw you and
yet: the restrained tremor behind a curtain of langour, the unmistakable gait, the feet almost dancing, the peculiarly erect head with
the neck thrust forward as if you were watching the horizon, the quick
glance darting and then sailing away. You were pushing a baby buggy
on the dirt path leading to the furthest bench by the water fountain
when you passed me. How well I observed the beauty that has with-
stood the distorting power of time, the sky-blue eyes encircled by shadowy lines, the noble forehead, arching back into the roots of your
hair. I couldn't take my eyes off you as you parked the buggy under
the shadow of a tree, walked to the sandbox, bent down, gathered a
fistful of sand and raised it to your eyes to examine it.

'She's counting the microbe,' sniggered the Bulgarian nanny, and
the other two nannies sitting with her roared with laughter. Every
so often a new nanny wanders into the park, makes her way to the
further benches and becomes the butt of the Bulgarian's mordant
laughter. The other nannies watch the impending duel with glee, hoping to fill another hour with giggles. But today I don't join in their
hilarity. As soon as I recognized you, the scenes we had witnessed

together simmered inside me like poison. Few people saw those sights and lived.

You know, for years I saw you in my dreams: you were always dressed in silken kimonos or in those lace blouses I had made for you. I'd see you walking down the palace stairs with your fluttering gait, or standing by the window in the upper room looking at the garden, a string of sapphires always around your neck and your hair braided at your nape like twined gold encased in a fine net. In the distance, even in my dream, the Germans laugh thickly or sing their songs, or hurry up and down the black marble stairs, cracking a whip once in a while with a flick of the hand. In the background, like horrid sound effects, the girls shriek and cry and howl day and night—but not you. You keep your dark silence.

'The heart specialist's daughter,' the Bulgarian chuckles. 'They interviewed two hundred women until they finally picked this one. She looks more of a lady than the professor's wife.'

Even in my dreams you never looked me in the eye. You looked over my head with that distant, languid gaze, but I noticed how your eyelids trembled. I would wake up from those dreams like a man escaping from a fire, suddenly remembering scenes much worse than the dreams: the girls bitterly crying on their first night, their voices soft, subdued, mingled with the rustling in the bed, sometimes a shriek pierced the illusory silence, ringing in my ears for a long time afterwards, like an echo in the desert. And the next day: their eyes were worn with weeping and their faces furrowed with shadows, and in the days that followed the spark of life slowly faded away.

A few weeks later the eyes were already dead, dried of tears, haunted by knowledge; the handsome bodies slowly wilting, and then the puzzled expression of a person refusing to understand what is happening.

In the cellar where I lived with my sewing-machine, I would listen intently to hear the loud thud in the backyard, learning to distinguish it from the other noises around the house: one of the girls had reached the end of her endurance, climbed stealthily to the rooftop or to a windowsill and hurled herself down. I would close my eyes and recite the only verse I still remember from the *Kaddish* prayer my father used to say at my grandmother's grave: 'Magnified and sanctified be His great name...'

Now you are vigorously shaking the grains of dust from your fingers, turning your head toward the toddler who is sitting like a prisoner in the buggy.

'Look how quickly she counted the microbes,' jokes the Bulgarian.

'I bet she'll never let her play in the sand. God forbid the professor's daughter's dress should get soiled.'

The day the German thrust you in my room and ordered me to find you a blue silk gown, I stared at you as if hypnotized. The girls brought into my room were all pretty. But you—there was something sinister, lethal, in your beauty. You darted looks around the room and asked nothing. Did you know what kind of place it was? Did you distrust me? You stood erect and regal when I dressed you, like a bride donning her wedding gown.

You are clapping your palms together and walking resolutely to your bench. Your body is amazingly lithe, your legs pretty, unblemished by the years, and your narrow waist shows itself clearly when you bend down to release the little girl's belt. My eyes follow you undisguisedly. Now that the initial shock is over my eyes are drawn to you as they were then. I see your iron hand clamp down on the girl like jaws, your fingers closing in on the tiny palm that flutters like a caged bird. The sight arouses my hostility towards you, towards the sights that have been buried inside me for decades with no respite. The many days that have passed have not softened your heart, cursed woman! From the first moment the black light in your eyes alarmed me.

Outside, the German laughed hoarsely, calling to one of his friends: 'I've brought you a present: a rabbi's daughter!' I looked at you and said to myself, trying to shield you from what I could see: before long she will be found dead. It's obvious she has no idea where she is, and when she realizes it, she will want to die. The little girl squirms in your arms and you rock and scold her. I was mistaken about you. You understood quite well, as soon as you placed yourself in front of the mirror in my room. How did you guard your soul in that place?

One of the nannies runs around the carousel, panting, grabs hold of the gate and shouts: 'If you don't eat the apple right now, I'm giving it to Michael. Do you want Michael to grow up big and strong, and you'll be puny and weak? He will never let you go on the swing. Is that what you want?'

Do you remember, at night, the girl with the auburn braid used to sing. She had the sweet voice of a schoolgirl. When she sang, the weeping in the room would suddenly stop. One day a new girl was brought into the room. The night before, she told us, she had married her beloved. In the camp, where they had been transported from the ghetto, two kerchiefs had been tied together to form a canopy and a rabbi had performed the ceremony. The girl with the braid sang a bridal song for her: 'The voice of mirth and the voice of gladness, the voice of a bride and the voice of a groom... ' And later, at night, the two of them would sing Sabbath songs and hymns.

One morning the two girls were found lying by the fountain in the garden, holding hands, their wrists slashed. A few days later I asked you about them and I noticed your fingers did not tremble as you stroked your hair.

A child jumps off the carousel, his knee hits a stone and he bursts out crying. From the other side of the carousel the nanny pounces on him: 'Why do you jump without looking first? Don't you remember we couldn't go out for three days because you jumped and hurt yourself last Monday? It was awful, you behaved terribly. Now you're jumping again? Do you think I want to be cooped up with you again in that prison?'

The German requests those magnificent Chinese kimonos for you. I never cease to wonder where they are found in such quantities. In my room you adorn yourself as though you are about to go to a ball. You alone, of all the girls, are an enigma: girls come and go, tear their hair, howl like wolves—you alone keep your head up. Week after week I observe you and see no change in you, unlike the other girls—the clear skin, the light pink tinge fading into the neck, the dark haloes around the limpid blue irises, the wide, rounded forehead sloping toward the high temples, the slender waist, the narrow foot, the hair reaching to the waist, the supple movements, the dancing gait.

Once I saw you being dragged out of the parlour by an officer. Another time, when you left my room, I heard the drunken laughter of the men greet you outside. And one day, just by chance, as I passed through the hallway to clean up some filth from the rug downstairs, I saw you on the floor, the Chinese kimono all awry, your hair wound around your face like roots, your hands tied between your knees with a string. One night you came down the stairs wobbling like a drunkard, feeling your way down by the railing, your arms bleeding. The next morning you stood serene, looking out the window, pieces of broken vase at your feet, sipping soup, quietly imbibing the thick liquid, putting down the bowl, and, without looking, picking up a slice of salami and biting into it noisily, your eyes all the while fixed on the lilac bush and your right hand holding the drapes. I picked up the pieces of broken vase, my eyes glued to your wicked hand clinging to the drapes: fingernail marks like furrows ploughed on your arm, on the back of your hand. On your elbow, like a painting, were three burn marks that resembled a flower.

A hag overtakes the girls overnight: their complexion becomes ashen, their eyelids swell, their hair loses its sheen, their bodies are drained of vitality. You alone never change, as if inured to vicissitudes and knowing that nothing lasts for long. And I watch in amazement while the bruises on your arms heal and your lovely skin triumphs.

The Bulgarian jumps to her feet, dashes forward and threatens, 'Yuvali, get off this minute. Don't climb up from the bottom. Don't you see there's a girl ready to slide down? Do you want such a fat girl to fall on your head? Climb the ladder and slide down after that fat girl, like you did before. Look at her hit the bottom—kerplunk! Lucky for you I noticed her, or you'd be on your way to the hospital.'

The night the girl from the Lodz ghetto told us about Passover eve, you were the only one who stayed in bed. All the others gathered around the girl, who told us in whispers how she and her mother had been left alone in the cellar where they had been hiding. Her elder brother had gone out a week before to look for food and never came back. The younger brother had been sent out to look for him, and he, too, never came back. The mother had picked up some bread crumbs and flattened them into squares which she wet with water, and before she went out of her mind and ran screaming out into the street, calling for her sons, she prepared the Passover meal, putting stones on the table instead of wine, fish, soup and meat, and the squares of bread crumbs that served as matzo. Then she went around the cellar singing: 'How is this night different from all other nights? That on all nights we eat . . .' The whole time she was telling us about the ghetto I kept looking at you. You were sitting facing away from us, motionless, as if you were a piece of furniture. Did you, like me, already know that the next day the girl from Lodz would collapse and the Germans would throw her out at noon?

'Why did you hit her?' The nanny's voice sounds thinner and shriller than the children's. 'I saw you hitting her. Don't lie to me. Why is she crying then? Just because you can't climb on the monkey bars, you have to hit her? Aren't you ashamed to play with girls anyway? Look at all the other kids playing nicely, only you go looking for trouble. You think you're so smart picking on little girls? Where is your nanny anyway? What's she being paid for? Why isn't she watching you?'

Often I wondered whether you would have triumphed over that place if it hadn't been for the senior officer who took you under his wing and kept the others away from you. For a while we were both protected: I by my sewing skills and you ensconced in your benefactor's room.

We both regarded the others as if their fate had nothing to do with ours. Do you remember the three girls who were taken out one night of revelry when the Germans were drunker than ever? At dawn two of them crawled back, their bodies lacerated. The third girl had been rolled up in a carpet, her long hair hanging out of one side. Then she was dragged out into the garden and set on fire. The drunken German stood there watching as the hair rapidly caught fire, and the smell of burnt flesh filled the room until a wind started to blow. One of the girls told us, before she was taken to the doctor from where she never returned, that the German had strangled her friend while he violated her body. In the morning the other girl was spitting blood. She came to my room for shelter and exposed the fist marks on her lower abdomen.

Sometimes, when I sit here on the bench in the public park among the nannies, listening to them bickering and chattering, watching the toddlers play in the sandbox under the trees, I am reminded more and more of the trees in that other house: the linden tops converging above the fountain, the goldfish swimming among corals gleaned from the ocean depths, the thick foliage, the sombre shade, the dew drops stored in the grass, the clear night sky. What are they doing now, those girls who used to sit on the Germans' knees, who rolled on the floors? Are they living their lives, carrying the memories from night to day, from day to night? I try to calculate how old they would be today, and the thought alarms me.

Do you remember that time, at a ball, when our eyes locked over a girl crouching on all fours, her forehead touching the empty boots, licking the bare feet of the officer, who was standing like an artist's model, his hands on his hips, his pants rolled down and his briefs hanging loose around the pillars of his legs. His companions laughed. One of them said: 'Not many people can brag that they've caught a German officer with his pants down.' What went through the girl's mind as she crouched there in the middle of the crowded room? Was she thinking of her mother? Of her father? Of the boy peering at her from behind a prayer shawl? What were you thinking of?

A young woman is dragging a weeping girl to an adjacent bench. 'Tell his nanny, my little angel. Don't cry, honey. There, there. I'll tell her! Your kid spat on her. Is this what you're teaching him? Sure, you're responsible. You sit here yakking about salaries and gossiping about your employers, while he's spitting on other kids. Some nanny! Come to the tap, angel and I'll wash your dress.'

You were beautiful in those days. You must have found a make-up kit somewhere, or else your benefactor gave you one. You put on mascara, rouged your cheeks, and I, who know your features like the back of my hand, noticed a new sparkle in your eyes; you braided your hair and searched in the jewellery box in my room for a string of sapphires, which you hung around your neck. You examined yourself in the mirror and waited for his arrival, as a lover would. Once after you had stayed in his room the two of you came out to the little porch. He put his jacket around your shoulders and you talked the whole night long. I saw you from my window, talking earnestly. What did you tell him, sitting so erect, wrapped in a German officer's jacket? What did he tell you?

In the spring the garden suddenly burst into my cellar with all its glory: the deep azure of Polish skies, the light clouds, the air laden with blossoms and pollen, heavy bunches of chestnut flowers peering through curtains of leaves, young boughs shooting from the treetops, the trickling of the fountain in the garden, hedges of white lilacs standing against the fence like ornate gowns lined up for a fashion show. And in the middle of the garden—the palace itself, where a prince used to live before the Germans came, with huge frescos, engraved doors, embroidered hanging rugs, inlaid cupboards, lion-footed armchairs, heavy silver cutlery, crystal chandeliers. And at rare hours, the profound silence between the walls, when the shrieks of the women and the thumping of jackboots on the marble stairs subsided; through the silence I could sense the glaring eyes, the quivering flesh, the nameless fear. One morning, amid the sweet lilac scent, I lingered by a wall in front of one of the rooms and noticed little dabs of blood behind the chest of drawers; the dabs forming letters: Shifra daughter of Shimon. What possessed Shifra to leave her father's name in that accursed place?

'You get down this minute! We're going home now! Do you want to tear your pants again? Your Mum won't buy you a new pair so soon. OK, a little bit more, just get off those bars and come play in the sand. Or go play with the girls that's better.'

On exceptionally pleasant summer nights the Germans would sit in the large garden, drinking beer from huge mugs, singing out loud, sometimes amusing themselves with a girl sitting on their laps by bouncing her from lap to lap around the circle. From my sunken window I followed you with my eyes. Your German had seated you on a chair by his side and offered you a drink, but you declined. Gently he caressed your cheek. I was shaken. In that place, the sight of endearment is hard to witness. You said something to him and he immediately bent his head towards you to catch it, nodding attentively. The two of you got up and walked down the path to the edge of the garden. A few minutes later shots were heard from that corner, and the Germans jumped to their feet. The girl remained as immobile as a statue. Soon it became clear: your officer was showing off his marksmanship to you. Loud laughter was heard from the edge of the garden.

You make sure the bench is meticulously clean, you pick out cigarette butts from the sand and put them in a garbage can lodged in a tree trunk. Then you lay a napkin on the bench and feed the child, wiping her mouth constantly, picking crumbs from her shirt—and all the while your back is straight and your knees are closed tight, like an actress in a movie.

In all the days that followed you were protected, sleeping in the officer's distant overheated room, standing by the window watching the sudden summer rain showers on the garden. Every day, by your master's orders, your meal was brought to you on a tray as if you were the mistress of a house, sitting in your armchair and gazing at a painting over my head, as I changed the sheets on your bed. Unlike the other girls, you never asked me anything. Did you understand everything? Or is it that you didn't want to understand more than you had to? I knew more about the Germans than about you.

The nanny who is sitting next to me pulls a crying child toward her. 'And his father is a doctor! Can you believe it, a big doctor, with such a stupid son? Always sticks his head where he can get hurt. Why don't you watch your head? Ask your father and he'll tell you how important it is to watch your head.'

One night, the house was suddenly empty and silence fell on the lawn and on the copse behind the palace. The girls, alarmed by the unwonted silence, gathered like somnambulists in the parlour; some lay on the sofas and on the rugs, eating candy from ornate boxes, drinking wine, whispering. One of the girls burst out crying uncontrollably. In the morning we were woken by the thumping boots of returning Germans. Later in the afternoon we found out that the officers had been summoned to a special meeting, and also that the golden-haired girl who had been brought in the day before from Majdanek had taken advantage of the commotion and disappeared. They sent the dogs after her and found her hiding in the bushes, under the porch columns. We saw the dogs dragging her into the thicket.

The morning your officer was found dead in his bed, you were not in the room. The doctor was called in and suddenly there was panic in the palace, with people dashing to and fro, exchanging short phrases like a secret language, passing each other on the stairs. Through the door I could see him lying in bed like a mountain, his neck red even in death. The doctor pronounced that his heart had given way. When the body had been removed, covered in a velvet blanket, the others swooped down on you. That day and night the Germans kept going to your room at the top of the stairs, doing to you what they had been prevented from doing while your defender was alive. In the morning I saw you staggering on the doorstep. I recognized you by the kimono.

You take no part in the general hubbub in the park. The child, too, keeps her distance from the other children, just pushing her buggy in circles around your bench. Her lovely sandals burrow in the sand. For a moment your eyes seem to focus on the baby sitting on my lap. Did you recognize me? Your hand seems to have lost control, your fingers feel their way along the bench, grabbing the metal edge of the wooden plank. Your body maintains its calm, your back is erect, only your whitened fingers tremble as they clutch the wood.

One morning the Germans were suddenly gone. They left in haste, yet they took two of the girls with them. We got up in the morning, seven girls, to a new silence. The doctor's daughter from Lublin was the first to realize what had happened. She climbed to the fourth floor and opened up all the rooms one by one, and her roar became louder the further she got. Leaning on the top floor railing she shouted: 'All the swine are gone!' She shouted in Yiddish, defiantly, and a tremor went through my body as I heard those words. The girl who had been the last to arrive, her paleness glaring against the dark room started rocking to and fro raising her eyes to the high frescoed ceiling and chanting, 'Blessed art thou, our God, Lord of the universe...' And a moment later the woman who spoke fluent German burst out laughing and started demolishing the paintings on the wall with her bare hands.

The Bulgarian is overcome by compassion as easily as she gives in to bursts of cruelty. 'Look what a heart of gold he has—every day he gives his chocolate milk to the cat. I tell his Mum that he shouldn't be so softhearted. When he grows up the girls will make his life miserable. You know what girls are like when they lay their hands on a good guy—they destroy him.'

We didn't know at the time that the Russians were already in town, we were still delirious, roaming through the rooms. You were the first to leave. You cocked your beret on your head, packed a small suitcase, broke into my room, opened the jewellery box, scooped up a fistful of jewels and put them at the bottom of the suitcase, picked two dark sweaters and a grey woollen skirt, packed them quickly, and left. At the main gate the vicious dog leapt at you, and you bent down, picked up a rock and hit him on the head. As soon as you left, all hell broke loose, as if you had given the signal for a new life.

You gather your things, harness the little girl, get up and turn to the park gate. Again, a pace away from me, I see the ice-cold eyes surrounded by black haloes. The nannies fall silent, following you with their eyes as you pass us by. For a moment I seem to feel your glance lashing at me. Do I awaken a memory in you? An echo of German voices? The contact of flesh against your flesh? The fluttering of silk against your skin? The smell of chestnuts? Were you ever able to forget? The girl who had aged within days, the one who swept the marble tiles, who removed the filthy sheets and put on fresh ones, who stitched the fancy dresses, ironed and sewed, and all the while never took her eyes off you, lovely daughter of Israel. How all that beauty was collected and destroyed—have you been able to forget?

Suddenly the steely eyes are on my face. And you say with a dull voice devoid of surprise, 'Which sandals?'

I reply, 'The little girl's.'

You look straight ahead. 'I don't know. I didn't buy her the sandals. Her mother did.' And you propel the buggy onto the gravel path and walk away.

I stumble back to my seat on the bench, the Bulgarian makes room for me and peers into my face, concerned.

'What's wrong, my angel? Come, sit down.' She pats my back amicably and smiles. 'How you ran after that lady! As if in her you had found Cinderella's sandal, the one she lost at the palace.'

And they all join in her laughter.

Translated by Marganit Weinberger-Rotman.

Ruth Almog

DORA'S SECRET

Ruth Almog was born in Petah Tikva in 1936 to an Orthodox family of German descent. After studying literature and philosophy she taught for a number of years. Since 1967 she has been working for the literary section of the daily newspaper Ha'aretz. She has been awarded many literary prizes, some for her children's literature. She has published novels, short-story collections, and children's books and stories. Ruth Almog's stories are often reconstructions of the inner worlds of children, conveying the manner in which children suffer intense feeling without understanding it.

When Dora said to me on the phone, 'Come and have lunch with me and we'll talk', I couldn't believe my ears. On my previous visit to Paris she had avoided meeting me. Or so, at any rate, it seemed to me. Now she told me how to get to St Cloud—which was where she lived—said, 'Au revoir', and hung up. When I replaced the receiver on its cradle, for some reason there were tears in my eyes.

On my way to the St Lazare railway station I went into a confectioners and bought her a fancy box of *marrons glacés*. It was a big box and looked impressive without costing too much.

In the Gare St Lazare I inserted a coin in the automat and a train ticket popped out. I had no idea that I was supposed to punch the ticket when I went through the gate to the platform, where my train was already waiting. Afterwards Dora explained to me that this was against the law. 'You could have been arrested for it,' she said, 'You're lucky a conductor didn't come into your coach.'

During the whole train trip I was very tense. I was afraid of missing St Cloud, and kept checking the names of the stations where the train stopped against the names on the map above my seat. This was the reason that I hardly paid any attention to the landscape.

The St Cloud station was situated deep in a narrow creek and seemed isolated and remote. Nevertheless there was a huge slogan painted on the wall in black tar, saying 'Down with Khomeini'. At that time there were violent clashes between Iranian students in Paris almost every day.

I climbed the steep wooden steps out of the station and set off in the direction of the flourishing garden suburb. After a while I turned into a street of pleasant new houses. The people who lived here were obviously well-to-do. I found the house without any difficulty. When I rang the bell the door opened immediately and opposite me stood a little old woman. For a moment I thought it was my grandmother come back to life. The resemblance was astonishing, and I almost cried out loud: 'Regina!' But I soon saw the differences. My grandmother's nose was prominent and hooked, obviously Jewish, whereas Dora's was small and dainty, almost retroussé. We kissed, and when I drew back the gold cross on her neck glittered in my eyes. I said: 'You look like Regina, my grandmother.' Dora said: 'I don't remember her. She only visited us in Vienna once or twice. Come inside.'

From the dark entrance hall we entered a salon full of light. Next to the door, on the right, stood a grand piano, and opposite it, on the far side of the room, stood a loom with an unfinished tapestry on it. The walls were crowded with large, pale, faded wall hangings. The transitions between the pale colours were so subtle that at first the tapestries seemed quite empty of content. It was only when I came closer that I saw how complex the pictures were: they all depicted scenes from the life of Jesus and his family and were imbued with an intense religious feeling which could not be disguised by the rich, detailed intricacy of the tapestries. The colours looked to me like the colours of snow or ice. Their compass was extremely limited: from white to dark grey, various faint yellows, pinks, and pale blues. A very little black and a little very dark burgundy. There was nothing bright about the colours. On the contrary, they were dim and muted, flowing in rounded lines without defined borders between them.

These tapestries filled me with wonder. 'Are they yours?' I asked carefully. She nodded. 'I thought you were a sculptor,' I said.

'Oh, not for a long time,' she said with a smile.

From close up it was possible to distinguish the astonishing wealth of the colours, which merged into a muted pinkish grey. They were like a secret which only revealed itself to a thorough examination. But from close up it was only possible to take in the details without getting a comprehensive view of the picture as a whole. Consequently, the viewer was obliged to miss something: If he saw the scene depicted,

he missed the details, and when he concentrated on the details he
failed to see the scene.

Dora said: 'I've been making these tapestries for years. Each one
takes a year of work. I've shown them all over. Two years ago I had
an exhibition in Rome, and there was a plan to show them in Jerusalem too. My husband and I wanted to visit Jerusalem very much. But
because of our catastrophe nothing came of it. Come and sit down.'

We sat down in comfortable armchairs next to a coffee table and
I asked her: 'What catastrophe?'

'My husband is very ill,' she said, 'I'll tell you about it in a minute.
But first, won't you have something to drink?'

She went into the kitchen and came back with a tray holding two
glasses of lemonade. I gave her my gift. 'You shouldn't have... ' she
said and tore the wrapping paper. From the fancy cardboard box
she removed a plain tin can. An ordinary, round, tin can, without even
a label on it. I had no idea that *marrons glacés* came in plain tin cans.
She went back to the kitchen and returned with a very small, ineffici-
ent can-opener, and began to open the can. The tin was thick and the
opener was no good and it made a jagged border round the edge of
the can. Dora was careless and cut her finger, which began to bleed.
'Oy!' I cried. I felt guilty and I didn't know how to apologize. Dora
put the tin on the table and said, 'Please help yourself.' But I couldn't,
because her finger, which she wrapped in a handkerchief that she took
out of her pocket, was still bleeding. 'You must bandage it', I almost
screamed, and she smiled faintly and left the room and returned with
a bandage round her wounded finger.

Dora sat down in the armchair, looked at me, and said: 'We were
extremely happily married. All our lives we loved one another to distraction. We never parted even for a single day and we never did anything without consulting each other. There was complete harmony
between us. And now I can't finish that tapestry. Soon it will be a
year that it's been stretched there unfinished on the loom. How can
I know if what I do is good and right when he isn't here to tell me.
You know, he never wrote a book without consulting me. In the morning he would write, and in the afternoon I would read what he had
written. Our lives were perfect. No, we were never apart, not even
for a day. And then, about two years ago, they found a tumour in my
body. Not malignant, but it bothered me. They said I had to have it
removed. But my husband was afraid. He actually cried. He didn't

want me to have the surgery. I put it off from month to month. I suffered, but I put it off. Until my children—they're all doctors, you
know—said it had gone on long enough, I had to have the surgery. I
saw how hard it was for him and we arranged a bed for him next to
me. We went into the hospital together and we weren't parted. The
night before the operation he slept next to me. In the morning our
oldest son came. He never left his father for a moment, but when
they took me into the operating theatre, my husband collapsed. He
thought he would never see me again. He went beserk, he tried to
follow me into the operating theatre, and of course they wouldn't let
him. My son was with him all the time, but he broke down completely. They had to tie him down and sedate him. When they brought
me back to the ward a few hours later, he was sleeping. When he
woke up he was no longer himself. He didn't know me. He talked
nonsense and he didn't recognize me, or our children either. His
mind seemed to have been wrung out of his body, it was gone, it just
wasn't there any more . . . We had to commit him to an institution.
I only go there to visit him once a month, the place is very far away,
but it's quite pointless. He doesn't talk to me. He doesn't know who
I am. He's like a vegetable. The whole thing is incredible, incomprehensible. Up to the moment they took me to the operating theatre
he was in full command of his faculties, at the top of his intellectual
form . . . Do you know how many books he wrote? Come, I'll show
you,' and she led me into another room whose walls were lined with
books, and there was one case there with a whole shelf full of his
books. I looked at the titles and saw that they were about philosophy
and religion and music. He wrote about Nietzsche and Fichte and
Beethoven and about German Romanticism in music and literature,
all kinds of books. 'He was a very learned man,' she said.

'How did you meet him?' I asked.

'Ah!' she said, and her face lit up, 'In Vienna. He was attending a
musicians' congress and my brother Henri met him there' (Why Henri?
I thought indignantly. His name was Henrik) 'and brought him home.
I was eighteen and he was twenty-eight. I fell in love with him. He
returned to Paris and I began to take instruction in the Christian religion. He didn't insist on it, I wanted it. And later on I converted to
Christianity, out of true faith, and we were married. My husband
was a devout Catholic, a true believer, and so am I.' 'I thought', I said
carefully, 'that you were already Christians in Vienna. Leon said that
your father converted to Catholicism in order to receive a government
post and the title of Hofrat.'

'Nonsense!' she cried. 'Leon was always making up all kinds of stories. My father converted after the war, when he returned from Mexico and came to live with me, just before he died. He had a revelation and he understood that Christianity was the true religion. He said that he wanted to die and be buried as a Christian.'

I knew that they, in other words, my mother's uncle and his son Henrik, had fled to Mexico. I well remembered the letters addressed to my grandmother with the beautiful big stamps which we would carefully remove. My father would soak the envelop in water until the stamp came off almost of its own accord, and then he would dry it and smooth it out and stick it in the stamp album. After the war, Henrik returned to Vienna. My friend, the painter Osias Hoffstetter, used to meet him there in a Bohemian café frequented by emigré artists. 'He was a fanatical communist,' he told me. I never knew that the father had gone to live with his daughter in Paris.

'He died like a saint,' said Dora. 'In his sleep. He fell asleep sitting in his armchair and reading the New Testament. The children grieved terribly. They loved him to distraction.' I said: 'A friend told me that he once heard one of Henrik's works, very modern, for twelve cellos.'

'Yes,' she said. 'His music is hard to understand. It's very modern.'

'I heard someone wrote a book about him. Perhaps you have it?'

And again her face lit up. She was still a beautiful woman. Very fine, blueish-white skin, and fine, almost golden hair. She went into the next room, her husband's book-lined study, and came back with a German book. I leafed through the book and looked at the pictures of Henrik at different stages of his life, but none of the pictures caught my imagination, I felt no closeness to him and he eluded me. I wanted very much to keep the book, but I didn't dare ask her to give it to me.

'Next week,' she said, 'I'm going to Vienna to pay him a short visit.' I thought to myself that perhaps one day I would go too. In the only letter he had ever written me he said: 'I'm glad to hear that you're a writer. I'm glad that there's still one exception to the rule, one artist left in our family of capitalists.'

I identified with him intensely, even though I didn't really know what he was talking about. So few members of our family had survived, and the truth was that he, too, had only known them by hearsay.

Suddenly Dora said in an animated tone of voice: 'Did you know that there's a Cardinal in the Vatican from our family?'

I looked at her in astonishment and incomprehension. 'Yes, yes,' she said emphatically, 'We have a Cardinal in the Vatican from our family, Cardinal Rubin.'

I had never heard this before and I didn't believe her. In fact, I had stopped believing her long ago. From the moment I set foot in this elegant, well-appointed house I hadn't believed her, from the moment I set eyes on those pale tapestries of hers, with the scenes from the life of Jesus so well disguised in them that it was almost impossible to make them out. But not long after my visit to Paris, back home in Israel, a friend told me that the entourage of the Polish Pope did, indeed, include a Cardinal called Rubin. If he was really connected to our own Rubin family—my mother's, Dora's, Henrik's, I couldn't find out.

For some reason I stared at the piano, and she caught my gaze. I had no doubt that the piano was a very expensive one. 'My husband's piano,' she said, nodding her head sadly, 'we had a perfect marriage, perfect.' After a moment she added: 'Did you know that we have four children, two girls and two boys, all doctors. But when they were small they each learned to play a different instrument and we had a quintet at home. We used to give concerts. On Sunday afternoons we used to invite people and play for them. My husband played the piano, the girls played string instruments and the boys the flute and the clarinet. It was perfect. Simply perfect. It's so hard for me to realize that he isn't here, with me. I miss him so much.' She fell silent and after a while I asked her about Kaethe, Jacob Rubin of Leipzig's daughter. I knew that she lived in France, in a provincial town called Beauvais. I knew that she too had converted to Catholicism and that her husband was a professor. Or maybe just a teacher.

Dora pulled a disgusted face: 'I don't have anything to do with her,' she said. I gave her an inquiring look and waited for her to go on, and she must have sensed my anticipation for she immediately said: 'She worked for the Gestapo during the war. An informer. After the war they caught her and shaved off her hair. She's lucky they didn't execute her. After the war they all got what they deserved, all those informers and collaborators.'

I said: 'I don't believe it. It's just loose talk. People say things like that about you and your husband too.'

It came out on an impulse before I could stop it. I realized that I felt some anger against her. 'What?' cried Dora in horror.

'Leon says you betrayed our cousins from Bonn to the Gestapo,' I said.

'What are you talking about?' she screamed. 'Do you know what they did? We hid them in our old house in Neuilly at great danger to ourselves. And behind our backs they were busy dealing on the black market. My husband was in the Resistance. They were putting our lives in danger. We had to tell them to go. If we'd been caught they'd have sent us all away.'

'Did the people around you know that you were of Jewish descent?' I asked.

'Nobody ever knew. Nobody knows to this day. Don't forget that I came here from Vienna. And I was already a Catholic when I came. And nevertheless, when they came and asked for help, we hid them in our cellar. But they dealt on the black market behind our backs. My husband's comrades in the Resistance warned him about them. They were ungrateful. I had small children, don't forget.'

I said nothing. I knew by then that there is always more than one way of telling the same story.

'My husband consulted me and we discussed what to do. I've already told you that we always did everything together. There were never any disagreements between us, never any arguments. Do you know that in over fifty years of married life we never had a single quarrel?'

Afterwards we had lunch. I apologized for troubling her, but she explained that the maid had already prepared everything. 'She comes in for two hours every day. It's hard for me nowadays. I'm not so healthy either any more. That's why I only go to visit my husband once a month. It's so far away. But they look after him very well there.' And then she added dully: 'In any case he doesn't know me. The only one he sometimes recognizes is our eldest son . . .'

We finished off the meal with an assortment of cheeses. I couldn't take my eyes off the bandage round her finger. The tin of *marrons glacés* I had brought her was standing on the low table where she had placed it. I had not taken a single one of them and neither had she.

Dora ate very little and it was obvious that she was upset. I helped her to clear away the dishes. Her kitchen was enviably big and modern.

We sat down again and she said: 'Leon's crazy. Why did he have to go and tell you such a pack of lies? And he didn't say anything about Kaethe?'

'No,' I replied. 'He never said a word about Kaethe.'

I didn't believe her story. I thought she had some unclear, hidden need to invent it. A shocking story to excuse her estrangement from her only relative in France.

Suddenly I sensed her anxiety. Hidden, unclear, but obviously present. I looked at her and I thought to myself that she was a very frightened woman.

'It was a terrible time,' she said suddenly. 'Terrible! Terrible!. . . . You understand that that is the reason you will never be able to meet my children.'

'No, I don't understand,' I said.

'They don't know. They don't know anything. And they never will know.'

'Don't know what?' I asked insistently.

'They don't know that I'm a Jewess.'

'What?' I asked, completely nonplussed. 'But you're not a Jewess. You're a Catholic.'

'You don't understand,' she explained, 'they don't know that I was born Jewish. We never told them. It was our secret, my and my husband's big secret. All my life I've been afraid of something like Hitler happening again. I don't want them ever to be in danger, to have something like that hanging over their heads, you understand. We decided to keep it a secret the minute the trouble started. In those days secrecy was vital. And afterwards we decided that we would never tell them.'

There were too many holes in her story. If her father had converted only after his return from Mexico, that meant that Henrik had remained Jewish, and if this was the case, how had she kept it a secret from her children? And what of the book about Henrik—didn't it say there that he was a Jew? And the name Rubin? How did she explain that? It was such an obviously Jewish name.

I felt increasingly uncomfortable, as if I were being stifled. The lies were choking me. What was true and what was a lie, I asked myself, and I knew that I would never know the answer to this question. In his one and only letter to me, Henrik had written resentfully that he had never denied his Jewishness, offering as proof the fact that he was a member of the Friends of the Israeli Philharmonic Orchestra. I thought about this and wondered if it, too, was a lie. I had never tried to find out and had no intention of checking up on him. Dora was now in deep distress. Her face was pale and drawn. 'You have to understand me,' she said, almost imploringly.

'I understand,' I said. 'It's not important. It doesn't matter at all . . .'

'I'm sorry you won't be able to meet them,' she said. 'I'm truly sorry. They're wonderful children. To this day they still play together when they find the time to meet, and they take care of me and their father devotedly. It's a shame you won't be able to get to know them. It's a privilege to know people like them. They really are wonderful.'

Now I saw how little she really resembled my grandmother, Regina.

There was something slack in her face, and in spite of the similarity in their complexions, their hair, the colour and shape of their eyes, there was an enormous difference between them. My grandmother's face expressed stubbornness and determination. And she really was a hard, uncompromising woman—something which had always bothered me. But now, faced with Dora, I found myself longing for her and making peace with her in my heart.

Dora seized the tin of *marrons glacés* and offered it to me. 'Please take one,' she said.

Her bandaged finger, the wound she had received because of me, because of my coming, because of my gift, suddenly took on a symbolic significance in my eyes. And so I didn't refuse, and carefully, so as not to hurt myself, I took one from the tin, and put it in my mouth. The *marron glacé* melted in my mouth and it tasted like Paradise.

'I think I had better go now, it's getting late,' I said and stood up.

She stood up after me, and when I picked up my bag she said: 'I hope you kept your ticket. You'll be able to use it on the way back. You saved yourself some money, but next time don't forget to punch your ticket. It's an offence against the law and they treat it very gravely here.'

Next to the door we kissed each other and when I embraced her I felt how small and fragile she was.

At the top of the steps leading down to the creek and the station stood a wooden hut painted white. I bought a ticket to Paris there, having thrown the previous one into the first trash can I came across after leaving Dora's house.

Opposite me, the gigantic slogan 'Down with Khomeini' glared with a kind of violence, as the train slowly entered the station.

All the way back I struggled with myself, restraining a fierce desire to look up her children in the telephone directory, call them up and introduce myself, resisting the urge to betray her—not in the name of truth and for its sake, but just so, out of a kind of childish need, out of the nagging compulsion to touch, over and over again, what appeared to me as my own living flesh, as if such a confrontation had it in its power to reveal an additional, hidden and unknown part of myself.

Would I be able to resist this temptation, the sweet temptation of betrayal, in the future too, if I ever found myself in Paris again? There was no guarantee.

Translated by Dalya Bilu.

Glossary

agal	the circular braid worn by Arabs atop the *keffiyeh* (q.v.)
ahlan usahlan	(Arabic) with pleasure
Aliyah	one of the waves of immigration to the Jewish Palestinian Settlement, 1882–1923
Ashkenazi	Jew from Central or Eastern Europe
bar mitzvah	celebrated by Jewish males on reaching the age of thirteen
brith	the ceremony of circumcision
Bund	abbreviation of *Algemeyner Yidishe Arbeter Bund*, the General Jewish workers' union in Lithuania, Poland, and Russia and Jewish Socialist party founded in Russia at the end of the nineteenth century; associated with devotion to Yiddish, cultural autonomy, and secular Jewish nationalism, and sharply opposed to Zionism
Chevra Kadisha	the Jewish burial society
Elul	month of the Jewish calendar corresponding to September–October
fellaheen	(Arabic) peasants
finever	fiver
galabiyeh	long, loose Middle Eastern garment
gonif	(Yiddish) thief
Hadassah	a large hospital in Jerusalem
Haganah	Jewish self-defence organization established in Palestine during the British Mandate
hakima	(Arabic) woman doctor
hamsin	hot dry desert wind
havdalah	benediction signifying the end of the Sabbath or festivals
heder	Jewish religious elementary school
hora	Israeli folk-dance
huppa	the canopy under which Jewish marriage ceremonies take place. It often refers to the wedding itself
Irgun Tzva'i Leumi	a Jewish underground armed organization in Palestine during the British Mandate
Kach	acronym signifying the extreme right-wing militant movement led by Rabbi Meir Kahane

Kaddish	the Jewish prayer for the dead, said by the son or nearest male relative
kamanji	(Arabic) Oriental stringed instrument, having one or two strings
keffiyeh	Arab headdress
Keren Kayemet	the Jewish National Fund
ketubah	marriage contract, often exquisitely ornamented
Kol Nidrei	lit.: 'all vows'; liturgy for the eve of the Day of Atonement
Kupat Holim	Israeli health insurance scheme or sick fund
Lag Ba'omer	the eighteenth day of the Hebrew month of Iyyar, corresponding to early May. This is also the anniversary of Bar Kokhba's victory over the Romans
Landsleit	someone from the same country of origin, compatriot
mamzer	bastard
matsos	the unleavened bread eaten during the festival of Passover
Men darf kannen redden	(Yiddish) 'One may speak'
mezuzah	a tubular case of wood, glass, or metal, usually a few inches in length, containing part of the *Shema* creed inscribed on parchment. The *mezuzah* is nailed at a slant on the upper part of the right doorpost at the entrance of a Jewish dwelling
Midrash	a voluminous talmudic literature consisting of an imaginative interpretation of the biblical writings, particularly the five books of Moses (the Pentateuch). The Midrash includes aphorisms, proverbs, poetic metaphors, legends, fables, anecdotes, and parables
minyan	a quorum of ten male worshippers, the number required for holding public prayer
narghiles	(Arabic) water pipe (for smoking)
Nisan	month of the Jewish calendar corresponding to March–April
Palmah	the élite corps of the Israel Defence Force (*Haganah*) in the War of Independence, 1948
Rabbi Meir Baal Haness	(Rabbi Meir the Miracle-Worker) A legendary rabbi to whom miracles were attributed. The traditional charity boxes for collecting funds for poor Jews in Palestine were named after him
Rosh Hashanah	the Jewish New Year
selikhot	penitential prayers recited during *Elul* (q.v.) preceding *Rosh Hashanah* (q.v.)
Sephardi	a Jew of Spanish origin, now predominantly from the Middle East and North Africa

Shalom aleikhem	greeting in Hebrew
shehakol	benediction over water or foods not grown
Shema	the first word of the Jewish creed, *Shema Yisrael, Adonai Eloheinu, Adonai ehad* (Hear O Israel, the Lord our God, the Lord is One)
shiva	the seven-day period of mourning
shofar	ram's horn, the only ancient musical instrument still used in the rites of the synagogue, particularly on *Rosh Hashanah* (q.v.)
Simhat Torah	the festival of the Rejoicing of the Law
sukkah	booth erected for the Festival of Tabernacles (q.v. *Sukkot*) where for seven days religious Jews live, or at least take their meals
Sukkot	the Festival of Tabernacles
tallit	prayer-shawl
Talmud	the vast body of rabbinic civil and criminal law, regulations, traditions, and the disputations of the rabbinic sages
tefillin	phylacteries
Tisha Be'av	(Hebrew: the ninth of the month of *Av*) A fast-day which commemorates and mourns the destruction of the Temple in Jerusalem in 586 BCE and 70 CE
Torah	the five books of Moses, the Pentateuch
Tsena Ur'ena	a compilation of stories from the Bible and Mishnah written in Yiddish for women
Yahrzeit	(Yiddish) the annual anniversary of a death
yarmulkeh	a skullcap worn by Orthodox Jewish men at all times and by all Jewish men when entering a synagogue or engaging in prayer
Yishuv	the Jewish population in pre-Israel Palestine; the Jewish Palestinian Settlement
Yom Kippur	The Day of Atonement

Publisher's Acknowledgements

The editor and publishers are grateful for permission to include the following copyright material:

Shalom Ya'akov Abramowitz, from *The Literature of Destruction*, ed. David G. Roskies. Copyright © 1989 by The Jewish Publication Society. Reprinted by permission of the Jewish Publication Society.

Yehuda Amichai, from *The World is a Room and Other Stories*. Copyright © 1984 by The Jewish Publication Society. Reprinted by permission of the Jewish Publication Society.

Aharon Appelfeld, from *In the Wilderness* ('Ah'shav' Publishers). All rights are reserved to Akhshav.

Yitzhak Ben-Ner, from *Rustic Sunset*. Used by permission of Three Continents Press, Inc., USA. English translation copyright © by Ann Oved Publishers and the Institute for the Translation of Hebrew Literature.

M. Z. Feierberg, from *Whither? and Other Stories*, 1972. English translation copyright © 1972 by The Jewish Publication Society. Reprinted by permission of the Jewish Publication Society.

Shulamith Hareven, from *Twilight and Other Stories* (Mercury House, San Francisco, CA), © 1992 by Shulamith Hareven. Reprinted by permission of the publisher.

Haim Hazaz, from *The Jewish Caravan*, selected and edited by Leo W. Schwarz. Copyright 1935 © 1963, 1965 by Leo W. Schwarz. Reprinted by permission of Henry Holt and Co., Inc.

Yehudit Hendel, from DELOS vol. II, No. 1, Spring 1989. Copyright © 1989 by The Center for World Literature. Reprinted by permission of DELOS.

Yehudit Katzir, from *Closing the Sea*, copyright © 1990 by Hakibbutz Hameuchad. English translation copyright © 1992 by Yehudit Katzir. Reprinted by permission of Harcourt Brace & Company.

Yehoshua Kenaz, from *Musical Moment and Other Stories*, trans. Dalya Bilu (Steerforth Press, South Royalton, Vermont, USA). English translation copyright © 1995 by the Institute for the Translation of Hebrew Literature.

Amos Oz, from *Where the Jackals Howl and Other Stories*, trans. Nicholas de Lange. Copyright Amos Oz and Am Oved Publishers Ltd. English translation